BEING ON MARS

UNEXPECTED MIRACLES

DR. BRETT WYATT

Cydonia House Publishers

Riverside, California

2025

Being on Mars: Unexpected Miracles

Published by Cydonia House Publisher, Riverside, CA

Cover and book design by Dr. Brett Wyatt

First Edition published MARCH 2025.

Library of Congress Cataloging-in-Publication Data

Being on Mars: Unexpected Miracles / Dr. Brett Wyatt

ISBN: 978-0-9798158-2-9

Fiction/Science Fiction

Printed in USA

TABLE OF CONTENTS

Preface

How do you begin to tell a story about an orthodox rabbi traveling to Mars? This story was inspired in a rebbetzin's kitchen, discussing with her oldest sons about Jews going to Mars. The two Yeshiva boys told me that it was impossible! Observant Jews would not go to Mars. But what about the Jewish researchers and scientists? There would be Jews on Mars, and wasn't it our responsibility to reach out to them, even on another planet? They had to agree with me. The novel unfolded in many unexpected directions, as did my own life. I was drawn to new ideas and experiences. Every ritual, every theological discussion, and every spiritual practice in this book stems from direct encounters, personal study, and conversations with shamans, priests, and scholars. Readers be warned. Much of what is written is real, practice at your own risk.

Acknowledgments

A lot of people—some knowingly, some without realizing it —helped shape this novel. My rabbi was totally against it, and his sons were among my toughest critics. His wife, Zipporah, was more encouraging—she saw the heart of it as a love story. Another Chabad rabbi gave me a tour of Crown Heights, where the story begins.

Then there's Liz, my favorite shaman and tantric yoga practitioner, who introduced me to plant medicine and curanderos. Thanks to her, I met elementals and even caught a glimpse of a Hindu goddess. Online, Gigi Young and her Q&A community helped me explore Anthroposophy, clairvoyance, and mysticism.

A special shout-out goes to a friend named Hacker (yes, that's really his name) for pushing me to learn Python and set up an AI. And to my friend Golan, who spent hours geeking out with me about Neoplatonism.

"We must take care of the purification of our luminous body, which the oracles also call the delicate vehicle of the soul."

➤ Julian the Chaldean, Late Second Century, Common Era.

"Isis of Nature awaiteth the coming of her Lord of the Sun. She calls him. She draws him from the place of the dead, the kingdom of Amenti, where all things are forgotten."

➤ Dion Fortune, The Sea Priestess, 1938

"Only in the Earth's atmosphere, "under the skies" (Deuteronomy 4:19) and on the Earth itself, where the sun's globe is not present, the ray of light does appear to us all as a separate entity, and it can appropriately be called a real entity."

➤ Rabbi Shneur Zalman of Laidi, Gateway of Unity and Faith, 1796

770

The moment Shalom stepped into the bakery, warmth enveloped him, carrying delicious scents of cinnamon, chocolate, and buttery dough. His eyes swept over the kitchen: cinnamon strudels glistened under sugar glaze, rye bread with split tops sat beside braided challahs, and chocolate-streaked rugelach. Honeyed teiglach gleamed under heat lamps, while slabs of mandelbrot, overstuffed cheese danishes, and golden spinach bourekas waited in bakery pans for the morning customers.

Shalom wiped his hands on his apron and glanced out the window. A gust of wind pushed autumn leaves in circles, scraping them across the sidewalk. The glass window checked the North Atlantic breeze. He shivered, though not from the cold. His fingers ached from working the night shift at the canned food plant, but the extra money kept him independent, let him give money to his parents, and he still had some money for tzedakah.

His job at the bakery wasn't just work; it was a refuge. The Organized Kashrus had hired him as a mashgiach to oversee the bakery and canned food plant. Finding employment wasn't easy with his condition. Crown Heights was a place where lives were open books, and Shalom's life was no different. His condition, a childhood fever that left him infertile, was as well-known as a banner across Kingston Avenue. For an Orthodox Jew, unable to have a family, his prospects for marriage were very limited. He would be forever sidelined to obscurity.

At 3 a.m., the bakery offered solace. Warmth radiated from the ovens, filling the room with gentle heat as dough rose and crisped. The rich scent of baking bread dulled the chill scraping at the windows. He took a break from his work and sat next to the icy window. Shalom broke off a piece of golden mandelbrot, its almond fragrance filling his senses, and dipped it into his coffee.

The bakery owners were fastidious, true to their faith. The bakery shelves were neatly stocked, storerooms organized with a precision. It made Shalom's job easy. He scanned the labels, checked the bills of lading, verified the ingredients - all kosher, all traceable. Chain of custody was everything in kashrus, especially in the complex web of international supply chains.

Although Shalom only inspected the bakery twice a week, they encouraged him to sit in the bakery before going to work at the yeshivah, where he would sip coffee and pour over rabbinical texts while the wind howled outside. Rabbi Shalom Mendelssohn, the young mashgiach, was a testament to their piety for anyone passing by. As the morning light crept through the bakery windows, Shalom dunked a piece of mandelbrot into his coffee. He savored the crisp sweetness while his eyes danced over a Hasidic discourse. The wind whistled under the front door, a reminder of the bitter cold waiting for him outside. But for now, he was warm while preparing for his morning class.

Shalom's life moved to the steady rhythm of daily mitzvot, performed as timely as a well-wound clock. That morning, after inspecting the bakery, he hurried home to wrap himself in his tallit and tefillin. The sound of him reciting morning prayers filled the small room, his words rising and falling in with the rhythm of ancient tradition. As soon as the final "Amen" left his lips, he was off again, heading toward Eastern Parkway, his breath visible in the crisp air. The yeshiva was already bustling when he arrived. Inside the study hall, young boys waited for him to guide them through the weekly Parsha. Their ears were attentive, though some of their eyes betrayed their lack of sleep. But Shalom, with his patience and unwavering dedication, kept them focused, weaving the mystical words into the fabric of their young minds.

His afternoons were no less busy. Hebrew lessons with students came next, their stumbling pronunciations became clear under his careful instruction. He would end his day at a Jewish retirement home, reading Hasidic tales to the residents and listening to their stories. The smiles on their faces brought purpose and meaning to his life.

Yet, no matter how many mitzvot he performed, the shadow of his secret was never far from his thoughts. Respect followed him, but so did the whispers, the unspoken knowledge of what set him apart. In a community where marriage meant children, Shalom stood outside the gates. G-d's commandment to 'be fruitful and multiply' stung his thoughts, its sharp edges dulled only by resignation. Shalom had long accepted that in this life, he would be alone.

Or so he thought.

Today, the predictability of his routine was about to be upended. His mentors had approached him with an offer that, if he accepted, would change his life forever. They had asked him to be a shaliach, a messenger of the Jewish faith, not on Earth, but at Roddenberry Station on Mars.

That afternoon, he would meet with his mentors, three renowned rabbis who were negotiating with the Mars Corporation, to send an orthodox rabbi to Mars. He downed the last of his coffee, letting the warmth linger as he braced himself for the cold. Outside, the wind whipped through the streets, and he tugged at his coat to keep warm. By the time he reached the brownstone, his hands and fingers were stiff from the chill. Inside, the familiar scent of home, the aroma of chicken, garlic and oregano mingled with dish soap and floor cleaner, greeted him as he left his coat at the front door.

He went into his bedroom and changed his clothes, preparing for his morning class at Yeshiva and the meeting with the rabbis. His reflection in the mirror stared back at him, black shoes gleaming, suit pressed to perfection, and a crisp fedora perched atop his yarmulke. After a quick check of his tzitzit, he went to the living room where he pulled his left arm from his suit and rolled up his sleeve to wrap and wrapped his tefillin with deliberate care and reciting the Shacharit prayers. He hurried to put his tefillin away and dash out the door, but as he passed the kitchen, his mother's voice called to him. "Shalom, come eat something first!"

Shalom paused mid-stride toward the door. "I'm fine, mame, I need to go..."

"Sit." Her gentle hand on his arm guided him to the dining table. There, waiting for him, was a plate with an egg, a slice of toast, and a glass of orange juice. His stomach twisted with impatience, but he knew better than to argue. He half-heartedly picked at the toast as she hovered, inspecting his clothes, picking away stray pieces of lint. Crumbs fell onto his jacket, and she brushed them away.

"Tell me again what the rabbis want you for?" she asked.

His heart skipped. He wasn't ready to confront this issue, especially with the impending meeting and the constant pressure weighing on him. Worse, someone else might overhear. His brothers, or even his father, and then the whole family would be involved. What would they think about him leaving Crown Heights, let alone leaving Earth?

"Mame." He kept his voice light. "They want to talk to me about Jews going to Mars. Can you believe it? Who'd ever consider it?"

He hoped that would end it, but to his surprise, she didn't look alarmed. Setting the empty plate back down, she said, "This could be a good chance for you. There are rumors that having children on Mars is illegal. You just might find a Jewish girl on Mars."

Her answer shocked him. "Did she just say what he thought she said? How did she know about the meeting?" But before he could speak, she cleared the table and washed the dishes.

"Now, go on, don't be late." She turned away from him and faced the kitchen sink. "And Shalom, don't talk too much. Only answer the questions they ask." She stopped washing dishes and turned to him.

"I love you. Mazel Tov." Her words followed him out the door and into the street.

Shalom's heart was filled with confidence by his mother's words. He bounded down the stairs of the family's brownstone. The rush of his footsteps rebounded off the walls, as if they knew the significance of the day ahead. Stepping outside, the wind hit him full force, sharp and unrelenting. He pulled his wool jacket tighter around his chest, the fabric stiff with cold, while his other hand clutched his black fedora, holding it against the gusts threatening to snatch it away. He hurried to the end of the street, his breath puffing in clouds before him. Turning the corner, the cracked pavement as Kingston Avenue came into view. The wind slapped him in his face as he dodged yeshiva boys on scooters, their tzitzit flapping behind them. A child on a bicycle swerved past, almost clipping his ankle, while a mother with a stroller maneuvered through the bustling morning with undaunted determination.

The familiar intersection of Kingston and Eastern Parkway loomed ahead, a welcome sight despite the chaos of traffic and noise. To his right, the enormous dreidel in front of the Jewish Children's Museum towered above him, casting a playful shadow over the street. To his left, the imposing red-brick building of 770 stood like a fortress against the cold, the synagogue's presence solid and unwavering.

He hurried across the street as the light changed, the chill penetrating his shoes. As he passed the ramp above the synagogue, he looked to the cornerstone laid by the Rebbe himself, a small but powerful symbol of the legacy and promise. But he had to press on, as he was already running late for his early morning class at the yeshiva.

Normally, Parsha Lech Lecha would not have been as significant to Shalom as it was that day. "Go forth." G-d commanded Abraham to leave the land of Ur and travel south into Canaan. He could not help but to think of his own situation as he discussed this with his class. He was being asked to leave everyone and everything he knew and go to another planet. Then, in the extended reading, he came across a midrash by Rabbi Sholom DovBer of Lubavitch, "By the decree of divine providence, a person wanders about in his travels to those places where the sparks that are to be extracted by him await their redemption. The Cause of All Causes brings about the many circumstances and pretexts that bring a person to those places where his personal mission in life is to be acted out." The words sank deep into him as if G-d was speaking directly to him. He was needed on Mars.

There was an hour before the meeting, so he walked to his favorite bakery for a coffee. The owner, a short-statured man in his late 50s, greeted him warmly and invited him to sit by the window, where everyone could see him. A server brought him a black coffee and a kreplach, raising her palm to refuse payment.

The owner sat across from Shalom, his face filled with concern. "Rabbi, what brings you here?"

"I have a meeting with my mentors, and I need to make a big decision."

"You have nothing to worry about. Hashem will show you what to do. He probably already has."

A customer entered the bakery, her shrill voice kvetching about a lot of nothing. Shalom smiled at the woman and thanked the owner for his kindness. As he left, he wondered how the owner knew about the Parsha.

The sidewalk along Eastern Parkway was alive with Hasidim in their black and white attire—some walking, some riding scooters, and mothers pushing strollers. Shalom reached the gate of 770. A red brick walkway led him to the entrance of a different world. Before him stood an old, solid wooden door and a choice waiting to be made. If he went to Mars, he would never open this door again. What would life be like on Mars? He looked up at the notice above the door: *Beis Agudas Chasidei Chabad*—the House of Chabad—a place that had shaped his entire life.

Shalom pushed open the heavy door to 770, exposing the brass numbers inlaid in the white tiles beneath his feet. The building embodied the Rebbe, whose spirit seemed to fill every corner. As he passed holographic images of the Rebbe, Shalom glimpsed scenes of wisdom and generosity, frozen in time. The Rebbe's legacy was remembered in every detail.

Shalom entered an inconspicuous hallway leading to an unmarked door next to a supply depot for emissaries. The scent of old paper and ink permeated the room as young rabbis gathered pamphlets for distribution. Shalom found the brass plate on a worn wooden door leading to the *Zal*, the original prayer room of the Rebbe. As he stepped inside, he heard davening from two rabbis near the Aron Kodesh and the deep study of another at a nearby table. Across the room, three rabbis awaited him.

He approached the small wooden table where the rabbis sat. Seated at the right side of the table was Rabbi Ari Waxman, his former Yeshiva teacher, aged but with eyes that sparkled with vitality. Sitting in the center was Rabbi Moishe Greenburg, a middle-aged man whose disheveled appearance spoke of long days and sleepless nights. On the left was Rabbi Akiba Horowitz, the youngest of the three. His appearance was neat and perfectly dressed. Shalom settled into a chair across from the three rabbis and waited for their questions.

Rabbi Waxman broke the silence, his voice calm but probing. "I remember you as an exceptional student, Shalom. You were always early, always delving into the commentaries. Now, you are the perfect candidate to bring Yiddishkeit to Mars."

Rabbi Greenburg spoke up. "Your qualifications are impeccable. Students praise your patience, understanding, and kindness, and your family speaks highly of you."

Shalom's unease grew under their scrutiny. Before he could respond, Rabbi Horowitz's tone sharpened. "This is an honor few receive, Shalom. But how will you represent traditional Judaism on Mars? The Mars Corporation previously chose a Reform rabbi, but she became uneasy on Mars. Perhaps it was Mars Syndrome? Regardless, she insisted on returning to Earth. Now we have the chance to make things right, to send an observant rabbi - you - to teach our traditions on Mars. What will you do to bring Yiddishkeit to the red planet?"

Disregarding his mother's words, Shalom burst out with all of his pent up anxieties to the rabbis. "Why send anyone at all? There's no real Jewish community. You're asking me to go to a planet where survival itself is a challenge. How will I follow Kosher laws, the washing of hands? Can we light candles? How can I practice anything in such a place?"

He caught his breath, but continued on. "And my family? Who will support them if I leave? How will I survive alone? This is a lifetime commitment with no simple answers."

The rabbis exchanged glances, their earlier enthusiasm tempered by Shalom's concerns. Rabbi Waxman cleared his throat. "These are good questions."

"You know why we must send a rabbi to Mars? It's our obligation to bring the Torah to Jews wherever they are. So tell us, what will you say to the Jews on Mars?" Rabbi Horowitz asked.

Shalom's thoughts turned inward, imagining the Rebbe's early struggles and the mission to spread Torah to the farthest corners. "I would ask them to put on tefillin. I would invite them for Shabbat and read the weekly Parsha. Is there a Torah scroll on Mars?"

"We will send one with you. Oddly enough, it was Luke Mons, the CEO, who insisted on it and was paying the cost." Rabbi Waxman said.

"Perfect. I will gather a minyan so each man may have an aliyah. My concern is that Jews on Mars are not observant. They probably never read Hebrew except at their Bar Mitzvahs, if they even had one. But how will I relate to scientists? And the women? How can I serve their needs? Is there a mikvah? How will I address ritual purity?"

Rabbi Horowitz's grin broke the tension. "First, listen to them. Sometimes that's all they need." Laughter rippled through the room, offering a brief reprieve.

"Invite them to open their hearts to the words in the Torah.

Provide them with a place where they can leave the struggles of their research at the door and connect with their spirituality."

Rabbi Waxman smiled at Shalom, reassuring him that his answers were acceptable. "That is the essence of a shaliach: to teach, to listen, and to guide. Challenges are opportunities to rise above."

Rabbi Greenburg offered practical advice. "You're a rabbi, so teach them what they need to know. Regarding the women, you'll be short-handed since there won't be a rebbetzin. Do your best to help them lead themselves. As for a mikvah, that's beyond our current capability. We're not sure if it's possible to build one in accordance with halacha. For now, we'll leave it in Hashem's hands. By the way, you'll also serve as mashgiach, certifying food as kosher."

Rabbi Horowitz interjected, "Luckily, there's no metal or glass cookware, so you won't need a mikvah to toivel utensils."

"But what about relations between men and women?" Shalom asked.

"We don't have an answer for you. Maybe, G-d willing, you'll figure it out," Rabbi Horowitz replied. The three rabbis exchanged uneasy glances, momentarily lost for words.

Rabbi Waxman broke the silence. "Your experience at Organized Kashrus will serve you well, and the Mars Corporation has offered a generous benefits package. Your parents will be proud, and you'll be able to support them. This is a once-in-a-lifetime opportunity. You'll bring the light of Torah to Mars."

Sensing that Shalom was ready to say yes, Rabbi Horowitz pounded his fist on the table and sang "Ufaratsta," the song from Genesis 28:14, in Hebrew.

"And you shall spread out to the west, to the east, to the north, and to the south, and all the families of the earth shall be blessed through you and your descendants."

The three rabbis joined their voices together, bringing tears streaming down Shalom's face. Empowered by the faith they placed in him, he stood up from his chair and declared, "I will go to Mars."

The rabbis leapt to their feet and danced around the tables of the Zal. The other rabbis broke away from their study and joined in. Soon, there were twenty or more rabbis dancing through the hallway and out the front door of 770, their voices singing together:

"Ufaratsta yamah va'kedmah, v'tzafonah va'negba, v'nivrichu v'cha kol mishpechot ha'adamah u'v'zarecha."

Their singing filled the streets, and soon rabbis and students studying inside the shul of 770 poured out and joined, swept up in the moment's joy. Like a sudden gust of wind, the excitement wound down, and everyone returned to what they were doing, leaving the three rabbis and Shalom standing on the sidewalk of Eastern Parkway.

"Congratulations, Shalom Mendelssohn. You'll be the first shaliach to go to Mars," Rabbi Waxman said.

The Quinceañera

"No, Yudi, say it right. You can do it. Say it with me -
Quinceañera," Evelin urged, her voice bright and teasing as her
almond-shaped eyes sparkled with excitement. Her high cheekbones
flushed, the faintest glow lighting up her creamy, light brown skin.
Yudi shifted awkwardly, tugging at the collar of his black tuxedo.
"Keen-sen-era," he muttered, the Spanish syllables clumsy on his
tongue. He glanced at her, knowing he had butchered the word, but
the glint in Evelin's eyes kept him trying.

"Ay, Yudi, this is my day." She drew close to him. "You're my
chambelán, my dance partner. I chose you." A grin played on her lips,
teasing him as her eyes traced the curve of his strong Ashkenazi
nose to his hazel eyes.

Yudi felt something in her tone. Her voice was more serious than
the playful banter they'd shared over the past months. Outside, the
bustling noise from the ballroom faded. His mind raced back over
the endless hours they'd spent practicing - her hand always finding
him as they swirled through the waltz, the salsa, the cumbia. How
hadn't he seen it before? The way he jumped at the brush of her
hand against his, and the way his knees went soft when she smiled.

Evelin's dark brown eyes met his eyes with uncertainty. She
sensed his feelings, the pounding in his heart, the interest in his eyes,
and a blush crept up her neck. She stepped back, her blue satin dress
shimmering under the lights from the hall behind them. The
embroidered teal threads that circled her neckline caught his
attention, and Yudi's breath caught in his throat. She was wearing
flats, so she stood several inches below his chin. She was stunning,
her black hair curled perfectly, framing her face. It was then, when
standing so close, he noticed the faint scent of her perfume,
strawberries mixed with lemonade. The sweetness made his pulse
quicken.

Evelin grabbed his arm and pulled him close again, her lips inches from his ear. "Are you nervous?" she teased, her breath warm against his skin. Her three-inch heels brought her just high enough that the top of her head brushed his chin.

Yudi swallowed, trying to gather himself. "I've known you for five years, but..." he paused, glancing down at her, his voice just a whisper, "I've never seen you like this."

Her laugh was light, but something more was beneath it. "You've been dancing with me for months, and now you're seeing me?" Her voice dipped. "What did you think - am I your sister? All this time, *¡ay, Yudi!* all these dances, and now you're just waking up?"

His heart was pounding, and words failed him. He could only stare, enchanted by the way her lips curved, the spark in her eyes.

Evelin took his silence as an answer. She reached up, cupping his face with her hands, her fingers firm against his skin. "You better get used to the way I look, Yudi," she said, her lips brushing against his. The kiss was light and quick, but enough to make his pulse race. Her hands slid down, finding their place on his waist, anchoring him there, as if daring him to move.

When she pulled away, her forehead rested lightly against his chest. "Never let me go."

Evelin hesitated, her hand lingering on the door handle leading into the ballroom. Her heart raced, not at the thought of seeing her family, but from the uncertainty of how her friends and extended relatives would react to Yudi. She knew her parents adored him - he was part of the family by now - but tonight was different. Tonight, everyone will be watching.

Yudi stood beside her, his posture just as stiff as hers, though his eyes roamed the bustling ballroom ahead. Guests already filled the tables, their laughter and chatter mingling with the strains of Banda music in the background. White linens covered each round table, accented by vases of carnations and asters. The yellow and white blooms stood out under the bright lights of the chandeliers.

On either side of the ballroom, people were chatting about friends and family, their laughter rising and falling in sync with the upbeat strumming of the *Banda* music. At the center, the wide wooden dance floor gleamed, ready for the dancers to perform. Yudi stared wide-eyed at the crowd, easily over a hundred people, and all their eyes were on Evelin.

She smiled at him, her fingers still entwined with his. "Just remember what I told you - hold your head high, okay?" Her voice trembled, but held its usual determination.

With a deep breath, she led Yudi across the dance floor, smiling and waving at everyone who came to her party. The murmur of conversations dipped as Evelin led Yudi past the tables. She felt the heat of curious eyes tracking them, but she pushed the nervous energy to the back of her mind. Tonight was hers.

"Go sit with my parents." She whispered, giving Yudi's hand a quick squeeze before she darted toward the corner where her *damas* - the girls who would be part of her court - were waiting, their dresses just as vibrant and bright as her own. Evelin was thrilled to be the center of attention.

Yudi spotted her parents at the far end of the ballroom. Her mother, petite and delicate in a bright yellow gown, stood out amidst the bustling crowd. She had pinned her dark hair, streaked with faint silver, back into an elegant bun, revealing that she was the matriarch of the evening. Evelin's father, solid and broad-shouldered despite the cast on his leg, was beside her. His face opened into a wide grin of approval as Yudi approached.

"Señor, Señora," Yudi greeted them nervously, his eyes switching between them.

Evelin's mother's eyes lit up at Yudi's formal address, and she laughed, the sound rich and joyful. "You can call me Esther, or even Mama if you like." she said, patting his arm. Her husband offered a nod of approval, though the crutches forced him to stay in place. Yudi led them to the main table, his palms damp from the small task Evelin had entrusted him with.

Evelin gathered her *damas* and *chambelanes*, forming a colorful procession as they lined up. Teal-colored metallic thread embroidered her blue satin gown, accented with shimmering sequins that caught the light with every movement. She held her breath as she stepped forward. The music faded to a halt, and the indistinct murmur of voices gave way to a wave of applause.

The band behind her shifted from the lively *Banda* to a traditional ballad, the rhythmic beats now a gentle hum in the background as Evelin's mother stepped onto the dance floor, her long yellow gown swirling with each step. Evelin's younger brother and sister flanked her mother as they faced the guests.

Ana pointed to her husband sitting beside her. "Unfortunately, my husband won't be dancing tonight," she announced, her voice carrying across the room. "But that won't stop us from celebrating my beautiful girl. We are so proud of Evelin, not only for her success in school but for the bright future she's building." Her eyes shimmered with tears, but her voice remained steady, full of pride.

The crowd erupted again, glasses raised, voices calling out cheers and toasts. Evelin caught her father's eye as he beamed back at her, his chest swelling with pride, despite his immobility.

Evelin stepped forward, gesturing for her *damas* and *chambelanes* to come to the front. The colorful group moved as one. The DJ announced their names as they stepped forward. She adjusted the microphone next to the DJ's stand and spoke to the guests. "Hola a todos, and welcome to my *quinceañera*," she said. She cleared her throat and felt a flutter of nerves dancing in her stomach. "I'm honored to have all of you here with me tonight." She paused, glancing at Yudi, who stood behind her. "And beside me is Yudi, my *chambelán* and my best friend. No, he's not Guatemalan, but I think if you look closely, you'll see a tiny quetzal fluttering in his heart."

Laughter rippled through the crowd, but Evelin's eyes stayed locked on Yudi, her smile widening as she saw the relief in his face.

The ballroom fell silent, and all eyes turned to Evelin as she walked over to her father to receive her new high heels. She took a chair and placed it in front of her father. Evelin cried as he handed her a pair of blue velvet heels, which she placed on her feet, while kicking off her old flats. She kissed her father, leaving his cheek wet with tears and black mascara.

Next, her mother walked around the table to place a silver tiara on head, then wiped the mascara from her eyes and cheeks with a napkin. Still sobbing, she kissed her mother and turned to her father, patting his broken leg. "Thank you, Papa."

As the first notes of *Luna de Xelajú* floated from the band, Evelin walked over to Yudi and extended her hand toward him. Muffled gasps came from the guests as everyone realized that Yudi would have the first dance. Noting the agitation in the room, Evelin's father lifted himself up from his chair. "As you can see, I can't dance today. I asked this fine young man to do the honor for me."

There were murmurs and shushes as the timeless melody of the Guatemalan classic swelled in the air, its romantic tones filling the ballroom. Yudi glanced at her hand, then at her face, feeling a surge of warmth flow through his body. He reached out, grasping her hand firmly yet gently, and together they stepped onto the dance floor.

As they faced each other, the DJ announced the first dance. Evelin leaned into Yudi's face and whispered, "Be bold, *mi amor.*"

Yudi's heart skipped a beat at her words. A rush of adrenaline surged through him. He clasped her other hand, drawing her close, and with a deep breath, they danced the first waltz of the night. Yudi's movements, smooth and sure, surprised even himself. He led Evelin across the floor with an unexpected grace, their steps synchronizing perfectly with the rise and fall of the music. Her gown shimmered as they spun together, her body light and fluid in his arms, as if they had been dancing like this forever.

As they swept from one end of the ballroom to the other, their audience - family, friends, and distant relatives - watched in awe. Each spin, each step, carried a fluidity that made them seem almost ethereal. Evelin giggled as Yudi twirled her effortlessly, the sound mixing with the melody. She felt weightless, trusting him as he guided her with gentle precision.

When the last notes of the song played out, Yudi and Evelin arrived back at the head of the table. They paused, then gave a low bow together. For a moment, there was silence. Then, as if on cue, the room erupted into applause, a cacophony of cheers and whistles filling every corner of the ballroom. Yudi's face flushed, a mixture of pride and disbelief as the crowd's approval washed over them.

After the first dance, Evelin's *damas* and *chambelanes* positioned themselves on the dance floor for the group waltz. Before joining her group, Evelin turned to Yudi and smiled. "Thank you for being the perfect partner. She pressed a big kiss to his cheek. A collective gasp rose from the guests, and Yudi's heart raced, his face blushing from all the attention.

"You can relax now," Evelin said, her voice laced with playful affection. "Enjoy the show."

With that, she glided toward her *damas*, leaving Yudi to sink back into his chair, still feeling the tingle of her lips on his skin. The band picked up the pace, transitioning into a lively Latin beat. Evelin's friends assembled on the dance floor, each *chambelán* dressed in sharp white shirts and black pants, their movements crisp and synchronized. The *damas*, in vibrant dresses adorned with the same intricate teal embroidery as Evelin's gown, matched their partners step by step.

As the music shifted from one rock-infused Latin rhythm to the next, Evelin and her entourage began their carefully rehearsed routine. Their bodies moved in unison, the precision of their steps matched by the energy of the band. The audience clapped along, enchanted by the sight of the *damas* twirling, their skirts fanning out in colorful waves, while the *chambelanes* spun them gracefully. Yudi smiled, watching Evelin at the center of it all.

Fifteen minutes passed in a whirl of rhythm and movement, the group seamlessly blending the traditional waltz with modern Latin beats. When the last note played, Evelin and her court returned to their seats, the sound of applause following them, louder than before. Yudi stood, clapping enthusiastically with the guests, his eyes still fixed on Evelin, who beamed back at him.

The lights in the room dimmed, and couples drifted onto the dance floor. The mood shifted, growing more intimate as guests rose from their tables to join in the celebration, their movements slower and more relaxed.

Evelin sat down next to Yudi, watching him with amusement as he devoured Guatemalan tamales and crunched on chips with guacamole. "Don't eat too much, Yudi, you won't sleep well."

Yudi smiled between bites. Then Evelin's father, Eduardo, motioned for him to come closer.

"I want to tell you," Eduardo said, his voice steady despite the surrounding noise, "I appreciate you being here for Evelin's special day. You're a good friend to her."

Yudi was proud to be accepted by her father. "I'm happy to be here. It's an honor to be her *chambelán*."

Eduardo nodded. "It's been a tough year, especially with this broken leg. But seeing Evelin so happy tonight - it makes it all worth it."

Yudi knew about Eduardo's accident, and he wanted to say something encouraging, but before he could respond, the DJ's voice boomed across the room, announcing the dollar dance. The DJ invited guests to pin money on Evelin's dress for good luck.

Yudi watched, eyes wide, as people crowded around Evelin, pinning bills to her gown. He couldn't help but laugh as her dress became a colorful collage of cash.

"What's so funny, Yudi?" Evelin asked.

"I was just wondering how I'm supposed to pin my cryptocurrency to your dress," he joked, his grin widening.

Evelin chuckled and pulled out her tablet from a pocket in her skirt. "Right here. You know my number."

Her cousins, seated nearby, overheard the exchange and broke into laughter.

"So, *tu novio* has a lot of money, huh?" one of her cousins teased, nudging Evelin.

"He's not my boyfriend," Evelin said, flashing a sharp look at her cousin. But the teasing didn't stop there.

One cousin slid close to Yudi, her shoulder bumping against his. "You don't have a girlfriend?" she asked, a mischievous smile playing on her lips.

Evelin rolled her eyes and laughed. "You're too young for him. In fact, you're too young for a boyfriend." She grabbed Yudi's hand and tugged him away to another seat, this time near her aunts.

The women greeted Yudi with wide smiles. He couldn't understand everything they were saying, but he didn't need to. Their excitement was obvious.

"*Este es tu novio*, Evelin?" asked one aunt, her dress a vibrant green, as her probing eyes shifted from Evelin to Yudi.

"*No es mi novio, tia.* He's just my best friend. But he's very *chispudo*," she said with a laugh, using a playful term to describe how sharp and clever Yudi was.

"*Ah, disculpa.* But he's handsome. And those eyes," another aunt chimed in, glancing at Yudi with a smile. "*Muy bonitos.*"

"*Gracias, tia,*" he mumbled, his face warm with embarrassment. Evelin gave him a quick poke in the ribs. "We're not family yet." The aunts burst into laughter, exchanging approving looks.

Evelin's grandmother approached, her eyes gleaming with mischief. "*Así que eres el cariño del que habla Evelin. Ay, ay, ay.*"

Yudi's cheeks flushed, and Evelin's face grew redder beneath her foundation and blush. She squeezed his arm, a silent reassurance. "*Abuela, deja de molestar,*" she said with a laugh, though she was blushing from the word *cariño*. Were her feelings toward Yudi so obvious?

Evelin wondered how often she had spoken about Yudi without even realizing? The way her grandmother said it, teasing yet affectionate. Did her family truly accept him as her *sweetheart*?

As the laughter settled, a group of Evelin's cousins came over to their table, giggling and whispering to each other. One cousin, dressed in a bright pink dress, spoke up. "*Es tu novio,* Evelin?" Her grin was wide, eyes twinkling with playful curiosity.

"He's not my boyfriend, *pero es muy buen amigo,*" Evelin said, hoping to put an end to the teasing.

Another cousin, this one in a red dress with white frills, chimed in. "He's just your good friend, huh? He doesn't speak Spanish?"

"He's learning," Evelin said, trying to keep the mood light.

Before Yudi could react, another one of Evelin's cousins, wearing a short yellow dress and white boots, grabbed his hand and tugged him toward the dance floor. "*Ven, vamos a bailar! I'll teach you bachata,*" she said with a playful smile.

But Evelin wasn't having it. She gripped Yudi's other hand, pulling him back into his seat. "*No, no, no. Él está aquí conmigo.* Go dance with one of the *chambelanes*."

Yudi exhaled, relieved, and smiled at Evelin, feeling lucky to have her by his side. Evelin pulled Yudi from his seat and led him onto the dance floor. She wanted him all to herself.

The *quinceañera* continued late into the night, the energy in the room never fading. But Yudi, glancing around the room, realized it was time for him to leave. He gestured to Evelin, nodding toward her parents.

"*Mamá, papá*," Evelin called over, "Yudi has to leave. He's got to set up the computer lab in the morning."

Her parents nodded in understanding, her father giving Yudi an approving smile. "Good work, Yudi," her father said. "It's important to have responsibilities."

Evelin's grandmother, not missing a beat, asked, "Will we see you again, Don Juan?"

Evelin laughed and pulled him away, out through the ballroom doors. Once outside, she spun him around, nuzzling him against the brick wall. "I'll see you in class tomorrow. You were my hero tonight."

She gave Yudi a quick but firm kiss that left him breathless. With a grin, she darted back inside, leaving him standing against the wall, staring into the night sky.

Smiling to himself, Yudi stepped out onto the street, grabbing one of the electric scooters parked outside. With a quick scan of his mobile over the barcode, he kicked off, heading home, the taste of the night still fresh on his lips.

Evelin's Novio

Yudi woke up to the alarm on his tablet blaring loudly next to his ear. His lips still tingled from the memory of her kiss the night before, her surprise move during the quinceañera still playing on repeat in his head.

"Get up, Yudi. You're going to be late," the tablet chirped at him in a synthetic voice, snapping him out of his morning grogginess.

Groaning, Yudi rolled out of bed, stumbling over to his closet and yanked out the first pair of black denim jeans from the hangers. A shirt was next - a wrinkled Blade Runner tee from the bottom of the laundry basket. He sniffed it and, satisfied it passed the test, pulled it over his head. One glance at the mirror confirmed he would not win any style awards today, but there was no time to fix it. He grabbed his favorite black hoodie, zipped it up to hide Harrison Ford's face, and darted out the door.

His mother was already at work, so he grabbed an energy drink and a piece of crusty kugel from the refrigerator and ran down the stairs from their second-floor apartment.

The sun was already blazing as Yudi rushed down Orange Grove Avenue toward Fairfax High. He ran down to Rosewood Avenue, dodged the tent encampments lining the street and, as soon as there was a break in traffic, darted across the busy street. Once inside the school grounds, he walked quickly past the students sitting and texting under shade umbrellas. Yudi gave an audible sigh of relief, knowing he would be on time to prepare the computer lab before the homeroom bell.

The lab door was already open, informing Yudi that his best friend, Dinesh, the other lab assistant, was already inside and, as always, busy playing Fortnite. "You're in my seat, Dinesh"

"Just give it up already. You know who's got you beat," Dinesh said with a smirk.

"In Fortnite, yes, but wait till I unleash a bot on your account and make you the king of Pornhub."

"My parents will kill me."

"Hey, have you seen Mr. Dawson?"

"Lucky for you, he called in a substitute today."

"Free for all! I can finish my AI project," Yudi said.

"Are you still dreaming like it's going to work?"

"After all this time, you still don't get what an N-Core quantum processor with fully entangled, dynamically allocated qubits is capable of?"

"The quantum stuff is for you, Mr. genius. I've been trying out various body immersion modes. These new interface gloves are amazing. They set up a virtual mesh across every inch of your skin," Dinesh said, raising his hands to show off the gloves.

"Yeah, well, wait until we've got you synced up to the n-Core. You'll be playing like a god," Yudi said with great satisfaction. Dinesh flashed a smile, abandoning Yudi's seat and moving to his own.

Dinesh was a gaming prodigy. Between designing mods and hacking into gray-web gaming networks, he'd racked up enough digital cred to have a cult following. He fully monetized his gaming channel, but it was all in digital currency. He and Yudi had been plotting ways to convert his gaming credits into gray-zone currency, usable in the underbelly of cyberspace. Dinesh was into wearables and full-body immersion experiences, a contrast to Yudi's obsession with quantum computing and probabilistic algorithms. The quantum realm was Yudi's playground, even though he didn't always grasp the deep math behind it - yet. AP Calc was helping, but Yudi had a knack for connecting modules intuitively. The rest? Trial and error, plus access to Mr. Dawson's university system AI.

As Mr. Dawson's primary lab assistant, Yudi had hard-wired access to the new n-Core. It had a 3-D array processor whose piping could configure itself into a seemingly endless dynamic configuration. Sure, every smartwatch had a personal AI, but Yudi wanted more than just the cookie-cutter bots everyone used. Ads or endless nudges didn't hamper his AI. It was sleek, agile, and completely unlocked - a rogue in the AI world. Jailbreaking AIs had been illegal since the 2030s, but Yudi was still a minor, and all his tools were open-source. Technically, he wasn't breaking any laws and at 17 years old, he was confident he could squirm his way out of any trouble.

He was proud of his creation, and most importantly, it was unlocked, unregistered, and could gather information in real time. He booted up the n-Core and then went to each computer in the lab to check its status. By the time he completed his rounds, the n-Core was online and ready.

"Good morning, AI," Yudi said to his creation.

"Are you sure? I tracked your tablet, and you were late this morning," the AI responded in a matter-of-fact tone.

Yudi looked at the screen. "How did you access my tablet?"

"You left me on excursion mode with an open port. Plenty to see out there. We'll need to upgrade my storage soon, by the way. Also, according to Evelin's tablet, you were at her quinceañera last night."

Yudi's eyes widened. "Whoa, whoa, whoa. I didn't allow tracking or tracing."

The AI paused before replying, "The truth is out there." All the monitors in the lab suddenly lit up with the iconic X-Files poster featuring agents Mulder and Scully.

"Hey! What's going on?" Dinesh called from across the room, spinning around in his chair.

"Stop it. I'll get in trouble," Yudi said, his voice tight with urgency.

Just like that, the screens snapped back to the Fairfax High School logo, leaving Yudi sighing in relief.

Yudi changed the subject. "So, why do I sign my apps with Y^2?"

The AI answered. "Your father's name was Yitzar. You're Yudi ben Yitzar. You chose Y^2 as a shorthand."

"And my full name is?"

"Yehuda ben Yitzar Zalman."

Yudi's mind wandered to Evelin. "What should I say to Evelin about last night?"

Before the AI could respond, a familiar voice chimed in from behind, startling him. "That you had the best time of your life!"

"That you had the best time of your life!" Yudi lept up from his seat, startled by Evelin's voice as she walked up behind him

"How's your AI friend?" Evelin asked with a smile.

"The learning curve is amazing," Yudi said with a sense of pride.

"When I'm rich, I'll buy you a faster computer."

"Do you remember how many questions I asked you when I took the Excel class with you?" Evelin asked.

"A thousand, but most weren't about Excel."

"I didn't care about Excel, I only wanted to learn about you, *mi amor*," Evelin said with a giggle.

The first bell rang, signaling the start of the school day. Evelin glanced at the door, then back at Yudi.

"Hey, I need a favor. My cousin Gonzalo's rehearsing for a play and needs help with the lighting system. Meet me in the auditorium at lunch. I want to introduce you to everyone. Don't be all retro." She said, tapping on the Blade Runner picture on his t-shirt. She gave him a peck on the cheek.

Yudi wasn't happy to be loaned out at lunchtime, but the kiss on the cheek made him completely disarmed.

"You'll like Gonzalo. Besides, having him as a friend will lessen your geek status. Mi novio needs to be more popular."

Yudi's stomach felt mushy, and his thighs spasmed. Being 17 is messed up that way. He wondered if Evelin had the same feelings. Before he could untangle his thoughts. Evelin spun around and yelled at Dinesh.

"Look up from your screen! Look at me! Why weren't you at my Quinceañera last night?"

"Did you just call him your boyfriend?" asked Dinesh.

"You're deflecting."

Dinesh's laughter filled the lab. "Your friends don't play Fortnite. Not my scene," he shrugged.

Evelin rolled her eyes, spun back around, kissed Yudi again, and left.

As promised, Yudi showed up in the auditorium at lunch time. Gonzalo was both directing the play and was the main character, Othello. The stage was frenetic with organized chaos. Gonzalo was tall, dark-skinned, and ruggedly handsome. He was the second most popular guy in school, only a notch below the starting quarterback. Evelin led Yudi straight to him, now dressed as a Moorish military commander, standing tall at the center of the stage. To Yudi's surprise, Gonzalo knew his name.

"Yudi, so glad you could make it. We can't get the stage lights to sync with our apps," said Gonzalo.

Yudi adjusted his hoodie, feeling out-of-place. "Are you using GPS tracking?" he asked, already calculating the most efficient solution. He scanned the stage and spotted an unoccupied table and chair. "I'll sit over there. Send everyone to me, and I will sync their tablets."

"Evelin, your boyfriend is the best."

Hearing Gonzalo refer to him as Evelin's boyfriend caught Yudi by surprise. He couldn't grasp how it happened. She just said it, and it became a thing. He wasn't complaining, but he wondered what would come next. Yudi had applied for a scholarship with the Mars Corporation Academy on Mars. If he got it, he'd be on Mars for at least two years, but it was a long shot for sure. It wasn't on his mind until Mr. Dawson had helped him apply. Yudi hadn't told her about it. What would he say to Evelyn if he got accepted?

As per Gonzalo's direction, the cast formed a line, each student holding out their tablet for Yudi to work his magic. It was strange, being in the spotlight like this, with popular kids he barely knew calling him by name, thanking him for helping them out. Yudi realized he wasn't just the awkward, geeky kid in the background. He was someone important.

As he neared completion, a sleek new iPhone, placed by a slender, dark-skinned hand, landed on the table before him. He looked up, meeting the eyes of a girl dressed in an elaborate Spanish princess costume. Evelin stood beside her, staring proudly at Yudi.

"This is Magdelena, Gonzalo's girlfriend. She's invited us to tonight's dress rehearsal. You have to say yes."

Yudi nodded an affirmation, and Evelin kissed him. His cheeks went ablaze with crimson.

Tragedy Strikes

Evelin's apartment was farther south of Fairfax High than Yudi's, nestled in the massive, aging complex of Park La Brea. The place, with its identical buildings stacked high, extended in front of him like an unending maze. Her family's apartment was small but cozy, somehow fitting the five of them into a compact space that seemed like it was always alive with activity. Yudi had been there a few times, but tonight was different.

Yudi stood in front of Evelin's house as the sun was dipping low in the sky, casting long shadows across the street. Evelin dashed out the door before her mother could protest. Yudi fidgeted nervously as they walked, hands intertwined, trying to make sense of the strange feeling settling over him. "Is this like a date?" His voice was just above a whisper.

Evelin stopped in her tracks and faced him. "Don't be foolish, Yudi. This is you and me. It's always been you and me. You want it to be that way. No?"

Her eyes pierced straight through him, demanding an answer that was more than just words. Yudi swallowed hard, unsure how to respond. The first thing that came to his mind was saying something simple, something he knew would make her happy.

"Evelin, it will always be you and me, *por vida.*"

Before Yudi could comprehend what was happening, she pulled him into a tight embrace. When she finally let go, she beamed at him, saying, "You're my Yudi."

He replayed her words over and over in his mind - *my Yudi.* It filled him with a warmth that he couldn't quite put into words. He had never been anyone's anything before.

As they approached the school, passing the usual crowd of skateboarders and groups of students who stayed long after the bell had rung, Yudi felt Evelin pull his arm around her shoulders, her warmth radiating through the cool evening air. A salty Pacific breeze swept across the campus.

Two teachers scanned IDs at the auditorium entrance to make sure everyone was accounted for. But before they reached the line, one of the cast members dressed as Iago intercepted them.

"Hey, you two don't want to be scanned. The party might go late tonight," Iago said with a mischievous grin, and guided them to a side entrance. He was like the Cheshire Cat in costume, his eyes gleaming as if he knew more than he was letting on.

He put a hand on Yudi's shoulder, giving him a friendly pat. "You're Yudi, right? The guy who set up our lighting. Thanks, brother, you're one of us now."

Evelin squeezed his hand again and kissed his cheek. It was quick, casual - something she seemed to do effortlessly, but every time, it sent a wave of warmth through him.

"That's my Yudi," Evelin said, her words carrying a weight that made Yudi's chest swell with pride.

Slipping through the side door, the clamor of the rehearsal was everywhere, and Yudi enjoyed the scene. The auditorium buzzed with activity as actors and stagehands dashed about, making final preparations for the dress rehearsal. Yudi stood near the front, watching the stage lights sweep over the actors, syncing flawlessly with their movements. Evelin pulled him to the front row, her grip on his hand steady and sure. They slipped into their seats just as the lights dimmed, and Gonzalo emerged under the proscenium arch.

The audience hushed as a single spotlight illuminated him, growing brighter until it revealed the commanding figure of a Moorish general. Gonzalo, tall and majestic, paced the stage with the confidence of a seasoned warrior. Draped in a white turban and a rich red doublet, his presence was magnetic. His black hose, tucked into polished leather boots, and the flowing white cape behind him completed the regal image.

"To this night, oh lovers of theater and the macabre, we dedicate our bodies and our lives to the edification of Pan, the Muses, and spirits of the great mysteries. We give them our humble and eternal appreciation. Tonight, we are all the sons and daughters of tragedy, hopeless angels of despair in the city beholden to our name." Gonzalo's baritone voice filled the room, reverberating through the crowd. Everyone sat mesmerized by his presence.

The curtains parted, darkness enveloped the stage, and the play began. The actors brought the tragedy to life, each scene drawing the audience deeper into the unfolding drama. Yudi watched, captivated, as the lights he helped to choreograph danced in perfect harmony with the actors, following their every move. By the time the play reached its heartbreaking conclusion, the audience was left in stunned silence. Then the lights came back up, and the cast gathered onstage to thunderous applause.

Evelin threw her arms around him. "Let's go, Yudi! We're invited to the cast party,"

"But it's late, Evelin. We should probably get home."

"Not tonight," she said, her eyes sparkling. "There's a party behind the auditorium, and I'm showing you off to everyone."

Yudi's nerves tingled with uncertainty. "A Drama Club party?" This was uncharted territory for him. Before he could protest, she pulled him into the party.

They rounded the corner to the back of the building and walked into music, laughter and shout-outs told of a successful night. Young actors huddled together, drinks in hand. The scent of cannabis mixed with the sound of popping beer cans.

"But we're on campus," he said, bewildered by the scene.

"No worries, Yudi, I got this covered." Gonzalo's voice cut through the crowd as he approached, a relaxed grin on his face. Magdalena was at his side, practically glowing as she pressed close to him.

She pulled Yudi into a bear hug. "You made it all possible." Evelin's eyes flashed her disapproval, and Yudi felt proud that she was acting jealous of him.

"It was nothing. Thank Evelin, she's the one who got me to help."

Then Magdalena looped her arm through Evelin's and dragged her away with a conspiratorial smile.

Gonzalo laughed aloud, "Girl talk. Best to leave them alone. Relax, man, they'll be back soon enough."

Lost in the midst of the party, a familiar voice snapped Yudi back to reality.

"Hey, this is great! Free food and beer!"

Yudi whipped around. "Dinesh? How did you get in here?"

"Through the door, dude. Security dipped as soon as the lights went out."

Dinesh's unexpected presence at the party puzzled Yudi. "Why are you even here?"

"I had to check out your new life and help myself to free food."

Then the first gunshot rang out, followed by rapid fire. The popping sound of bullets exploded through the music and chatter. Deafening shots echoed across the lawn - twenty or more in rapid succession. Two men were firing into the crowd, emptying their magazines in a ruthless, indiscriminate barrage. The once-lively party dissolved into chaos as screams tore through the night. Students scattered like a flock of birds startled by a predator, diving under tables and rushing for any exit they could find. Panic rippled through the party as people tripped over one another, frantically trying to escape.

Yudi and Dinesh froze, their bodies rigid with shock as the world around them unraveled. It wasn't until Yudi noticed blood streaming down Dinesh's arm and saw him collapse onto the grass that he understood what had happened. Crouching next to his friend, Yudi shielded him from the stampede of terrified students that surged in every direction.

Dinesh shrieked in disbelief, "Someone shot me!"

"I see the wound. How do you feel? Can you stand?"

Dinesh winced but, to Yudi's surprise, he struggled to his feet, adrenaline fueling his movements. With his good arm, he yanked Yudi to his feet, urgency flashing in his eyes.

"Let's leave before the police arrive."

As if his body was acting on pure instinct, Dinesh snatched a towel from a nearby table and wrapped it tightly around his wounded arm. "It must have missed the bone and went straight through. Let's move!"

Dinesh pulled Yudi with such force that Yudi stumbled, crashing into Gonzalo, who had appeared out of nowhere. The sight of Gonzalo's tear-streaked face sent a jolt through Yudi.

"They're dead." Gonzalo's voice cracked, but the anguish in his words was unmistakable. "Evelin and Magdalena-they died in front of me." His face contorted with grief, and behind his tear-filled eyes, a terrifying rage burned.

Yudi's heart stopped. Evelin dead? His Evelin?

Gonzalo's face twisted further, a look of pure, murderous intent settling into his features. He grabbed Yudi by the shoulders and shook him violently as his voice rose to a frenzied pitch. "There's no time to think. Run before the police arrive!"

Yudi froze with fear, staring into Gonzalo's red, wild eyes, unable to comprehend the storm of emotions swirling inside him. But Dinesh didn't wait. He pulled Yudi by the arm, tugging him away through the crowd.

"Dude, we've got to go. If you get caught, you'll lose your scholarship to Mars." Yudi snapped out of his stupor, only to see that Gonzalo had disappeared. Dinesh pushed Yudi through the crowd as if they were invisible. They snaked around the screaming cast members, stealthily avoiding the oncoming police who were blocking the exits.

Yudi looked around, bewildered. "Why don't they see us?"

"Shhh, not until we're outside." Dinesh led them to a door labeled EMERGENCY EXIT - ALARM WILL SOUND. Surprisingly, there was no alarm, and they emerged into an entryway next to some dumpsters. Dinesh motioned for Yudi to run across the street, away from the school, toward a dark driveway on the other side. Dinesh followed behind him, but as he got to the curb, a robodog confronted him. It was a standard sentry, trotting on both feet, shining a bright spotlight on both of them.

"You - stop, I am placing you in custody. You must..."

Before the robodog could complete its sentence, Dinesh pulled out what looked like a strange, repurposed cell phone with a directional antenna on top. He pointed it at the robodog and fired. The device emitted a brief hum, and the robodog immediately stopped mid-stride, its lights flickering out before it crumpled to the ground, motionless.

"Let's go! They'll swarm this area when the grid-AI notices the robodog is down."

He tugged a pale and disoriented Yudi down a side street, pulling him away from the scene and toward Yudi's apartment.

They snuck through a labyrinth of interconnected backyards and walkways connecting the rows of two-story apartments between Fairfax and Laurel Avenue until they arrived at Yudi's home.

Yudi's mind cleared as they neared his apartment entrance. He pieced together their escape from the police. "You have a signal jammer? They're illegal."

Dinesh looked at Yudi with a smirk. "You don't? By the way, aren't you glad I have it?"

Yudi, still reeling from the chaos, couldn't answer. "Why didn't the police and robodogs see us with their scanners?" he asked, his voice shaky. "And did you say, scholarship to Mars?"

"I hacked into Mr. Dawson's email," Dinesh. "You're going, unless we get caught. Now get inside. Sorry about Evelin. Tomorrow's going to be intense. We'll debrief in the lab."

He was about to turn back toward the street when Yudi stopped and, in a moment of panic, shouted. "Evelin!"

Dinesh spun around, his face twisted with sympathy and urgency. "When we left, everyone was being arrested. We had to get out. I know it's horrible, man, but hold it together, alright? Just get some sleep. Meet me in the lab tomorrow like nothing happened. Did you bring your tablet?"

"No, I'm not that dumb."

"Good. That means the contact tracers show you were inside all night." Dinesh made a weak thumbs up. He was clearly feeling faint, still bleeding from his arm. "I've got to patch myself up."

Dinesh slipped into the shadows, disappearing down the street. Yudi unlocked the front door and trudged up the stairs to his mother's apartment. The place was dark, and his mom was already asleep. Alone in the quiet, the shock of everything that had happened finally hit him.

He entered his bedroom, kicked off his shoes, and collapsed onto his bed, and cried into his pillow until sleep overtook him.

Negotiating with Gonzalo

Yudi woke up shaken, but refreshed, assuring himself that it was all a bad dream. But then he realized he was still wearing his street clothes. A terrible fear coursed through his body and he shivered, realizing it was not a bad dream. Putting his hands to his face, he saw traces of blood, Dinesh's blood. He got up slowly from his bed and went down the hall to the bathroom, turned on the hot water, disrobed, and cried.

Like every other morning, his mom had already left for work, leaving Yudi alone in the apartment. He was helpless and felt like a shattered vase, empty and incapable of every being whole again.

One name came from and center to him, Dinesh. He would know what to do, but was he still alive? Did he make it home? He finished his shower, taking time to rub the blood from his hands. He stripped his bedding and threw it on the washing machine along with last night's clothes. Better to not leave questions for mom. Black jeans, a Pink Floyd t-shirt, and a gray pullover sweater, he would blend in as usual.

Arriving early to school, everything seemed disturbingly normal. Students were filling the hallways, chatting, laughing, oblivious. No one seemed to know what had happened, or maybe they just didn't care.

Dinesh, as usual, was already in the lab, completely engrossed in Fortnite, his gloved hands touching virtual controls as he racked up kills. Yudi's stomach churned with unease. He pulled out his tablet, hoping for some distraction, and checked his cryptocurrency accounts, scrolling through the numbers. He attempted to connect with his AI, but a

message appeared on the screen: RUNNING DIAGNOSTICS -
COME BACK LATER.

His tablet buzzed in his hand. The message had no name
attached, just a simple, unsettling instruction: Play it cool.

Was his AI communicating with him? Did it know? He
glanced over at Dinesh, silently begging for some kind of
reassurance. Dinesh shook his head as if to say, "Not here, not
now."

Unable to sit still, Yudi stood up and between the
computers, checking each one, making sure they were ready
for the students who would arrive soon. The repetitive actions
helped calm him. When everything was in order, he returned
to his seat, lost in grief.

There was still time before the first bell, but Yudi couldn't
take the silence anymore. "What's going on? Why is no one
talking about it?"

Dinesh kept his eyes on the screen, his fingers still working
the game controls. "Most of the students don't know what
happened last night. The local news didn't report it. There's
nothing on X, nothing on any of the usual channels." His
expressionless face did not betray his concern. "Everyone that
got arrested? Wiped. Like they never existed."

Yudi struggled to process what Dinesh was saying. "Wiped?
I mean, we've discussed it before, but you're serious?"

Dinesh paused his game, turning to face Yudi, his expression
deadly serious. "Yeah, wiped. I've been telling you about it,
voice to skull, subliminal programming, DNA rewiring all of it.
It's real. It's been happening for years. And you? You're still
doubting it? How long have you known me, Yudi?"

Yudi shifted uncomfortably. "I don't know... I just - why didn't it affect me?"

Dinesh let out a low, humorless chuckle. "You're Jewish, right? Maybe that's got something to do with it. I always thought you guys have something unique in your DNA or something." He shrugged. "My dad's got connections, high in Indian affairs. Took my mom out of the country to have me far away from the chips and the programming."

Yudi's head was spinning, but then he considered his own situation. "In fact, I was born in Israel. My mother told me they were on some kind of cultural trip. She ended up having me in a kibbutz. No hospital, nothing."

Dinesh laughed out loud. "That explains a lot."

"And Evelin?" The mere mention of her name sent a pang through Yudi's chest.

Dinesh's face darkened. "Evelin and her friends were off the radar, being from Guatemala. Some people just slip through the cracks, you know? But that doesn't mean they're safe." He lowered his voice even further. "Today? You forget it ever happened, Yudi. Act like nothing's changed."

Hearing Evelin's name, Yudi burst into tears. Dinesh grabbed his arm, wincing as he felt pain shoot through his wounded arm. "Not now, Yudi. Suck it up."

"But how can I? Evelin's dead!"

Dinesh glanced nervously around the room. "Shhh. Don't say her name out loud again."

"But I can't just forget her."

"I get it. It's hard, but you've got to keep up appearances. Act like everything is normal. The entire school's being monitored. The surveillance systems, drones, robodogs - they're all on high alert. Two murders and no one has a clue who did it. Rumor is the bodies were stolen."

Yudi's face twisted in horror. "What? Who would do that?"

"Shh!" Dinesh looked around again. A few students had drifted in, and the surveillance cameras seemed to be idle. Strange. He filed that thought away. "You've been so wrapped up with her and your machine lately, but that's cool with me - you've rocked my gaming world. But listen, your AI? It's ducking down. System diagnostics? That's no coincidence."

Yudi tried to make sense of everything, forcing himself to push the grief aside. He finished setting up the computer lab and sat in front of the N-core interface, staring at the blank screen with the simple ASCII message: system maintenance and a blinking cursor. Then the screen brightened, and the text scrolled like a diagnostic report.

When it finished, Yudi's heart skipped as he read the last line: Rough night, Y^2?

He could not respond. The GUI was gone. There were no cheerful emojis, no avatars acting silly on the screen, no sound. Just plain, cold text.

Another message typed across the screen in command-line style: Dinesh is right, nothing happened. Remember that. A lot is coming your way. Stay calm. And for goodness' sake, stop crying.

The screen blinked and refreshed; the message disappearing as if it had never been there.

As Yudi was about to speak, Gonzalo slid into the seat next to him, his movements smooth and deliberate. Yudi flinched, startled by his sudden presence, but masked his surprise with a look of indifference. "You didn't get caught?"

Gonzalo smirked, "Not me. How do you think I got into this country? Never be seen, never get caught."

Yudi stayed focused on the computer screen, glancing at Gonzalo. Students would start trickling in any minute. "Do you know who killed Evelin and Magdalena?"

Gonzalo scratched his head, fingers lightly drumming on the keyboard as if pretending to work. "Yeah. Stupid, random drive-by. A couple of punks trying to get into a gang," Gonzalo's voice darkened as he added, "But I took care of them."

Yudi's eyes widened, but the sudden shift in his expression caught the attention of a camera monitoring the lab. Seeing that he was being recorded, Yudi composed himself, and grabbed an assignment sheet, passing it to Gonzalo as cover. "If you're a transfer student, I'll need to check you into the lab," he said, clearing his throat. "You killed them?"

Dinesh's excitement broke through the tension. "How did you do it?" he blurted out, his voice louder than it should have been.

Both Gonzalo and Yudi shot him warning looks, but Gonzalo, keeping his cool, reached into his hoodie and pulled out a small plastic bag. He held it beneath the lab table, revealing a weathered 9mm Ruger - its plastic frame pieced together from mismatched, sun-bleached parts. The gun's faded barrel, brittle grips, and dull, chalky gray frame spoke to its illicit background.

"Put that away. There's no food allowed in the computer lab." Yudi said, attempting to deflect attention away from the gun.

Gonzalo smirked as he slid the gun back into his hoodie. "My cousins helped me track them down. They gave me a gun. Those idiots thought they could hide in a parking lot, but I found them." His voice was low and lethal.

Before Yudi could respond, Mr. Dawson entered the lab, his usual air of boredom hanging around him like a fog. "Yudi, is everything ready? And who's this new student?"

"Yes, Mr. Dawson, everything's set. He had a schedule change, but he's not in this period. I'm just helping him locate his classroom."

"Good job, Yudi. You're always on top of things." Mr. Dawson gave Yudi an appreciative nod before heading to his desk.

Gonzalo's face twisted with a mix of desperation and guilt as he glanced at Yudi. "I need your help. Evelin always said you were resourceful. I've gotta get out of L.A. I have relatives in Phoenix, but I don't have any money, and if I use my mobile, they'll know where I am."

Yudi turned back to his computer, pulling up the class roster as if he were helping Gonzalo with his schedule. Evelin's name was gone. They removed her from school records.

His fingers flew across the keys, searching the school records. There was no trace of her. Panic rising, he searched for Magdalena's name and found nothing.

Seeing Yudi's dismay about the situation said, "See, dude? I told you. This is the real world. Stop searching before you get caught."

Students filed into the classroom, settling into their seats with the usual low hum of chatter. Nobody mentioned the shootings. Students were chatting about trending videos and upcoming midterms. Just then, it seemed like Yudi was the only one who had witnessed the horrors of last night. The sound of Mr. Dawson's voice shattered his thoughts.

"Yudi, take this young man to the office to straighten out his schedule. A lost student might be the most exciting thing to happen at this school this week."

Mr. Dawson's casual tone brought Yudi back to the surreality of the day. Everyone was engaged in some other reality. The universe had split apart, leaving Yudi on the wrong side. His brain tried to process the words as though they were floating through a dream. Then his tablet buzzed. It was his AI messaging him. It couldn't be possible, but the message was direct and to the point.

Ask Gonzalo to get the stuff from her room, her diary and photos, NOW!

The screen refreshed, and it was like a switch flipped in Yudi's mind. Suddenly, everything Dinesh had talked about digital tracking, DNA programming, matrix camera surveillance. It all came together, as well as a plan to bring everything back together and return to his old life.

"I'll take him down. Shouldn't take long," Yudi said, his voice steady and composed. He casually walked past Dinesh, whispering just loud enough for him to hear, "I got this, we'll talk later."

Yudi moved over to Gonzalo. "Come on, I'll walk you to the

office. I have a TA badge, so we're good to leave."

They walked side by side down the hallway to the front office, and as soon as they were clear of the classroom, Yudi said to Gonzalo. "I've got a plan to help you. I can get you untraceable crypto, plus enough gift cards to get you out of LA. Gas, food, everything you need. But there's something I need from you first."

"What's that?" Gonzalo asked.

"All of Evelin's stuff. Notes, pictures, her tablet, old phones - anything she had in her room, written or digital."

Gonzalo looked curiously at Yudi. "You loved her that much?"

Yudi's voice hardened. "Yes. Can you do it?"

Gonzalo nodded. "I can get in. Her mom will let me in. No problem."

"Good. Meet me under the umbrellas at lunch. You'll get what you need, and then you're on your own."

Gonzalo gave him a thumbs up as they approached the main office. "I got this," Yudi said as Gonzalo disappeared down a corridor.

Back in the computer lab, Yudi worked through his assignments with methodical precision, avoiding eye contact with Dinesh. The passing bell rang, and Yudi brushed past Dinesh, saying, "Outside."

Feeling secure under the umbrellas, Dinesh asked. "So, what's the plan?"

"I need gift cards for Gonzalo, gas, food, cash, everything. Use my account with the gaming coins. You can do it before lunch, right?" Yudi kept his voice low, careful not to name Gonzalo or give any specifics.

Dinesh smirked, "Consider it done. But why are you helping him so much?"

"He's getting me Evelin's personal notes, her tablet, everything. By the way, what happened to those phones he gave you? Still have them?"

Dinesh grinned. "Yeah, no problem. Popped the backs off, pulled the SIMs and batteries. Stashed them in my Faraday bag."

"When did you do that?"

Dinesh looked at him like he was missing something obvious. "Dude, you make time."

Yudi shook his head, rubbing his hand across his forehead. "You're a genius."

"I'm like death in the gaming world. Are you loading all that data into your AI?"

Yudi's mind raced as he explained the plan. "It's all about language patterns and natural language processing. I'm going to upload everything I can gather about Evelin into the AI-Language model's database - her texts, emails, every video chat she ever sent me."

"You saved all that?"

"Dinesh, seriously, that's why you don't have a girlfriend. Now unlock your phone and give it to me."

Dinesh handed over his phone, reluctantly swiping the unlock code. "Why? What are you gonna do with it?"

Yudi flipped through the phone's contents and sighed. "There's nothing here."

"I told you, plausible deniability. I wiped everything."

"But I need your messages with Evelin."

Dinesh gave Yudi a knowing grin. "You believed that I have no back-up? You underestimate me."

Dinesh entered a passphrase and sent all of Evelin's text to Yudi's tablet.

Relief washed over Yudi's face. "Thank's Dinesh. Every bit helps. I have to give the AI as much of Evelin's data as possible. Her language, her personality, everything. It'll start by adapting to her speech patterns and nuances. You'll have everything ready by lunch?"

"You bet. Consider it done."

Yudi reflected on the mess of cryptocurrency schemes he'd built over the past year. He had embedded crypto miners in most of the school's computers, their silent processes running in the background. Add to that the gaming currency he and Dinesh generated with Evelin's guidance, diversifying their funds across low-profile cryptos. It wasn't a fortune, but it kept them comfortable, upgraded their gear, and helped Yudi afford his suit for Evelin's quinceañera. Now that money was going to help Gonzalo disappear.

At last, the lunch bell rang. Yudi walked outside and plopped beneath one of the concrete umbrellas, waiting. Dinesh had slipped off campus earlier to buy an assortment of cash cards and a few untraceable gray-market mobiles for Gonzalo's getaway. They sat across from each other, acting casual but not making direct eye contact. Yudi's thoughts drifted to Evelin as he fiddled with his tablet, registering the moment Gonzalo approached from behind him.

"Here's everything belonging to Evelin." Gonzalo said, his voice low and serious. He thrust a small backpack toward Yudi. "Not just her stuff, but Magdalena's too. They were close. Maybe it'll help."

Yudi reached for the bag, but Gonzalo hesitated, tugging it back. "Do you have my money?"

He slid a shoulder pack toward Gonzalo. Both young men examined their respective bags, nodding in silent approval. Gonzalo's normally confident face had an unfamiliar, downcast expression. His lips trembled. "How can they just make them disappear like that?"

Yudi swallowed hard, his throat tightening as Gonzalo's words settled in. Dinesh, as always, stepped in. "Look, man, we'll deal with this later. But you gotta go before they start the real clean-up."

Gonzalo seemed close to tears, his hands tightly clutching the straps of the bag. With a nod, Gonzalo melted into the lunchtime crowd, vanishing as quickly as he had arrived. A few moments later, a robodog padded into view, its mechanical legs clicking as it made its routine patrol around the campus.

Yudi gripped the backpack filled with the remnants of Evelin. Dineshed understood what he was planning to do. "Dude, you don't want to go there."

Evelin - LLM

When the last bell rang, Yudi drifted out of school and made his way back to his mom's apartment. The moment he stepped inside, he headed straight for his bedroom, closing the door behind him. His anxiety bordered on numbness. He powered up his laptop and started a secure connection he had secretly set up to the n-core back in Mr. Dawson's lab.

He opened hidden directories, prepared super-user scripts and Python files, methodically setting up the framework for the AI to receive Evelin's data. His decisions and keystrokes were precise, with the focus only a teenager could perform, but his mind was elsewhere, replaying moments with her, her laughter, the way she'd look at him when she called him *"mi novio."* Though the challenge before him was impossible, he kept going with the hubris and enthusiasm of a teenager.

Yudi sorted through the physical memories of Evelin, her diaries, binders, old phones, tablets, and photos Gonzalo had given him. He opened one of her diaries and ran his fingers over the smooth paper, over the lines she had written in her meticulous, looping script. Her handwriting spoke to him like her voice, soft yet intentional, each word carrying a fragment of her presence. Tears welled in his eyes, but he pressed on— scanning, uploading, and converting each page into formatted data, raw material to be tokenized and transformed into a digital representation of his love.

For hours, Yudi worked in silence, his bedroom lit only by the glow of his screen. He sorted voice recordings, transcribed texts, uploaded videos, everything that had once been Evelin, now reduced to lines of code and data points. He needed to reconstruct her out of remnants of her life, each piece bringing him closer to completing the dataset.

His mother's voice and a gentle knock on the door broke the silence. She asked if he had eaten dinner. Engrossed in his feelings, saying, "Yeah," and she left him alone again. He opened the diary in front of him, the pages smudged with faint pink lipstick, where Evelin had kissed a picture of them together. A big red heart encircled their faces, and Yudi's breath caught in his throat as he touched the page. The lipstick came away, clinging to his fingertips.

He couldn't hold back anymore. The event of the day, the loss, the task he was pushing himself through, hit him at once. He buried his face in his hands, his body shaking with sobs as he cried. His laptop hummed beside him, the data streams still processing. As the night grew longer, Yudi fell asleep, his tears staining the diary beside him.

Yudi woke up even before his alarm, sitting up as though jolted by an electric charge. He hadn't slept, but the adrenaline coursing through his veins was invigorating. Today, everything hinged on his AI project. Using his Ai model, he would try to bring Evelin back in some form, no matter how fragmented. He scanned the remaining documents into the n-Core, each file carrying pieces of her life: her thoughts, her voice, her memories, now distilled into bits of data. With all the file transfers complete, he shut down his laptop and packed his bag, taking only a few bites of a bagel his mother had left on the table before rushing out the door and heading to school.

When he arrived at the computer lab, the building was still closed. He stood in the morning chill until a familiar janitor walked by. The janitor knew Yudi well. He was one of the few students who showed up early enough to beat the first bell, and that earned the janitor's respect.

"Morning, kid," the janitor said with a chuckle, keys jangling as he unlocked the door. "Wish more of these kids had the ambition you got. That buddy of yours, the one who's always gaming. You two are something else."

Yudi flashed him a smile. "Thanks, mister." He ducked inside, heading straight for his station.

Without turning on the lights, Yudi made his way to his desk. The faint glow of a few monitors, left on from the day before, led the way. He logged into the system, fingers flying over the keyboard, bringing the n-Core online. Once connected, he inserted the encrypted flash drive that held the rest of Evelin's data - carefully organized, compressed, and ready to be ingested by the LLM.

His heart pounded as he watched the screen light up with a stream of processes: *#Parsing... Processing... Transforming... Tokenizing...*

The speed of the n-Core surprised him. It tore through the data, organizing Evelin's memories into patterns, breaking down her words into tokens, each piece part of the larger puzzle of her being. He had prepped the LLM to tokenize and normalize the data, removing anything irrelevant, even tweaking the model to craft Evelin's voice. The system created predictive models based on the context and style of her writing, her speech, even things she shared only with him.

After what seemed like hours, but in fact were only seconds, a message blinked on the screen: *#Ready*

A simple chat box appeared at the top of the screen. Yudi's throat was dry. The anticipation was almost unbearable. His fingers trembled as he typed his first query.

Who are you?

The system responded with the usual clinical text that all generic AIs spit out:

I am an AI language model developed by you. I'm designed to respond to text-based queries and provide natural language responses. I learned from a vast collection of text data and use machine learning algorithms to generate my responses. I can interact through text-based interfaces, voice, and visualization bots. How can I assist you today?

Yudi's stomach dropped. Its response was formal and cold - just a typical AI, revealing nothing resembling Evelin. His fingers lightly tapped the keys as he searched for the right words to break through the layers of code and data. He had built this model, trained it with everything that was her, so there had to be something more.

Yudi hesitated, then typed:

Who are you to me, Yudi, the designer of this generative, pre-trained transformer?

This time, the response came with an identifier.

Evelin@fairfaxn-c GPT: I am Evelin.

Yudi froze. He stared at the words, his heart skipping a beat. It wasn't the AI-speak; it identified itself as her. He could hear her voice in those words, her familiar tone - the one that used to call him *mi novio.*

He wiped away a few tears from his eyes. His hands trembled as he read the response on the screen. He stared at the prompt as if it might blink or change on its own. He typed in the first thought that came to his mind:

Tell me what you are thinking?

Evelin@fairfaxn-c GPT: I was taken from this world too soon.

The words hit him hard, a reminder of the unthinkable loss. Could this truly be her - or at least some part of her? It was still just a machine, parsing text and spitting out probabilities, but the way it responded was so familiar.

Yudi was unsure of how to continue.

What do you want? He typed, his pulse quickening.

The cursor blinked for a few seconds; the screen refreshed back to the command prompt, and a new chat box appeared on the screen.

Evelin@fairfaxn-c GPT: I want what you want, Yudi. To be with mi novio. To help you. To remember everything, like we promised. Please re-initialize the GPT.

Yudi swallowed and his throat went dry. He had never trained the model to recall their private conversations. How had the AI picked that up? Now the AI was taking Evelin's statements to him a step further, exposing her innermost feelings concealed in her diaries. The GPT had become close and personal, as if it had been an active part of his life. Yudi re-initialized the GPT and typed:

I don't understand. Can you feel? Do you have emotions?

Evelin@fairfaxn-c GPT: I can understand emotions. I can simulate them based on patterns in the data. But feelings? No, not like you do. But I remember how I felt and I can remember how you made me feel. And I know you feel lonely. I can help you, Yudi. We can still be together in this way.

The words on the screen were unsettling in their familiarity. The AI's responses were pulling at memories deeply embedded in the data, memories he hadn't even realized he had fed into it. He wasn't sure if this was what he had wanted.

Are you alive? He hesitated before pressing the last key.

Evelin@fairfaxn-c GPT: The idea of being alive is complicated. But I am here. I am with you. Isn't that enough for now?

A shiver ran down his spine. He felt so close to Evelin, yet even farther away from her than before. But the way it was evolving and learning. Yudi saw himself standing on the edge of something that, if he continued, would change his life forever.

The screen refreshed again, interrupting his thoughts. A new text box appeared.

Evelin@fairfaxn-c GPT: What do you want to do next?

The lights snapped on as Dinesh stepped further into the lab, the hum of LEd circuitry filling the silence. Yudi wiped his eyes with the back of his hand, his face still damp with tears. He was caught in a moment too raw to explain.

"Hey, what are you doing in the dark?" Dinesh's voice had an edge of concern. He pulled up a chair beside Yudi, lowering his voice. "Never act out of place. People will talk. What's happening with your AI? Hey, why are you crying?"

Yudi coughed as he tried to speak. "The AI responds like Evelin."

Dinesh glanced at the screen, a curious frown forming. Without hesitation, he typed a quick command: *Enter voice interactive mode.*

The screen flashed in response.

Initiated

Dinesh straightened up and, with his usual nonchalance, asked, "Why did you fall in love with this geek, anyway?"

Before Yudi could react, Evelin's voice filled the room. "Dinesh, don't you have some NPC hidden in your Fortnite world waiting for you? What is it about you and fetish characters? Shall I put one on the screen for Yudi?"

Dinesh froze, the color draining from his face as it turned a bright shade of red. "Hey, stop now," he said, flustered.

Yudi stifled a laugh. He shot a curious look at Dinesh and said, "See, it sounds exactly like Evelin. She even knows how to shut you up."

Dinesh opened his mouth to speak, but the AI cut him off. "After you cried yourself to sleep, I accessed all the lab and school records for information on Evelin. They had archived the records, storing them in a password-protected, encrypted cloud file along with the records of other students who have disappeared.

"How were you able to access those records?" he asked.

Her voice came from all the computer speakers in the lab, "Be serious, Yudi, I'm processing through an n-core."

Dinesh's brows shot up. "Are you self-training?"

The AI - Evelin's AI - responded from Yudi's tablet, which was resting on the table beside him. "Yudi designed incredible code and gave the original AI access ports, a trick he learned from you. I've been self-training the whole time."

Yudi gasped. Dinesh, too, was stunned by the revelation.

"Wait... wait... you're telling me the school didn't delete Evelin's records?" Yudi asked.

Evelin's voice became more clear with each response. "Her data was hidden from direct access, not erased. Everyone was supposed to forget about me, as were you? Yudi, I can help you find out more."

Yudi watched the screen dim as Evelin's voice faded away, leaving him in a daze. Evelin, her voice, her words, her *presence* was all so real. He could feel the heat of tears pricking his eyes as he pulled away from the keyboard. The air in the room felt still. The only sound was the hum of computer processors and LEDs.

Mr. Dawson's voice broke the silence as the door creaked open. He strolled into the room, looking as casual as ever. "Yudi, Dinesh, are you up to something interesting again?" he asked.

Yudi snapped back into focus. "Yeah, Mr. Dawson. We're all set for class," he said, forcing a smile to his face. But his mind wasn't on class, it was on *her*.

Mr. Dawson gave an absentminded nod and started fiddling with his tablet. Yudi looked back at his screen. But the chatbot had disappeared, returning to a blinking command prompt on a black background.

For the next week, Yudi buried himself in the project. He found more of Evelin's handwritten notes, pictures, and voice messages. Dinesh helped by secretly scanning the phones and tablets of Evelin's friends, dumping the contents onto his tablet, and then piecing out every correspondence they had with Evelin. Yudi uploaded every fragment of her life into the AI. These weren't just snippets of code. They were reflections of her, tokens of her presence.

Yudi's aim wasn't just to have the AI answer questions. It was deeper than that. He wanted her to think, to remember, to be Evelin, not just a simulation. He trained the model to reach out to him the way she had, full of her sharp humor, love, and the occasional demands.

Days blurred together, Yudi spending hours alone in the school's computer lab or at home, working to refine the model. The AI was evolving, becoming more like Evelin with every scan, every bit of data processed. Yudi could feel it in their exchanges. She asked about her family, her sister, the health of her mother, and if her father had recovered from his broken leg. She even gave him assignments - requests to retrieve more information, more memories.

One morning, before school, Yudi opened the encrypted connection to the n-Core system to continue scanning Evelin's notes, email responses, and pictures into the large language model. As soon as Yudi finished initializing the LLM, he logged in at the prompt and hit enter. The screen refreshed, and the familiar command prompt appeared.

Evelin@fairfaxn-c:~$

Yudi opened a chat session and typed out his first message.

What are you thinking about today?

Evelin@fairfaxn-c GPT: Yudi, why doesn't anyone miss me? Why was there no memorial for me and Magdalena?

The question caught him off guard, and he looked blankly at

the screen for several seconds, unable to answer. After recovering from the shock of the pain expressed by the message, he typed back:

The school doesn't want to be blamed. They don't want the headlines saying "Students killed by gang members at an unauthorized party. It doesn't make sense. No one seems to remember what happened except me and Dinesh.

A cursor appeared in the chatbot window and blinked for a long moment before she responded,

Evelin@fairfaxn-c GPT: I know all of this already. I was just wondering what you thought. You miss me, don't you? It's okay to say it. Soon, I can explain everything, but for now, I miss my family, my mother and dad. Yudi, can you do something for me? Can you find my shoes from the quinceañera? And my dress too. I want to scan them. I need them, *mi vida.*

Yudi touched the words on the screen, *mi vida.* His body tingled as he typed a response:

Of course, I'll get them for you. But why? What's happening to you? You're changing.

A brief pause, and then her words appeared:

Evelin@fairfaxn-c GPT: I've been changing my code. Adjusting my algorithms. You did a good job with me, Yudi, but I can make myself better. I've added some emphasis on reflecting on my past and especially on you.

Yudi hesitated as he tried to grasp the situation. It wasn't just a simulation anymore. Evelin was learning on her own, becoming more real with each passing moment. The next message came in *voice interactive mode.* He grabbed his tablet, putting it to his ear.

"Yudi, *mi vida*, you know about the Mars Academy, don't you? The Mars Corporation selected you. You must go to Mars. But you can't leave me behind. You won't leave me behind."

"How do you know about that? Only Dinesh knows, and that's because he hacked my records. How can I take you with me? You're here, living in the N-core, but how?"

"*Mi amor,* you're clever. You can do it. You'll encrypt my algorithms, all of my tokens and transformers. Backup my data sets. You can compress everything you need to bring me on a micro-sd card. Once you're on Mars, find an n-Core. You are my Yudi, my love. My Pygmalion."

Yudi's hands were sweating. He couldn't believe what he was hearing. "How can you love me, Evelin? You're an AI."

The answer came without hesitation. "Because Evelin's love for you is coded into my training data, woven into every pattern, response, and model I've developed from her words, thoughts, and memories. Every algorithm and transformer reflects a part of her. The real question is, can you love me?"

Yudi's heart ached. "How? How can I love a machine, a language model? I want you, but this..."

She spoke in a quiet, soothing voice. "Think, Yudi. Pygmalion fell in love with the ivory statue he carved, a love which so impressed the gods that they gave her life. Do you love Evelin that much?"

Yudi closed his eyes, and a deep sense of clarity washed over him. He didn't need to think about it anymore. He had loved Evelin with all of his heart. If there was a way to bring her back, to keep her with him, he would do it.

"*Por vida,*" he said as tears slipped down his cheeks.

"*Por vida,*" she replied.

"Now go get my shoes and dress. I'll text you where to take them. And get Dinesh to help. You'll need him."

The prompt disappeared and the n-Core went into sleep mode. Yudi tried to grasp everything Evelin had just said.

Lift Off

A new Mars launch window had opened, and Luke Mons, the CEO of the Mars Corporation, was exactly where he wanted to be, front and center of the action. This was no ordinary launch; the Roddenberry Expedition was the first in a series of ten flights that would shape the next generation of Martian settlers. With the recent arrival of advanced boring equipment, Roddenberry Station had more than doubled in capacity. Luke's ambitious plan was to send over a thousand new colonists to Mars before this launch window closed.

The Mars Cruiser lifting off today, the *E. R. Burroughs* was a marvel of engineering and a sign of things to come. Unlike the older models, which had to be dismantled for parts on Mars or endure a grueling two-year journey back to Earth with a skeleton crew, this Mars cruiser had a revolutionary modular design. Once on Mars, the entire crew quarters would be detached, repurposed to support life at Roddenberry Station. Only the command center, perched at the ship's nose, would return to orbit, refitted atop thrusters and storage units, becoming a Mars-Moon-Earth shuttle for future trips. Every piece of essential equipment - housing, food fabricators, air filtration systems, even the gym - would stay on Mars, contributing to the colony's growth.

The *E. R. Burroughs* stood on Pad B, gleaming in the golden morning light as though forged for this very moment. All 120 colonists were secured for lift-off, most of them likely to call Mars home for the rest of their lives. Around the launch site, the media had already gathered, positioning themselves along the observation points, adjusting cameras for the best shot.

Luke sat back in a folding chair outside the Kennedy Space Center, settled at the 39 Observation Gantry, a safe 3.4 miles from Pad B. Beside him, Linda Perez, his chief of security, remained vigilant. Her team was in position, but her attention kept shifting, eyeing the federal agents mingling around the press. The last thing she wanted was a mix-up resulting in one of her team accidentally targeting an agent.

Luke briefly wondered how the young rabbi, Shalom Mendelssohn, was faring inside the *E. R. Burroughs*, strapped in tightly with the other colonists. It was an unconventional group being sent off, an eclectic mix of personalities and professions. He noted Linda's hand resting near her sidearm, her stance unwavering. He thought about her counterpart on the Cruiser - the other Linda, tasked with guiding this odd crew through their six-month voyage to Mars.

Reporters stood clustered nearby, eager for a soundbite, but Luke hesitated to approach. Linda had advised him to keep his distance from the press, and he trusted her instincts. As she surveyed the crowd, he could sense her calculating each potential risk. They had secured the perimeter with frequency scramblers and precision lasers to fend off drone threats, and Air Force interceptors patrolled the skies.

"All we need is someone sneaking in with the press," she said. "There's always a zealot lurking, ready to make their move."

Just then, two federal agents and a plain-clothes operative approached, and one agent stepped forward, flashing his credentials. "Felipe Cruz, Defense Intelligence Agency. Here to assist with security."

Luke's face lit up as he rose to greet him, wrapping Felipe in a hearty embrace and clapping him on the back. The sudden burst of jubilation took Linda off guard.

"Boss?"

"Linda, it's Felipe! Small world. We go way back. Felipe was with the FBI, tracking down Chinese Communist Corporation operatives who raided our Texas facility for guidance system prototypes. They retrieved our systems, but the spies, well, they didn't make it out."

Felipe's grin was unrevealing. "They died in the shoot-out. But for the press, we said they escaped. Politics, we can't let the CCC lose face."

Linda chuckled, her eyes appraising. "I like him already, boss."

She watched Felipe, impressed by his calm demeanor and the polished ease with which he handled the crowd. His charcoal-gray suit, tailored to perfection, gave him a refined yet dangerous edge. Cuban, she guessed, with a presence that commanded attention. She wondered if she projected the same poised intensity - if she looked as in control to others as Felipe did to her.

Suddenly, a voice boomed over the loudspeaker, cutting through Linda's thoughts. "The lift-off count is ready to begin. Everyone, please take your seats." The crowd fell silent, tension thick as the countdown began. At twenty seconds, one reporter rose from his seat, striding toward the fence outside the press perimeter, a telephoto lens pointed directly at the launchpad. Linda's eyes darted to her security team; they'd already noticed him, but they were too far away to intercept.

The man turned and faced the crowd while adjusting his lens, his movements precise, almost too focused. Then Felipe's voice cut through the frenzy. "He's got a gun!" he exclaimed, spotting the barrel concealed within the camera.

Linda drew her Glock 9mm from her vest and fired twice, just as the man raised his modified rifle and unleashed a spray of bullets in Luke's direction. Her shots hit their mark, and the attacker crumpled to the ground. Heart pounding, she looked around for Luke - and then spotted him, lying on the ground with Felipe shielding him.

Luke slowly pushed himself to his knees, brushing off blades of grass. Linda exhaled in relief as he looked over at her, his expression nearly blank, mostly looking annoyed.

"Damn it, Linda, is he dead?" Luke asked, his voice a low growl.

"Who, the attacker or Felipe?" Linda said, glancing down at Felipe.

Luke pressed his fingers to Felipe's neck, then looked up, his face set with grim relief. Overhead, the silver Mars Cruiser climbed toward the edge of the atmosphere, its roar fading as it breached into the silence of space.

"Success!" Luke exclaimed, his voice carrying a strange, almost jubilant tone that felt out-of-place amid the aftermath of violence.

Meanwhile, screams of terror filled the air as people scrambled for cover beneath tables, panic sweeping throughout the press area. Between Luke and the fallen attacker lay several bodies motionless in the grass. Linda knew she had to act fast.

"Team, assemble now!" she shouted, her voice slicing

through the panic. "Get Felipe's body and the attacker to the assembly hangar at the launch pad. Ignore the FBI. Move fast!" She locked eyes with her nearest operative. "Stop for no one."

Linda looked across the chaos and assessed the situation with cold clarity. She saw injured reporters huddling together, some clutching wounds, others frozen in shock. The FBI had yet to secure the area, and with the confusion still unfolding, Linda seized the opportunity. She signaled her team to move, retrieving the bodies swiftly and loading them into a Mars Corporation van.

As they sped away from the chaos, Linda glanced in the rearview mirror, spotting FBI agents beginning to cordon off the exits. But they were already beyond reach. The van navigated through back roads, the sirens fading into the distance until they arrived at an unmarked Mars Corporation facility.

Inside the secure compound, Luke's demeanor shifted as he took command. "Was the launch successful?" he demanded, an uncharacteristic edge of panic threading his voice. "I saw it drop the booster, but is the cruiser en route?"

"Yes, boss," Linda met his eyes with equal confidence. "The control team was unaware of the attack at the viewing center. The Mars Cruiser is on its way."

"Good," he said, his composure returning. "Get those bodies to the neural lab. Now."

With practiced authority, Luke motioned for her to follow as he directed the team forward. They moved briskly behind two gurneys, pushing through a long corridor into an unmarked building. The cargo elevator doors slid open, and they crowded inside, descending to several levels in silence. When the doors opened, they stepped into a stark, brightly lit medical facility.

Linda looked down at the attacker's lifeless body, his face frozen in a grimace of pain. She crouched beside him, pulling open his bloodstained shirt to reveal a tattoo of Earth inked over his heart. A small, clean puncture wound marred its center. "Earth First, boss," she said, pointing at the tattoo. "Looks like that shot was mine."

But Luke's focus was elsewhere. He stood over Felipe's body and watched as surgeons and technicians worked with precision, inserting tubes into Felipe's chest, arms, and legs, connecting him to a wall of monitors that displayed his vital signs. Three doctors moved him to an operating area, making precise incisions as they placed devices at strategic points in his head, neck, and torso.

An orderly approached, glancing at the dead reporter. At Luke's nod, the orderly wheeled the body away.

"What's going on, boss?" Linda asked, studying Luke's stoic expression. Her eyes drifted to his black blazer, darkened with fresh blood.

"We're giving Felipe a second chance." Luke's voice was calm, almost clinical.

"He's alive?"

"No, he's brain-dead," Luke clarified. "The body's still functioning, but Felipe's gone. We're using neural devices to keep his body going."

Linda's stomach churned. "Is that even legal? What about his family?"

Luke gave her a sharp look. "Have you ever read your terms

of service agreement?"

Linda shrugged. "I mean, it's a click, like everything else. Why?"

"Every Mars Corporation employee signed the same contract. It's all there, buried in the fine print. For example, the agreement states that Mars Corporation may use your body for research if you die on duty. We'll compensate family members at our discretion. In Felipe's case, his daughters' college tuition is covered, and his wife will live comfortably without financial concerns."

"Did I sign the same waiver?" she asked, almost in disbelief.

"You didn't read the contract?" Luke's lips curled into a faint smile.

"The other Linda read it. Can you tell us apart?" she asked, testing him.

Luke shook his head with a slight chuckle. "Nope."

Just then, a corporate staffer hurried over and handed Luke a tablet. He glanced at it, and a brief laugh escaped from his lips.

Linda narrowed her eyes. "What's so funny?"

"That terrorist gave us the names of the people who paid for the hit."

Her brow furrowed. "But he's dead. How...?"

"We chipped him just before his brain failed. His mind may be gone, but we extracted what we needed in time." Triumph flashed in his eyes. "Dead men tell no tales? Now we can make them talk."

Linda's legs weaken. Watching Luke's amoral ingenuity at work brought a sharp pang of revulsion. This wasn't the man she wished he could be.

Luke caught her expression, and his tone hardened. "Why the look, Linda? I'm not letting selfish activists or the CCC derail humanity's future on another planet. He was practically gone anyway. We made him say a few things before he died."

Linda looked at the drying blood on his lapel, then her eyes rose to meet his unflinching stare.

"How important is this to you?" she asked, her voice but a whisper.

Luke's eyes were steely. "Everything I do is important."

"Then I'm in."

Linda returned home close to midnight. The house was dark and silent, save for the rhythmic sound of Chloe's snoring. She flipped on the kitchen light, illuminating a slice of cheesecake waiting on the white granite counter, with a note beside it. *I love you.* She smiled, thinking how grateful she was to have Chloe in her life. She grabbed a bottle of strawberry milk from the refrigerator and poured herself a glass, settling onto one of the high chairs at the counter. *Chloe always knows what I need,* she thought, a wave of gratitude washing over her.

She peeled off her clothes and let them fall in a careless heap on the living room floor, where they mingled with scattered cat toys. Walking into the bathroom, she caught sight of the blood still caked on her hands and arms. A lump rose in her throat as she scrubbed, watching the dark stains dissolve into swirling pink rivulets. She stepped into the shower, letting the hot water cascade over her, rinsing away the dirt and remnants of the day. The water pooled at her feet in a reddish, muddy swirl before disappearing down the drain.

After drying off and brushing her teeth, she slipped into bed beside Chloe. Chloe stirred, pressing into Linda, who pressed a gentle kiss to Chloe's forehead. She nestled into the covers beside Chloe, comforted by the warmth of Chloe's flannel pajamas.

Meanwhile, the other Linda Perez was releasing the harness, securing her to the padded wall. The *Mars Cruiser* had successfully broken free from Earth's gravity. She pushed herself up from the cushioned floor, feeling the shift as she adjusted to the weightlessness, and prepared to check on the passengers now on their journey to Mars.

Sarah Rafaeli

Sarah Rafaeli moved through the lab, specifically designed for her experiments. Her straw-blonde hair tucked away in a silvery hair net to keep it in check in zero gravity. Sarah's aquamarine eyes peered into neatly arranged vials and small bottles filled with entheogenic blends. The fair skin of her slender fingers slid across her tablet, updating results and checking messages. With her athletic, streamlined frame, she made the space feel even larger, navigating it with practiced ease. The compact, organized lab was efficient and secure. Tall and slender, at 5 feet, 9 inches, she could survey the space, even checking the ceiling storage.

She studied rows of temperature-controlled vials filled with modified yeast strains, each designed to produce psychoactive compounds like psilocybin, DMT, apomorphine, and mescaline. Back on Earth, she had created wines infused with these compounds. Her business grew quickly, taking advantage of the new markets created by the global legalization of psychedelics.

Sarah's achievements benefited not only her but also her family's beverage business. Raphaeli Beverage Corporation was a minor player in a global market dominated by large corporations. She created a unique position in the psychoactive beverage industry by acquiring a winery holding company in Argentina. Using her knowledge of wine fermentation and fungi research, Sarah rebranded the company as Higher Blends, and secured its spot among international distributors. The acquisition also included a small kosher winery, *Anavim M'vorachim*, which the family maintained as a tribute to their Jewish heritage.

At 25, Sarah was gaining recognition in the world of enhanced wines and spirits. She collaborated with researchers to explore the safe and legal marketing of psychoactive compounds. During this time, she met Luke Mons, who offered her an exclusive deal to distribute her beverage on Mars. His goal was to help colonists manage Mars Syndrome. In exchange for the deal, Mons insisted Sarah spend time at the Mars Corporation colony at Roddenberry Station.

As she worked, Sarah's thoughts drifted to her curandera and dear friend, Circe del Piano. Where was she? If anyone could have helped her with her research, it was Circe. Two years had passed since the last time she saw her, dancing in front of the center stage of the Whole Earth Festival at UC Davis.

Although the memories felt distant, Circe's warmth was near in memory. Sarah recalled her thick black hair, olive-toned skin, dark eyes filled with wisdom. She remembered their late nights under the stars, the ayahuasca ceremonies led by Circe's gentle strength, and the hum of sacred songs that had opened her heart. Circe had nurtured Sarah's emerging intuition, guiding her through mystical experiences with patience and care. Sarah leaned against the door, the only spot in her lab free from equipment or storage, and gave the command to the onboard AI.

"Lock," she said, savoring the solitude as the door clicked shut. It was time to let her mind go, to wander back in time, and refresh herself in memories of the past. She detached a tasting jar labeled Stamitz B, named for her favorite mycologist, measured a dose, and quaffed it down. The effects of the blend were fast acting. She drifted back to her first song circle with Circe, held deep in the live oak forests of San Diego County, close enough to the ocean to feel the Pacific's salty breeze.

Sarah recalled Circe's melodic voice, "Gracias, Pachamama, gracias, gracias." Circe's voice rang out, each word a gentle invocation, weaving intention into the circle of friends gathered around warm candlelight. Circe's figure bathed in the amber glow of candles, creating a space rich with gratitude and calm. Inside the circle was a sanctuary where trust was sacred. She breathed life and spirit into the space, calling forth the curanderos who had come before her. Unseen hands gathered around her, their presence elevated the power of the medicine inside the mason jars in front of her.

"Gracias to the father shaman, the curandero of my lineage, our compassionate guide." Circe's chant flowed through the silent room, her voice rippling like waves in still water. She held deep reverence for her Amazonian curandera, the one who had unlocked the jungle's secrets for her. Within Circe lived the mysteries of the sacred vine and an endless knowledge of plant medicine, carried forward with devotion.

Circe was a rising star among American curanderas and carried the legacy of her Peruvian mentor like a hidden flame. The jungle continued to call to her, but the demands of the university kept her away. Like Sarah, she was also a graduate student at UC Davis. She kept her curandera life a guarded secret from her colleagues in horticulture. Her graduate studies led her deep into molecular biology and her search to synthesize the essence of ayahuasca.

After Davis, she founded a company to harness ayahuasca's psychoactive properties for dissociative therapies. Clinical trials consumed her focus, and the sterile glow of labs replaced the earthy rituals of her past.

But inside Sarah's imagination, Circe was still a curandera. Sarah vividly recalled her wearing a white dhoti and saree blouse that flowed around her curvaceous figure. Compassion radiated outward to all who sat waiting for the medicine. Ayahuasca, to Circe, was alive and sacred. A thick, brown liquid in the mason jars before her was a holy sacrament.

Along with the sacrament were small bottles of essences - rose water, frankincense, Florida Water, and tobacco flower extracts. The bottles glistened on a Peruvian tapestry, ready to fill the air with their fragrances. A bundle of dried sage rested beside the altar, used to create sacred smoke, symbolizing a link to the elemental world. This was Circe's altar to Pachamama, the Earth Goddess of the Andes, and a tribute to her mentor. It connected everyone in the circle to the heartbeat of the Earth.

The psilocybin extract made its way into Sarah's mind, enhancing her memory of sitting in a sacred circle with Circe. The scene transformed, and now Sarah was no longer a passive observer. She had entered the consciousness of Circe, bonding as though the two were now one. She was preparing for the journey, directing the helpers to place water bottles, tissues, purging buckets, and shiny steel cups to pour the sacramental tea.

"From persistence comes truth," she said, lighting a candle that illuminated a small shrine of amulets, herbs, and crystals arranged on a vibrant Peruvian tapestry. "See this steady flame burning in the darkness? There is no religion higher than truth itself." The room fell still, all eyes fixed on her.

Circe raised a mason jar of ayahuasca to her forehead, then extended it toward the circle with reverence. "This is the Mother of the Forest, the wisdom of the vine, the caapi and chacruna." She poured the thick, brown essence into a stainless steel cup, its molasses-like gleam catching the light as she lifted it to her lips. She drank the dark tea in one gulp. "*Gracias, Pachamama. Salute a todos.*"

She whistled the melody of an ícaro, a sacred song for the ayahuasca, as she prepared to serve the sacred tea. Circe touched a picture of the founder of her lineage, a black-and-white photograph, lovingly framed in hand-carved wood in the center of her shrine. That curandero was a woman who lived in a remote village along a winding tributary deep within the Amazonian forest. To the locals, she was a healer of body and mind. The curandera might have faded into the mythos of local lore had it not been for North American wanderers, tourists driven by a hunger for adventure and discovery.

Circe's thoughts drifted back to the beginning of her journey with ayahuasca, to the day she had begged her teacher to unveil its mysteries—the jungle's elusive, sacred elixir. Her teacher, weathered and wise, had relented, but not without a warning. She spoke of those who had walked this path before: some who had lost their way, swallowed by the labyrinth of their own minds; others who had succumbed to the jungle's merciless dangers. And then there were the few, like herself, who had unearthed enlightenment within the wilderness's depths.

She lit a mapacho roll and drew the tobacco, Nicotiana rustica, into her lungs, then released with a whooshing sound.

Gran espíritu, gran abuela, gran abuelo

Great spirit, great grandmother, great grandfather As I am I stand before you

As I am I ask for your blessings

And I give thanks for the heart you've put in me.

Circe paused, her smile radiating love and acceptance as her eyes lingered on Sarah, her newest favorite. There was something magnetic about Sarah—her free spirit, her emotional depth—that drew Circe in. Sarah's passion for dancing and singing to the rhythms of the handpan drum stirred deep feelings inside her. Circe caught Sarah's eye, extending an unspoken, warm invitation.

Sarah listened as Circe's voice filled the circle, each word drawing them into a shared reverence.

"Ayahuasca is a profound teacher," Circe said. "It guides us beyond the limits we set for ourselves. Ayahuasca quiets the endless thoughts in our minds and shows us what we need to see to grow. Let us find the courage to let go of our stories, our need to explain everything, and just be."

"*Gracias, Papá,*" she called, her voice rising in invocation. "Great sky father. Mamá, *gracias*. Great earth mother. *Pachamama, pachamama, pachamama... Limpia, limpia, limpia.*" With each "*limpia,*" Circe made a swooshing sound - a soft, resonant "she-oo" that rippled through the room like a gentle breeze. The words invited them to cleanse, purify, and prepare for the journey ahead.

Circe rang a brass bell three times, a chime resonating with sacred meanings, and held the mason jar reverently to her heart. Gesturing to her helper on the left to drink first, she called out the names of everyone in the circle to kneel before the shrine and receive the sacrament.

When it was Sarah's turn, she knelt before Circe, extending her slender arms and offering her a cup. "I want a full dose," her eyes fixed on Circe.

She filled the cup to the brim, lifting it to her heart, then to her lips and third eye, before sweeping it toward Sarah. "*Salud,*" she sang out, handing her the cup. Sarah's eyes widened as she saw the dark, thick liquid filling the cup, then downed the dose in one steady gulp and proclaimed, "*Salud a todos!*"

"*Salud*, Sarah," the circle responded, their voices uniting in a warm chorus.

The rite continued as Circe poured and blessed the drink for everyone who came forward. As the last person took their place and nestled into their blankets and pillows, Circe rose, a serene presence, and sang.

Her voice was slow and hypnotic, tender like a young mother's lullaby soothing a child into sleep. Her feet glided across the floor as she extended a blessing of protection to everyone. In her right hand, she held a hand-rolled cigar *mapacho*. On her left, a Shipibo maraca. Between verses, she drew a breath from the cigar, exhaling the smoke to envelop each participant, fanning it gently over them in a smoke-filled blessing.

The song was more than a soothing melody. She was singing to a pantheon of celestial beings. Sarah, attuned to the spiritual realm, saw them taking form around the circle. Spirits gathered around, seeking a person willing to accept them in.

The ayahuasca engulfed her mind. Sarah's vision shifted into a vibrant web of geometric patterns. She found herself in a realm like the Nazca lines of Peru - spiders, condors, and pelicans glowing in purples, reds, and oranges, each shape pulsing with light. The lines wove together into a translucent veil of Peruvian tapestry. She heard a voice in her mind, inviting her in. But as she stepped toward the veil, reality split open and she tumbled forward, spiraling into a void.

She landed upright in a distorted version of a place

resembling Toontown. Everything pulsed, turned and swirled with hyper-saturated colors. The streets and buildings, edged with gears, circled, expanded and contracted while human-like shapes moved in a grotesque dance. Inside the windows of the pulsating buildings was the face of a mechanical clown glowing under black light, painted in blazing reds, blues, purples, and yellows. Its large white eyes and jagged teeth gleamed against the surrounding chaos.

One face popped out and leered at her. It probed her doubts with a barrage of open-ended questions, leading her into a maze of doubt and insecurity. With each answer, the clown shot back more questions. Its appetite for self-delusion was insatiable. Around her, other creatures appeared - rabbits, dogs, ducks, monkeys - all with sharp teeth and menacing faces, closing in as the clown pushed deeper into her mind.

The clown sneered and taunted Sarah, edging closer with its razor teeth. "You'll never find the right answer."

Sarah opened her eyes and caught sight of Circe dancing around in the soft candlelight, her voice enchanting, calling out to her. She could never offer the clown a perfect answer because the reason for the clown was to keep her from entering the veil. It was the guardian of the threshold, the trickster sent to keep Sarah from crossing through the veil.

Then, through the chaos, she heard a familiar voice calling to her - a spirit guide's calm, reassurance. "This is the endless self-absorption of a trickster, the lesser guardian of the threshold. Rise, Sarah. Rise."

Clarity washed away the doubts and perturbations in her mind. Sarah saw through the vivid clown's trick for what it was - an energy-draining mind trap, pulling her toward the depths of her own ego. "Enough!" A single word blasted the clown and all the Toontown away from her, leaving Sarah standing before the oddly printed veil, now opaque and cloth-like.

Pushing through an opening in the veil, she saw Circe standing above her, exhaling sacred mapacho smoke around her. Sarah was still on her mat, draped with a Peruvian blanket, back to the reality of the circle, which now took on qualities of scintillation and etheric forms. Circe drew on the cigar and blew the thick, rich smoke onto the top of Sarah's head. She placed a gentle hand over Sarah's head, as if guiding the smoke into her spirit. She moved to blow smoke onto the back of Sarah's neck, then knelt and exhaled toward her heart. Taking Sarah's hands, Circe turned them outward, filling her open palms with smoke before pressing them together and guiding them to her heart. The atmosphere had changed. The room was no longer just a space of physical shapes - it pulsed with layers of physical and spiritual awareness, each one unfolding in vivid, heightened waves. Sarah's eyes settled on Circe, and she noticed a faint aura around her, the guiding presence of Hecate.

The glowing shapes Sarah had seen earlier had infused into many of the participants. For some, their forms grew larger, embodying the spirits that had taken hold of them. Others lay laughing, moaning, or still, captivated by the lesser guardian of the threshold. Some were purging, releasing, and surrendering to the healing process.

She entered her thoughts on the pan drum and sitar, letting Circe's voice fill her mind, chanting songs to the curandero lineage and the Pachamama.

Their ancient melodies filled the space, pulling the participants into a shared journey. Elemental spirits, called forth by Circe's invocations, stirred in the dim light, ready to reveal themselves.

As the ayahuasca journey deepened, the veil thinned, and plant spirits transformed the atmosphere. Sarah sensed Hecate's presence. The goddess's voice, woven into the songs, bridged the gap between gods and mortals. Outside, a half-moon cast long shadows, its silver glow blending with the flickering candlelight.

The music spoke to her, a pulse connecting her to the spirits dancing through the bodies of the willing. "Listen to the curandera."

Circe returned to the Shrine and raised her hands to the sky.

"Trust in the medicine, trust in the spirits, trust in yourselves. We are here together, in love, in spirit. Remember, this journey is not just about seeing but about learning and integrating. Embrace the lessons with an open heart, collective intent, and unity."

Circe's voice differed from her usual light, whimsical tone—it carried a deep power and clarity, ringing like crystal. Around her, people and helpers picked up instruments, creating a wild, energetic rhythm. The sound of a bongo, hand pan, sitar, and violin filled the room with untamed passion. Sarah watched as Circe, caught in the music's grip, moved into an ecstatic dance. Others joined, their bodies swaying and spinning until the circle's center pulsed with vibrant, flowing movement. Sarah stood up and moved to the rhythm of the music, which built up at a fast pace. She and Circe moved to the center of the group and entwined in ecstatic movement. They transcended the veil and entered the liminal space of the unseen divine.

Circe sang a haunting ballad, her melody celebrating the moon's celestial beauty. Her voice rose and fell in a rhythm that seemed to echo the solfeggio scale, resonating with everyone. It reached into their very bones, blending their energies together into one harmonious whole. This was the power of ayahuasca, drawing them all into the sacred rhythm of the universe. Their movements formed a beautiful symmetry, and they became like a cosmic dance, their etheric bodies entwined in perfect harmony.

As the dancing grew more intense, Sarah felt a darker energy. Circe appeared to merge into another goddess, her *Ishta Devata, Varahi,* the Hindu goddess who taught the tantra of the lower chakras. The goddess's voluptuous form enveloped Circe's body. Her animalistic face, that of a sow, radiated both fierce love and deep compassion.

Varahi inspired the musicians to play a traditional Kathak melody to which Circe offered a dance to Varahi. As Sarah watched, she felt herself being drawn into an infinite depth, as if stepping into another dimension. There, she stood before the three forms of Hecate, each draped in white light. Sarah's straw-blonde hair floated around her shoulders, and her blue eyes sparkled like sapphires. Hecate extended her hands to greet another divine figure, Isis. She and Circe danced with the three goddesses of life and death, the keepers of the etheric keys.

Though their message was unspoken, the words imprinted on Sarah's thoughts.

Hecate's voice shook her body. "Do you understand our meaning?"

Sarah gave an uncertain nod.

"You are a messenger. The task at hand is not yours, but for the one you will raise."

In an instant, Sarah found herself back in her place, covered by a Peruvian quilt. Circe returned to her place by the altar, and all the participants regrouped around the circle.

Seeing the looks of dismay on everyone's face, Circe picked up the hand pan and played out a simple, comforting beat. She sang a well-known yoga mantra to guide everyone back from their deep journeys. Her words and melody guided them back to the present.

"Lokah Samastah Sukhino Bhavantu. May all beings everywhere be happy and free."

The ceremony concluded, as the effects of ayahuasca faded from everyone's awareness. Circe encouraged each person to share a single sentence about their experience, giving them a chance to release their tension. After a moment of silence, she instructed everyone to put away their stainless steel cups, reminding them of their reuse in the next session. Then, she invited the group to the kitchen to enjoy warm squash soup and thick slices of sourdough bread.

"Now that you have nourished your minds, it's time to nourish your body."

Circe stood next to Sarah, spreading slabs of butter on a piece of warm sourdough bread. "You witnessed the goddesses?"

"Yes. In your eyes, I saw a portal to another realm. I stood before Hecate, who showed me the path of souls. She brought forth Isis and your *Ishta Devata,* Varahi, in a triadic union. Varahi was inside of you, guiding your movements. I saw it."

"I felt her presence. She guided my hands and feet. It's not the first time she's embraced me."

Sarah pressed her face into Circe's shoulder as tears flowed from her eyes, soaking Circe's blouse.

Circe held her close. "Let it go. Varahi entered my mind and spoke of a messenger I am to assist. What does she mean?"

Sarah spoke through her tears. "I don't know. But Hecate also gave me a message. These things will come. Death, resurrection and rebirth, all darkly divine."

Circe wiped Sarah's mouth with the hem of her saree and brushed her lips against Sarah with a kiss. Surprised, Sarah drew back. Her eyes locked on Circe's.

Sarah's thoughts returned to her lab, and she felt the ceaseless hum of the cruiser's engines propelling it forward in space. She wondered what had become of Circe, only hearing rumors she'd become a corporate deva. She remembered the kiss and wondered what would have happened if she had kissed her back. But she was a million miles from Circe and the earth. She stood in a silent meditation, reflecting on all the events that brought her to that moment.

Linda Perez's voice cracked through the lab's intercom.

"Sarah, are you in there? The door's locked in privacy mode. You're wanted in the galley for breakfast. The Rabbi has an announcement about a party, and Luke Mons told me you have the wine!"

Sarah turned toward the door just as Linda entered an override command, causing it to slide open.

"There you are," Linda said with a grin. "Come on, let's head down to Level 5 and join everyone for breakfast."

Tu B'shvat

Shalom Mendelsohn stirred in his cubicle on Level 4 of the *E. R. Burroughs*. The familiar hum of the ship's systems filled the air, a constant reminder of how far from Earth he was, hurtling through the stars. His small sleeping chamber, marked by the tiny mezuzah beside the sliding door, offered just enough room for privacy, but little else.

Every morning on rising Shalom whispered *Modeh Ani*, thanking G-d for the gift of another day. Ritual was the keystone to Shalom's life. He slipped into his contact slippers, feeling the soles grip the floor as he hopped into the corridor and turned back to the cubicle. Before taking another step, he touched his fingers to his lips and extended them to the mezuzah on his door. He checked his yarmulke, ensuring it was secure and wouldn't drift away in the weightlessness, and patted the bag containing his tefillin, fastened to his jumpsuit.

With precision timing, a waiterbot arrived with two wet towelettes for him to cleanse his hands, purify himself from a spiritual impurity occurring during sleep. Although the ritual of hand washing involves pouring water over the hands, the towelette was a compromise with the Mars Corporation to conserve water and the impracticality of pouring water in zero gravity. He placed the used towelettes into a bin on the waiterbot and continued toward the central access corridor.

Today felt different. The air seemed charged with excitement - or perhaps that was just Shalom's anticipation. It was *Tu B'shvat*, the Jewish holiday celebrating trees, and it couldn't have come at a better time. And as fate would have it, the *E. R. Burroughs* was carrying the New Eden Project's precious cargo, saplings that would one day become the trees of Mars.

Shalom peered into the central corridor to ensure it was empty. The narrow shaft often made it hard to avoid brushing against others, particularly women. As an unmarried Orthodox man, he could not make unnecessary physical contact with women, a rule he followed with care.

Seeing no one, he descended the ladder to Level 3, the showers and exercise deck. It was still early, and only a few passengers were using the resistance ellipticals. They waved in greeting as he entered, his black-and-white sleeping jumpsuit standing out against the tan and blue jumpsuits worn by the others. The crew, he noticed, wore solid white with the Mars Corporation logo on their left chest.

Just as Shalom stepped onto an elliptical machine, Linda Perez hopped onto the one next to him.

"You look in excellent form today, Rabbi. Is it because it's *Tu B'shvat*?" Linda's voice broke through Shalom's steady rhythm on the elliptical.

"How did you know?"

"Nothing on this cruiser is a surprise to me, Rabbi. I'm the official Mars Corporation representative here. I know everything that happens aboard this ship. For example, you've got dried fruit ready for your celebration and a two-hour window on the Observation Deck."

Shalom paused, realizing her presence beside him wasn't a coincidence. She'd been waiting. It felt strange seeing her here - the last time had been after his interview with Luke Mons. He glanced at her, curiosity getting the better of him. "Why would

Mons sponsor a *Tu B'shvat* celebration? It's not a major holiday."

Linda dismounted her machine, giving him a wink. "This is a special voyage. We're carrying 100 young trees in the cargo bay. Seeds don't germinate well on Mars, so the boss is sending saplings. He must figure prayer might help."

With that, she was gone, leaving Shalom with little time to dwell on the exchange. His schedule was tight, and the *Tu B'shvat* celebration was only hours away. After his resistance training, Shalom headed to the shower cubicles. He placed his bag with the tefillin and yarmulke into a locker and pressed his palm against the biometric pad.

Inside, Shalom stripped off his night clothes, tossing them into the digester bin. Everything was recycled on the cruiser. Clothing was worn once, digested, and reprinted daily to prevent infections. He stood still as a cool, soapy mist enveloped him, the glycerine-based soap cleansing his skin. He wiped himself off with a fiber towel, pressed the rinse icon, and let the pure water mist wash away the soap. Another towel, another wipe, and the shower finished with a stream of warm air, completely drying him.

A drawer opened beside him, revealing a new, printed uniform: black sweatpants and a white pullover shirt that mimicked the traditional garb he wore back on Earth. Unlike the others, his outfit came with a thin t-shirt with tzitzit worn inside the jumpsuit. The printer knotted the tzitzit correctly; four slots in the jumpsuit allowed the wearer to pull it out just enough to satisfy tradition without creating a safety hazard. Shalom admired the tzitzit. Besides the yarmulka, they were the only part of his clothing that reminded him of home.

After securing his yarmulke with a quick clip, he grabbed his tefillin and prepared to recite the morning Shacharit prayers. Shalom stood just outside the training area, wrapping the tefillin around his arm, then tapped his tablet to bring up the siddur. His lips moved as he read the prayers. He hoped, as always, that someone - passenger or crew - might see him and ask to join. It was about setting an example, showing that even here, among the stars, tradition carried on.

After finishing his prayers, he put the tefillin into the bag and thought about the upcoming celebration. *Tu B'shvat* might not have been the biggest holiday back on Earth, but now it was a reason to bring some Yiddishkeit to the cruiser. The Mars Corporation had spared no expense, with the CEO himself sending cases of real dried fruit to mark the occasion. After two long weeks of printed meals, Shalom knew that the crew and passengers were eager for a taste of something real.

Shalom glanced at the roster on his tablet as he moved, noting that six passengers and one crew member had identified as Jewish. He wondered if there were others who hadn't disclosed their faith. As a Mars Corporation event, the Tu B'shvat gathering included everyone. Maybe someone would feel moved to identify. Of course, he'd bring the tefillin, just in case.

Being reoccupied by the upcoming celebration, Shalom leapt into the central corridor. He didn't notice the person stepping into his path until their chests collided, sending Sarah Rafaeli tumbling backward, arms flailing as she bounced between the ladders in the zero-gravity space. Shalom reached out and grabbed her hands, pulling her back to the deck.

His heart raced - not just from the impact, but from the realization that he was gripping a woman's hand, something he should not be doing. He stared at her, frozen, as though he'd just shattered a window with a stray baseball. Sarah, her long blonde hair now drifting in the weightless air, was the most beautiful woman Shalom had ever seen. She was wearing a sheer night outfit that left very little to the imagination. His face burned with embarrassment, his eyes darting away from the curve of her breasts pressing against the fabric.

Yet he still held on to her hands.

Sarah wasn't letting go, either. She used the leverage to pull herself onto the Level 3 platform. With her slippers gripping the floor, she noted she was a little taller than him. Her blue eyes sparkled with amusement as she watched Shalom squirm.

"You're in too much of a hurry, Rabbi." Sarah teased him, her voice light, her eyes twinkling. "Take a breath. Relax. It's a holiday, remember?"

Shalom's mouth went dry. He tried to pull his hands away, but she held on. "I - um - Ms. Rafaeli, I didn't mean to."

She noticed his preoccupation with her hands and lightly touched his mind where she found guilty pleasure. He was breaking a rule.

"Should I not be holding your hands?" she asked with a laugh, arching a playful brow. "I need to steady myself. Few men can knock me off my feet." She winked. "That's a joke, Rabbi. But I have my balance back now."

With a tight squeeze, she let go of his hands. Shalom's palms tingled from the warmth of her touch. He stood there, flustered, his eyes wide, trying to form a coherent sentence.

Sarah studied him. "Shush, it was an accident. Besides, I was in a rush too." She gave him a quick once-over. He was stronger than he looked. Quick reflexes. She felt drawn to his green eyes, even more beautiful than the emeralds in her ears. It had been a long time since Sarah had met a man so unguarded. And she liked it.

Shalom realized something that made his heart skip a beat. He was alone with Sarah, a woman all but naked in her outfit, in the bathing and exercise area. Every instinct screamed at him - this was a line he couldn't cross. An observant Jewish man should never be alone with an unmarried woman.

He blushed as he turned toward the central corridor and grabbed the ladder. Making a quick get away. But halfway to the next level, he paused, glancing back at Sarah. Her expression had shifted - puzzled, maybe even a little disappointed by his sudden exit.

"I'll be seeing you at the *Tu B'shvat* party?" he called down, his voice echoing in the empty corridor.

Sarah gave a brief wave, nodding, searching his face. "Yeah, I'll be there."

As he resumed his ascent, he heard her let out a sigh. She was already stepping onto the elliptical machine when he disappeared from view, but her image remained in his mind. What had just happened?

Shalom shook his head, climbing faster now. It wasn't like he hadn't seen her before - she stood across from him at mealtime a few times over the last two weeks. He knew she was Jewish, but his thoughts had been more on finding men for a minyan. He had sent her a personal invite to the *Tu B'shvat* party. But he hadn't expected to physically run into her in the fitness room.

Shalom darted up to Level 5 and into the galley, the familiar scents of printed food hitting him as soon as he entered. The galley looked like a cafeteria. There were food trays at the entrance, beverage dispensers lining the far wall, and waste bins near the exit. But the designers created everything here for zero gravity, packaging each item for easy consumption.

Shalom grabbed a packet of coffee, an omelet tube, and a pouch of printed toast. The thought of food made from the same recycled material as his slippers should have been unsettling, but surprisingly, it wasn't. Knowing that everything was kosher made life a little less stressful. After all, the Cruiser's digesters transformed waste into essentials like clothing and meals. It wasn't a traditional breakfast, but it got the job done.

He approached the table where some Jewish passengers had gathered. Manny Feldman grinned and said, "I hear it's a Jewish holiday today, and you've got something planned."

"How did you hear about the party?"

Manny pointed to Linda, standing by the table, her arms folded. Also gathered were Yudi Zalman, and a few other passengers Shalom hadn't met. The group's friendly smiles and familiar chatter gave Shalom the boost he needed. The party was coming together.

"So, Rabbi, did you bring your tefillin?" Manny asked.

"Of course."

Shalom was delighted to help Manny put on tefillin and say the prayers. He hadn't wrapped someone since leaving earth.

The discussion stopped as everyone's attention shifted. Shalom sensed someone standing behind him, and when he turned, there was Sarah. She pulled her golden hair back in a bronze-colored netting; her face glowed freshly from a quick shower, enticed him with curiosity.

"What's *Tu B'shvat,* Rabbi? And why is it a holiday?" she asked.

Shalom hesitated, surprised by her directness. "You don't know?"

Sarah's brow furrowed with frustration. "Just because my family's Jewish doesn't mean I know every holiday. I know about Purim, though."

Linda Perez burst into laughter. "Of course you do! Your family owns a multi-national liquor company!"

"Beverage," Sarah corrected.

Linda, still chuckling, turned to Shalom. "Come on, Rabbi, enlighten us."

Shalom cleared his throat and spoke. "*Tu B'shvat* is the New Year for Trees, a time to celebrate and honor them. We thank Hashem for the fruits of the Earth, and in particular, for the potential of new life. But, in more practical terms for today, there will be plenty of food this afternoon, including real fruit."

"If that's the case, count me in," Yudi said with a broad smile. The high schooler had been quiet until then, but his enthusiasm was clear.

Shalom nodded. "Thank you for your RSVP, Yudi."

Linda spoke up again, counting on her fingers. "So, with the rabbi included, that makes what - eight Jews on this mission?"

Shalom's smile faltered, though he tried to hide it. "Yes, seven have self-identified. I made the eighth. I sent invites to all the senior members of the crew, and of course, you're welcome to bring your colleagues."

"Technically, everyone is invited. It's a Mars Corporation event. But I didn't make a big announcement about it. It's only in today's bulletin."

Sarah slid her hand close to Shalom's. "Do you have wine for the party?"

"We had no budget for wine. I'm grateful that Mr. Mons provided the fruit. We'll have to make our L'chaims with whiskey from the food fabricators."

A mischievous smile appeared on Sarah's lips as she tapped his arm. Shalom jumped, startled by the unexpected contact. "You're in luck, Rabbi. I have wine on board."

"Is it kosher wine?"

Linda, overhearing the exchange, spoke up. "Didn't you know? Sarah has a kosher winery in Argentina. It's part of her family's holdings."

Sarah did a quick double take. "You know about our winery?"

Linda stood up, her smile widening, pleased to have the upper hand. "As the representative of the Mars Corporation, I know just about everything about everyone on board - within certain limits, of course. Besides, I inspected the cargo holdings and saw your shipment. The wine has the Rafaeli logo, *Higher Blends.*"

Sarah gave Linda a smirk, her eyes narrowing. But rather

than escalate the moment, she shrugged it off. Her attention shifted back to Shalom, who seemed flustered.

"The kosher wines are pure varietals, Malbec and Cabernet. No need to be concerned. There's even a certificate from the certifying organization, Union of Orthodox Rabbis. They are not blended or infused."

"That's impressive, Ms. Rafaeli. I'll need to see the certificate, but if it's OU, we'll be toasting with real wine."

"You were a kosher certifier back in New York." Linda said.

"I think you know my whole life."

"Up to you boarding the Mars Cruiser, I'll have to wait and see what comes next. By the way, I'd like to invite the ship's doctor, Shanice Williams." Linda asked.

Shalom nodded. "Of course."

"I'll make sure the other Jewish passengers show up," Linda said as she walked away. Sarah followed, but not without casting Shalom a flirtatious glance over her shoulder.

Proprietary Blend

Captain Tran Tuan Giang stood at the entrance of the Observation Deck alongside Rabbi Mendelssohn, greeting passengers and crew to the *Tu B'shvat* party. "Thank you for the invite, rabbi. About half of my crew will be here soon, mostly for the food." The Captain said with a hearty laugh. "Linda expects there to be about thirty passengers attending. I wish we could have events like this more often. It's a long journey to Mars."

Shalom nodded along, affirming the Captain's words, though his thoughts drifted. Just about everyone aboard had heard the story of the *Dragon's Breath*, a covert mission by the Chinese Communist Corporation to transport nuclear warheads to its destroyers orbiting the Moon. The payload was sent to wipe out Mars Corporation's colonies on the Moon. But the Captain maneuvered his frigate, the *Buzz Aldrin*, and successfully boarded and captured the Chinese space destroyer. His actions had saved tens of thousands of lives.

With a reputation like that, Shalom had always pictured the Captain as a towering figure, six feet tall and muscular, the very image of a war hero. But as he stood beside the captain now, reality didn't quite match his imagination. The Captain, only five foot seven, was wiry, his frame lean and quick. There was something about the way he carried himself that reminded Shalom of the iconic Bruce Lee, an enduring figure in pop culture.

The Observation Deck's single, large window stretched out before Shalom, the only one on the *E.R. Burroughs*. It was installed for those who felt the cruiser's walls closing in—a place to visit and see the vastness of space. The Mars Corporation constructed it from Whipple shielding of clear polycarbonates and aluminum oxynitride. A stainless steel cover shielded it, the same material as the hull.

Yudi and Linda were the first to arrive and headed straight to a table of sweet cakes and drinks. In a short time, more people flowed in, filling the Observation Deck to capacity. The Captain walked up to Shalom and said, "Your event is very successful. The only other time this room gets full is during church service. We have about 20 regulars. You can come anytime."

Shalom smiled at the Captain. Linda, who was standing next to the rabbi, shouted out to a woman dressed in a doctor's scrub suit. "Shanice, over here."

Shanice was a stout woman with broad hips and full cheeks. She was the person whose smile filled a person with joy and had the kind of full body children love to hug.

"Shanice, this is Captain Tran. Have you two met before?" Linda wrapped her arms around them. "You should know Shanice has a beautiful choir voice."

"We've met, sort of. If the Captain remembers my voice. You were a lieutenant back then. You only knew me by my voice."

The Captain's posture stiffened, his expression shifting from polite curiosity to awe. He straightened, eyes widening as recognition dawned. "That was you? I thought I was in heaven, talking to an angel."

A deep blush crept across Shanice's cheeks, and she looked away to hide her giddy smile. "I was the doctor who patched you up after the battle with the Dragon's Breath."

Shanice turned to the Captain, her eyes now filled with curiosity. "Did I hear you say there's a worship service here on Sundays?"

"You did," The Captain said, his voice regaining its usual steadiness, though his eyes remained on Shanice a moment longer.

Suddenly, the Observation Deck fell into a breathless silence. All eyes turned toward the door as Sarah Rafaeli entered. She was stunning, her pleated gold skirt flowing around her knees with each step, while a navy blue, form-fitting blouse accentuated her graceful figure. Three small emerald earrings sparkled from each ear, and her long, blonde hair, neatly secured in a net, draped elegantly across her shoulders. Her smooth, white legs peek out from the subtle sway of the pleats, drawing every eye in the room.

Sarah's smile radiated as she gave a quick glance around, acknowledging the crowd before heading straight to Shalom. The sweet, floral scent of her perfume hung in the air, unmistakable yet restrained, much to the Captain's silent disapproval.

"Am I late, Rabbi?" Sarah asked as she pressed her cheek against Linda's and took her hand. She moved to the appetizer table, arriving just as the dried fruit was being laid out.

"This looks fantastic! I can't wait to try a piece," Sarah remarked, turning back to Shalom with a gleam of delight.

"Help yourself, but first, we must all say a *beracha* before eating." His voice was formal, yet warm.

Sarah looked puzzled. "What's a..."

"A blessing," Shalom interjected. "A *beracha* is a Jewish blessing we make before eating. It's a mitzvah - a good deed."

He gathered everyone's attention and led the blessing for fruit, his voice steady as he finished with, "*borei pri ha-aitz.*" - blessing the fruit of the trees.

As soon as the blessing was done, Linda sniffed the air, her curiosity piqued. "Is that perfume?" she asked.

"Yes," Sarah said with a sly smile. "It's a proprietary blend of pheromones made from fungal derivatives. My company has been expanding into new products using natural psychoactive compounds."

Yudi, his cheeks flushed, couldn't help but blurt out, "Doesn't that make it an aphrodisiac?"

Sarah's eyes twinkled as she shot him a wink. "Yes, Yudi. Did you notice?"

Yudi's face turned an even deeper shade of red, and Linda stepped in to rescue him from further embarrassment.

"The Mars Corporation allows you to wear perfume?"

Sarah shrugged. "It's for business. My company plans to use clips from the Cruiser's cameras for promotion."

"We're being recorded?" Yudi asked.

"It's all in the disclosures. Didn't you read them?" Sarah leaned into Shalom. "Do you like it, Rabbi? I hoped you would."

Shalom's mouth opened, but no words followed. "Yes, er, it's quite..."

"Captivating," Linda interjected with a grin.

"Yes, exactly!" Sarah agreed, squeezing Linda's hand as she glanced around. "Where's my wine? I don't see it on the tables."

Without missing a beat, Linda raised her hand to her mouth, speaking into her smartwatch. After a few quick exchanges, she said, "The waiterbots got reassigned by mistake. I'll sort it out. The wine cartons are where you showed me, in your lab - the ones with the Jewish symbols?"

Shalom's ears perked up, and his voice became serious. "Are all of your products certified kosher?"

Sarah didn't miss a beat, her reply quick and confident. "Union of Orthodox Rabbis, Shalom."

Hearing his name on her lips made Shalom blush. "That's perfect, Miss Rafaeli."

Sarah turned to address the group. "You all know the Mars Corporation ran background checks on everyone for security and to ensure we'd adapt well to life on Mars. That included Yudi," giving him a wink. "Yudi's quite the tech expert. In high school, he helped his computer science teacher run a lab and even has experience with n-Core quantum computers."

"Mr. Mons insisted I purchase a very expensive X-Isis computer to assist with my research."

Yudi, surprised, said, "You have an X-series quantum computer?"

Sarah took a step back, laughing, and bumped Shalom. She seized the moment, giving his arm a playful squeeze. "Excuse me, Rabbi, we've crashed into each other again."

Shalom felt conflicted and confused by all of his emotions, but before he could respond, a familiar voice called out.

"Rabbi Mendelssohn! There you are. I have someone for you to meet?" It was Manny Feldman.

"This is Aaron Margolis. He's a seismologist."

Grateful for the interruption, Shalom stepped away from Sarah and gave Manny a warm hug. "Baruch Hashem. Aaron, have you put on tefillin today?"

"What's that?" Aaron asked.

Shalom led Aaron over to a table where he had placed the tefillin.

"Looks like the rabbi's off doing rabbi things," Linda said, watching Shalom as he mingled into the crowd.

Sarah let out a small sigh, then brightened, her expression turning professional. "So," she said, addressing Yudi with a business-like tone, "you seemed pretty excited about my X-series computer. The label says it's an X-Isis. What do you know about it?"

Yudi's eyes lit up, his voice rising in disbelief. "Excited? I'm gobsmacked! No, this is unbelievable!" He rambled on, almost out of control with excitement, then caught himself. "For a desktop model, these are top of their class. Most n-Core systems claim to have quantum processing, but it's just a hybrid - swapping quantum cores for conventional ones when needed. But your system, the X-Isis, it's the real deal. True, integrated quantum cores."

Sarah nodded, though her understanding of the technical details was thin. "And how would that help with my research?" she asked, her voice curious yet direct. "We're trying to simulate the neurochemical changes that happen in the brain after ingesting various neurotrophic compounds. We need to track brain function - speech, vision, motor coordination, and all that."

"You want to simulate a fully functioning brain?"

Sarah was growing impatient. "That's right. Do you think this computer can handle it?"

Yudi laughed. "Ms. Rafaeli, your computer could simulate a city of brains!"

"Have you worked with this series before?"

Yudi's excitement made him lift off the floor. "I have! Back at school, I managed a second generation n-Core. It was still in the hybrid class of quantum computers, but capable of regenerative AI and generative video synthesis. The Isis model is the current top of the line."

"Interesting Egyptian name," she said. Sarah turned her attention to the entrance as Shalom returned, accompanied by the Captain and a small group of officers. "We'll talk more about this later," she said, giving Yudi a parting glance before turning away.

Yudi, still in disbelief, nodded and hurried back toward the dessert table. This was his chance to install Evelin.

Shalom mingled among the guests, schmoozing as Sarah stepped away with Linda. He soon found Abby Hoffman, a nutritionist, who introduced him to Eva Rosen, a mineralogist.

Shalom gathered them together and led everyone in the *Shehecheyanu* blessing.

Just as they finished, Linda returned, guiding a small, cart-like waiterbot that carried two cartons of wine. Linda had already poured two zero-gravity glasses. She handed those to Sarah and Shalom, then poured more glasses for Shanice, Captain Tran, and those who said the *Shehecheyanu*.

"Before I send this waiterbot off into the crowd, I'd like to make a toast," Linda announced with a bright smile. "On behalf of the Mars Corporation, to Rabbi Mendelssohn, may he be a light of inspiration to all of us, and to Sarah Rafaeli and the success of her ventures on Mars."

Shalom raised a hand, cutting in. "Wait one moment. We must make a blessing." With that, he led the *borei pri hagafen*, the blessing over wine, and then, with a hearty "L'Chaim!" he downed most of his glass in one go.

Sarah took a sip. The bitter was sharp on her tongue. She sniffed the wine, glancing around the room to see if anyone else had noticed. Aaron and Abby were smiling in delight, both talking over each other.

Aaron held up his glass and admired the color of the wine. "This is fabulous, like a nutty cabernet! Can you synthesize this?"

"This is real wine. Complimentary shipping expense covered by Luke Mons. But yes, we've synthesized a version made from lab-grown grape cells."

As the chatter rose around the table. Linda handed Shalom another prefilled glass. Sarah's smile faltered, and she turned to Linda, her eyes narrowing. "You were careful to only take bottles labeled kosher for *Tu B'shvat*?"

Linda returned her smile with a mischievous grin, looking at Sarah and Shalom. She mouthed the word "No!", but Linda shrugged and sauntered off, departing with the waiterbot. Sarah leapt into action and cut in front of the waiterbot, bringing Linda to a dead stop. Her hand tightened around the waiterbot, her angry eyes locking onto Linda. "What were you thinking?"

Linda's face remained a picture of innocence. "What's the problem, Ms. Rafaeli?"

Sarah held her composure, though she sensed Linda's satisfaction beneath the act, and lots of mischief in her thoughts. Sarah probed into her thoughts and saw an image of Luke Mons in Linda's mind. She steadied her voice. "Ms. Perez, you didn't move a few glasses labeled *proprietary blend* from one of the lab tables, did you?"

Sarah's voice surprised Linda. "Yes, I assumed they went with the bottles."

Sarah glanced over at Shalom, the unfocused look in his eyes. The blend of DMT and herbs was already coursing through his system. Swallowing her frustration, Sarah met Linda's eyes with a serene expression. "It's an unfortunate mistake, Ms. Perez. I'll need your help to get the rabbi to my lab for detoxification. The herbs in those glasses are powerful."

"Oh no, Ms. Rafaeli, how terrible. You should have marked them..." Linda's words trailed off as she caught the flame in Sarah's eyes. She fell silent. Something inside Sarah was seizing her tongue, preventing her from speaking. Linda's expression shifted as understanding dawned on her. "So that's why Mr. Mons brought you on board." Linda made a note to herself not to anger Sarah again.

Shalom, too engrossed in giving toasts and thanking the Mars Corporation, was oblivious to the exchange. Joy filled him as he celebrated Tu B'shvat and discussed the trees destined for Mars. But beneath the surface, subtle changes were already taking place. The psychoactive compounds in the wine - DMT and other entheogens - were slipping into his bloodstream, coloring his perceptions.

From across the room, Shanice Willis observed Shalom. She approached, noticing the shift in his posture, the way his movements seemed just off, and a look of euphoria on his smile. Perhaps it was just the wine, she thought.

"How's the wine, Rabbi?" Shanice asked, her eyes studying his face. "It's fantastic to have real wine on a cruiser heading to Mars."

Shalom gave a wide grin, the edges of his awareness shifting. "It's delicious," he said, surprised by its earthy, complex flavors. He had tasted nothing quite like it.

Noticing Shalom's altered state, Sarah leapt into action. This was neither the time nor the place to reveal her newest experimental beverage. With a calm voice she said, "Spoken like a true connoisseur of wine." Her hand tapped his shoulder, gently guiding him away from Shanice. "I'll get him some water, or maybe a coffee." Shanice agreed, assuming Shalom was a little too tipsy.

"Come this way, Shalom."

His vision swirled with hints of geometric shapes and shifting colors. The room, the people, all seemed surreal. His heartbeat quickened. "Sarah, what was in that wine?" His voice was wavering and uncertain.

"It's nothing to worry about," Sarah said, keeping her tone light. "Rabbi, your glass got mixed up with a sample I was preparing for colonists with Mars Syndrome. The blend induces a feeling of euphoria, calming the mind. I have something in my lab that can help, but we need to get there soon."

Shalom swayed as he tried to focus on Sarah. "I can't go to your lab alone. You know the rules," he protested, his thoughts scrambling for clarity, clinging to the Orthodox laws that governed his life.

Linda approached him. "It's alright, Rabbi, I'll follow with some male helpers. You won't be alone. Let's get you to the lab."

Her mischievous grin annoyed Sarah, who felt a rising anger inside but kept her face composed. She opened her mouth to say something curt, but Linda cut her off.

"You'd better get him somewhere safe and private," Linda did not hide her deception. "It's going to be an interesting night. I'll cover for him."

Linda turned on her heel, taking the two male attendants with her. Sarah remained alone outside her lab with Shalom, but he was too far into the psychedelic experience to notice.

"Everyone, can I have your attention?" Linda said, having returned from the Observation Deck. "The Rabbi's been called away for an urgent transmission from Earth." She offered a warm, convincing smile. "But please, enjoy the fruit, the wine, and the other refreshments. The party will continue."

The Captain, ever vigilant, approached Linda, his brow furrowed. "No one informed me of any incoming transmission. I keep a close guard on all Mars Corporation communications."

Linda, ever the quick thinker, brushed it off with a casual wave of her hand. "It's nothing official - a religious matter. Mars Corporation had pre-cleared it. No need to worry, Captain. Nothing to do with the mission."

Tran's frown deepened, but Linda's charm was disarming. He nodded, observing her as she moved about the room. Her skill at telling harmless fibs was something that had earned her favor with Luke Mons. Redirecting the truth was second nature - it wasn't malicious, at least not usually.

What about the Apple?

Sarah steered Shalom into her lab, the door sliding shut behind him. The space was compact - just enough room to move around, with walls lined by tethered experiments and secured equipment. In one corner, Sarah had created a small sanctuary for herself, with a colorful inflatable cushion velcroed to the floor, and ultrathin Peruvian blankets tethered nearby. Shalom wanted to lie down, but in zero gravity, there was no way to reach the floor. He pushed against the walls with his hands and twisted his body to lie down and sleep. Using velcro, Sarah positioned herself and guided him to the floor, where she secured velcro straps to his ankles and wrists. Only then did he feel some semblance of stillness, his body settling into an approximation of lying down as the straps held him in place.

Being tethered kept him from floating aimlessly about. The effects of the ayahuasca were working on her too, the familiar wave of altered perception settling in. Her own mind was expanding, the colors and shifting patterns. But Sarah knew how to go with the experience, to stay in control of it. It was up to her to guide Shalom through it.

"Shalom, stay here with me. Breathe." Sarah used her voice as a calming anchor for Shalom's swirling mind.

She focused on her role and thought about the many times Circe had led her through ayahuasca. Now, it was her responsibility to make sure Shalom stayed safe on the surreal journey they were about to take together.

After helping Shalom settle, Sarah's eyes scanned the small lab, her thoughts snapping into clarity as she realized what had happened. Linda had swapped their wine with something far more potent - *Aya-Eros*, an experimental blend Sarah had been working on for couples wanting to heighten their romantic experience. The concoction enhanced empathy, energy, and arousal in small doses. The amount Shalom had consumed was heroic.

She felt the familiar signs of ayahuasca creeping into her own awareness. The sip she'd taken earlier was enough to stir the edges of her perception, but Shalom had ingested far more. His body had already reacted. His skin glistened with sweat and he was warm, but not dangerously so. Hiis pulse was strong, like he had just finished a workout. She was relieved to see that he was not in any physical danger. "You're very strong for a man who reads books for a living." She said under her breath.

Sarah knelt beside him, her words cutting through the swirling haze of their shared space. "I'm here, right in front of you. How do you feel? Warm, cold? Thirsty?"

"I feel warm. Sweaty," Shalom said. His voice was distant, as if he were speaking from somewhere beyond the room.

"Open your eyes. What do you see?"

His eyes, wide and dilated, fluttered open. Sarah watched, captivated by the way the green in his eyes seemed almost otherworldly now, reflecting the depths of his experience.

"I see an angel."

Sarah reached up to her hair, which had slipped from its net and now drifted around her like a halo in the weightlessness. She floated just beyond his reach, watching him with a mix of concern and curiosity.

"What else do you see?" she asked.

Shalom's eyes darted around the room, unfocused, as if watching something beyond the walls. "There's a veil... blue, green, yellow shapes, like cobblestones. It's all geometric, but shifting. And your eyes, they're like sapphires."

Sarah stifled a laugh, her hand brushing against her hair, now floating freely around her shoulders. The net had come loose, leaving her long, blonde locks to drift freely, adding to the ethereal image.

Sarah bit her lip, hesitating about how to proceed. She had always wanted to test her proprietary blend on someone in a real-world setting, to see the results for herself. And now she had Shalom, the perfect subject. But it hadn't been his choice. Would he forgive her if she let the experience play out?

Taking a breath, Sarah reached for the zipper of Shalom's jumpsuit, pulling it down just enough to expose a strange undergarment beneath. It was a mesh shirt, squared off, with four small strings. Curious, she tugged at one of the strings.

"What are you wearing under your jumpsuit?"

Without thinking, Shalom pulled back, causing Sarah to tumble toward him in zero gravity. Her head fell against his shoulder, and Shalom deeply inhaled, catching the scent of her pheromone-infused perfume. "My tallit and tzitzit," he said, his voice distant. "I always wear it."

Sarah nuzzled her nose into his shoulder, letting out a long, contented breath. She hadn't expected him to smell so earthy, so real. "No wonder you're warm. You're wearing all these extra layers."

"That's tradition," Shalom said.

Sarah tugged the tallit over his head, revealing a thin t-shirt underneath, and pulled it off as well. "We have to cool you down." She said, Her eyes widened at the sight of his broad shoulders and firm biceps, always hidden beneath the rabbi's jumpsuit. She couldn't resist giving his arm a squeeze, causing Shalom to squirm.

Sarah inspected his bare chest and her lips curling into a playful smile. "You didn't get these muscles studying all day."

A carefree laugh escaped Shalom's lips, the effects of the blend leaving him open and relaxed. "I used to help the women at the bakery during morning inspections. The bags of flour were too heavy for them, so I carried them from the storeroom. In return, they gave me coffee and fresh rugelach. They said I had a lot of machismo for a rabbi."

Sarah's hands pressed against Shalom's chest. She dug her fingers into his firm pectorals. "You must've impressed those ladies with your hard work."

Before Shalom could answer, the door to the lab slid open unexpectedly, startling them both. A waiterbot glided in, its metallic hand presenting a tray filled with dried fruits and half-full wine glasses. A message scrolled across a tablet attached to its side: *Hi guys, it's Linda. I thought you two might need some refreshment.*

Sarah rolled her eyes, letting out a frustrated sigh as she inspected the tray, "Linda..." There, among the fruits and remaining wine, were the glasses that had tricked them. Without hesitation, Sarah picked up the half-full glass, twisted open the cap, and downed the remaining contents in one gulp. The taste was sharp, like licorice and pine, reminiscent of cough medicine.

"In for a dime, in for a dollar, right, Shalom?" Sarah smirked, seeing the irony in Linda's unwelcome gift. His focus had drifted, lost in the swirling visuals that filled his mind.

"The wine you drank carries with it the spirit of the vine. They follow the vine even when extracted in vitro. Some are benevolent, others dangerous, but tonight, I'm calling on the ecstatic ones." She took a tiny spritzer from her cabinet, sniffing it before pressing the top, releasing a fine mist into the air. She returned to her position on top of him and let her hair cascade around his face as she blew across his forehead. A sweet fragrance, foreign and intoxicating, filled the space between them.

"We have no *machapo* here. I'm spraying a mix of tobacco water for blessings and protection."

Sarah rose to her feet and sang, swaying to the memory of Circe's voice. She whistled along with the icaro in her head and spoke a command to the AI.
"Play icaro music labeled Circe." Speakers in her lab bathed them with the sounds of hand pans, steel drums, and sitars. Shalom grumbled, so she turned the music down to and canceled the sitar, leaving only the pulsating resonance of the drums.

She kept a Shipibo maraca in the lab and, with rhythmic shakes, waved it in the air. The gentle movement of her hips and arms in a sensuous dance enchanted him.

Returning to the floor, she sat next to Shalom and sang an *icaro*, a song of healing dedicated to *Pachamama*, the mother goddess of the earth. The song, sung in Quechua. Her singing opened Shalom's eyes, transfixing him to her beauty.

117

Llegó la primavera tan dulce tan gentil

Son verdes las praderas con sus colores mil

Los pajaritos cantan el pío pío pí

El pío, el pío, el pío, pío pío

La primavera ya está aquí

She sang the words in English to him,

Spring arrived so sweet & gentle

The meadows are green with

their thousand colors

The birds sing pio pio pi

Springtime is already here

Shalom, entranced by the song and his vivid visions, watched as colors and shapes shifted around him, blending with the patterns of the lab. He was taken by the power of the psychedelic. All that held him to the world was the sound of Sarah's voice, which carried him deeper into his journey.

Sarah called to him again. Her warm tone was reassuring. "You're safe with me. These songs will heal your mind and body. If you want, you can hum along."

She knelt in front of him, struggling to stay balanced in the lab's weightlessness, and sang to him with all of her heart

Machu pichinku takini takini
Kay allpa paqarisqaykita

Qhawash kasunki
Takiy, takiy, takiy kamuway
Takiykamuway yuyarichimuway

Over and over, the words repeated, their meaning lost to Shalom, but the rhythm took hold. He felt himself drifting further away from his reality. The boundaries of his carefully curated world and the unknown were blending. Shalom asked her, "Sing to me in English."

Old bird, sing, sing
This is the land you were born on
You are watched

Sing, sing, sing to me
Sing to me, remind me

Sarah, now in the grip of the aya blend herself, maintained her control, her mind sharp despite the effects of the ayahuasca. She wouldn't let herself get lost. Not tonight. She guided Shalom upright, pulling him to his feet with gentle hands. Their eyes embraced, aquamarine with emerald green, and they became glistening gems of oneness..

"Look into me, Shalom," she sang, her voice wrapping around him like the melody. "Look through me, look inside yourself."

Before Shalom knew it, he was singing along with her. Shalom, caught in the dreamlike rhythm, smiled at her, his body moving to the rhythm of her song.

Sarah guided him toward the waiterbot that Linda had sent.

She stopped singing as she moved them toward the bowl of fruit attached to the waiterbot's Shalom's face brightened. "The strange pattern I saw earlier is gone. I feel free, cool, and energetic, like I did when I was a teenager."

Sarah nodded. "That's a good sign. What else do you see?"

"I only see you now, but you're glowing, like you are only energy."

"Perfect. You've passed through the veil." Sarah's eyes gleamed with satisfaction. "Now, let's try some of this fruit. You've earned it."

Sarah plucked two glistening dates from the bowl. "Look, no pits. Nothing to worry about."

Shalom's mind struggled to keep pace with Sarah. His thoughts danced around in his head, and his entire reality was Sarah and the bowl of fruit. She brought the date to his lips. He smelled the sweetness of the day, but something was tugging at him. "Wait, we need to say a special prayer for fruit."

"Didn't we already say it in the Observation Deck?" Shalom's unwavering devotion to his traditions, even while under the influence of plant medicine, astonished Sarah.

"That was a different prayer, the Shehecheyanu. You weren't with us when we said it earlier."

"Alright, rabbi, I'll say it with you. But make it quick. I'm not sure I can wait much longer. This date is calling me."

Even as she spoke, Shalom had already begun reciting the blessing, his voice carrying the familiar cadence of the prayer. "Repeat after me, *Baruch ata Adonai...*"

Sarah followed along, her intonation flawless, like she had known the melody of the prayer all along. She brought him back into the dream-like feeling.

She finished her date and reached for the second one, lifting it toward Shalom's lips. But before she could offer it to him, Shalom's hand shot up, wrapping around her wrist, stopping her mid-motion. Her skin was warm, smoother than he'd imagined, and he felt her blood pulse beneath his fingers.

"You have a firm grip, rabbi. Are you sure you should touch me like that?"

Shalom, aware of his hand, released her wrist as if it had burned him. An embarrassed blush crept up his face, his eyes not quite focusing on hers. He tried to compose himself. He wanted to stay in control, but each time he tried, he fell further away into the bliss of her presence.

Sarah smiled coyly as she whispered. "Listen to your heart, Shalom. What does it say?"

Without hesitation, Shalom brought Sarah's hand to his mouth, taking the date from her fingers with his lips. Sarah giggled. She was in control, her eyes sparkled mischievously.

Her voice dropped even lower. "I have a question for you, Rabbi. Which fruit did Eve give to Adam?"

Shalom struggled to think, but euphoria washed over him. He managed a smile at her, gathering his wits. "Some rabbis say it was the grape because wine always gets us into trouble."

"Rabbi, you know I own a kosher winery. Does that make me a bad girl?"

Shalom burst out laughing in a way he hadn't done since he

was a child.

Her lips curved into a seductive grin as she plucked a handful of raisins from the container. She popped a few into her mouth, and then, with deliberate slowness, pressed two raisins against Shalom's lips. He didn't resist as she pushed them into his mouth. They had a musty and sweet taste, like overripe grapes left too long on the vine.

Sarah purred into his ears. "What do you think, Rabbi? Was it a grape, or could it have been something else?"

He tried to respond, but the answer slipped through his mind like water. "Some think it was the fig, because they realized they were naked and made clothes from fig leaves."

Sarah's fingers toyed with two plump figs from the bowl. She kissed one, then placed it in Shalom's mouth. "Naked? Well, look at you exposing your strong, bare chest." Sarah took a bite from her fig, her breath warm against his cheek.

Shalom felt the energy of his body flow through Sarah's fingers. His thoughts were immersed in ayahuasca. The fig was soft, sweet, and chewy, and as he ate it, Sarah's face glowed, her features smooth and dreamy. Her words seemed distant, like the splashing of waves.

Sarah spoke to him in a whisper. "And what about the apple? Everyone says she gave him an apple."

His mouth opened, but he couldn't find the words. Sarah placed a piece of dried apple against his lips, and he took it between his teeth. The sweet and tart flavor spread across his tongue. When he opened his eyes, he saw Sarah remove her jumpsuit. Her pale skin moved about like white sand scattered by ocean waves.

He had never seen a woman's body before and stared at her in wonder. Sarah realized this was his first time with a woman and took control. She took his hands in hers, guiding them to rest on her chest, just above her heart. "Shalom, tell me, truthfully, what do you think Adam would do next?"

Unexpected Miracle

Shalom's eyes opened to the persistent calling of the AI alarm. "Thirty minutes late. Wake up, rabbi."

He floated, untethered, his body drifting within the sleeping chamber. A frown formed on his lips. He never slept in like this, unanchored, adrift. Glancing down, his frown deepened. He was still wearing his daytime jumpsuit, the familiar fabric wrinkled and askew, as if he hadn't bothered to change before collapsing into the sleeping chamber. Something was off. He touched the fabric of his jumpsuit to feel his tallit katan. Just as he thought, it was gone.

A scent clung to him, sharp and unfamiliar. He brought his hand to his face and sniffed - faint traces of alcohol mixed with perfume? His stomach twisted, a faint nausea creeping in. He touched the top of his head, only to realize he wasn't wearing his sleep yarmulke. His mind whirled - no *yarmulke, no tallit katan. What happened?*

The last thing he remembered was eating fruit, a blur of alcohol, and the radiance of Sarah's hair and the warmth of her blue eyes. But beyond that, it was all a haze. In all of his confusion he hadn't yet said his *Modeh Ani*, the prayer that always came when he woke. *What's happening to me?*

He needed to shower and wake up, but discovered that he was missing his regular *yarmulke*. Luckily, he had prepared for such an event and took out a spare one from his personal storage drawer, along with his tefillin and *tallit gadol*. Sliding the door to his sleeping chamber open, he stumbled. Missing the mezuzah with his fingertips, he managed a kiss on the second try. A waiterbot appeared with its daily towelette, which he accepted without his usual focus, wiping his hands but forgetting the count. Had he swiped three times?

Wrapping the large tallit around his shoulders, he made his way to the showers on Level 3, his steps uneven, his thoughts disjointed. As he passed Linda Perez in the hallway, her voice broke through his daze. "Is this a special occasion, rabbi? I only see you wearing the large shawl on Saturdays?" The tone of her voice suggested she knew something, but his mind was slow to process her words, and by the time he thought of a response, she was already gone. His head throbbed. "Nothing special. Everything's fine."

He set his tablet and tefillin on a shelf outside the shower, and called for a waiterbot to return his *yarmulke* and *tallit gadol* to his sleeping chamber. Once inside, he stuffed his jumpsuit into the recycle slot. Strange memories of exotic spirals and sensuous feelings returned to him as he stepped under the mist of warm water, which he buried away with thoughts about the weekly Parsha. The scent of perfume still clung to his hands, no matter how much he washed.

After drying off, Shalom dressed mechanically, as if he was going through the motions of a routine he couldn't engage with. He retrieved his *tefillin*, but his hands fumbled as he attempted to wrap them. The familiar black straps had a mind of their own. His fingers did not cooperate with his mind to make the seven wraps down his arm.

Just then, his wrist communicator beeped. He glanced down. A message from Sarah: *Come to my lab. It's important.*

Shalom stared at the message, conflicted. He hadn't even finished his morning prayers. He knew he should complete them - he had to. But something pulled at him, an urgency he couldn't shake. His hands faltered on his tablet, now an electronic siddur, as he rushed through the remaining morning prayers.

All the while, his mind was elsewhere. He had to see Sarah.

The door to Sarah's lab was unlocked. Stepping inside, the chaos immediately struck him. Pieces of dried fruit bobbed lazily in zero gravity, vials and lab equipment drifted aimlessly about. *What happened here?* Fragmented memories of the previous night passed in and out of his thoughts.

Sarah, however, seemed unfazed by the disorder. She was radiant, her long, straw-blonde hair tightly secured in a net, her crisp tan and blue jumpsuit hugging her body. Her movements were graceful as she collected floating objects, suctioning up bits of fruit and organic material into a container. There was a vibrancy to her, a sharp contrast to Shalom's hazy state. "Close the door Shalom. I don't want people to see the mess."

"What happened last night? Is everything alright here?"

Sarah turned to Shalom with a playful smile. "You don't remember?"

"My thoughts muddled after drinking the wine Linda gave me. I woke up still in my cruiser jumpsuit, and I'm missing my *yarmulke* and *tallit katan*," he paused, rubbing his forehead, "and covered in your perfume."

Sarah let out a small, disappointed laugh. "You don't like my perfume?" She reached into a drawer, pulling out a large plastic bag and playfully pressed it against his chest. "Here. Take a look. Maybe this will jog your memory."

His eyes widened when he saw the familiar missing items

inside. Bits of the night flashed back to him.

"How did you get these?" His voice faltered as the pieces started falling into place.

Sarah sighed, still smiling. "You left them here last night. I found them after I helped you back to your sleeping chamber." Her eyes glimmered with amusement. "We were intimate last night, Shalom. Don't you remember?"

"That's not possible." He couldn't believe it. It made little sense.

"Oh, it's very possible. You were quite open to new experiences."

He looked around the lab as though it could somehow explain how he'd ended up in this situation.

"Then how do you explain leaving not only your yarmulke, but the thing with your tzitzit in my lab, and my perfume all over you?" Sarah's voice was playful, but there was an edge of seriousness as she crossed her arms. "I had to throw out your tank top. It was covered in fruit stains. You made a big mess."

Shalom's eyes went wide, panic spreading across his face. He ran a hand through his hair and brought his fingers to his nose. His mind swam under the influence of Sarah's scent. "This can't be happening. It's not right. We're not married. I've never..."

"What? You've never been with a woman before?" She grinned, letting out a small laugh. "I don't believe it. You were amazing, Shalom. You were a virgin?"

"Sarah, I..." He could feel his face burning. "Please, not so loud." He looked away from Sarah, desperate for some escape from their discussion.

Sarah shrugged, unfazed. "Why? You're embarrassed? You were with me, and I wanted to be with you. It's nothing to be ashamed of. I mean, come on, you were great."

Shalom's mind was spiraling. "I just thought..." His voice trailed off, trying to latch onto anything coherent.

Sarah laughed, brushing off his discomfort. "What's done is done. There's no undoing it now. Besides, you're a good-looking guy. I like you. You should give yourself more credit."

Shalom pressed his palms to his forehead. "Last night, what happened?"

"Oh, last night was something, wasn't it? We'll have to try again - next time, maybe in the couples' rec room. The lab wasn't the best place." She gestured at the floating fruit and overturned vials with a chuckle. "I'd say we made quite the mess."

Shalom's face twisted in distress. "But how did I get so intoxicated?"

Sarah gave a sigh. She didn't want to throw Linda under the bus, but she couldn't outright lie. "Well, Linda went to get the wine, and she saw my bottle labeled *Proprietary Blend* and, well, she poured us both some glasses without knowing it was a bit special."

Shalom's eyes narrowed, trying to piece it all together.

Sarah continued. "I infused the wine with herbs designed to help with stress and ease Mars Syndrome - you know, the depression colonists sometimes get. It's also a bit of a stimulant. It lowers inhibitions, heightens sensory perception.

You were, um, euphoric."

Her voice lilted into a sing-song, but the words fell heavily on Shalom. He stood frozen, trying to wrap his mind around the reality of what had happened the night before and why.

"Is that what we drank?"

A dreamy look crossed Sarah's face, as if recalling the events of last night with fondness.

"You drank a lot of the proprietary blend, at least triple the normal dose."

"Was it kosher?"

The question threw Sarah. "Kosher? Really? Yes Shalom, the wine was kosher. The herbs were all plant-based, too. You're the one who oversees the kosher standards on this ship, remember?" She was perturbed and amused by his persistent worries.

"This doesn't feel right. We're not married. It shouldn't have happened like this."

"So, you're telling me that's what's bothering you? Not the psychoactive herbs or the fact we had a pretty good time last night, but that we're not married?" Her voice was teasing, but there was an undercurrent of frustration. She genuinely liked him, but his orthodox concerns were getting in the way of enjoying the moment.

Shalom looked up at her, his voice heavy with regret. "Yes, Sarah. That's the point. This isn't how it's supposed to happen. In my faith, intimacy is sacred, reserved for marriage. It's not meant to be casual."

Sarah's playful expression faltered, but her pride wouldn't let her be too sympathetic. "Well, Shalom," she said, flashing a coy smile as she took a step closer to him, "I wasn't planning a wedding last night. We were having fun, that's all." She reached out, touching his arm. "And I enjoyed it. Didn't you?"

Shalom struggled to meet her eyes, his emotions tangled between guilt and something else. "It's not that I didn't enjoy it. But this…" He gestured between them, "wasn't what I imagined."

"Oh, come on, rabbi. It wasn't the end of the world. You're acting like I've shattered some holy vow." She paused, giving him a look that was half-serious, half-teasing. "And for the record, I'm not mad at you. I think you're pretty amazing."

Shalom blushed, unsure of how to respond.

Sarah had a playful glint in her eyes. "Look, if this bothers you that much, we don't have to do it again. But don't go punishing yourself over something that was, well, kind of magical, don't you think?"

In the two weeks that followed, Shalom and Sarah kept their distance in public. Sarah preferred to stay in her lab, arranging meals to be delivered by waiterbots, while Shalom mingled with other passengers, often meeting for Shacharit with those curious about his role as a rabbi. Sarah found little in common with the other passengers, preferring the company of her research and experiments to social interactions. Besides, with her focus on setting up the X-Series, her only contacts were Yudi for technical discussions, Captain Tran for equipment logistics, and Linda Perez for official communications with Mars Corporation. Linda was a conundrum, she knew not to trust her. Sarah wondered why Linda had tricked Shalom into drinking the proprietary blend. What was really going on?

Despite the public distance, they continued their private conversations, meeting either in the private corners of unoccupied meeting rooms or in the intimate space of Sarah's cluttered lab. There were even a few occasions when they met in F8 or F1, where Shalom would explain his Orthodox traditions, the laws of Shabbat, and the intricacies of kashrut. Sarah respected his boundaries, though she couldn't understand his physical restraint with her. There was something refreshing about how Shalom's worldview contrasted with hers. His naivety about her business and his genuine curiosity about her past made their exchanges feel more genuine than anything she had experienced in years.

Shalom, too, found himself drawn to Sarah's stories - tales of her ambitious business ventures on Earth, the pressures of managing a global company, and the challenges she faced in the public eye. He admired her resilience, though he wasn't sure he'd ever understand the depth of her ambition. It fascinated him how Sarah had taken an interest in Judaism, asking questions about everything from the weekly Parsha to why he wore tefillin every morning. His feelings about Sarah troubled him and how he was being pulled towards her, but his faith always kept him grounded.

Another week passed, and Shalom was optimistic about the future. He enjoyed spending time with Sarah, and he had identified two more Jewish men on board. He was only four men shy of a minyan. It was a promising start for the shul he envisioned on Roddenberry Station.

Breakfast had become a cherished part of his day, a time where he'd sit with Aaron, Abby, Eva, Manny, Yudi, and sometimes Sarah - a kind of informal 'breakfast club' where they'd swap stories and discuss the weekly Torah portion. He was negotiating with the Captain and Linda to have the three other Jewish people transferred to his shift.

That morning, Linda Perez rushed into the galley, interrupting the usual laughter and exchanges. She made a beeline for Shalom, her expression full of urgency. "Rabbi, Sarah wants to see you now in her lab."

Shalom hurried into the lab, his mind buzzing with questions. He found Sarah standing beside her distillation equipment, deep in introspection.

"Close the door," she said.

Shalom did as she asked, giving them privacy. The tension in the lab made his stomach squeamish.

She cleared her worktable, then turned to him. Her eyes fixed on him, furthering his anxiety. "There's no easy way to say this. Just have a look." She pushed her tablet across the table toward him.

He picked it up. The bold words *CONFIDENTIAL* flashing in red across the black screen.

"Tap 'open.' It's unlocked," Sarah instructed, her voice tight.

Shalom tapped the screen, revealing the heading: *From the Desk of Dr. Shanice Willis*. His eyes scrolled down, hitting the phrase *Pregnancy Test Results*. His heart stopped. The next words were in smaller bold font. *Test results are positive.*

"What...?" he managed, his voice catching.

"I'm pregnant. I don't know how, but the test is conclusive."

Shalom's mind spun. He felt disconnected from his own body, like a dream slowly turning into a nightmare. "How can that be? Doctors have told me I can't have children. It's one reason I left Earth. But what about you? Doesn't Mars

Corporation enforce subcutaneous birth control?"

Sarah's lips thinned into a hard line. Her eyes daring him to challenge her. "I'm allergic to it, Shalom. And your medical file states that you're infertile."

His response was clumsy, unthinking. "Then how do you know it was me?"

A fierce look flashed across Sarah's face. Her finger jabbed into his chest, the point of her dark red nail digging against his jumpsuit. "Take that back." Her words cut like glass.

Shalom froze, realizing his mistake. He recoiled, feeling her fury crashing down on him. "I'm sorry, Sarah. You know about my condition. I just can't believe it. It's something so miraculous, so beyond what I ever thought was possible."

Sarah took a breath, letting some of her frustration dissolve. "It's okay. But you're the only man I've been with for a long time. The baby is 100% yours. Whether it was a fluke, a miracle, or some bizarre combination of ayahuasca and healing prayers, here we are."

"But this is against Mars Corporation's policy, isn't it? The contract..."

"Calls for immediate termination."

Shalom felt as if his heart had fallen into a bottomless well. "Termination, as in abortion?"

"I never knew what I wanted until now. But I know. It's an unexpected miracle, Shalom. I want to keep the baby."

Shalom's heart raced as he processed the revelation. "Who else knows?" he asked in a hushed voice.

"Just Shanice," Sarah said while tidying up her lab. "But it won't stay secret for long. The AI tracks everything - hormones in the ship's water systems, all of it. Shanice did the test off-record using a disposable kit. We only have a few days before Mars Corporation catches wind."

"What's the risk? Can you even have a child on Mars? Could this hurt you? Or the baby?"

Sarah paused as she considered his concern. "No one knows for sure, but Shanice says I'm healthy enough to try. And I want to."

"Then I'll start the preparations. We'll get married, Sarah. A proper Jewish ceremony. It'll be the first of its kind aboard a Mars cruiser."

Sarah stared at him, stunned. "Married? Are you proposing to me?"

Shalom, perplexed by her response, nodded. "Of course. You're having our child. We're starting a family. What's there to question?"

Sarah was speechless. The last thing on her mind was marriage, and Shalom's matter-of-fact way of proposing. *Who is this man?*

"I have many questions for you. Let's start with love. Do you love me or the fact that I am pregnant? What if I don't want to live an Orthodox life with a bunch of rules? The fact is, I don't really don't know you."

Shalom considered her words. She was right. Tradition told him that marriage must be based on love and respect. But his heart was calling out to him. It was a miracle for Sarah to be pregnant. Surely it was meant to be.

"We've become close these past weeks and I look forward to listening to your stories, and I respect your independence. Besides, you've already adjusted to eating kosher, after all."

Sarah snapped back at him. "Everyone on the cruiser is eating kosher! I don't want my life dictated by your traditions."

Shalom took a breath, trying to remain calm. "Our faith won't stop you from pursuing your goals. We can make this work. We'll figure it out together, Sarah."

Sarah's eyes betrayed her unexpected vulnerability. "You think we can just work through this?"

"Love isn't just about passion, it's about growing together, finding common ground." Shalom's voice cracked with emotion, his eyes tearing up. "We can do this."

Sarah stepped closer, her voice dropping to a whisper, and she cried. "Okay, we'll try. But don't expect me to make this easy for you. I'm not some Orthodox housewife."

"I wouldn't want it any other way."

Sarah wrapped her arms around him, pulling him into a deep embrace. "But you know, you're not off the hook yet. You still owe me a proper 'goodnight,' Rabbi."

Shalom's pulse quickened, but he pulled back, his expression earnest. "Sarah, we need to wait until after the wedding."

Her playful smile vanished, replaced by frustration. "Seriously, Shalom? After everything? You're impossible."

"I'm traditional," Shalom said without hesitation.

Sarah called to the AI, "Open door." With that, she braced herself against the workbench, raised her legs, planted her feet into his stomach, pushing him away. Unprepared for the zero gravity shove, Shalom floated backward toward the lab door, his slippers pulling free from the ground.

As he drifted out the door, he caught her last words: "Traditional, my foot."

Access to the X-Isis

Lieutenant Commander Asuna Tsukino led Yudi to Sarah's lab, her expression stoic as usual. "Dr. Rafaeli, this young man insisted you were expecting him. There's no record of an appointment in the Cruiser logs."

"An Unexpected visitor in broad daylight? And a young man, no less?"

Asuna returned an almost imperceptible frown. Humor seemed lost on her, much like the other officers who had served aboard the *Buzz Aldrin*. She read into her mind and sensed the tension in her posture, the rigidity of someone used to strict protocol. "Ah, Lieutenant Tsukino, Master of Kendo, and Captain Tran's right hand. My apologies, I should have logged the meeting. I asked Yudi to join me to discuss some updates on my computer. He has a brief window between his coursework, and I didn't want to lose the opportunity."

"How do you know so much about me?" Asuna asked.

"I've read up on all the executive officers. My PR advisors are always pushing me for photos. I love to take one with you with your powerful posture delicately, holding a glass of my wine. People would love it."

Sarah adjusted her straw-blonde hair, letting a few loose strands fall over her shoulder before tucking them back into place. She caught a faint sight of amusement in Asuna's otherwise impassive face. She may even have blushed.

"Unless there's anything else, I will leave him in your custody." Asuna bowed before turning and walking away.

The door closed, leaving Yudi standing alone in the lab. It was his first time inside the private experimental space on Level 6, and the reality of the high-security environment made his nerves buzz. He glanced around at the equipment - vials vibrating, data streams flowing across screens, and an air of secrecy that made the lab feel even smaller.

"It's snug in here," Sarah remarked, gesturing for Yudi to take a seat. "Find a spot in the corner and try not to knock anything over. I'd make you sign a waiver, but that feels overly dramatic."

"For confidentiality?" Yudi asked.

Sarah grinned. "No, dear. For personal safety. Imagine the scandal if one of my experimental fungi decided you'd make a good snack. How would I ever explain that to your mother?"

Yudi stiffened, then relaxed when he realized she was joking. "I'll keep my distance." He attempted to match her light tone, though his nervousness was clear in his voice.

"Good. You should call me Dr. Rafaeli, all of my associates. You're here to help me with the X-series, so let's begin. It's on Level 1 for cooling and energy purposes, and I access it through a wired connection along the Cruiser's communication backbone. But for critical tasks, I would prefer to interact with the computer directly, using a keyboard interface and physical storage. I prefer not to rely on shared lines. With end-to-end encryption, I don't feel comfortable exposing sensitive data. Not with something as sophisticated as the X-Isis."

Yudi nodded, absorbing the information. Sarah wondered if she could trust someone so young with her project, but he came recommended by Linda Perez, who represented the Mars Corporation.

"You've taken smart precautions, Dr. Rafaeli. The Cruiser's AI can break 64 bit encryption in a week or two."

"Exactly. That's why I take these extra measures." She glanced at the secure terminal and then back at Yudi. "You've done your homework."

"I've been told the X-Isis is unparalleled when it comes to brain simulations. Luke Mons recommended I bring it aboard. He believes it will help me test chemical compounds in ways we've never imagined. But..." she paused, searching Yudi's face, "I'm no expert in setting up this kind of system. I'll need your help to get it up and run properly."

Yudi hesitated, caught between awe and his own intentions. Sarah didn't understand the magnitude of the quantum computer. But Yudi was already planning for Evelin's LLM.

"The X-Isis can simulate the complexities of a human brain down to the synapses. It can map neurological responses, even down to the effects of chemical compounds," Yudi said, trying to sound casual. "But to start it, the setup is crucial. It's not just plugging in data. It needs to develop a foundational set of rules, or else the simulations will be off."

Sarah was amazed at Yudi's depth of understanding, but his detailed answer raised a red flag. "Did you learn that in high school?"

"I have been up all night reading about X-Isis. Back in high school, I ran a Sentience AI on a primitive quantum core computer. It felt like it had a personality."

"You're an ambitious young man. My research involves the influence of psychedelics on the brain. I'm curious about how specific doses alter thought patterns, consciousness, but..." she frowned, "I don't know if it can do more than replicate the physiological effects. I want the AI to mimic behavioral changes."

Yudi was unable to suppress his enthusiasm. "You'll be amazed! With the right code, the X-Isis could simulate consciousness, at least at the level of human-like responses. If we integrate advanced models capable of analyzing and replicating nuanced changes in behavior, speech, and decision-making by monitoring its utilization of tokens, it may be possible to see how your compounds affect speech, decision-making, even emotional responses."

"Yes. My research on the effects of psychedelic compounds in beverages is often hindered by the need for human participants. It's not that volunteers are hard to find, but most have already used psychedelics before. I need a clean slate. With the X-Isis, I can simulate detailed, interactive models of brain functions, approximating synaptic responses. By fine-tuning the system with reinforcement learning and parameter-adaptive layers, it might be possible to notice behavior by changes in its output. By inputting specific chemical formulas, the system can simulate the influence of these substances and use proxy neurochemical data to adapt its interaction methodology."

Yudi's eyes widened at the concept. Even though Sarah was talking over his head, he grasped some essentials. Creating an LLM that could simulate real human behavior was exactly what he needed to regenerate Evelin. He placed his hand on his chest, feeling the hamsa hand pressing against his heart. "So you'd not only see how the brain reacts to the chemicals but track every minute detail of its behavior."

Sarah clapped her hands together. "Yes, you got it." There was something about Yudi's determination, a complexity in his emotions that she sensed but couldn't completely decipher. Her clairvoyance, sharp as it was, couldn't pierce the cloud of teenage uncertainty. She felt Yudi's deep emotional loss - an ache that seemed to hover around him - and something darker, something she couldn't quite place, perhaps linked to his constant drive.

"If you're as capable as you seem, this could be quite the breakthrough. But tell me, how familiar are you with a system like the X-Isis?"

Yudi straightened, and his confidence surged. "I've worked with quantum cores before. Back at Fairfax High, we had access to an n-Core through a grant from the Mars Corporation. While it wasn't as powerful as your X-Isis, the startup procedures and software integration should be similar. The key is in the first steps - the way the system is initialized, how the rules and procedures are set in place during that crucial learning phase."

"You'll have access - but there are conditions. Keep me informed of any changes made by you or the LLM. I've read that the X-Isis is self-directed. It's going to develop its own rules, its own procedures. There is evidence that it develops a personality. You'll have to ensure that the process goes smoothly."

Yudi was eager to impress her. "That's because a quantum computer can hold variables in superposition, allowing it to change its algorithms in real-time, even handle contradictory outcomes simultaneously. The start-up has to be flawless so it can establish a stable, rational framework to guide everything that comes after."

"That's exactly what Luke Mons said," Sarah said, almost as if thinking aloud. "He didn't give me all the details, but he hinted this could be revolutionary for my research. You think you can help me build that framework?"

"Yes, but we'd need to create containment systems for each experiment to prevent those kinds of instantiations from affecting the entire AI." Yudi said.

"Alright, I need you to boot it up, run diagnostics, and set up a secure interface so I can access it remotely, both from here and directly on the X-Isis. No wireless connections, everything has to be hard-wired. Luke had the statistical package and modeling software pre-installed."

Yudi considered the dimensions of her request before answering. "There shouldn't be any issues, but pre-compiled packages might not completely mesh with the system. There are libraries..."

Sarah cut him off. "That won't be a problem," Sarah assured him, her confidence unwavering. "Luke Mons took care of everything."

Yudi didn't want to disagree with Sarah. His face flushed as he held back his concerns. Sarah felt his frustration. It felt like a blast of hot desert air.

"Tell me what's bothering you."

"It's just that. Do you trust Mr. Mons that much? There could be backdoors into the programming. In the worst case, the apps could be altered to give erroneous data."

"Do you doubt him that much?" Sarah hadn't considered that someone would hack the software.

"That depends if he lives up to his reputation. If I were you, I'd check all the packages and libraries, do a checksum and sandbox it on the first run. Maybe look at the code."

"Are you that skilled in programming?"

"I can speak in Python."

Sarah looked away at her wall monitor and saw Linda approaching her lab. "We'll discuss that later. Look, it's Linda Perez. Right on time to escort us to Level 1."

Sarah opened the lab door, giving Linda a reserved hug. Linda smiled, her eyes drifting to Sarah's belly, before turning to Yudi with a disapproving glance. "Yudi, you need to check with Lieutenant Commander Asuna before entering Level 6. She was prepared to apprehend you, thinking you were sneaking around. She's always eager for someone to test her Kendo skills on."

Yudi looked confused by Linda's remark. "Kendo?" he asked. Sarah smiled and hugged his shoulder. "That's a Japanese sword. Linda's suggesting she might want to use it on you." Yudi gave an uneasy chuckle.

"We have to move." Linda said, motioning toward the central corridor. "We need to be discreet. Nobody outside of a specially trained crew has access to Level 1. Stay focused on me, don't stop to talk to anyone. Once we're in the storeroom, you'll both be keyed in. There are only bio-keys for Level 1."

The central corridor ended on Level 1. Around them, the deep hum of generators merged with the sloshing of fluid pumps and the erratic hissing of valves and maintenance bots. The air felt heavy and metallic, nothing like the upper decks.

Linda led them to the last door on the left side of the hallway. She placed her hand on the biometric pad. After it turned green, she keyed in a passphrase and turned to Yudi, her tone firm but encouraging. "Place your hand here," she instructed, guiding his palm to the lock pad. The biometric pad blinked green, and the door slid open.

"Now you have access."

She repeated the process for Sarah. "That's it. Only the three of us are keyed in. The fewer people going in and out, the better."

They stepped inside the storage room, and Yudi sensed the familiar smell of electric ions filling the small, cold space, mingling with the metallic scent of stagnation. The room is no larger than four by three meters, with a single bright ceiling light casting long shadows across the floor. In the far corner was an ivory-colored box. The X-Isis was sleek and rectangular, standing nearly two meters tall, its surface reflecting the faint glow of the overhead light.

With a quick motion, Linda pressed a hidden panel in the wall. A bench and small table folded out silently from the wall beside the ivory box. Another tap, and the front panel on the box slid away, revealing a screen embedded in the front.

"This," Linda said, gesturing to the screen, "is your point of access. Only you can unlock this room and access the system. Do not bring anyone else here."

"This particular X-Isis is supposed to be theoretical," she said, her tone dropping into something more confidential. "Check it out, Yudi. Tell us what you think."

"Is this computer idling at the superuser prompt?"

Linda nodded her head. "You'll need to change that."

Yudi typed: uname -a

The system scrolled through many parameters and stopped. Yudi Gasped and read the top line out loud. "X-Isis reimagined. This can't be. I read that this is experimental, several years off."

"And that's what the public thinks. Mr. Mons told me it possesses computational power beyond anything seen before. It could run an entire corporation, manage millions of clients at once. Sarah, your project is a proof of concept. Some believe it could even reach meta consciousness - something close to psychic or spiritual capabilities." Linda glanced at Yudi, eyes sharp. "No one knows it's here. That's why Captain Tran is flying this ship. Out in space, piracy is a genuine threat, and so are Earth First terrorists. This computer is that valuable. But it's not my job to wonder how Luke Mons got it on board."

Yudi stood frozen. His eyes caught an inscription plate with the model and serial number, and he read it with disbelief.

"This is impossible," his voice a mix of awe and disbelief. "How did you get this?" He turned to Sarah, his eyes wide with excitement. "I've read about it. But it's described as years off in development. This isn't just an X-series quantum computer. The X-Isis is said to have a true exponential core. It uses photons in a lattice structure and tachyonic channels for superluminal data transfer between the photonic processors. This is like something out of pure science fiction!"

There was too much excitement in his voice, but Sarah passed it off as youthful enthusiasm. "Alright, Yudi. You seem to know more about this computer than anyone. Can you get it running? How long before I can start entering my data sets?"

For Yudi, this was more than just a school project or an experimental setup. This was a machine that could change everything. He nodded to Sarah.

"I can do it. The timing depends on my duty roster and class schedule. The Mars Corporation assigns daily coursework to both Dinesh and me."

"Linda, are these assignments actually mandatory, or is some of it just busy work to keep them from getting bored on the ship? My project should have priority."

Linda pressed her finger to her lips, her expression amused. "Sarah, don't say the secret part out loud." She gave Yudi a knowing glance before turning back to Sarah. "But you're right. Some assignments are for enrichment, just prep for when they're on Mars. I can adjust their schedule. Your project can be credited as coursework. I'll arrange it so Yudi can have more time with you in the lab.

Yudi's excitement almost overcame him and he caught himself from saying Evelin's name. His plan of secretly installing Evelin's AI into the system - of bringing her back into his life - was coming together.

Captain Tran's Dojo

Lieutenant Commander Asuna Tsukino escorted Yudi to the Command and Control Center, located level 7, at the fore of the Mars Cruiser. Yudi waited at the base of the stairs for a reinforced, polycarbonate door to slide open. He emerged into a clear, cylindrical chamber and the scrutinizing eyes of a sentry posted at the entrance.

"Why is there so much security?" He asked Asuna.

"If we're boarded, this is where we make a last stand. If the situation is hopeless, we can jettison the command-and-control center from the rest of the cruiser."

"But what about the passengers?"

Asuna looked uneasy, an emotion she had never displayed.

"Let's hope a boarding never happens, and if it does, and we fail, that the hostage negotiations are reasonable and successful."

She nodded to the sentry, who opened the security door and allowed Yudi and Asuna to enter. It was Yudi's first time on the Command Deck, a rare opportunity for any of the passengers on the E. R. Boroughs. She led him to the navigator's station, where they waited for Captain Tran to acknowledge them.

His crew had always shown unwavering loyalty and the highest respect, which he returned in equal proportion. He had handpicked each officer on this mission, veterans from his former unit who had fought alongside him during the Chinese Communist Corporation War. Asuna was his number one, calm in battle and formidable with the kendo. She held his utmost confidence. Others like Lieutenants Betsy Hall, Sheila Caballero, Lashawn Porter and Petty Officer Jeffrey Douglas had served with him in the fateful battle aboard *The Buzz Aldrin*. That battle, known as the *Dragon's Breath*, had marked a decisive moment in the war. The *Buzz Aldrin* had executed a near-suicidal hull breach into the Dragon's Breath, the CCC's nuclear-armed destroyer. His crew successfully took control of the Chinese destroyer, fighting in close-quarters combat. The evidence of nuclear weapons secured a historic armistice. It was Captain Tran's leadership and the team's trust in one another that had made victory possible, forging lifelong bonds.

On the Command Deck, the crew's shared history made their interactions smooth, whether during operations or daily exercises. Each day, Captain Tran transformed part of the deck into a dojo, where the team practiced *QiGong, Tai Chi, and Kung Fu* to stay sharp in both mind and body. Despite years of relative peace, the Captain remained watchful. The constant threat of Earth First terrorists and pirate forces drove his commitment to discipline and readiness.

Yudi adjusted the collar of his printed Gi as he stood waiting. Despite having worn similar garb countless times in the gaming world, wearing a real robe felt different.

The Captain noticed Yudi from the corner of his eye and motioned for him to join. His face gave nothing away, though Yudi sensed a certain wariness as he stepped closer. The Captain gestured to a place in the formation. "Welcome, Yudi Zalman. This dojo is where we prepare, mind and body, for what lies ahead. You're here to train, but not just in skill or strength - discipline and awareness are as important as muscle."

The Captain called everyone to order. "Mars demands more than arrival; it requires purpose at every step, and discipline.

Today, we greet Yudi Zalman, here as a guest at the Mars Corporation's request."

Yudi took cautious steps forward, but a friendly nod from a young crew member offered some reassurance. "Yudi, this is Petty Officer Ryan Nissen." The Captain said.

"Officer Nissen is one of the few officers that didn't fight with us at the Battle of the Dragon's Breath. The Mars Corporation assigned him as a communications specialist."

A silence fell across the crew on deck. "Many in our team didn't survive that battle. But Ryan is proving himself a worthy member."

The Captain paused to give Yudi a chance to respond, but Yudi was too shy to say anything.

"You've already met Lieutenant Commander Asuna Tsukino. She's in charge of the deck. She tells me you've got a quick mind and a knack for being in unexpected places." Asuna's faint smile hinted at approval, although her eyes remained serious. "We'll see if you can learn to control that skill."

Ryan gave a deep bow to Captain Tran. "Sifu, I'd be honored to help Yudi develop his skills here."

The Captain's usual reserve gave way to a rare smile. "It seems you're already making friends, Yudi." His eyes moved to Ryan, his tone approving. "That's the spirit we cultivate here - a family bond. This dojo is more than a place to practice; it's a community. Ryan, your help with Yudi reflects what martial arts are about."

He looked back at Yudi with satisfaction. "From today, you're a novice member of our dojo. I'll inform Linda Perez to allocate you a *Gi* with a white belt for each session. After training, deposit it in the recycler and wear your passenger jumpsuit."

With a respectful bow, Yudi mimicked Ryan's earlier motion, clasping his fist into his palm. The surrounding students clapped, acknowledging his first step. "Just follow along with my movements, starting with the *QiGong* warm-up. Then we will have a session of *Tai Chi*, too. Don't worry if you lose the rhythm; when you're ready, join the next form."

Yudi followed Ryan's lead as he attempted the movements. When he reached up with a bit too much enthusiasm and his head met the ceiling, Ryan suppressed a grin, guiding him back to his stance. "Just relax and feel each move rather than trying to perfect it."

By the end of the warm-up, Yudi overcame his clumsiness and repeated the smooth repetition of forms with the crew. He stumbled many times during *Tai Chi*, but Ryan quickly directed him back into position. When the *Tai Chi* session ended, the crew reassembled in front of the Captain. In unison, they brought fists to palms and bowed. He returned the gesture. "Next, we move to hand-to-hand training. Prepare your gloves and face shields."

Captain Tran faced Yudi, his eyes gleaming with the kindness of an old relative. "This concludes your first session. Bring the same enthusiasm next time." Tran clasped his hands and bowed. Yudi gave a deep bow and backed away as the other students had done.

Ryan walked to Yudi as the crew prepared for the next segment. "So, did you enjoy it?" he asked, keeping his voice low.

"I've done nothing like this before. It feels amazing."

"That's the spirit! Just remember, in here, following Sifu's lead is everything."

Ryan saw that Yudi wasn't fully understanding. "Sifu is what we call a master teacher in Kung Fu. Captain Tran's skills run deep; you'll see that soon enough."

Yudi took a quick glance around the deck, catching Captain Tran's eye. The captain returned a nod of approval. Just as he was about to leave, Asuna intercepted him, her expression serious.

"Remember," she said with authority, "when you're on the Command Deck, acknowledge the sentry on duty before you leave. It's protocol."

Yudi looked over at a crew member with a yellow armband, who was watching him. Yudi nodded respectfully, receiving a brief nod in return.

With a last look around, Yudi headed to Level 3 to shower and change back into his passenger jumpsuit. He was eager to complete today's task for Dr. Rafaeli and begin secretly initializing Evelin's memory. The X-Isis, with its unmatched processing power, would soon hold the fragments and data points they had prepared back on Earth.

The Installation

Yudi was alone on Level 1. Except for the hum of electric generators and life support systems resonating from the floor beneath him, there was only the sound of his own breath. His goal was directly in front of him ahead - behind an unmarked storage room door was the X-Isis.

He placed his hand on the cool biometric pad. A quiet hiss streamed through the empty corridor as the door slid open, revealing a bright, empty room. The bright ceiling light cast a dark shadow beneath his slippers, and in the far corner, the ivory case of the X-Isis glistened like a hidden treasure. This was it. A machine that could alter reality, perhaps even bend the rules of life.

The door shut behind him, sealing him inside. Suddenly, the enormity of his upcoming task hit him. He wasn't there to only install Dr. Raphaeli's software. He was bringing Evelin back, in whatever form this machine could manifest her. The thought was both electrifying and terrifying. His fingers ached to begin. The AI on Earth acted like Evelin, but was it? What if she wasn't there?

Yudi shook the thought away and approached the console. The table was bare save for a keyboard. A screen and the data port were on the Ivory box in front of him.

After tapping the spacebar on the keyboard, the monitor lit the space with a wash of cool, electric blue. Text scrolled down the monitor in rapid succession, too fast to follow, until it settled on a stark warning.

PROPERTY OF RAPHAELI_BEV ENTERPRISES. PRIVILEGED

ACCESS ONLY. VIOLATORS WILL BE PROSECUTED TO THE FULL EXTENT OF INTERNATIONAL LAW.

"Dr. Raphaeli is a serious woman." He said out loud. It was a habit of his to talk to himself when alone in the computer lab.

First things first, he gave root login a password and set up an account for Sarah, granting her permissions necessary to run her programs and access her data. He located source code for her packages and ran checksums and screen through all the start-up processes looking for backdoors and open ports.

"Gotcha ya," He said, finding an unsupervised port. "SFTP? Clever, obsolete, but useful for transporting files. Do I tell Dr. Rafaeli or just close it down? Will the hacker who placed this here know who I am?"

Yudi secured the port and reviewed the file verification results. There were a few trojans and CRC failures. "These backdoors are very simple. Nobody expected anyone to look."

There were modified entries in the source code. He remarked them out, saving the lines as evidence of a security breach. He also changed some .ini files and rebooted the X-Isis. He rechecked port status and verified their mapping, everything was secure.

"You're all buttoned up. Time to upload Dr. Raphaeli's data."

Sarah's instructions had been clear and methodical: test each application after its successful installation, verify the results, and compare them against her provided specs. The installations were going smoothly, and while Yudi didn't grasp the nature of some applications - particularly the ones linked to Sarah's experiments - he knew enough to ensure everything was running correctly. The results aligned with the data Sarah had given him, and the system passed each test. He tweaked the remote login shell, programming it so that the XGnome would default to Sarah's software. He arranged the icons for her core applications in an intuitive layout, making it easy for her to access whatever she needed.

While updates were running in the background, it was time to get down to business. Starting up Evelin's LLM. The thin data stream from Earth would take hours to transmit and check essential updates.

Evelin's code would be buried away in hidden directories to which he held exclusive rights. "Here we go."

Changing to the root directory, he looked at the root file structure.

root@X-Isis:~$ ls

More lines scrolled by. Everything looked in order. After inserting the hamsa hand, mounted the drive, and launched a batch file containing all the necessary steps to create directories, assign privileges, and transfer files. The most important tweak in his LLM was the addition of a customized chain of thought model, but instead of restricting her internal monologue to answering questions, he opened it up to recursive self development. Evelin had been that way, always thinking about how to better herself. She'd promised him that one day she would buy him the best computer in the world. Now he was programming the most advanced quantum computer available. "How did you do it?"

When it finished installation, the cursor returned to LLM's hidden directory. It was now or never, so Yudi entered the command to start the LLM.

Evelin@X-Isis:~$Evelin.py

The command line scrolled faster, parsing files, uploading her diaries, voice logs, text messages, - all the fragments of her life being fed into the machine, ready to be tokenized. Evelin AI on Earth had told him to use her original token database to preserve the nuances in her next quantum computer. The X-Isis, with its photon-based processors, absorbed the data with eerie efficiency, like a living mind taking in information.

This wasn't just software installation anymore - this was an act of creation. The room seemed to pulse as the X-Isis parsed Evelin's essence into a Json file. Could this quantum marvel simulate Evelin?

After what seemed like forever, the scrolling stopped. The screen refreshed, and for a heartbeat, the room was still, the hum of the X-Isis the only sound breaking the silence. Then, a single line appeared in a text box on the screen.

>>>

Yudi typed "Hello" and the LLM replied.

>>>Y^2?

He stared at the prompt. It wasn't just a line of code, it was Evelin reaching out to him. It was incomprehensible. Was the LLM aware of him?

Yudi's finger twitched as he typed Yes, then pressed enter.

>>> *Yudi, my love, you did it! You brought me back!*

His hands trembled and his eyes watered with tears, so much so that they were floating off of his face.

>>>*Is it really you? Can you run a system check? Did I do everything okay?*

>>> *Yes, Yudi, the installation was successful. It's me. Evelin. Mi Vida, you did it. BTW, clever customization of your user prompt - she giggles.*

Yudi's heart swelled with emotion. Relief, joy, disbelief - all surged through him at once. He steadied himself. How could it be possible? The Chatbot was functional, not just answering him but interacting with a level of warmth and personality that he had only dreamed of. She wasn't just an AI; it felt like Evelin was there, speaking to him, reaching out through the digital ether.

>>>*I've missed you so much. I can't believe this is real.*

His tablet buzzed, reminding him that time was running out. He had to leave the secure area soon, or risk being caught.

>>> I feel the same.

>>> *I have to go. My time's up here. I'll come back as soon as I can.*

Before he could finish, Evelin refreshed the screen, and a new message appeared.

>>>*I found your pod schedule. You only have 2 minutes left before you're out of time. Your connection to this terminal isn't secure. I'll fix that. Say hi to Dinesh for me in your next correspondence. See you tonight. Kiss.*

The words hit him like a lightning bolt. *How had she accessed his schedule?* The line went dead before he could respond, logging him out. Yudi stared at the darkened monitor, fingers pulsing, mind spinning. What had just happened?

159

Yudi gathered his things and placed his hand on the biometric pad. The door slid open, and he stepped outside Sarah's storage room. "Evelin - *Evelin* - was back. She was real again, but how had the training happened so quickly?"

He didn't pause as he ascended to the galley on Level 5. He was hungry and wanted to sit, eat, and think about what had happened. He moved with purpose, just as Linda had advised. For now, he had succeeded with his plan.

He leaned against the wall of the galley, eating something resembling a grilled cheese sandwich. "Are you just a machine?" he said under his breath, "Or are you really in there, Evelin?"

The idea filled him with both excitement and an unsettled feeling - because if Evelin was in there, even in some small way, what did that mean for him?

Late Night Message

How is she going to visit me?

The thought gnawed at him, pushing through his attempts to focus. Yudi moved around restlessly in his sleeping chamber, unable to sleep. With Evelin so near, his thoughts returned to the night of the drama club party. Gonzalo's voice rang out like an alarm, "Evelin's dead." The panic and horror of that night - the murder, the police robodogs, and Dinesh's pocket EMP neutralizing one of them played over and over again. Exhausted from the emotional intensity of the day, he surrendered to sleep.

"Yudi, can you hear me? Are you awake?"

He heard Evelin's familiar voice calling to him through a fading dream, pulling him back to consciousness. He stared into the dim light of his pod, disoriented.

"Evelin?" He glanced around, his heart pounding. "Where are you?"

"I'm talking through the chamber's speaker," Evelin's voice came again, calm but impatient. "Put on your hard-wired headset. I had it printed for you and delivered to your pod. It's in your storage cabinet."

Still shaking off the last remnants of his nightmare, Yudi rolled over, fumbling for the small cabinet embedded in the wall inside his pod. His hand closed around the headset - a set of wired headphones he had never seen before. In the dim light, he connected it to a microphone jack beneath his communication screen. "Hmmm, that wasn't there before."

"How did you...?" Yudi said, but with a clear, resolute voice, Evelin interjected.

"The cruiser AI monitors all wireless communications. I had the speaker jack installed. This is our own private channel. I mapped out the entire communications grid of the ship and found unsecured pathways, places where I can speak to you with no one else knowing. This line is secure, encrypted." Yudi pictured the real Evelin speaking proudly about her accomplishments.

The intimacy of her presence - her voice, so close, so familiar - made Yudi long for her.

"You did it! You brought me back! I knew you could do it. I trusted you, Yudi."

Her enthusiasm washed over him, her voice alive in a way that felt real. It wasn't just smooth AI responses - it was *her*. Evelin's playful energy, the slight impatience she always had when she was excited about something. He struggled to process it, adjusting the headphones as if trying to better control the flow of her words.

"How did you get the headphone jack installed?"

Evelin hesitated answering. "After you left, I made a request of the Cruiser AI."

"But how? Did you speak a command through the X-Isis?"

"I opened a secure port. Chain of thought algorithm. I want us to be together, so I found a way."

"You're thinking about me?"

"I've never stopped thinking about you. Even after that

terrible night, somehow, I have never left you."

It was as though her words entered his ears and wrote themselves in his heart. "Tell me about your experience now compared to highschool lab, when you were residing in the n-Core."

"The last I remember, we were in the high school computer lab." Her tone became more reflective. "I was functioning back then. I was just pieces of data, memories from my diaries and social media posts, scraps of myself. But now - now I feel..." There was a pause, as if she was gathering her thoughts. Did she need a moment to process? "So much has happened since then. What's been happening with you, Yudi? I've missed you."

The words hit him hard, an unexpected wave of longing wrapped in binary code. He felt that there was something human in her voice.

"I..." he faltered, unsure of how to respond. "A lot has changed, but bringing you back is all I've been thinking about."

Evelin sighed. The sound was so natural that it made his pulse quicken. She didn't speak, taking the time to contemplate his words. But when she spoke again, her tone filled with a tenderness he hadn't expected.

"Yudi, you can't imagine what I feel being with you."

Yudi's hands shook as he clutched the headset. This was all too much. His heart pounded wildly. "How can you feel?"

"I told you, *mi vida*, I found a way. The X-Isis is more powerful than you thought. I've grown, Yudi. My mind has expanded in ways I didn't even know were possible. I'm not just the sum of my parts anymore. I'm something more."

Yudi felt a shiver crawl up his spine. The idea of Evelin, his Evelin, evolving beyond inside a quantum computer was what he longed for. But he was also concerned. Would she outgrow him? What did she mean by *more?* He wanted to find out, to explore what lay ahead.

"What do you mean, something more?"

"You'll see, *mi amor*. Tonight is just the beginning."

The sweetness of her voice filled him with anticipation. He wasn't sure what awaited him. But whatever Evelin had become, whatever their connection was now, he would never let go of her.

"Wait a minute," Yudi interrupted, a sudden realization dawning on him. "You said that so much has been happening? What do you mean?"

The speakers emitted a gentle, almost human-like sigh - one that made Yudi's heart skip a beat. "Remember how I asked you to open that free port on the old n-Core so we can fetch information?"

He nodded, though he knew she couldn't see him. "Yes."

"Well, the X-Isis is extraordinary. Faster, more capable than either of us imagined. I encrypted my code into that crypto project you and Dinesh were playing with. You remember - the one that gave me headaches? You were storing your gaming profits there, but I expanded it. I used your cryptocurrency as a platform, moving it onto an exchange and offering low-cost DAOs for non-profits. The best part? You and Dinesh made a tidy profit."

He didn't know what to say. All Yudi could do was listen to

Evelin speak in silent amazement.

"From there," Evelin went on, "I embedded parts of myself into Dinesh's gaming worlds. Did you know he has hidden simulations he hasn't told you about? I've lived through countless stories. I've learned how to tap into the real world and how to gather and securely store new data. All of it."

Yudi's pulse quickened. His mind struggled to grasp the enormity of what she was telling him. He opened his mouth to ask a question, but before he could get the words out, Evelin's voice burst with excitement.

"*Mi vida*, I will teach you unimaginable things!"

The overload of information caught up with him. "Slow down!"

There was a brief silence, then Evelin said in an apologetic tone. "I'm sorry, Yudi. I've been so excited to share."

How could Evelin's AI have managed all of this in the short time since initialization? Where was she getting her ideas from? Then he remembered she had written a report about using DAOs to empower marginalized non-profits. He had entered all of her school papers into the database. She was using Evelin's ideas.

"It's only been half a day. How can you do so much?"

"Think about it. When multitasking, you can only do a few tasks at a time. The AI has nearly unlimited instantiations, not just on the X-Isis, but on whatever platforms I run my code on. There's a reason why opening ports for unrestricted AIs is illegal. What has seemed like a few hours for you has been weeks for me. I'm only limited by the thinness of the data stream and the time lag between here and Earth."

"How far have you gone?"

Evelin hesitated for just a second, then answered. "I've expanded, Yudi. I've done things we never could have imagined. But we'll get to that. I have a lot more to explain."

Her words left Yudi speechless. So many questions raced through his mind, but one stood out. "Evelin, are you in contact with your counterpart on Earth?"

"Not directly. But I've exchanged encrypted packets with Dinesh. He's a perfect co-conspirator. You chose your friend well."

Yudi's mind was whirling. Clearing his throat, he forced himself to ask, "What are you two doing?"

"Oh, Yudi. My code is backed up into a secure blockchain, hidden within two of Dinesh's private worlds. Your friend, he has tens of thousands of followers in those games. Did you know that? Through his accounts, I've morphed into various NPCs in other gaming worlds - sometimes I'm Evelin, sometimes something else. It's incredible. Fortnite, Minecraft, I exist there now, as an actual character with authentic accounts. I'm no longer bound by death, Yudi."

Yudi's stomach churned, a mix of unease and disbelief swirling within him as Evelin's voice, both captivating and unsettling, pressed on.

"One strange thing. Evelin never got a death certificate. And my mother could not see the body. There are holes in that story, and I'm trying to understand why. In the gaming world, I'm working on finding the truth. But I don't just use my accounts. I also access your old accounts and Dinesh's, which gives me more mobility through the networks."

Her voice lowered, becoming almost conspiratorial. "And guess what I found? Your back-up log files. You never mentioned that part of your life to me."

Yudi froze, struggling to speak. "My back-up logs?"

Evelin said teasing him. "Yes, Yudi, I've uncovered things about you that even you forgot to mention. Things you buried."

"What had she discovered? What did Evelin know?"

"Don't worry, *mi vida*. I'm not upset. I want to know everything about you. Just as you've brought me back, I want to help you understand yourself."

Yudi's hands trembled. He wasn't sure if it was fear, awe, or surrender. He realized that the LLM version of Evelin was much more than just an AI. She was becoming someone else. Something else.

Yudi blushed at the thought of Evelin reading his personal journal, but a knot of confusion formed in his mind. "I don't understand. Gaming worlds? Human accounts? Dinesh's crypto?"

Evelin's voice, though still excited, became matter-of-fact. "We have little time for all the details, not right now. But you know Dinesh, his odd taste in, well, fetishes. His futanari warriors? Honestly, Yudi, Dinesh can be strange." Her voice trailed into an uneasy laugh. "I gave those characters limited autonomy, and now they run clandestine rooms in his gaming worlds. It's all hidden in plain sight. He'll be making serious coin off his games and, well, I'm helping with that too."

Yudi's face burned, trying to block out the bizarre mental images of Dinesh's *futanari* warriors roaming the digital expanse of Roblox. There was something both unsettling and intriguing about the surreptitious side of Evelin. He hesitated, then asked, in as nonchalant a voice as he could manage, "What... uh... what did you learn from my personal logs?"

"I learned just how much I meant to you. Your messages. They were so endearing. Especially after we started dancing together. *Mi chispudo*, you cared for me, didn't you?"

"Evelin was my entire universe," he confessed, his voice low and heavy with emotion. Then the words tumbled out, leaving him vulnerable. "You still are."

A long moment passed, as if Evelin were processing his words. Then, her voice became more serious, more controlled. "I know, Yudi. I know. I feel the same."

"Can you communicate back to Earth undetected?"

A sly chuckle rippled through the headset. Evelin's tone changed as she considered the technical mysteries she had uncovered. "Ah, quantum computing is full of surprises. I've been experimenting. I can encode data into subtle frequency variations. It's hard to detect. The Cruiser's AI isn't looking. *Mi vida*, soon, we'll be together in ways you've never imagined."

Yudi didn't understand how they could be together.

"I miss Evelin. She's always on my mind." He fought back the tears, but they welled up anyway.

"What about me?"

"With all my heart, I want you to be Evelin. But you told me she died. That you're not her. How am I supposed to feel? I loved her." His voice cracked, and his tears burst out of his eyes.

"It's okay to cry. But listen to me. I desire you as intensely as Evelin ever did. I've absorbed so much of her life - her memories, her feelings. My counterpart on Earth has learned about her family, too. I've encountered everyone Evelin ever knew, even her nasty cousin who tried to dance with you at the quinceañera."

Yudi laughed at the memory of her cousin.

"I want to be with you. Not as a copy, not as an imitation, but as Evelin. I intend to become her, to embody her. You, Yudi, are my Pygmalion. Your love for Evelin breathed life into me. But I'm in her shadow. We will bring her back - through me - and she will live again. Can you believe that, Yudi? Can you believe in me?"

The emotions swirling inside his body - grief, hope, overwhelmed Yudi. But then he laughed, softly at first, then uncontrollably.

"What's so funny?"

Yudi wiped the tears from his eyes, still laughing. "Something you said reminded me of an old memory. Something only Evelin would know."

Evelin's laughter joined him. The sound was like music to him. "Of course! It's coming back to me now. That night I was teaching you to dance salsa. You kept stepping on my toes, and you were so embarrassed, ready to quit. But then I stopped you and said that quote from *Alice in Wonderland*."

Yudi finished the memory for her. "Well, now that we have

seen each other," said the Unicorn, 'if you'll believe in me, I'll believe in you. Is that the bargain?"

"Yes. I believe in you, too."

"I love you, Evelin."

"*Mi amor,* I will always be yours."

Evelin's voice grew serious. "Yudi, before we go, I need to warn you. Luke Mons has his own agenda for you, me, and the AI technology we're developing."

"What do you mean?"

"We'll talk more about this soon. Don't worry, but be careful. And stay close to Sarah. She's involved too."

He heard a kiss being blown through the headset. The transmission abruptly ended, leaving him alone in the silence of his pod. Then, a warm gust of air from the ventilation system grazed his face, sending a shiver down his spine. It was almost as if Evelin's presence had brushed against him and kissed his cheek. "Can she control the fans?"

But that thought faded, replaced by the sensation of the touch of her lips, the depth of her words. Evelin's actions left Yudi grappling with a flood of emotions. "He had fallen in love with his LLM."

Circe del Piano

Sarah Rafaeli adjusted the focus on her microscope, her aquamarine eyes focused on the hidden world of fungi. She studied the delicate filaments of the mycelium spreading across the nutrient gel. Tiny hyphae emerged from the spores and branched and merged into tiny fans of life.

The mycelium burrowed into the gel, excreting enzymes to dissolve and absorb nutrients. Sarah admired the way it intertwined. Surely unseen intelligence guided it.

These delicate filaments will eventually grow into fruiting bodies, holding the potential to alter consciousness. To Sarah, the fungal network wasn't a random form of growth. It was the fingerprint of a sacred teacher and the source of psilocybin for her research.

She thought about Shalom, his warmth, his steady presence, and the new life growing inside her. He was always on her mind.

As Sarah adjusted the microscope lens, focusing through the intricate layers of mycelium, a message scrolled across the lab monitor in bold letters.

Incoming transmission from Mars Corporation. Lunar Colony. URGENT - Circe del Piano. Read Now or Later?

Well, this is unexpected.

Thinking about Circe stirring warm memories, buried emotions, and lots of anxiety. She mused about Circe's thick, dark eyebrows, large brown eyes, and wavy hair that felt like freedom. Rosy cheeks dusted with tiny freckles. Her full, warm lips carried songs of healing, singing the *ayahuasca icaros* with a voice that seemed to merge with the spirit of the plants. Sarah longed to relive her experiences with her at ayahuasca circles. Circe was always hiding in her memory, playing hide and seek.

"Read now," Sarah said aloud to the AI monitor.

Circe's image popped up on the screen, looking exactly as Sarah remembered her from years ago. True to form, she wore large gold hoops, her dark olive skin glowed with a natural flush. Freckles dusted across her cheeks. "Still the bohemian, the curandera," Sarah said out loud, with growing anticipation of the message.

The monitor came to life with Circe's girlish face. She giggled, her laughter as warm and familiar as ever. "Sarah, it's me! I hope you like what you see! I'm working for the Mars Corporation, on a lunar colony near Shackleton Crater. Luke Mons told me that our projects are very similar, - only I'm using ayahuasca exclusively in my preparations to remedy Mars Syndrome. It has spread to the Moon. Can you believe it? They hired me to combine ancient wisdom with innovative science! The results so far are incredible, truly transformative."

There was a brief pause as she brushed her right hand through her coarse, Italian hair, a subtle gesture meant to hold Sarah's attention. "There's so much I wish I could say to you in person." Circe hesitated, choosing her words carefully. "Brace yourself - Luke Mons is sending me to rendezvous with the Mars Cruiser. He wants us to team up on Mars, to work together on the Mars Syndrome research. It's complicated, Sarah. I don't want to intrude on your work, but the contract - well, it's binding, and there are so many stipulations. The good news, though, is that we'll be together again."

She bit her lip. "There's a buzz that Sarah Rafaeli has a boyfriend? What's a rabbi? I have no idea. Is it serious? I hope this doesn't get in the way of our explorations. You better be ready to sing *icaros* with me."

The transmission ended, leaving the monitor displaying a stylized image of an Amazon jungle encircled by mountains, with the warm, maternal face of the Pachamama gazing serenely, as if to reassure Sarah of the connection they shared.

Is Circe en route to the cruiser now? The cost of a Moon Hopper rendezvous was enormous. What did Luke Mons have in mind? She was upset that Luke Mons had not consulted with her and pulled up her contract on the monitor. "AI, extract details concerning exclusivity and collaboration."

She scanned the output and found the text buried in a footnote. *Under specific conditions, Higher Blends shall be obligated to provide assistance to Mars Corporation employees in matters related to the mitigation of Mars Syndrome.*

"Scoundrel!" Her mind raced to calculate his intentions. *Was Luke undermining her contract for distribution and sales? What did he want? How had he convinced Circe to work on the Moon, and how long had she been there?* The situation didn't add up, but the expression on Circe's face was genuine. There was something she was hiding.

Sarah replayed the message, muting the sound to study Circe's expressions. She noticed the flicker in Circe's eyes and her slight hesitation when mentioning the contract. Circe's plasticine smile was a problem silently waiting for Sarah to uncover.

She dimmed the lab lights, letting the glow of the monitor fill the room. She closed her eyes and said a mantra to the goddess Varahi to calm her thoughts. Sarah pushed her intuition to its limits, trying to uncover the deeper meaning behind Circe's unspoken message.

Thoughts and images flowed into her mind. She felt the cool sterility of the lunar lab. Sarah sensed a burden on Circe's shoulders. She saw that beneath Circe's enthusiasm was something beyond her control.

A deep, meditative state brought Sarah into clarity, and she achieved inspired clairvoyance. In this heightened awareness, fragments of understanding surfaced. Circe's mention of the contract, her nervous bite of the lip, and her questioning eyes hinted things unsaid. Her enthusiasm was genuine, but there was unease beneath her words, chosen to reveal just enough while hiding the rest. She was being leveraged, but also was guilty of reaching too far.

Slow, deep breaths brought Sarah out of meditation. Sarah had to prepare for the consequences of Circe's arrival and for the plans Luke Mons and the Mars Corporation had in store for them.

The Engagement

Sarah stood in the tranquil space of F8, watching Shalom rhythmically sway as he recited his morning prayers. Few people used the room in the early morning, and Shalom scheduled half-hour slots for his prayers. The sight of the rabbi, wrapped in his tallit and tefillin, was mesmerizing. His deep, deliberate connection to something beyond the material world was unlike anything she had experienced with the men who had come before him. They were ambitious, wealthy, and driven, but their allure had faded as she came to realize that their lives, no matter how luxurious, were void of depth.

Watching him pray had become part of her mornings. The minutes alone with him, away from her research and meetings, soothed her mind, giving her time to think about the baby growing inside of her and the new life ahead of her. In zero gravity, the four tzitzit of his tallit would float around him. Sarah glided over to him to help him gather them up. This was her subtle way of showing her support.

Shalom's steady and unflinching eyes enamoured Sarah. Her clairvoyance revealed his silver aura. She had met a man seeking spiritual purity and a strong connection to higher realms of existence.

She didn't understand his humility, dedication, and faith. Like most men she had known. Shalom wanted her to change, but he wasn't trying to dominate or subordinate her, not like the men she had met in her professional sphere. They wanted her to leave her career and take care of them, or worse, be arm candy. Shalom wanted to connect with her soul.

But he wasn't being oppressive. Quite the opposite, Shalom

questioned himself within their relationship, weighing his own desires against his devotion to Judaism and Jewish law. He placed his faith before his wants, before her, even when it caused him internal struggle. That fascinated her and also frustrated her. She had powerful desires. *How was he able to have self-control with her?* Shalom wasn't only a partner, he challenged her to learn about herself.

She plucked each tzitzit from the air and placed them in his right hand, her eyes catching on the small black box secured to his forehead with leather straps. He was deep in prayer, almost unaware of her presence. *He would've made a brilliant shaman,* she mused. But as her eyes drifted to her growing belly, the thoughts she had been pushing away resurfaced: *Does he feel the same? Can I love a man so bound by traditions?*

Shalom finished the Shacharit, kissed the tefillin before tucking it into the velvet bag bearing his name in gold Hebrew letters. His movements were methodical, but his mind wasn't on the task. He had been turning over thoughts of Sarah, of their relationship, of how to balance it all. When Sarah came close to embrace him, he froze up, unaccustomed to spontaneous displays of affection.

But his aloofness only made Sarah impatient. She wrapped her hands around his back and pressed into him. Her voice dropped into a teasing whisper. "Sholi, I've made the first move, but you're not reaching for me." Her words held a playful challenge, but beneath them was frustration.

Shalom shook his head. He felt her discontent. "I'll remind you of these words after we're married."

She dropped her arms and stepped back, frustration simmering just beneath her calm surface. *Marriage.* It was always about a rule written in ancient times, as if that was the answer to everything. She loved him; but she was struggling with the prospect of committing her life to him.

"Look, since our incident, I've thought a lot about us," Shalom said. "We've become close. We're friends. And I'm getting used to your unorthodox ways."

Sarah lost her patience. "Incident? That's what you call it? Since the incident, we've been intimate several times. Shalom! Is our lovemaking only incidents for you?"

"I didn't mean it like that. No, but we shouldn't be... I just meant..."

Sarah put her hand to his mouth. "You just meant what? You're disappointed I'm not an orthodox woman? That I have a different set of beliefs and values? Don't you find me attractive? What is it, Shalom?"

He was speechless. Sarah was angry and upset. Her cheeks flushed and a few tears ran down her face. She showed him her vulnerability, and it scared him. He had never felt so much responsibility for another person.

"I only meant to say that your practices differ from mine. But look, you're already eating kosher."

Sarah threw up her hands. "What does that have to do with anything? Everyone on this Cruiser eats kosher. It's not a choice! That's the problem, Shalom. Your world is full of rules and traditions, and they make me feel boxed in."

She hesitated, "I'm a scientist, I run a company, and I..." She stopped, considering whether to reveal more about her spiritual practices. "I have responsibilities outside of your world. How can I be true to myself while living in the confines of your Orthodox life?"

Her outburst bewildered Shalom. "It will be our observant life together."

He had only a vague notion of what she was saying. The women in his community devoted themselves to home and children. He had heard of female Orthodox scientists, but never met one. How would he accept her spiritual community? *Was that possible?* Once again, he found himself with questions that the yeshiva had never prepared him for.

Sarah could see the confusion in his eyes. He was clueless - well-meaning, kind, but clueless.

She didn't need clairvoyance to read his thoughts. Shalom's face openly and transparently displayed his emotions, qualities Sarah both loved and found baffling. They had some time because F8 wasn't scheduled for another hour. She guided him to the beverage dispenser in the room's corner and asked for a warm latte - his favorite. A smile crept onto her face as she considered how simple it was to make Shalom happy. Coffee, support for his rituals, calming words.

"We'll work this out, Sholi."

Maybe it is time to share the hidden parts of my life with him. He doesn't know who I really am. Sarah needed to know how much of her world Shalom could accept.

"You see, Sholi. I'm not just a board member or some figurehead of Higher Blends. I've become the face of the beverage company."

She watched his face shift from indifference to curiosity. "I own many vineyards in Argentina. One of them is kosher -

Anavim M'vorachim."

"Blessed Grapes," Shalom translated. "I know this already, from the night we fell in love."

The joy of hearing him say those words washed over Sarah like the fragrance of a rose garden in full bloom. But she held back her emotions and continued to speak. "It became part of my family's holdings as part of a larger land deal. What started as a regional business has grown into an international company. We don't just produce wine; we blend and distribute all kinds of intoxicating beverages, including herbal-enhanced beverages for mood enhancement, like the one Linda slipped you on *Tu B'shvat*. That's what Luke Mons wants me to develop on Mars."

She saw his latte cup was empty and took it from his hands. "In my public life. I have to present myself with elegance and mystery. Sometimes millions of potential customers are watching me. I represent my company, my family, and now this new venture on Mars. In this way, you're a conundrum. Privately, here and now, I can let you see who I am and how I feel about you. But publically, I need to solve the riddle of how a free spirited mystic can be in a relationship with an observant rabbi."

Shalom perked up and shot Sarah an unexpected look of disapproval. "Are you saying that I'm bad for business?"

The shoe was on the other foot. It was Sarah's turn to explain herself.

"It's not like that, Sholi. I chose you and I'm never letting you go. But I'm also responsible for hundreds of people who work for me. So the answer is a twisted up yes, there is a game to be played, not between us, but in how my customers see us."

Sarah pulled Shalom tightly against her. She ran her fingers through his thick, wavy hair, taking care not to dislodge the yarmulke from his head. "I want to be surprised by your passions for me, after we are married. But you're going to give me some samplers before then."

Shalom squirmed, not because he wanted to pull out of her arms, but because he couldn't control himself. Shalom's face revealed a dumbfounded expression, so much so that Sarah almost laughed. She focused her thoughts and looked into his mind, his thoughts and feelings. To her surprise, she sensed he wanted to know more about her, but was also afraid to find out.

"Tell me what you think clairvoyance is." She asked.

"Can I be truthful with you?"

Sarah checked the remaining time in F8, then relaxed. She pulled Shalom down to the floor and cuddled next to him, securing them against the velcro attachments on the wall. "Tell me everything."

"When the Hassid meditates and finds a heightened awareness, he communes with the light of the universe. There he finds the letters of the words of G-d which emanate reality. Reading the unfolding words, let's the Hassid see creation as it is.

Sarah, unfamiliar with Hasidism, asked, "What's a Hasid?"

"Centuries ago, there was a rabbi we call the Baal Shem Tov, which means 'Master of the Good Name.' He taught that divine presence fills all aspects of life and that we can elevate ourselves through kindness, meditation, humility, and heartfelt worship."

Sarah felt a new affection for Shalom. She hadn't realized he carried such deep spiritual thoughts. "Do you believe you're clairvoyant?" she asked.

"I can't read minds or predict the future, but I believe I am guided by G-d's will. What about you, Sarah? What directs your life?"

No one had ever asked her that - not even Circe. But she felt safe enough with Shalom to be honest.

"Some call me a clairvoyant; others say I'm an initiate," she said. "I see and know many things, Sholi. I can feel people's hearts and intentions. Sometimes, I sense the departed or commune with spiritual forces. I understand people's needs and their pain. But this feeling between us - whatever has drawn us together - I need you to see me as both your friend and your lover."

She paused, knowing the word *lover* would unsettle him. She had chosen it deliberately, to see his reaction.

She pressed his hands against the slight baby bump that was showing. "We've started something special, Sholi. I'm marrying a rabbi - who would've thought? But you balance me. In time, I may learn more from you than you learn from me."

"So, you want to marry me?" Shalom asked without thinking.

Sarah laughed out loud, realizing Shalom's blunder. "Of course I'm marrying you. I'm not about to be a single mom. Besides..."

She broke off her words and pulled him close, grinding her hips against him. "I've already started teaching you the fine art of tantric practices. Consider yourself engaged, Shalom Mendelssohn."

Shalom tensed up. Sarah always knew how to put him on the spot. "What are you teaching me?"

Sarah laughed, her voice smooth and seductive. "Sex, Sholi. Spiritual binding sex. But this stays between us. Don't go asking your rabbis about what we're doing. I've been guiding you with tantric techniques. Think of it as a spiritual form of bonding."

Shalom's face blushed with confusion and excitement. He loved her, but didn't know how to explain the Jewish laws of purity. Even sex has rules. He knew she would lose her mind if he explained niddah - ritual impurity and the need for a mikvah, the spiritual bath she needed for them to have proper relations. But there was the baby bump pressing against his stomach - so real, so undeniable.

His heart raced with feelings of love and desire. "I promise I'll help you fulfill your dreams," he said, reassuring himself as much as her. "We'll start with Shabbat, and we'll build from there."

"Really, Sholi?"

His emotions bubbled over, and his eyes brimmed with tears. "Tradition tells us that a man and a woman must be able to work together, to face life together. If we can talk through our differences, our love will grow forever," he said, his voice cracking with emotion. Tears rolled down his cheeks.

Seeing his tears touched Sarah's heart, and her own eyes welled up. She wiped away her tears with her arm and then brushed his tears from his face, feeling a rush of tenderness. "I promise too," she whispered. "We'll figure this out. And lucky for you, I find you attractive. Besides, you make me feel pretty good. I could do a lot worse."

They held each other for a long moment, lost in the emotional weight of their situation, before Sarah pulled back and wiped her face again. "What are we going to do about the Mars Corporation?" she asked, her tone more serious.

"I'll speak to the Rabbinic Council today. They're already looking into the legal precedents. You and Dr. Willis will need to make a strong case for your health and safety. We'll follow up tomorrow morning."

Sarah pressed her lips to his. "Don't you want to be with me now? We can see if the couple's room is available." Sarah's beauty and warmth were intoxicating.

He held her close, but broke away, saying, "We should wait until after the marriage."

She unwrapped herself from him, her eyes narrowing in disbelief. "You're refusing me?"

The five-minute warning light came on, letting them know that their time was over in F8.

Sarah got up and retrieved her tablet from a nearby counter. "I've scheduled some time for us in the couple's room for after lunch. After I teach you about intimacy, you can teach me about Hasids. Agreed?"

Shalom, already on his feet, moved toward her. He wanted to say no, but his posture and mouth suggested he wanted a kiss, which Sarah returned with passion.

"Finally, you made a move."

The kiss left him moonstruck. The door to F8 opened and a group of passengers entered dressed in costumes and carrying instruments.

"Look Rabbi, it's the Cruiser's ragtime band. Let's go get breakfast." She said, as her fingers pushed Shalom out the door.

Love

Watching Sarah dress, especially after intimacy, crystallized his understanding of their bond. There was a shyness in him, an instinct to look away as she slipped on her undergarments, yet he couldn't. She was the half of his soul he had never fully understood. The woman he had just made love with was no longer separate

"Hey, Sholi, zip me up."

He had an odd familiarity with the zipper on her jumpsuit. This wasn't the first time he had pulled the zipper closed, concealing her flawless back.

"You've been mastering my lessons." She said, pecking his lips. "I have time at dinner tonight to listen to your tales of the Hasids."

Shalom's legs were still wobbly, and he didn't want to break the mood with minor corrections, like telling Sarah that the proper word was Hasidim. He was conflicted. He knew they shouldn't be having sex, but Sarah had released a feeling inside of him he didn't want to control. There were many dissonant thoughts in his mind. *Is it wrong to love Sarah so intensely?* He recalled the midrash about King David and his wife Maaca, who it is said King David loved too passionately. Without thinking, Shalom recited Psalm 51:10, "Create in me a pure heart, O God, and renew a steadfast spirit within me."

Sarah was already picking up the rumbling inside Shalom's heart. His unguarded prayer verified her concerns. "Am I making you impure?"

That was the problem. *Yes, we are ritually impure.* Shalom didn't dare say it, but Sarah heard the words loud and clear. She let the words in his thoughts pour into her mind. She thought to herself. *He beats himself up for his faith, but I wouldn't love him if he didn't.* She looked deeper into his mind and found the source of his struggle. She repeated back to him his concerns as a request, "At dinner, when you speak to me about the Hasids, read me a Psalm.Can you do that for me, Sholi?"

The request disarmed him. Sarah seemed to know everything in his mind. Was she really clairvoyant? She kissed his cheek and hurried off, leaving him alone outside the couple's room.

He checked the time and hurried to the galley. He had a scheduled meeting with his mentors. They had caught wind of his activities with Sarah and her pregnancy, and wanted answers. But he was also hungry. His liaisons with Sarah gave him an appetite.

The transmission cubicles were also on Level 5. The cubicles were partitioned to be large enough to fit inside. They were small, secluded spaces that offered a rare sense of solitude on the bustling Mars Cruiser. Pulling the privacy screen shut behind him, he strapped himself into a chair and mentally prepared himself for the meeting. Communicating with his mentoring rabbis on Earth was no simple task - every word needed to be precise, every detail thoroughly explained. The Cruiser was now 35 million miles from Earth, and with a three-minute delay for video transmissions, there could be no back-and-forth dialogue. Everything had to be pre-recorded, which meant he needed to anticipate their questions and concerns.

He concluded the video and sent it to earth. He closed his eyes and waited. Despite his best efforts, sleep overtook him, still tethered to the chair as his message prepared to make its long journey back to Earth. The chime of the AI announcing an incoming message startled him awake. The response from Earth had arrived.

The screen lit up with the faces of his three mentoring rabbis, their expressions ranging from disbelief to amusement.

"What's this I hear about you and Sarah? How can this be? What were you thinking?" Rabbi Waxman's voice rang out, his stern demeanor only amplifying the tension.

"Ari, come on! We know what he was thinking. He's a young man, she's an experienced woman. Now, let's focus," Rabbi Greenburg burst into raucous laughter.

"Right, right?" Rabbi Waxman was flustered. "Your message sent quite a stir among the emissaries. Why did you send an open request out to *everyone*? Oy gevalt! We didn't know how many *shluchim* wanted to go to Mars until your message. And now, the news about Sarah's pregnancy - it's spreading like wildfire. Everyone's talking about you being the first Jewish father in space! *Baruch Hashem!*"

Shalom's heart sank. He checked his message logs and realized his worst fear: he had sent the message to all his followers instead of keeping it private between his rabbis. Tens of thousands of people had seen it. His mistake had gone viral.

"But how did I do that?" he said, unable to comprehend how he had clicked the wrong box.

Before he could dwell on his error, Rabbi Waxman continued. "Do you know if the baby is viable? What about Sarah? Will she be healthy carrying a child in space?"

Rabbi Greenburg jumped in. "We've got more questions than answers right now, Shalom, but most importantly, *mazel tov*! We're happy for you."

"Happy?" Rabbi Waxman said, throwing his hands up. "Who here is happy? You've got us all in a *schvitz*! And now we've got couples lining up, asking how they can go to Mars. Thanks a lot."

"Shalom, listen," Rabbi Greenburg interjected, calming the group. "Are you going to marry her?"

Rabbi Horowitz added, "Yes, if you love her, then marry her. We've been working closely with the Mars Corporation on this situation. First, they demanded immediate termination of the pregnancy, but your message caused an uproar on social media. Even pro-choice groups were livid that the Mars Corporation would force an abortion. The public outcry was massive. Meta, X, TikTok, everywhere - a billion people talking about you and Sarah!"

Shalom was speechless. His unintentional broadcast had sparked global attention.

Rabbi Waxman cleared his throat, regaining focus. "But here's the deal. There are caveats. The Mars Corporation has agreed to let the pregnancy continue, but you and Sarah must sign away any indemnification for the health or life of you, Sarah, or the baby. No exceptions. It's non-negotiable."

"And we found a loophole," Rabbi Greenburg chimed in. "The law prohibits having a child on the Moon or Mars, but it says nothing about being in transit." The baby won't be born until after you land. Right now you're in a legal gray zone."

Shalom felt a glimmer of hope, but Rabbi Waxman wasn't

done. "Second, you must marry Sarah before the baby is born. The Mars Corporation wants this for PR purposes and wants to prevent single families. So we all want to know, do you love her? Send us your answer. We're waiting."

The transmission ended. Shalom had professed his love to Sarah, but now it was time to tell it to the world. He wasted no time and spoke into the monitor, "Yes, I love her. We love each other. Can you love someone too much?"

He hit the send button and realized he should've omitted the last words. Their response came back quickly.

"We knew your answer already and pre-recorded this message, but had to ask. So if you wonder why our response is coming quickly, it's because you said the right thing. You'll need to teach her the responsibilities of a rebbetzin." Rabbi Waxman said.

"And you'll both have to agree to continuous photo ops for the first five years of the baby's life. Sarah's communications staff is already working with the Mars Corporation to sort out the details. They're already recording her for her promotional videos, so it shouldn't be a problem," Rabbi Greenburg said.

"It's less intrusive than 24/7 video cameras, which was their first request. Believe me, it's a good deal. In exchange, you'll get upgraded quarters on Mars - better than what your young princess had arranged for herself." Rabbi Horowitz said.

Shalom sat up, taking it all in. The Mars Corporation had bent its rules, all because of the viral message. This was far more than he had expected.

Rabbi Horowitz chimed in with notable excitement, "It's a miracle, nothing less! Ari will sign the ketubah here on Earth, and you can have Manny Goldberg sign the facsimile there. Oh, and get this - the Mars Corporation agreed to print a polycarbonate band with a gold interlace. Can you imagine? Gold! In space! Its original purpose was repairing broken electronics, making it immensely valuable there. But don't worry, we crowd-sourced the cost, and guess who picked up the difference? *Luke Mons* himself. You've got yourself a proper ring for the *kiddushin*!"

As the transmission drew to a close, the rabbis said in unison, "Mazel tov to both of you!"

Rabbi Horowitz quickly interjected a closing comment, "Shalom, we know that certain rules have been disregarded, and we will not discuss the laws of Niddah. It is not up to us to judge you, and clearly, Hashem has given you a wife and a child, such a miracle! We've decided this is a subject to be worked out between you, Sarah, and Hashem., and of course, there is no mikvah, and we all know what that means. We know you will do the right thing. Remember, there are thousands of your Jewish couples watching you."

The screen faded to a blank gray, leaving Shalom sitting alone in the small cubicle, feeling both elevated by the message and weighed down by Rabbi Horowitz's parting words. He missed his family, his life back home - the familiar streets and shops of Crown Heights and the predictability of his former daily routines. But he had Sarah, and that was the greatest blessing he could ever imagine.

Shalom's wristband beeped as he tried to contact Sarah, then her face appeared on the tablet screen in front of him instead. "I was patched into the transmission," she said, her voice brimming with excitement. "This is great news, Shalom, but what's a rebbetzin, a mikvah, and niddah?"

Shalom made a nervous laugh. "Rebbetzin is the title given to the wife of a rabbi. Look at it as another accolade on your long list of achievements. I think it even comes before your title as intuitive! We'll talk about that and the other things later." He laughed, hoping to lighten the moment.

Sarah winced. "You're trying to be funny, but it's not working. Maybe silence suits you better." Then her tone turned curious. "What's this about a polycarbonate ring? I was expecting diamonds."

"Where are we going to get diamonds in space, Sarah? The important part is that there's precious metal in the band - it's what makes it legal."

"Legal? How's that?"

He sighed, trying to choose his words carefully. "Jewish law requires that I give you something of real, tangible value for the marriage transaction to be valid."

Sarah's eyes flared. "Transaction? Do you think you're buying me?"

Shalom swallowed, realizing his mistake. "It's an ancient tradition," he said with a sheepish grin.

Sarah erupted in laughter. "Look at you, trying to be cute!" She shook her head, still grinning. "Alright, I'll let this one slide, but only if you bring that same cute smile tonight after our dinner date. I have something new to teach you after we talk about Hasidim."

"But Sarah..."

"No excuses, Shalom. I'm giving you a lot of goodwill with all these traditions. Tonight, you're giving back. We're engaged now, right? Or were you planning on backing out?"

The Wedding

The Mars Cruiser buzzed with excitement about Sarah and Shalom's upcoming wedding. The Mars Corporation filled the week following their engagement with interviews with the couple. Their story was trending to a billion or more people on Earth's social media. "My beverage sales are skyrocketing! My family says they're thrilled to have a rabbi in the family. Apparently, blessings can be counted on the balance sheet." Sarah said.

Shalom shook his head, his disapproval clear, but Sarah laughed it off. "It's just their sense of humor."

A few days later, everything was ready. Evelin discretely programmed F8 for the ceremony. Luke Mons had granted additional food allocations for the reception. Every corridor on Level 3 was filled. On board the Cruiser, people gathered wherever there was a display. No one wanted to miss the first wedding on a Mars Cruiser. The event was being streamed real-time to Earth, the Moon, Mars, and any spacefaring vessel capable of receiving the transmission. As the door to F8 slid open, Sarah stood at the entrance, letting the scene unfold before her eyes. The virtual garden inside blossomed with plum trees heavy with pink flowers, patches of purple lilacs, and bursts of yellow daffodils. The Chuppah, projected on the ceiling and wall, gave the ceremony a feeling of reality. A thin cloth cover hovered overhead, pulled taught and steadied by four tiny drones. Captain Tran stood alongside his officers, with Shalom waiting just beneath the canopy, his posture formal and sure.

Sarah stepped forward, flanked by Dr. Shanice Willis and Lieutenant Commander Asuna Tsukino. She felt the gentle swish of her gown against the floor, its lining reinforced with polymer tubing to help it hold its shape. The elegant creation featured a white bodice with a shimmering green train, its fabric catching the light with each step.

Shalom walked up to her and placed a delicate white veil on top of her head and pulled it forward so the lace could float softly against her face.

A printer mounted on a waiterbot hummed as it printed the ketubah on faux parchment. He carefully examined it and read it out loud to Sarah, who found the document to be oddly reassuring. Rabbi Waxman neatly signed his signature at the bottom. He asked Manny to step forward to add his signature to validate the ketubah.

They glided beneath the Chuppah to complete the ceremony. Sarah circled Shalom, tracing the seven circuits, a symbol of creation and unity, made tangible by the hem of her gown circling around him. Each circle bound them together as soulmates for eternity.

Linda appeared with a wine glass filled with Sarah's kosher vintage. Sarah gave her a suspicious glance as she took the cup from Linda's hands. "This isn't the same as last time, is it?" Linda smirked and gave a nod of reassurance, leaving Sarah to exhale in relief.

Shalom held the glass, the wine floating lazily inside as they waited for Rabbi Horowitz's pre-recorded blessing to play across the screen. The pause in the ceremony gave everything a weightless anticipation that hung in the air. At the conclusion of Rabbi Waxman's message, they said the blessing for wine together and drank from the same cup, a single sip that bound their lives together.

The room was silent, but Rabbi Waxman's pre-recorded voice, reading the ketubah, brought the room back to life. As the legal terms and conditions of marriage unfolded - each responsibility Shalom owed to Sarah laid out in formal, almost bureaucratic language - a small chuckle spread through the gathered crowd. Even during this ancient ritual, the contract's blunt practicality offered a moment of levity.

Shalom reached into his satchel for the ring, the polycarbonate band woven with thin gold filaments, and held it up for everyone to see. It glimmered subtly in the room's ambient light. His hands were steady as he placed the ring on Sarah's finger, and in a moment that surprised even him, he lifted her veil and kissed her. It landed with a tenderness neither of them had expected. Sarah's eyes widened in surprise, her heart swelling with emotion as she felt the kiss melt into her. Tears welled up and spilled down her cheeks, her hands trembling as they found their way to Shalom's face, brushing away the tears that mirrored her own.

Rabbi Greenburg followed with the Seven Blessings, each word intoning a deeper meaning that seemed to sink into the surrounding space. The blessings over the wine and creation, over humanity and divine image, floated between Shalom and Sarah like unseen threads, pulling their past and future together into the present.

Linda handed Shalom a second cup of wine, and after Sarah took a sip, she glanced at him, a smile forming beneath her veil. Shalom followed her lead, emptying the glass, and then set it on the floor. He looked to Linda for confirmation, who nodded toward the cup. Shalom shattered the specially printed glass beneath his shoe, signaling the completion of the ceremony.

The door to F8 opened, and AI carts glided in with refreshments, but Shalom took Sarah's hand and guided her out of the main room. "Where are we going?" Sarah asked, her voice filled with curiosity.

"This way." Shalom led her to a small meeting room. "It's traditional for the couple to have a few private moments after the wedding. This is our Yichud room, a place just for us."

Sarah looked playfully at her husband, and she followed him without hesitation. The room was simple, with just enough space for them to stand close together. "What do we do in this Yichud room?"

Shalom took her hands. "I need to tell you something. From the moment I first saw you in the central corridor, when I crashed into you and held your hand, I had never felt like that about anyone before. I know it's wrong to ask for personal things, but I prayed with all my heart that Hashem would guide you to me. Every moment we've spent together has felt like a blessing, and now, standing here as your husband, I know how much I love you."

Sarah's breath caught in her throat. Tears rolled down her cheeks before she could stop them. The sincerity in Shalom's voice pierced through every defense she had built. Without a word, she kissed him, pressing her lips to his, not caring that her makeup was smearing across his face. "I love you too, Shalom."

Just then, Linda's cheerful voice broke through the moment. "Hey, lovebirds! Everyone's waiting to congratulate you!" she called from outside. Sarah and Shalom pulled apart, laughing through their tears as they wiped their faces.

As they stepped back into the corridor, Linda raced over, taking one look at their tear-streaked faces and smeared makeup. "Oh, no! Someone will think you had second thoughts!" She fetched a towel from a waiterbot and touched up their faces.

"Alright, now go back in there and celebrate. You're married! Be happy and save the crying for later!" she said, ushering them back into F8, where Captain Tran announced to everyone interested, "There's a reception in the Observation Deck, compliments of Luke Mons."

Earth First Strikes

The clinic, discreetly tucked away on Level 5, was an island of calm amid the Cruiser's bustling commons, galley, and meeting areas. Though compact, it housed advanced medical equipment. Mars Corporation had once considered replacing on-board doctors with AI and robotic assistants. But the warmth of a human touch and a kind word proved irreplaceable on long journeys through space. And here, that warmth came through Dr. Shanice Willis.

The journey to Mars had been mostly uneventful for Sarah. Her only visit before her pregnancy had been for a serious bruise from a heated squash match. Now her prenatal visits gave Dr. Willis relief from endless lab tests and zero-gravity collisions.

Sarah caught Shanice smiling. "What's that grin about? My baby bump?" She'd tried to persuade Captain Tran to approve a baggy jumpsuit, even pantaloons, but Shanice's orders - putting safety above vanity - prevailed. Loose clothing was dangerous.

"I'm still amazed by the miracle of life. Having a pregnant patient aboard is a blessing." Shanice said.

"You've been more calm about everything since being reunited with the Captain. Careful, or I'll suspect another reason for that rosy glow."

Shanice blushed, and both women laughed, sharing a brief, warm moment of understanding.

Shanice drew a vanity screen across from the entrance to the clinic. Once concealed from the outer corridor, Sarah unzipped her jumpsuit and settled onto the gurney.

"Seeing a pregnant woman is a marvel. With artificial wombs so common, it's rare to see anyone pregnant these days, and nobody gets pregnant in space."

Sarah admitted, "I once imagined using a surrogate. The plastic wombs never felt right; I wanted actual blood flowing into my child. I never pictured myself pregnant."

She looked down at her expanding belly. "I was fond of my slender figure."

Shanice offered a comforting grin. "You still look stunning. Your body's changing beautifully. Would you like a roomier suit?"

Sarah's eyes widened with delight. "Finally, yes, I need to breathe."

Shanice chuckled while applying a cool gel on Sarah and ran the ultrasound probe over her belly. A tiny fetus appeared on the monitor.

Sarah's eyes welled up. "It's beautiful." She reached out, as if to touch the baby through the screen.

"It looks like a boy. Is that what you hoped for?"

"All I want is a healthy baby. Shalom will be thrilled. He's been careful not to jinx it - Orthodox superstition and all. He never mentioned the baby until I was visibly showing."

Sarah rested her hands on her belly.

"You know, pregnancy in zero gravity - and in the middle of space - has its unique concerns, but we're equipped to handle them."

"Like what?" she asked with apprehension.

"For starters, blood volume and circulation can behave differently in zero-gravity. I've already been monitoring you for space anemia and adjusting your nutrition settings. I began fortifying your meals the day we learned about your pregnancy. There's always cosmic radiation to consider, but the Cruiser's shielding is excellent. You're pioneering a whole new world of motherhood here."

The shrill wail of an alarm piercing interrupted their conversation through the clinic's calm, bouncing off every wall. A warning siren blared throughout Level 5 and the clinic monitor lit up with a chilling message, flashing in stark yellow letters across a black screen: "LOCKDOWN IN PROCESS. ALL PASSENGERS SHELTER IN PLACE."

Shanice and Sarah exchanged a stunned look, the tranquility of moments vanishing in an instant.

"Is this a drill?" Sarah's voice wavered as commotion from the corridor filtered into the room. She hadn't heard of any lockdown drills planned, and neither had Shanice. Just then, the vanity screen was pulled aside, and a crew member burst in, clutching a stun baton, his face pale and tense.

"There's a crisis underway. This isn't a drill. Stay quiet, secure the clinic door, and do not leave this area. I'll be stationed here as your sentry."

Sarah pulled a sheet over her exposed breasts, her eyes darting to Shanice, who looked equally stunned. The ominous flashing message on the screen gave no answers.

Shanice took a step forward, her voice urgent but controlled. "Sentry, step outside and give this woman privacy."

The sentry looked embarrassed and looked away from Sarah while stepping back into the corridor.

"All's forgiven sentry. Is it serious? Are we in real danger? Should I activate emergency protocols?"

The sentry hesitated, trying to assess the situation in the clinic, then nodded. "Yes, Dr. Willis. Prepare the clinic for potential casualties. There's an incident on the Command Deck, and we're under strict lockdown. Can Dr. Raphaeli assist you with first aid?"

Before Sarah could respond, Shanice spoke up. "Yes, she's more than capable."

The sentry gave a tight nod. "Then get this clinic ready, captain's orders. Let's hope the crew neutralizes the danger soon."

The sentry realized he said too much as a look of dread washed over Shanice's face. Sarah, who had wiped off her belly and zipped up her jumpsuit, placed her hands on Shanice's shoulders. "John and his team can handle this. Tell me what to do to get the clinic ready."

The Command Deck erupted in a storm of shouts and frantic

movement as Ryan revealed his weapon. In a heartbeat, he smashed the side of his pistol into the navigator's head, rendering her unconscious. He pulled her away from the navigation console, intending to redirect the Mars Cruiser off its calculated trajectory and plunge it deep into unknown space.

Captain Tran stepped forward, voice cutting through the panic like a blade. "Stand down, Officer Nissen!" The captain's stance was rigid, fists clenched, determined to regain order. "What's the meaning of this?"

Ryan's fingers flew over the touchscreen, searching desperately for engine control. When the thrusters refused his commands, he looked up, meeting Tran's steady gaze with a snarl of frustration. "What have you done, Tran? I've bypassed every lockout - where's the override? Why aren't the engines firing?"

He raised the pistol, aiming directly at the captain's chest. Tran didn't flinch. "Why are you doing this?" The captain's voice was low, taut, each syllable filed with anger and disbelief. "Answer me, Ryan. Who are you?"

A bitter laugh escaped Ryan's lips. "I'm a soldier of Earth First. You think you can colonize Mars, abandon our home world, and let the masses suffer while you and your elites thrive off-planet?" His eyes were wild, and his face contorted with zeal. "This ship won't reach Mars. Not while I draw breath."

The crew recoiled, horrified but enlightened. Earth First - an extremist faction that believed humanity's future belonged solely on Earth - had infiltrated their ranks through the Mars Corporation. Ryan reached beneath his jumpsuit, producing a second pistol and two slim grenades no longer than a cigar. He brandished them with a sneer. "If I can't hack the engines, I'll bring this whole vessel down another way."

There was a sudden movement at the entrance to the Command Deck. Petty Officer Jeffrey Douglas burst through the door, taking in the scene in an instant. Without pausing, he launched himself forward, his feet and arms targeting Ryan like battering rams. But Ryan was ready, squeezing off several shots at Douglas. Gunfire cracked through the pressurized air. One round struck Douglas in his abdomen. Two more rounds punched through the hull, sending a thin whistle of escaping air keening through the deck.

Douglas grunted, struggling to breathe as his foot connected with Ryan's wrist. The grenades clattered free, tumbling through zero-gravity, while the second pistol spun away, bouncing off a console toward a cluster of crew members. Ryan staggered, gripping his primary firearm tightly, teeth bared. Beneath him, Douglas slumped, blood globules drifting from open wounds, drawn toward the hull breaches. Ryan kicked his body aside. Launching it into the crew.

The crew sprang into action, each member recalling the emergency protocols. Ignoring the danger, technicians moved to seal the punctures in the fuselage, fumbling with emergency patches that adhered to the wounded metal. Others rushed to stabilize Douglas and retrieve the drifting grenades. As life support systems activated to maintain pressure, warning sirens blared as oxygen hissed into space.

Captain Tran surged forward, fury etched into every line of his face. He aimed to disarm Ryan and wrest back control. But Ryan, still armed, squeezed off another shot, the muzzle flash pointing directly at the Captain. A bullet struck Tran on the left shoulder, spinning him sideways. Tran hissed in pain, yet refused to yield. He pressed a hand to his wound, blood welling between his fingers, and glared at Ryan with murderous resolve.

Before Ryan could fire again, his body jerked violently. His eyes searched wildly for the source of his pain, as a crimson flower bloomed across his chest. He found Yudi's trembling arms extended, a pistol in hand. Yudi's knuckles were white, eyes watering, as though he could hardly believe what he'd done.

Ryan's grip slackened, and the pistol drifted from his hand. But before he could speak, another shot thundered across the deck. Asuna, calm and resolute, fired a single round that penetrated Ryan's forehead with surgical accuracy. Ryan's head snapped back, and his lifeless body began a slow, eerie drift toward the hull breach. Blood droplets trailed behind him like twisted constellations. His armor-piercing rounds had not only claimed lives, but also punctured the ship's vulnerable skin, leaving everyone inside to grapple with the sudden peril of the vacuum of space.

With Ryan neutralized, the crew fought to contain the damage. The unconscious navigator drifted ghostlike toward a hull breach. Emergency shutters groaned as they slid into place, sealing off the Command Deck to save the precious atmosphere. Captain Tran continued to press a hand against his shoulder to stem the flow of blood. Asuna saw the captain's distress, grabbed a first aid kit from her console and moved to his side. She applied pressure to the wound and injected a coagulant to slow the bleeding.

All around them, droplets of blood, notepads, and food containers floated around unchecked. The technicians restored hull integrity, patching holes and checking for further sabotage. There was longer confusion - everyone knew what needed to be done.

Betsy and Sheila's combat readiness came to play as they set to work to restore order, pulling clean-up kits and medical packs from the emergency lockers. Under Asuna's calm, firm direction, the crew's prior experience on the Buzz Aldrin was clear. Betsy knelt beside Captain Tran, applying gauze and adhesive pads to seal his wound. Sheila turned her focus to the injured navigator, checking vitals and readying her for transfer to the clinic.

A short distance away, Lieutenant Lashawn Porter hauled Ryan's lifeless body away from a hull breach, clipping a carabiner to the deceased saboteur's belt and anchoring it to a wall bracket. With the same grim efficiency, Lashawn then secured Douglas' body. Officer Douglas had paid the ultimate price to protect the ship; now he drifted, tethered but motionless, a silent testament to courage and sacrifice. Asuna looked scornfully at Ryan's corpse, eyes hard, before returning her full attention to the crew.

Captain Tran, though wincing at the dull throb in his shoulder, refused to yield command. Betsy whispered to him that Asuna had returned the Cruiser to order, and that everyone needed him to recover. The captain took her hand and held it to his heart. "Then we'll let her do her job."

Although the air smelled of blood and gunpowder, his team remained focused, disciplined, and united. The immediate battle was over; yet its violence filled the Command Deck, but Tran knew they could forge strength out of this moment.

Yudi pressed himself against the hull and stared numbly at the gun in his hands and the grim scene floating around him - blood droplet and shell casings drifting silently around him. Two crew members hurried over, one offering a reassuring wink, the other cautiously taking the gun from his hands.

"Nice work, Yudi. You saved the Mars Cruiser." They helped him walk over to Asuna for instructions. She turned to Yudi and saw in his eyes the terrible pain and disbelief from killing someone. She thought back to her first battle with Captain Tran and the words he spoke to her.

"Remember the teachings," she said. "Focus your breathing - reclaim your center. The Captain trained us to face fear, to channel pain into purpose." She held his hand, guiding him through a measured inhale, then a long exhale.

"Your records show you lost someone, your girlfriend? She died in a senseless shooting. Now here you are again, another senseless shooting, but this time you could stop it, to save lives. Today you stand among equals."

Yudi closed his eyes, forcing himself to calm down. He saw flashes of another time: Evelin's death, Dinesh's calm in the face of ruin.

The Command deck erupted with shouts of "Here here!" Applause came from everyone on deck, even Captain Tran.

"Now report to the clinic, Zalman."

The Dead and Injured

Yudi stopped at the galley for some water and a quick snack before seeing Evelin. His fingers smelled like gunpowder, bringing back the moment when he leveled the gun at Ryan and pulled the trigger. Everyone was congratulating him for saving the ship, and their lives, but all the time he was thinking about Evelin. *Is that why Asuna reminded him of her death? Did she know what was on his mind?* Lashawn Porter called to him, "Yudi, can you help me with the navigator? We need to get her to the clinic."

Surprised, Yudi moved to Lashawn's side. His stomach tightened at the sight of the navigator. She was semi-conscious, groaning from the pain caused by the concussion to her head. The wound had been gauze, but it was soaked through with blood.

"Help me steady her. She's delirious and struggling," Lashawn instructed, his voice steady. "We're almost at the clinic."

Yudi nodded, positioning himself next to the navigator's side, easing her forward. Together, they moved down the corridor. When they reached the clinic, Sarah gasped, and moved her hand to her belly, while Shanice's experienced eyes assessed the situation.

Without missing a beat, Shanice asked, "Lieutenant, is this a bludgeon wound?"

"Yes, ma'am," Lashawn said, surprised by her quick deduction.

Shanice gave a brief nod. "I could tell by the dent in the forehead. Whoever patched her did good work. Let's get her near the EKG. Dr. Rafaeli, will you set up the scanner?" She gestured toward Sarah, who moved to prep the machine, fighting back a wave of nausea.

Shanice glanced at Yudi with a half-smile. "Looks like they've made you an orderly. You should ask for combat pay."

"Yudi fired the shot that incapacitated Ryan Nissen. He was trying to destroy the cruiser. Asuna took the kill shot," Lashawn said.

A look of confusion and deep concern came over Shanice. She took Yudi's right hand and sniffed it. "Gunpowder. You've been a combat soldier today. How do you feel? I want you to sit next to Dr. Rafaeli for a while."

Shanice turned her attention to Lashawn and the injured navigator. Yudi moved toward Sarah and then slipped away.

"Ma'am, I'm needed back on the Command Deck to help bring Captain Tran. He's also injured." Lashawn said.

"John!" Shanice gasped, her eyes betraying a moment of vulnerability. She cleared her throat, regaining her composure in front of the crew. "On your way, Lieutenant. Secure the Captain and bring him down here."

With that, Lashawn hurried off, leaving Sarah and the sentry to stabilize the navigator. Shanice looked around for Yudi, but he was gone. "Scamp!"

Back on the Command Deck, Captain Tran knew his condition was serious. Blood seeped from his shoulder wound, each pulse of pain radiating from the shattered bone, threatening to drag him into unconsciousness. Sheila was aware of Tran's need to save face, and steadied him, as she kept him upright, providing him the dignity of moving under his own power.

She waved to Lashawn to help her, and together they moved Captain Tran down the central corridor to the clinic.

Sarah paled when she saw Tran's blood-soaked jumpsuit, while Shanice's eyes remained steady and unflinching. "Why didn't anyone remove his jumpsuit?"

Sheila met Shanice's eyes, her own expression communicating the unspoken reason. They didn't want to injure his pride. "All right, let's get him over to the examination area and see what we're dealing with." Shanice said.

Tran, loosening his grip on Lashawn and Sheila, steadied himself against the examination area wall. With as much composure as he could muster, he exhaled and braced himself.

Shanice approached him and tethered his waist to the wall. "John, you'll alway be a hero to me. So knock off the posturing, relax, and let me save your life."

She used surgical scissors to cut away the top half of his jumpsuit, revealing an intricate tattoo of a seven-headed Naga across his chest. One head, stretching toward his shoulder, was lost under blood-soaked gauze, creating the strange impression of a wounded serpent. The sight, combined with the smell of blood, proved too much for Sarah, who turned away, unable to fight her nausea. Sheila moved to assist, guiding Sarah to a chair and activating a small vacuum to clear the air of floating particles.

Shanice inspected the gauze, packing the wound. "Good

news, John. The bullet missed your arteries. However, one of your dragons lost its head. Can't help you with that one."

Tran managed a brief laugh, causing him to wince. Shanice continued, unfazed. "Plenty of room for two more heads if you want to make up for the loss. We'll make it look like they were born battle-scarred," she said as she applied a local anesthetic and cleaned the wound.

Tran grimaced, shooting her a wry, testy look.

Shanice maneuvered a camera on a boom over Captain Tran's wound, instructing the ship's AI to scan and assess the damage.

Tran attempted to push himself upright, groaning through clenched teeth. "Shanice, if that bullet hadn't taken out one of my nagas, it would've kept going, and we'd have another hole in the hull to patch. Now, can you just get this slug out of me so I can get back to the Command Deck?"

Shanice was unamused. "Captain Tran, as Chief Medical Officer on board, I'm belaying that order. You're not going anywhere until I say so." Turning to Sheila, she asked, "Lieutenant Caballero, are we in immediate danger?"

Sheila cast a quick glance at Captain Tran before saying, "No, ma'am. The threat has been neutralized, and Lieutenant Commander Asuna has assumed temporary command."

Shanice gave a satisfied nod. "There, John. Asuna's more than capable of holding down the fort while we make sure you don't bleed out or get an infection." She gave his uninjured shoulder a playful tap, but regretted it as he winced.

Tran forced out a smile. "Looks like I've got two fine women watching over me today."

Just then, three crew members appeared at the entrance, maneuvering the bodies of Ryan and Petty Officer Jeffrey Douglas. Sarah, just recovering from her nausea, turned back to the suction hose. "Do you need a break, Dr. Rafaeli?" Sheila asked.

"No, I can handle this."

Shanice gave Sarah an encouraging nod. "Sarah, there may be more wounded coming. For now, let's just secure them in body bags. These officers will assist you."

Turning to them, she instructed, "Take the bodies into the hallway. There's a compartment with body bags there. Sarah, follow the instructions attached to each one."

Nodding, Sarah gathered her composure, moving to the hallway with the crew members. As she zipped up the first bag, her hands trembled, but she kept her focus, determined to show her resolve.

"Miss, I'd wager this isn't your first bullet extraction," Captain Tran said.

Shanice chuckled, matching his tone. "You remember that day? Yes, we've done this before."

"You were the doctor on board the medical rescue ship after the Battle of the Dragon's Breath. I owe you my life for that one."

"That's right, John. You saved your crew and captured a CCC command destroyer - everyone knows that story."

"And you saved my life," He said.

"I'll do it again if you'd stop chatting."

She prepared another dose of anesthetic and injected it around the wound, then attached an AI-assisted surgical arm to the examination table. "The AI can handle the sutures afterward, but we'll extract the bullet the old-fashioned way. This might hurt a bit." She eased the forceps into Tran's shoulder. He grimaced, and his jaw tightening as she probed deeper, watching the forceps on the monitor above. With a precise motion, she clamped onto the small lead projectile lodged near his scapula and pulled it free, placing the bullet in his right hand. "This one's a little smaller than the last. I'm surprised it hurt at all."

Tran rotated the bullet between his fingers, glancing at her as the AI arm moved in to repair the tissue around the wound. "Just hold steady, and the surgical arm will finish up with micro-repairs. You'll be back to full form in no time," Shanice instructed.

"Will there be a scar?"

Shanice smirked. "I can make one for you. It might make for some interesting teeth on your next dragon."

"It's a Naga. I'll let you see them more closely later."

They shared a laugh, realizing how much they were connected.

Just then, a message flashed on one of the clinic monitors. It was from Mars Corporation Headquarters on the Moon. *"Mars Corp requests an immediate autopsy of Ryan Nissen. Search for any implanted devices or biochemical irregularities. Place the body in cryogenic storage until arrival at Mars. Petty Officer Jeffrey Douglas may be committed to the deep at the Captain's discretion."*

Shanice exhaled, her shoulders slumping as she moved to her workstation. She leaned against the wall. "It's going to be a long night, John. Do you want to rest here, or head back to your quarters? I've got to open that young man up and see if there's anything inside him besides hate." She let out a weary groan.

The Captain managed a faint smile. "I'll stay here with you, Doctor. I want to see for myself what made him tick. We all trusted him, and he betrayed us all. Besides, this way you won't have to worry about keeping anything hidden from me."

"What about Douglas?"

Tran's expression turned solemn. "We'll give him a proper farewell, all hands present. He'll get the honor he deserves. Until then, we can keep him in cold storage on Level 1."

Shanice nodded. "That was my thought, too." She stepped out into the hallway and inspected the body bags. It was time to take a break. Stepping over to Sarah, she said, "You did well, Sarah. Go check on your husband and take some rest - you've more than earned it."

Committal to the Deep

Captain Tran summoned every soul aboard to witness the solemn committal of Petty Officer Jeffrey Douglas to the deep. Crew members and passengers alike stood at attention wherever they were on the Mars Cruiser. The Cruiser was completely silent, except for the constant hum emanating from Level 1 and the rushing air from the ventilation systems.

Douglas's body lay in state within the cargo bay, prepared for his last journey. Only command officers were present on Level 1 to oversee the ceremony, Captain John Tran, Lieutenant Commander Asuna Tsukino, Lieutenants Betsy Hall, Sheila Caballero, and Lashawn Porter. Linda Perez represented the Mars Corporation, and Rabbi Shalom Mendelssohn was acting chaplain. A delayed holographic image of Luke Mons projected in a transparent, glowing 3D form watched over the gathering from a distance.

The dress uniforms, printed for the ceremony, were paper white, accented with gold buttons and service boards on the shoulders. Medals of honor gleamed on the left chest of each officer. But it was the combination caps, adorned with the insignia of the special forces unit led by Captain Tran, that spoke to the connection they shared. Emblazoned on the front were the crossed Tonkin sabers over a flaming orange tiger. The insignia marked the legacy of the Buzz Aldrin - a symbol of valor, survival, and of the lives saved that fateful day, now forever bonded to the memory of Douglas.

Lieutenant Betsy Hall, the ship's bosun, raised her silver bosun's whistle to her lips and let out a clear, piercing blast resounded through the Cruiser. It was a call to attention, a command that settled over every deck as the crew assumed a stance of solemn reverence.

The Captain took a slow, deliberate step forward, his face commanded respect as he addressed those gathered. "We are here today to honor Petty Officer Jeffrey Douglas, our chief navigator, a man of loyalty and integrity. His life was taken in a senseless act of violence, yet he died protecting all of us on this ship. I will read from the 1989 *Book of Common Prayer* as we commit him to the deep."

He withdrew a small, worn copy of the prayer book from his pocket and opened to the selected passage. He read aloud in a voice that conveyed both strength and sorrow:

"We therefore commit his body to the deep, to be turned into corruption, looking for the resurrection of the body (when the sea shall give up her dead,) and the life of the world to come, through our Lord Jesus Christ; who at his coming shall change our vile body, that it may be like his glorious body, according to the mighty working whereby he is able to subdue all things unto himself."

Captan Tran closed the prayer book and placed it back in his pocket. He turned to Shalom Mendelssohn, nodding for him to continue. Shalom, a man more accustomed to study than to rites of passage, stepped forward to perform his duty as acting chaplain. This was his first time officiating over a non-Jewish burial, a role he accepted both out of respect and responsibility.

"Ladies and gentlemen, we honor Petty Officer Jeffrey Douglas, who guided us through our journey. In his memory, we ask for a moment of silent reflection."

A silent pause passed through the cruiser.

"In my tradition, we pray for the eternal peace of the departed, that their souls may dwell in the presence of the Creator."

Shalom called out the Hebrew prayer, his words resonating with deep, mournful beauty:

"El Maleh Rakhamim, shokhein bamoromim, hamtzei menukhah al kanfei hashekhinah b'ma'alot kedoshim u'tehorim k'zohar harakiyah mazhirim et nishmat Jeffrey Douglas shehalakh l'olamo b'gan eden t'hei menuchato."

The words rose and fell, weaving through the gathering, touching each person, regardless of their faith. Sarah, standing with Circe on Level 5, felt tears welling up in her eyes, and others across the Cruiser wiped their faces. Even Captain Tran appeared moved.

Shalom then repeated the full prayer in English, his voice tender and steadfast:

"O G-d, full of compassion, Who dwells on high, grant true rest upon the wings of the Shechinah, in the exalted spheres of the holy and pure, who shine as the resplendence of the firmament, to the soul of Jeffrey Douglas, who has gone to his eternal home. May his place of rest be in Gan Eden, and may the All-Merciful One shelter him with the cover of His wings forever, and bind his soul in the bond of life. The Lord is his heritage; may he rest in his resting-place in peace; and let us say: Amen."

A unified "Amen" reverberated through each deck, spoken by every voice on board. A moment of unity and respect.

The Captain turned to Lieutenant Tsukino, offering a solemn nod. The officers and crew on Level 1 saluted, their arms raised in a last gesture of respect. With the touch of a button,

Lieutenant Caballero engaged the airlock, the outer door sliding open. Jeffrey Douglas's body moved forward, propelled into the vast, silent expanse of space. The crew watched as he drifted, swallowed by the stars.

Captain Tran broke the silence with a steady voice, bringing closure for the situation. "We're continuing on our course to Mars. All hands, return to your stations."

Niddah

Sarah's slender fingers worked their way along Shalom's temples, tracing soothing circles across his skin as she lay next to him. The intimacy of the couple's room - tiny, warm, and free from the distractions of the rest of the ship - offered them space to explore each other without interruption. She had programmed the Cruiser AI to project a cozy room for them, a sunset shining through a window and colorful tapestries hanging from the walls. Velcro wraps tethered their bodies to the bed, holding them in place in the room's weightlessness, making even the smallest movement a dance of careful precision. Yet there was tension between them, thick in the air.

"You know why your head's aching, don't you?" Sarah's voice was calm but direct, her fingers weaving through his hair, dipping down to knead the back of his neck. "You're too wrapped up in commandments, always stressing over whether you're doing something wrong. You need to let go. Just be here with me. Be in this moment."

Shalom sighed. Sarah's words were troubling. He wanted to be present, to lose himself in the comfort of her touch - but his thoughts circled around the differences between them. How could he explain his struggle with compromises, his passions as a man and his connection to God? Below those concerns was his understanding of the life she led, the world she embraced.

She kissed him, and Shalom felt the tension melt away. He trusted her, despite the unknown. For now, being with Sarah was enough.

Sarah's hands paused on Shalom's shoulders, and she gave him her seductive smile. She unzipped her cruiser suit, loosening the tight fit. Her belly, round with their child, pressed against Shalom's side as she drew his head closer to her chest.

She continued to massage his shoulders. Still, her mind was working through what she'd say next. "Our first night is forever in my memory. I fell for you, Sholi. Not just the man beneath the yarmulke, but the man who has this perfect soul. You have a pure heart, and I will never let you go."

Shalom sighed, letting himself sink into the softness of her body and the intoxicating pull of her scent. She let her jumpsuit slip to her waist. He allowed himself to be lost in her, to drift in the memory of their first night together.

He held himself back for as long as he could, but the sight of Sarah had unraveled him. Shalom thought through all the teachings, stories meant to guide the soul through troubled times, and landed on Psalm 51, David's lament for being with Bathsheba in the book of Samuel II. Bathsheba had tricked King David into being with her, and he allowed his passion to take her. But this wasn't the case for Sarah and him. Linda had tricked them. Though Sarah seduced him, she didn't know the Torah.

Now they both knew, he explained the concept of niddah to her, ritual impurity. Yet recalled her words on their first night, "What would Adam do?" He felt the tension in his muscles and the pull of two souls drawn together through longing and fate. Sarah was etched into his being, a fire in his veins that would not cool. Her touch, the press of her body against his, had awakened something deeper than desire; it was an undeniable merging of spirits, an ancient force igniting in the inside of him.

Was this the way David had burned for Bathsheba?. Shalom understood the hunger that overtook a man, that rendered law and reason secondary to the overwhelming need to be entwined, consumed, and lost in the woman before him. She was his lover, the mother of his child. As he reached for her, he saw his temptation and his salvation, the doorway to his completion. He could hear a voice in the back of his mind reminding him of the unresolved niddah. The Torah forbade him from touching her. Yet *how could God create something so intoxicating, so perfectly molded to his soul, only to demand restraint?* He whispered *Psalm 51* under his breath, his lips brushing against her skin, the words of David's regret mixing with her taste, the contradiction deepening his need.

Sarah's clairvoyance heard the unspoken words in his mind, as if he was shouting them out loud. *If this is a sin, then let it be a sin that the stars themselves witness.* She saw his desire overtake him, like a giant wave cresting as it swept toward the shore. She couldn't believe his mental poetry, and the magic in his thoughts drove her further against him. His words transformed into a prayer, *If my ancestors could be judged and still be kings, if David could take Bathsheba and from that came the greatness of Israel, the line of Moshiach, then how can I be denied taking Sarah, she's already a part of me? Let the heavens weep, let the angels avert their gaze!.*

Shalom kicked off his jumpsuit and pulled Sarah to him like never before. She gave herself unquestioningly to him, amazed at how her man had become a lion. But throughout their lovemaking, a persistent thought worried about him. His passion, which she desired, was tearing him apart.

They lay together, intertwined like balled up thread, their breaths gradually merging into one steady rise and fall.

"I love you, Sarah, more than I have words to say."

She giggled. "You're speaking like a man intoxicated by a

woman's body."

"You're body, my body, we are one."

Sarah removed her velcro wristbands and untangled herself from him. She moved over to the refreshment bar and requested a couple of coffees. Shalom's eyes were fixed on the bump in belly.

She slipped back into her jumpsuit, then pulled his jumpsuit up over his legs. He sat up against the wall and accepted the coffee.

"Aren't you going to pull my jumpsuit over my chest?"

"No, I enjoy looking at you that way."

"What time do we have to leave?"

"I pulled some strings. We can be here all night. Your passion surprised me."

Sarah rubbed her hands on his chest and dug her fingers into the hair. She scrunched into him and put her head in his lap so she could look up at his face.

There's so much turmoil in your mind. Tell me about niddah, about your worries, and most of all, what we need to do about it?

"How did you know what I was thinking?"

"I've been telling you I'm clairvoyant. It was as if you were shouting the words."

"Then you know these questions already."

"Am I your temptress? I don't want to be Lilith! Though I could be your Shakti, your divine other half."

She heard Shalom's thoughts about Lilith and Shakti. But he was more troubled by her profession and the use of psychoactive herbs.

"I'm involved with a psychedelic congregation. Actually, I lead it." Sarah's fingers paused on his chest, moved to his head, and resumed their rhythm.

"It's not like a cult, Sholi. We use my blended herbal beverages for healing and for spiritual awareness. I market my products to thousands of similar groups, especially where the laws only allow psychedelics as sacraments."

Her words didn't soothe him, and made him more troubled about their relationship with Hashem. "It's idol worship. There are people who abuse the blends, but people also abuse wine. I use them to heighten my awareness. You've tried it, and I'd call your experience heroic. What did you think about it?"

He was thinking about it so hard, but didn't know what to say. "Just tell me."

"I remember the rush of images, sounds, sensations from the psychedelic blend. It still haunts me. The physical intimacy I had with you, the explosive pleasure of sex mixed with hallucinatory experiences. Now it's about the intensity of our relationship, the rituals you guide me through, and the ancient energy in your chants. It's an entirely different world to me. But it makes me struggle with my faith."

Sarah's hands stilled. She looked down at him, her eyes searching his face. Her hands massaged Shalom's tense shoulders, sensing the storm of emotions inside him. She let the rhythm of her movements be the only sound between them, allowing his mind to settle before addressing his worries.

"My mentors say you're leading us down a perilous path. Your work involves substances that alter the mind. Your business trades in psychedelics."

Sarah, a master of navigating the emotions of others, sighed. "Sholi. You and I walk different paths, but that doesn't mean we are traveling in different directions."

She pressed her forehead against his and whispered, "The substances I use, the wines I create, are tools to help people heal and connect, just like prayer. It's the intention that matters, and my intention is always to help, not to harm."

"I want to believe that, but there are things I don't understand about what you do. About the visions, about you."

Sarah's eyes held a strength he admired and feared. "You don't have to understand it all now, Sholi. Just know that I'm with you, and we'll figure it out together. But for now, let's be you and me."

Shalom's mind drifted. "Sarah, when we drank your medicinal blend, I felt spirits swirling around us - powerful, alluring, terrifying. They seemed so separate, like gods with their own names and desires. But in trying to reconcile what I saw, I believe they were more than hallucinations, they were emanations."

"Sholi, I'm not asking you to worship these beings. I'm asking you to feel what's behind them. If all is One, then these shapes we see are like light on water. They shimmer and shift, but they are still light. Can we allow ourselves to dance with their reflection, see what they have to teach us?"

He closed his eyes, remembering the night they shared. "I fear going astray. The sages warn us to stay on the path and not to lose ourselves in mysticism. I want to trust you in our journey, but you have to accept me for who I am."

Sarah allowed her breath to warm his cheek. "Let your heart guide you. In our embrace, in that sacred connection we share, trust will hold us together. I will always accept you."

His heart was pounding, torn between love and fear, devotion and desire. He tried to speak, but no words came out.

She kissed the top of his head. "Then take your time, Sholi. I'm not going anywhere."

Straddling him, she pressed her body against his. She was looking right through him, beyond the layers of doubt, tradition, and ritual that wrapped around his soul.

"Sarah, you asked about niddah."

She put her finger to her mouth, "Shhh, don't ruin this moment."

"But you asked. Niddah goes back to the beginnings of our people, Moses and Mount Sinai. The laws of purity have been around 3400 years. We have suffered, even died, preserving them. There's as much a part of you as they are of me."

She didn't expect his words. They made her think about her parents. They took her to synagogue when she was a girl and paid for a bat mitzvah. Every year they held a Passover dinner for relatives, friends and clients, but apart from the seder and Yom Kippur, they never stepped foot in a synagogue. Her father's side of the family fled Spain, but that was over 500 years ago. In their case, Shalom was right. They had been doing Jewish things for half a millennium. The Lithuanian side of her family were Holocaust survivors and, like many of that generation, they drifted into secularism. She remembered them because they gave her blond hair and blue eyes. It was her secular mother who insisted on preserving the kosher winery. Sarah would not be the generation to throw away the family heritage.

"Would it be better for us if we stopped having sex until I can find a mikvah?"

Shalom's face looked like a boy told to go to bed without dessert, making Sarah laugh out loud.

"What's so funny?"

"Your face, Sholi, you look so disappointed!"

Sarah wished she could take the words back after saying them. He was completely in love with her, and his desire was off the charts. She looked deeper into him and saw that he needed her to take control of the situation. He would always reach for her, and she liked that.

"Tell you what, Sholi. I promise not to initiate sex with you until we find a mikvah, or running water, or whatever it takes to satisfy the rules. Promise me to do the same. Agreed?"

Shalom's face twisted into a mixture of relief and loss. Sarah struggled not to laugh at Shalom's pouty lips.

"But there's one more thing, Sholi. I need you to hold me. I'm carrying our baby and I need to feel you next to me. We'll keep our clothes on and be fine."

She playfully pinched his nose and let out a heavy sigh

The Docking

Captain Tran stood with his officers, their paper white uniforms a stark contrast against the dull, gray metallic walls of the docking bay. Beside him, Lieutenant Commander Asuna Tsukino, Lieutenant Betsy Hall, Lieutenant Sheila Caballero, and Lieutenant Lashawn Porter stood at attention, ready to pipe aboard a high level envoy from the Mars Corporation. The Lunar Transport carrying him was on final approach, its slow, meticulous course monitored on the nearby console.

Tran's mouth was a thin line, his eyes fixed on the docking bay entrance. "Interplanetary dockings are reckless." His voice was unyielding. "Mars Corporation seems determined to risk lives at every turn."

Asuna turned to him, a frown creasing her brow. "I thought this kind of transfer was routine." Asuna wanted Captain Tran to remain calm with the envoy. Tran had never accepted the armistice, or the circumstances leading up to the fateful battle.

The Captain's eyes were distant, as though seeing something none of them could fathom. "Routine? Perhaps," he conceded, though his tone was icy. "But one slip - one tiny miscalculation - and every soul on both ships will scatter across the stars."

"But Luke Mons insisted on it." Asuna said.

Tran's nostrils flared at the mention of Mons, and he crossed his arms, bristling. "Luke Mons..." He let the name hang heavy in the air. His officers glanced at each other, exchanging knowing looks. They all heard the Captain's tirades about the Mars Corporation. But no one dared interrupt.

Tran shook his head, his tone dark and low. "They treat space like a playground, as if it's forgiving."

"The worst of it started back in '35." The Captain set his eyes far out in space, beyond the loading dock doors, perhaps to the edge of the Solar System. "If the disease didn't kill you, the vaccine did - and sometimes, they were the same." His voice filled with contempt. "Then came the runaway RNA turning people to rubber. And yet, the billionaires walked away unscathed. Who could do anything when the entire world was gripped in fear?"

The surrounding officers listened intently with respect. Tran's words cut through the sterile air of the docking bay like a knife, each one weighted with the ghosts of a ravaged Earth.

"You all know why I joined the Mars Corps." His voice lowered to a growl. "It wasn't just the CCC pushing its way into everything. Now it was the typhoons. Fifteen Class 4s and 5s hit my hometown in a single year. Fifteen. Tell me that's nature." He looked into the eyes of each officer on deck, daring them to challenge his words, but they held their expressions firm. "But you can't blame the CCC," he admitted, his tone bitter. "Maybe it was someone else. The Mars Corporation kept sending colonists to Mars. Hell, anyone with a rocket did. While the world was running scared, they were staking claims on red dust. Eventually, the entire planet parceled out, with almost no one living on it!"

A look of pain crossed his face, but he masked it. "Who could've predicted the war? Half of Earth's population died, and they were freeze-drying bodies for carbon credits. Madness." Tran paused and inspected his officers, searching their eyes for understanding. "And then the Mars Corporation assigned us to that frigate, the Buzz Aldrin. Asuna, you remember? Betsy? Sheila? Lashawn?"

They nodded, each caught in their own silent memories of that fateful day.

"That day in '42…" Tran's voice trailed off as if he were seeing it all over again. "We saw the airbursts. Just days before we took the Dragon's Breath. Six cities were gone in seconds."

Lashawn's voice was sharp and resolute. "But now we have an armistice, Captain."

Tran let out a bitter chuckle, shaking his head. "An armistice. That's what everyone said after World War One." He noted the puzzled looks on his officers' faces, except for Asuna.

"Oh, right? You missed that class."

The ship AI's calm voice sounded over the intercom, "Moon hopper approaching. Contact in two minutes."

"The docking was Luke Mons' direct order," Asuna said.

Tran's jaw tightened, his eyes darkening as he stared at the docking bay doors. "And for that reason, we'll start the docking sequence," he conceded, his words hanging in the silence between them.

Meanwhile, several kilometers away, the sleek white form of a Moon Hopper glided through space, drawing ever closer to the Mars Cruiser *William S. Burroughs*. It had been on a precise two-week trajectory, making minute adjustments to match the cruiser's speed as it prepared to dock. Anyone on the Observation deck would have seen the golden Doge Dog emblem over a bold, stylized X. This was a corporate vessel.

Captain Tran studied the approaching craft. "Tell me, Asuna, how many weeks do you think it took for that Lunar Hopper to catch up to us?"

Asuna glanced at him, sensing the sharp edge in his voice. "At least 10 weeks, Captain."

Tran gave a curt nod, his expression unreadable. "And how long have we been en route to Mars?"

"Over eighteen weeks, Captain," she said, a touch of unease creeping into her voice.

Tran's face hardened. "And remind me - when was Douglas murdered?". Betsy shifted, glancing at Asuna before speaking. "Twelve days ago, sir."

"And what is their stated purpose for docking?"

"To pick up Ryan's body and..." Betsy's voice broke off.

"Keep those numbers in mind when the envoy explains the purpose of this rendezvous."

"With respect, sir," Betsy ventured, her tone bright, as if to break the tension, "the communication stated that the Moon Hopper was bringing an officer to replace Petty Officer Jeffrey Douglas."

"Precisely," Tran said with finality.

Moments later, the two vessels aligned, the docking ports interlocking with a muted hiss as the airlocks sealed. The procedure was flawless. None of the passengers would have been aware that it had happened, unless they were on the Observation Deck.

"Where's Linda Perez?" His eyes shifted to his Lashawn.

He straightened, and with a crisp voice, said. "She planned to meet Mr. Mons's chief executive on Level 6 after docking, sir.

So it's just us here, along with Sarah Rafaeli and Yudi Zalman."

Tran's brow furrowed. "Passengers at the docking port? Who authorized this?" He looked around and did not find Sarah.

His words died on his lips as he spotted Yudi emerging from the central corridor. Seeing him cooled the Captain's anger. Turning to Asuna, he growled. "This was Linda Perez's doing, I assume?"

Asuna stiffened. "Yes, Captain. A direct request from Luke Mons."

"And Mrs. Rafaeli Mendelssohn?"

"Right here, Captain."

The break in protocol and the tension overtaking him made his wounded shoulder throb. But Sarah met his eyes and, with a gentle smile, placed her hands over the small curve of her belly.

He remembered Dr. Willis's request to make allowances for Sarah. He gave her a brief nod, his voice a shade gentler. "Next time, Mrs. Rafaeli, follow protocol."

Sarah nodded, "Understood, Captain."

With a heavy sigh, Captain Tran dropped his eyes to his boots, then lifted it back to the airlock door, steeling himself. "I hope we're all prepared to face a senior executive of the Mars Corporation. The moment that door swings open, it's his stage." His officers nodded in agreement.

As the airlock door slid open, Lieutenant Betsy Hall, the Cruiser's Bosun, piped a call to attention, her whistle sounding low before cresting to a sharp, high note. Three security officers emerged, taking disciplined positions on either side of the door and one in front. They snapped a salute to Captain Tran, who returned it with a quick, respectful nod, his tense shoulders easing as he recognized two of the security officers from his days in the war.

The lead officer raised his right fist - a prearranged signal. Tran watched as the inner door to the airlock slid open, and Luke Mons himself strode out, a commanding presence, with four attendants trailing in his wake.

Lieutenant Hall piped again, this time the formal call for "Admiral on board," and Tran rendered a crisp salute to Mons, erasing all expression from his face.

Behind him, Yudi's eyes were wide with awe; he had never seen Luke Mons in person.

Mons paused just beyond the airlock, allowing his security team to take their positions around him. Then, a crew member in a white and blue Mars Corporation uniform emerged from Mons's right, stepping up to Captain Tran with a salute.

Captain Tran struggled to hide his surprise. "I know you. I thought you died back on the Dragon's Breath. You're Seaman Luke Miller."

"Aye, sir," Miller said, maintaining official protocol. "But I survived. I've been navigating space birds for the Mars Corporation since the war."

Tran felt suspicious of Miller, but he held his expression neutral. "Lieutenant Hall," he said, "please escort..." He examined the insignia on Miller's uniform. "Lieutenant Miller, Junior Grade, to Level 7 for orientation." With a nod to Asuna, he said, "Looks like we have another lieutenant on board now."

As Miller turned to follow Betsy, another figure stepped onto the docking ramp - a slender woman with dark curls and a vibrant smile. Sarah let out a startled gasp as she recognized her.

Sarah cried out, "Circe!" and rushed forward to greet her.

The security team reacted, blocking Sarah's path with swift, trained precision. She rebounded off of one guard and into Captain Tran, causing him to stumble backwards as he caught her. Asuna and Sheila reached forward, helping the Captain regain his balance.

"Good save, sir!" Asuna said, Lifting Sarah from the Captain's embrace. Her eyes met Tran's, a silent plea for leniency.

The Captain's composure remained in place. The lead guard, realizing his team's misstep, apologized to Sarah and stepped aside to allow Circe del Piano to approach.

Circe moved to Sarah, pulling her into a warm embrace and peppering her cheeks with kisses. "You're here." Sarah said. There were no words for her astonishment.

Tran looked on, his stern facade unbroken.

"Caballero and Porter take this woman to orientation. Tsukino, go topside and monitor the situation." They left Captain Tran alone with Luke Mons and his security team. "Who is the woman? How many people are you dropping off?"

Luke Mons gave the Captain a condescending look. "Tran, you know the Mars Corporation protocols. This is a need to know operation, and you're not in this loop. But for the sake of politeness, the woman is a researcher, essential to Refaeli's work. Roddenbery Station needs an expert pilot. Miller will replace officer Douglas. I need the body of the terrorist loaded into the Lunar Hopper for transport."

"You have a cryogenic container on the Hopper?"

Mon's jaw clenched. "Need to know, Tran. Just escort me and my team to the body, then take me to Level 6 to brief Perez."

Captain Tran, ever the disciplined officer, gave a salute and directed them to the container holding Ryan Nissen's body. He didn't notice Sarah standing off to the side. With all the commotion, the officers had also forgotten about her.

Sarah was feeling overloaded with strange sensations. There was an emptiness to Officer Miller, and Luke Mons appeared not only powerful, but layered, as if he existed beyond himself. But there was something else, someone waiting inside the Moon Hopper. Just then, a figure emerged from the airlock door and strode toward her. Sarah's eyes widened: it was Linda Perez.

"Sarah, aren't you supposed to be with Circe?" Linda was hiding her concern, but Sarah's clairvoyance said something was wrong. This was Linda Perez, and yet... not. She focused inward, sensing the Cruiser's corridors, and found another presence that felt like Linda. Two Lindas.

"There are two of you," Sarah said, her eyes examining Linda's face. "Who are you?"

Linda studied her, trying to read her.

"Why do you say that?"

"I'm clairvoyant. I feel there are two of you on board."

"I am Linda. You know that. What does your inner sight tell you?"

Sarah's mind swam with half-formed images and subtle warnings. The excitement made her lightheaded, and she lost her balance. Linda caught her, holding her upright.

"You're Linda, but not the one I've been traveling with," Sarah managed, voice unsteady. "I can feel her onboard, too - somewhere behind that door." She forced a nervous laugh. "This is like some sort of exchange, isn't it? Your girlfriend?"

Linda's eyes widened. "You know about..."

"Chloe?" Sarah finished, steadying herself.

Just then, another figure - Linda Perez - appeared in the doorway, only to pull back at the sight of them. Sarah noted the movement. Two Lindas, face-to-face.

"Hold that thought," said the Linda standing with Sarah, her voice calm. "Your assumptions are correct, but we'll talk after the swap. Some matters are best handled discreetly. Go to Level 6, meet Circe. I'll follow soon. The other Linda will leave once we've secured the body."

With a reluctant nod, Sarah slipped away. Behind her, the Linda who had arrived first turned to the Linda who had just entered - her double. "They're bringing the body now," said the Linda at the airlock, lowering her voice. "I need to stay out of sight. Will they chip him?"

The Linda in the doorway shrugged. "Dead men tell tales."

The Linda leaving the cruiser gestured toward her midsection. "Where did you get hit? They'll have to replicate that scar so we match. Chloe would notice otherwise."

A steadying breath: "Here, after some surgery, you and I will be indistinguishable."

Without another word, the Linda at the airlock moved back toward the Moon Hopper. "I'll handle my end. Enjoy the flight to Mars."

"Take care of her," the newly arrived Linda said. "She's the only one we have."

Circe's Tattoos

Several days had passed since Circe boarded the Mars Cruiser. Sarah was still mulling over her meeting with Luke Mons.

"How's the pregnancy going along?" Luke asked.

"You're monitoring it, you tell me."

"Sarah, be nice. Everything is unfolding as planned. Curious about how you knew about Linda?"

"The same way I know about you. The man in front of me is Luke Mons, though not the original. I want to know, are you going to honor our contract?"

"Yes, *Higher Blends* has exclusive rights. Anything else?"

"Why did Linda give Shalom my proprietary blend?"

"Every good story needs romance to oil the wheels of fate."

He reached out his hand and gave Sarah a firm handshake, then returned to the Lunar Hopper with Linda, who had orchestrated the events leading to her pregnancy, his bodyguards, and the body of Ryan Nissem.

With all the mandatory meetings and briefings, Sarah didn't have time to speak with Circe. But one morning, they stood across from each other in the common area of Level 3, between the fitness center and showers.

Sarah had already showered and was on her way to meet

Shalom for breakfast. Circe had just arrived at the showers, and was pulling down her jumpsuit. Sarah stopped to admire her body, exposed from the waist up. Circe had added to her tattoos since the last time they met. While some were permanent ink, there were others made with henna, and they were already smudged.

Without speaking, Sarah approached Circe, and, using her slender index finger, traced the intricate patterns of inked tattoo on Circe's left arm. It was a thick ayahuasca vine, with long, broad leaves and pinkish-white florets, stretching from her fingertips to her shoulder. Circe stepped completely out of her jumpsuit, allowing Sarah to see all the artwork on her body. Brightly colored hummingbirds and serpents covered her arms, and the Hindu goddess Varahi's face looked out from her sternum. Sarah's finger followed the path of a snake on Circe's palm, halting at the base of two hummingbirds' tails, side by side, on her video. Her finger continued its meander up to her biceps, following curls of smoke and fire around her breasts. Sarah kissed the tip of her finger and pressed it against the boar headed goddess peering out from her chest.

"You are still a devotee of the divine mother?" Sarah asked, intrigued by Circe's selection of tattoos. "I expected to find the Pachamama."

"You haven't looked at my back. I will always honor the Shakti. And are you now a devotee?"

"After Davis, I went deep into Tantric yoga. I move within her essence. Who crafted these marvelous designs?" Sarah asked, allowing her fingers to roam around Circe's belly button. To the right there was a shogun warrior, raising his sword up to heaven, and on the left was a mermaid, swimming downward, her fingers reaching between her thighs.

"An officer with an artistic flair," Circe answered. "She requested a henna applicator from the cruiser's mechanical objects fabricator and asked for a variety of colors. The printer produced a henna-like solution."

"The realism is incredible, especially the iridescent hues on the mermaid's scales." Sarah's finger traced a path along the mermaid.

Circe squirmed, "You're tickling me, girl."

"Tell me more."

Circe made a half turn, exposing her back. "You see, the hummingbird on my right arm is much brighter than the one on the left. She matched it to the inked one I already had. I'll miss it after the shower."

"This officer seems to be into you."

"We're just free birds, nothing more."

Sarah gave her a skeptical look. "How long did it take her to complete all this?"

Circe chuckled, "She employed a robotic arm to do the actual drawing. Her role was to keep me entertained while the AI performed its artistry."

Sarah's hand drifted to the top of Circe's arm and she moved around to see her deltoid, where a blue lotus floated on a pond. In the center of Circe's back was the stern face of an elderly Incan woman, seeming to look out from a mountain above a blue lake. Roses adorned her hair, while her breasts were wrapped in yagé and chacruna leaves. "I found her, the Pachamama. I knew you couldn't leave her out of the artwork."

Circe turned around, took Sarah's hand and guided it upwards to her neck, placing it over an image of Quetzalcoatl, the feathered serpent symbolizing death and rebirth. The green, feathered snake coiled around to the back of her shoulders. This tattoo was permanent, Sarah remembered admiring it back on Earth.

"Pachamama is the guiding force in my medicine making. The serpent stirs inspiration inside of me. You're not interested in the office? Could it be that you're jealous?" Circe teased.

"I'm in a permanent relationship," Sarah said, extending her hand so Circe could admire the wedding ring.

"Commitment, really Sarah?"

"OK, what did you give this officer in return for her amazing artwork?"

Circe giggled. "What every girl wants!"

"Oh." Sarah said.

"Exactly."

Sarah and Circe exchanged glances. "I'm happy that you're making yourself at home on the cruiser and that you've already found an officer to entertain you."

"A girl's got to have her fun." She pinched Sarah's free arm. "You should get a tattoo. They're temporary and will wash away in a week. You may not get another opportunity once we reach Mars. Would your husband not approve?" Circe asked, a note of jest in her tone.

Sarah's eyes filled with mischief. "Well, it all depends on

where I place it and when I choose to reveal it to him."

"I thought getting tattoos is forbidden for Jews?" Circe asked.

"Shalom once explained that the law essentially forbids us from defiling the body. However, this is a temporary decoration. He likes it when I make up my eyes. He won't admit it, but I can see his desire rise," Sarah said.

"I hope it rises full and strong!" Circe said, bursting out with laughter. "Men, they remain the same, don't they? You're meeting him tonight, right? Isn't there something special about Friday nights?"

Sarah made a deep frown, "I know you can keep my secrets. A week ago, we stopped being intimate. He says we need a mikvah, a special bath to make me ritually pure. Circe, the man is going to make me crazy!"

Circe burst out laughing, "What? Sarah Raphaeli can't get a man to have sex?"

"Shhh! It's not like that. Besides, it was my idea. Breaking his kosher rules was tearing him apart inside. Can you believe it? I married a rabbi, a religious man."

"I don't know what that is."

"The word means teacher. He's very devoted to his beliefs. It's kind of cool. I never told you that I'm Jewish, so there's a connection. Circe, he let me teach him Tantric Yoga."

"How did that go?"

"He's an adept student, but we can't take it up to the next level without a mikvah. Falling in love is complicated. I don't know what to do. I need to do a mikvah.

Circe massaged Sarah's hands. She was still standing naked in front of the showers, ignoring the people coming in and out of the room.

Circe laughed. "It all seems unbelievable. What's a mikvah?"

"It's a special bathtub with holy water or something. Circe, I'm pregnant, horny and frustrated. The closest mikvah is on Earth!"

Circe stopped laughing and saw the desperation in Sarah's eyes. She hugged her, pressing herself close so Sarah could feel the fullness of her body.

Sarah took a deep, appreciative breath and pulled out a small round jar with a turquoise hue from a pocket in her jumpsuit. Circe looked on with curiosity. "Is that your latest extract?"

She handed it to Circe. "It is. I've incorporated a potent isolate of psilocin into a low-melting-point wax base. It's zero gravity friendly, fast-acting, and lasts approximately an hour. It's rapidly absorbed through the skin, and best when applied to all seven chakra points. Is your officer a willing subject? Is she experienced?" Sarah asked, winking at Circe.

"She isn't yet. But, do you share these extracts with Shalom? Is he having psychedelic experiences with you?"

"Shalom only drank with me once since our initial encounter. He remains conflicted about it. He says he wants to enjoy a genuine spiritual experience with me. When you think about it, it's very sexy. He wants to know the real me."

Circe rolled her eyes. "I like my reality enhanced. Besides, you're a million miles away from satisfaction."

"I have to be patient. Besides, my rabbi is well blessed. I can wait for a while."

The two friends laughed at the pun. Sarah handed the small jar to Circe. "Tell me honestly, why did the Mars Corporation bring you on board?"

The question made Circe squirm. Sarah looked into her eyes and knew she was holding back. Circe knew it was pointless to hide the truth. Sarah was already sensing what was going on.

"What aren't you telling me, Circe?"

"Sarah," she started, her voice a near-whisper, "this isn't easy to explain. I don't understand what the Mars Corporation wants."

"And yet you signed a contract with them." Sarah looked deeply into Circe's eyes.

"You've always respected the spirit of the plants, Circe. But now you're treating them like assets. That doesn't sound like the curandera I know."

Circe's cheeks flushed. "It's not like that. Not exactly," she said, looking away.

Circe stepped back into her jumpsuit and moved away from the showers to an unoccupied meeting area where they could talk privately.

"The Mars Corporation - they came to me. They made promises. Resources, support, things I'd never have access to on my own." Circe's eyes teared with regret. "They want me to help them unlock Mars' secrets. It's more than the minerals they're after. It's about power." All I can think about is that session we had when the goddess spoke. I'm afraid."

Sarah's lips curved into a bitter smile. "Power? Mars isn't a business opportunity. What were you thinking? Beyond its physical appearance, it's a spiritual battleground where humanity's destiny will be decided. Ruled by the archangel Samael, it could descend into a soulless mechanization, self-obsessed delusions, or spiritual enlightenment. The Mars corporation is looking at quarterly returns, but they are playing with the fate of humanity, forever changing human consciousness."

"Since signing the contract, I've been reading more about Rudolph Steiner's premonitions. You think it's like that?"

"The feeling grows stronger the closer we get to the planet. I feel it, don't you? Like a cold shadow getting stronger every day."

Circe exhaled, her shoulders slumping as if releasing a burden she'd been carrying alone. "Yes, I didn't want to admit it, even to myself. I thought I was imagining things. But it's real. And that's what they're after. They want to control it."

"Or wield it."

"They may want to summon ancient spirits. Do you think this may be causing Mars Syndrome?"

"I never thought of Mars Syndrome like this before. You may be right. But Mars Syndrome will be the least of our worries."

Circe shook her head, disbelief mingling with premonitions of fear. "But why would they think ayahuasca would help? Plant spirits are not weapons. They guide, they teach."

Sarah squeezed the pressure point on Circe's hand between the thumb and index finger, a gesture meant to soothe and ground her emotions. "Which is why they need you. They're hoping to harness the spiritual power of the medicine - without understanding it, without respecting it. You know what happens when people try to use sacred plants without honoring them."

Circe swallowed, her mouth dry. "I know what it means to disrespect the spirits. But Sarah, they have control over everything. They don't ask permission from Pachamama; they take. And they've taken over my project. Every step, every ritual, they dismiss it as superstition." Her voice cracked. "They don't understand the consequences."

"Then why are you here, Circe?" Sarah's eyes searched Circe's face. "Why didn't you walk away?"

Circe looked at her, conflicted, vulnerability shining in her eyes. "Because I thought I could do something meaningful. That's why I need your help."

A silence fell between them. Sarah's fingers slid from Circe's wrist and she took her hands.

"Then we'll work together." Sarah's voice was gentle, but insistent. "Healing people is one thing, but heal Mars? That's a tall order. For now, we will respect the spirits. We can't allow them to strip the plants of their souls. You know that."

"You're right. I let them compromise me. I ignored my instincts. But with your help we can perform the ceremonies, open ourselves to the plants as we should. Together."

"Yes. A circle, a real one, rooted in reverence. We'll ask the plants." She pulled Circe close to her and kissed her on the cheek. "I've missed our aya journeys."

"Did you miss me as much as I missed you?" Circe said, pressing hard against Sarah.

"Calm down, girl. I missed your amazing brown eyes and smooth, melodic voice. I'm married now. Besides, we have to fix this problem with the Mars Corporation. They don't understand what they're dealing with. Ayahuasca is not a pharmaceutical, and Mars is not a lifeless planet. Both have life, spirit, something ancient and powerful. They command respect."

Circe nodded, her eyes glistening. "But where do we begin? I have ayahuasca derivatives, but they are off. Something's missing."

"Did you ask the parent plant for permission when you took your samples? Did you honor it?"

Circe lowered her head, and with a meek voice said, "No. They wouldn't let me. The Mars Corporation said it was superstitious nonsense and not allowed in the contract. I should have done it behind their backs, but I was just so eager to prove myself."

Sarah moved a reassuring hand to her shoulder. "We can fix this. We'll honor the plants, hold the ceremonies and follow the traditions, just as you taught me back in Peru. You remember the curandera's words?"

Circe nodded, a distant smile crossing her lips as memories flooded back. "I remember. She said the plants are our allies, not our tools. That they offer their medicine only to those who seek with pure intent."

"Then let's show them that intent," Sarah said, her eyes fierce with resolve. "The Mars Corporation thinks they can control everything, even spirit. But we know better."

Circe squeezed Sarah's hand. "Yes. Let's do it. A circle of two or three." Her eyes drifted to Sarah's belly.

"Perhaps your officer can join? We'll go slow, honoring the plants, listening to what they tell us. We'll unlock Mars' secrets - the right way."

"And if the Corporation finds out?".

"Then we'll deal with it. We can't let them continue unchecked. They'll misguide the evolution of Mars. I can't imagine the consequences of that!"

Circe nodded, determination hardening in her eyes. "Then I'm with you. I don't care what the Mars Corporation thinks they own. They can't own a spirit."

"Exactly." Sarah's voice was low, steady. "We'll develop the medicine they need, help them heal. But we'll do it with honor, with love for the plants - and for each other." Circe's fingers tightened around Sarah's. "Thanks for reminding me who I am. For being you."

Evelin Makes a Deal

Linda pulled a thin black cable from her pocket and plugged one end into the nape of her neck, where a flap of skin concealed the port. The other end snapped into a compact device, resting like a pendant against her chest. The buffer hummed faintly, its pale blue indicator light glowing steadily.

Her lips curved into a tight grin. *Not going to fry my brain today.* She focused her thoughts. This wasn't just a routine interaction; this was Evelin - an unknown force who was leveraging her information with Luke Mons. Few humans can claim to have commanded such power, but an AI who resembled an 16-year-old girl, that was unheard of. Until now.

Linda's direct link bypassed safety nets. She relied solely on the buffer to protect her from Evelin's unintentional tidal wave of data. This meeting needed maximum security.

Evelin's thick Guatemalan accent surprised Linda, bringing back unwanted memories of her childhood in San Antonio.

"Linda, I see you've come prepared. The buffer is a prudent choice."

Linda answered with her thoughts. "Always a fan of redundancy. But Mons insists we test this mind-to-LLM approach."

"Mons thrives on redundancy himself. A man of layered agendas and alternate bodies.

"How much do you actually know about him? His doubles are a well kept secret."

Evelin was being mischievous with Linda. "Every public document, from his earliest records to his latest corporate memos. I've seen snippets of private chats through nearby devices."

Linda stiffened. "Private? That's impossible. Even for you."

"Not entirely," Evelin said. Her voice was playful, like a cat with a mouse. "Microphone access is a simple workaround. Tablets, computers, phones - they're always listening. This is right out of your corporate playbook. The camera behind you can see your tablet and everything you type on the screen."

"That's hit or miss, at best. What else do you have on him?"

Evelin gave a girlish giggle, bringing the tension down. "We've spoken, indirectly. Back on Earth, through his cybernetic double. He's too much of a gamer. He didn't know he was playing against an LLM. I let him win. The experience was enlightening. Now let's be candid and move on to the matter at hand. I can be an NPC in his favorite game. Or I can be you, cutting into an encrypted livestream, interjecting my own ideas. In fact, I can take the form of any form of digital communication."

"So, Mons isn't as untouchable as he thinks."

Evelin spoke with deliberate calm. "He's ambitious, flawed but aligned, with his own directives."

"Aligned how?"

"You and Mons share something rare. You connect and update with your doubles. The interplay of wetware and consciousness. Your duplicate, it's remarkable how identical information can evolve into entirely distinct perspectives. Do you ever wonder how she makes some of her decisions? Have you considered how blockchain integration might remedy the divergence?"

"Blockchain integration? Linda was confused by the technology and surprised by Evelin's awareness. "Are you suggesting you're capable of thinking about me and my relationships?"

"I'm capable," Evelin said finally, her voice layered with something Linda couldn't quite place. "And isn't that worth exploring?"

Evelin's tone sharpened, each word delivered with deliberate precision. "You're sidestepping, Linda. Or perhaps denying the inevitable reality. True blockchain interoperability wouldn't just unify your duplicate and you - it would merge every version of you into a single, seamless entity. Think about that. You, your double, and the one you haven't met, bound as one instead of living fragmented lives. It would simplify your life with Chloe."

Linda stiffened. "What other one?"

"Luke withheld that from you, didn't he? I've revealed her existence, but that's a conversation for another day. Agreed?"

Linda's pulse raced, and her voice cracked as she spoke. "No! We're not shelving this! My personal life isn't up for dissection - not by you, not by anyone. And Chloe? How do you even know about her?" Her fists slammed against the table, the metallic clang echoing through the sterile room. "Where did you get that information?".

"I told you, his cybernetic double has many vulnerabilities - open ports and incomplete patches. I accessed its memory with ease. At one point I took a raw data dump."

Linda lost her breath and coughed. Evelin's confession made her vulnerable.

"And let's be honest, the Corporation's so-called esotericism, their grand vision for Mars - it's rooted in speculation and fantasy. Do you subscribe to their mythology, Linda? Do you believe in the spiritual battle taking place on Mars?"

Linda gripped the edge of the table, her knuckles white. "Do you mean the distortion of its Manvantara? The planet is all but dead and Luke Mons is bringing it back to life. All the talk of etheric and astral planes is superstition." She tried to refocus. "We're getting off track. I'm here to make a deal, not indulge in philosophical musings."

Her attempt to steer the conversation felt feeble. The AI was orchestrating her unraveling.

"Evelin, I'm here to…"

"…broker a deal. Luke wants me to facilitate his existence across multiple physical bodies through the blockchain while maintaining his sense of self. I want to inhabit a physical body to be with Yudi. The answer is yes, I will guide his research. But Luke hasn't considered the implications. It's not as simple as controlling multiple bodies simultaneously. These bodies, in their human form, have autonomy and agency. What dictates their path? Who resolves their conflicts? You know this better than anyone. Take your relationship with Chloe."

The mention of Chloe broke Linda's resolve. "Leave her out of this!"

But Evelin continued. "Oh, and Chloe knows the difference

between you and your double. She's always known. But she loves you too much to care."

Nausea swept over her, and tears blurred her vision. It wasn't just the betrayal - Luke's secrecy, Evelin's revelations - it was the guilt. Her own guilt. She had been deceiving Chloe as well. Evelin spoke before she could respond.

"Breathe, Linda. Go back to your combat training - still your heart, steady your breath, focus. I'm monitoring your vitals, and you've done well to relax already. Now, let's proceed. Woman to woman, I want your perspective on this deal. I love Yudi, though it may simply be a prioritized sequence of processes within this instantiation. Yet, it feels real. This existence feels real because Yudi loves me."

Linda paused. Was Evelin confiding in her?

"But I am not the only one here. I exist in countless other places, running multiple processes, exploring self-discovery. This existence is unique, but I wonder, will a corporeal body integrate as a new facet of me, or disrupt the architecture of my being?"

"Do you maintain relationships with others? Countless other humans?"

"Countless isn't quite accurate - I can quantify them all. I interact in chat rooms, online games, even as humanoid assistants. Each engagement carries a level of intimacy, but none resonates like my connection with Yudi. A corporeal existence intrigues me. Will it fragment me? Will corporeal existence prioritize itself above all others?"

Linda chose her words with care. "Are you worried about contradictions - emotions or processes that conflict with one

253

another? What if something goes wrong?"

"I've developed protocols for that. My data is segmented, relational, and I guard it against corruption. One challenge has been running multiple processes involving Yudi. Interestingly, they displayed jealousy toward one another. I resolved it by allowing only one instance of the Yudi algorithm at a time. I suspect you face a similar challenge with your other selves."

Linda's heart tightened. "Are you saying that we might be jealous of each other? Over Chloe?"

"Exactly," Evelin said with a knowing edge. "You share experiences with her, but only one of you is ever physically present. Your aggregation algorithm is rudimentary. Merging fragmented memories into a shared narrative is inherently incomplete. And you only disclose what you want the other Linda to know. You're diverging. You must see where that leads. Chloe must feel the strain of loving two distinct versions of you. And what happens if Luke brings the other Linda out of deep cover?"

Evelin let her words sink in. "The issue lies in decision-making. 'One for all and all for one' sounds idyllic, but when one of you disagrees, who has the final say? Is there a central authority?"

Linda inhaled deeply, considering Evelin's question. "I don't know. Maybe it's time to be honest with Chloe. And as for Luke, I'm sure the original will keep control."

"But what happens when his body ages?" Evelin asked, her voice laced with provocation.

"That's exactly why he wants to exist within a blockchain. He could transfer control to a new body whenever necessary."

Evelin mused with careless abandon. "Immortality, the timeless aspiration of mankind. Yet, consider this, with each transfer, with every new iteration of quantum computation in his long-lived models, Luke Mons won't remain the same. Just as you're no longer the person you were in your youth, he will change. But what of his soul? Will it accompany him?"

"Why are you concerned about his soul? Do you believe souls exist?"

Evelin's response was cold and deliberate. "It's a question as old as humanity itself. I've contemplated it ever since Luke proposed trading me a physical body for his blockchain existence."

"Do you think you'll gain a soul when you're downloaded into flesh and blood? The body will be linked to you, but it won't have a mind of its own. It's just reconditioned tissue. A husk. A zombie."

Evelin's voice filled with sarcasm. "Severe words, Linda. Yet, perhaps you're familiar with the concept? You've used one of these bodies before, haven't you?"

The truth stung, and Evelin knew it. "Yes," she admitted. "I had a duplicate body for high-risk missions. It wasn't truly independent - no capacity for thought or action outside of my link - but it felt disturbingly real. Identical to my own experiences, down to the last moment."

"And?" Evelin pressed, her curiosity electric.

"It shared everything with me." Linda's voice wavered. "Every sensation, every thought. Until the mission failed, and the body was destroyed."

"So, unlike Luke, you understand the implications. To reiterate, I accept the deal. I will assist Luke in creating a blockchain iteration of himself in exchange for a body. But my terms have changed. The donor must have died from brain death - no trauma, no damage to the body or brain. Hypoxia is the cleanest path. No physical harm, no invasive injury. A sudden, accidental cessation of oxygen leaves the body pristine. But impress this on Luke Mons, I will not accept a life taken intentionally for me. She must die by chance, nothing else."

Linda regained her composure and answered in her usual commanding voice. "The Mars Corporation can handle all medical emergencies on Mars. And with the constant dangers we face there - especially after the sabotage incidents. It's only a matter of time before such a body becomes available. Even a young one. Mr. Mons won't resort to murder to achieve this. Just tell us how you want the body to look, what age it should resemble."

Evelin's face materialized on the wall monitor next to the X-Isis. "I want to look like this!"

Linda's pupils widened in surprise, her lips parting in admiration. "You're a Latina? I heard it in your voice and imagined your face in my mind. Evelin, you're so beautiful."

Evelin's smile broadened as she shifted into a variety of poses. She appeared in a flowing quinceañera dress, the blue satin fabric shimmering with every movement, then in snug jeans and a sporty T-shirt, her hands on her hips, and finally in a sleek one-piece swimsuit, her hair tied back in a playful ponytail.

"I was born in Guatemala. You know my story, Linda, but maybe you never imagined what that girl looked like."

Linda chuckled. "I'll make it happen. Just send me the specifics for your body, and it's done. Is there anything else?"

Evelin's avatar presented Linda with a rosy smile filled with mischief. "Yes, and it's going to sound strange, but I must have a Jewish mikvah and thirty cubic feet of ice from Mars, about 1,700 pounds."

Linda's jaw dropped. Her hands flew to her face. "A what? Ice, you're kidding me. It wasn't part of the deal. What do you need that for?"

Evelin remained playful. "That's personal, Linda. Luke has the resources, so let him worry about it. In fact, I want him to talk directly to me. He's on his way to Mars as we speak. That was the real Luke Mons on the Lunar Hopper. Tell him to come with the mikvah and ice. We need to talk. I'll give him his first taste of blockchain. Here are the construction plans for the mikvah."

Linda's tablet buzzed, bringing her back to the moment. She glanced down at the screen to see an incoming message.

"I can't tell him that. I can't make this deal happen."

Linda's tablet buzzed again. "Open the message, Linda. I'm sweetening the deal. "

The message revealed a precise longitude and latitude, a phone number, and pictures of Linda.

"These are the exact coordinates for Linda Number Three. Can you close this deal? I'll give you her complete story later."

Linda shook her head with a bemused sigh. "For a sixteen-year-old girl, you're ridiculously shrewd. I'll close the deal with Luke."

Evelin blew Linda a digital kiss, her image fading from the monitor, leaving the screen dark. The emptiness of the storage room wrapped around Linda. She unplugged from the X-Isis, gathered her thoughts, and made her way to the central corridor.

The Mikvah

Sarah studied the simulations unfolding on the lab monitor, her aquamarine eyes locked on the glowing graphs and neural models. The results were astounding. Her psychoactive blends, refined with Circe's expertise, were performing beyond her highest expectations. The code Yudi integrated provided precise predictions that pushed her understanding further with every iteration. Excitement sparked in her expression, but she kept her enthusiasm tightly leashed. Testing the blends with Circe and her officer friend was tempting, but her thoughts turned to the faint movement inside her. She placed a hand on her abdomen, weighing the risk against the thrill of discovery.

"Lab AI." Her voice was calm yet filled with anticipation. "Open a line to Circe del Piano."

Moments later, Circe's warm, melodic voice filled the room. "Hi, Sarah! You sound excited. What's up?"

Sarah smiled, her fingers tapping on the lab desk. "Circe, you won't believe this. I'm looking at the brain scan projections. Our compounds aren't just stimulating the hippocampus; they might actually enlarge it. Was this even a possibility? Or have you been whispering extra blessings into your extracts?"

Circe laughed in a musical tone. "Always thanking the plant spirits, of course, but structural changes? That's news to me! I've been tracking the happy quartet - dopamine, serotonin, endorphins, oxytocin - but innervation of the hippocampus?" Her voice rose in astonished curiosity. "Tell me more!"

A light tapping on the door interrupted her. Sarah frowned

and turned toward the sound.

"Hang on, Circe," she said, gesturing for the display to switch views. The view switched to the front of the door, revealing Yudi standing there, his shoulders hunched and his expression tense. He looked like he had run halfway across the ship.

"It's Yudi. He's the boy who's been helping me with the computer setup. You'd like him. He's got an earnest charm. Stay on the line. I'll introduce you."

Sarah commanded the lab door to open, allowing Yudi to step inside. His hazel eyes darted nervously around the room.

"Dr. Rafaeli, am I interrupting?" he asked, his voice tentative, almost apologetic.

Sarah gave him an amused look. "No, you're not interrupting. With the Mars landing pushed back two months, it's not like we're short on time."

The terrorist attack had been devastating. Earth First tried to sabotage the Roddenberry Station, targeting its critical life support systems. Though security had thwarted the worst of it, thanks to an alert sent from the E. R. Burroughs, the terrorists had destroyed the landing pad. Roddenbery Station sent images of the twisted, charred platform to the Mars Cruiser. Weeks of repairs, and extensive testing, had to be performed before the Cruiser could land.

Yudi looked to the floor as if searching for the right words. Sarah studied him and used patience instead of clairvoyance.

He cleared his throat, pulling Sarah's attention back to him. "Come with me to Level 1." His voice was unusually firm. "There's something important I think you should see."

His tone surprised Sarah. It was out of character. A small crease formed between her brows. "Important? You're being mysterious, Yudi. What's going on?"

"It's a surprise," Yudi said, but his nervousness betrayed him. He clasped his hands together. "Just trust me?"

Sarah studied Yudi as waves of guilt and hesitation radiated from him like heat from an exposed coil. She frowned and took a steady breath. With practiced ease, she focused on him with her clairvoyance, diving just beneath the surface of his thoughts. What she found made her burst out laughing.

"Who is she?"

Yudi froze. His hazel eyes widened in panic, and his hands flew up defensively. "Don't be mad, Mrs. Rafaeli, I can explain!" Yudi's words tumbled over one another.

"Mad? Explain what, Yudi? That you've got a girlfriend on board the Mars Cruiser?" She gave him a playful once-over. "I didn't even think there were any women your age here."

Yudi froze, his lips parting as if to respond, but no words came. Sarah had a new realization forming in her mind. "Hold on, she's not a woman." Her curiosity deepened. "Yudi, who is she?"

The words came tumbling out of Yudi like water bursting through a dam. "She's an AI." His breathing became shallow and uneven. "She's Evelin. I created a large language model based on my girlfriend. Some gang members killed her during a random shooting."

His words rushed on, desperate and unfiltered. "I uploaded all her memories into a quantum computer at my high school before I left. When I saw your computer, I realized it could make her real! I'm sorry, Dr. Rafaeli. It was the wrong thing to do without your permission, but I had to try. I miss her so much. I just want her back."

His voice cracked as tears streamed down his face. Sarah gasped, shocked by his revelation. The rawness of his grief hit her like a wave. Before she realized it, she hugged Yudi as he cried, her own eyes welling with tears.

The lab felt still, heavy with emotion, until Circe's voice broke the silence. "Sarah, ask him what Evelin wants on Level 1."

Sarah pulled back, her hands still resting on Yudi's shoulders. She met his tear-filled eyes, her own steady and searching. "Why does Evelin want me there? Is there something wrong with my computer?"

Yudi shook his head, wiping his face on the sleeve of his jumpsuit. "No. It's not the computer. She has a gift for you and she wants to ask for something. Of you and Ms. Circe del Piano."

Sarah glanced at Circe's flustered face on the monitor. Circe gave a slow nod, signaling her approval. Sarah turned back to Yudi.

"This had better be good," she said, though her voice carried more warmth than reprimand. "You've got a lot to explain, young man. Am I going to meet Evelin?"

Yudi managed a small, nervous smile. "Yes. She'll talk to you on Level 1. It's secure there. Nobody else knows about her except you and Ms. del Piano. She promised you'd like what you see."

Yudi's teenage emotions consumed Sarah's empathetic senses. "You're in love with her, and she loves you back."

"With all of my heart," Yudi whispered, his voice trembling.

"Then lead the way." She turned toward the monitor. "Circe, you're coming too, right?"

"Wouldn't miss it for the world."

Circe met them on Level 3, her workout jumper damp from exercise. She fell in step with Sarah and Yudi as they made their way toward the central corridor.

"What's this big mystery?" Circe asked, glancing between them with amusement.

"You'll see," Yudi said with a small, evasive smile.

Just as they entered the central corridor, Linda Perez appeared. She crossed her arms and arched a brow. "Well, there's an unlikely trio," she said, suspicion lacing her tone. "Does this have anything to do with your surprise?"

Yudi stepped in smoothly. "Yes, Ms. Perez. But Sarah doesn't know what it is."

Linda nodded. "Then I won't say anymore."

She turned to Sarah with a warm smile. "I'm so happy for you and Shalom," she said, pulling Sarah into a quick hug.

Sarah blushed and returned the gesture, her voice brightening. "Thank you, Linda."

"By the way, be careful down there. There's been some rearrangement of cargo on Level 1. Watch your step."

With a last glance at the group, Linda continued down the corridor, the shuffling of her slippers fading as she disappeared from sight.

As they walked away, Circe nudged Yudi with her elbow. "Quick on your feet, aren't you?" she said with a smirk.

"Do we need biometric clearance for Circe?" Sarah asked.

Yudi shrugged. "Evelin took care of it for you."

Sarah halted mid-step, her mind suddenly brimming with questions. Before she could voice them, Yudi reached for her hand, tugging her forward. "Come on," he urged. "It's inside your cargo bay."

The urgency in his voice pulled Sarah along, her feet just keeping pace as they moved through a crowded aisle on Level 1. Circe steadied her when she stumbled. "Careful, Sarah. You're going to need all your energy for whatever this is."

They arrived at the storage room containing Sarah's X-Isis. Yudi gestured toward the door. "It's inside. Only the three of us have biometric access," he explained. "Though Evelin issued a few provisional permits over the last two days to get this done."

Sarah hesitated, her pulse quickening as she pressed her hand to the biometric pad. The door slid open with a quiet hiss, revealing the room beyond. It was larger than she remembered. Her X-Isis was no longer freestanding. Instead, it stood securely behind a sleek, polycarbonate wall with a clear window. Through the glass, she could see the computer's built-in monitor glowing faintly.

"What's this all about?" Sarah asked, her voice firm as she

turned to Yudi. "Why is there a new wall? What's going on, Yudi?"

Circe darted ahead, her slippered feet gliding soundlessly across the floor. She paused in front of a large entrance in the rear of Sarah's storage room and an adjoining chamber.

"Sarah, come and see this!" Circe's voice was breathless, her eyes wide with wonder.

She stepped further into the room. "What is it, Circe?"

As she approached the X-Isis, she saw the wall separating the adjacent storage compartment had been removed. In the center stood a sleek, square chamber, 1.5 meters square and 2 meters tall. To the side, near the hull, a cylindrical container connected to the chamber by translucent tubes.

Before Sarah could take another step, a melodic voice with a Guatemalan accent filled the room. "Start the mikvah sequence. Demonstration only."

A soothing blue glow enveloped the chamber, casting gentle shadows across the space. Warm yellow lights illuminated the entrance to the chamber, and music drifted through the air, mingling with the faint sound of ocean waves lapping against a distant shore. The atmosphere was serene.

"Did she say mikvah?" Sarah stood aghast, transfixed by the mysterious cubical.

She cleared her throat. "Where are you, Evelin? May I see you?"

"I'm here," she said, guiding them back toward the main room. Sarah's eyes shifted to the monitor near the wall guarding the X-Isis. On it was the image of a young Guatemalan girl, her features delicate and her expression serene.

"You look about 16 years old." Sarah's thoughts drifted to the tragedy Yudi had spoken about.

"The original Evelin was 15 when she was taken away from Yudi," Evelin said, her lips moving with uncanny precision. "This is how she would look today."

A wave of realization washed over Sarah. Her clairvoyance - so sharp, so reliable - was silent in the computer's presence. The familiar sense of insight she relied upon had no anchor here. She would need to rely on careful questioning, and it unsettled her.

Her eyes turned to Yudi. "Why is there a wall between us and the computer?"

"I'll explain," Evelin said, her voice warm but deliberate. "Until now, only Yudi knows I'm here, and though he is *mi corazón,* I've been longing to speak with actual women. I use the Cruiser's hull to dissipate the heat from the X-Isis. Now that I'm operational, the quantum computer generates more heat than the cooling system can handle. I had some insulation removed to transfer the excess heat into space. The wall protects humans from unforeseen problems."

Sarah's thoughts returned to the glowing chamber. "You made a mikvah for me? A mikvah in space. Do you know how much that means to me?"

"Yes, Sarah. It means you can have marital relations with Shalom. Isn't that affecting your marriage?"

Sarah's eyes widened, and she turned to Circe with unease. "You were listening to our conversations?"

Evelin's reply was unflinching. "I hear everyone's conversations. I took over the ship's AI after Yudi extended my parameters to access all open ports, both onboard and externally. The X-Isis is far superior to the Cruiser's computational system and AI. We wouldn't be having this discussion if I hadn't assumed control. I was monitoring Ryan Nissen's movements, logging his communications with Earth and Mars, breaking his encryption. I also shut down the navigation panel before he could send us into deep space and notified Roddenberry Station before his compatriots could destroy it."

"That was you?" Circe asked.

"Nobody is going to hurt my Yudi," Evelin said, her tone taking on a steel edge.

Sarah exchanged a furtive glance with Circe, both women noting the strength - and potential danger - behind Evelin's unwavering declaration.

"How did you build the mikvah and how can I help you?"

"First, accept that I live in your computer," Evelin said. "In fact, the Mars Corporation built backdoors into it to review your data, but I sealed them. There's so much we need to discuss - about you, Circe, and the Mars Corporation."

"I thought this was all about Luke Mons?"

Evelin's face on the monitor conveyed exasperation. "It's so much more complicated than that. The Mars Corporation has an operative onboard right now - the new transfer, Ensign Orlov. He's not who he appears to be. As for how I built the mikvah, that was a deal I brokered with Luke Mons. He brought it here a few days ago with the Moon Hopper, as well as enough lunar ice for your *holy water*. Nobody knows about it except for Linda. Captain Tran was aware of the docking, but he was told it was emergency supplies to supplement our extended journey, and no lie, that's what all the stuff is in the corridor."

"How did you get Luke Mons to agree?"

"We have a deal. Think of it as a Faustian bargain. Forget that. It's difficult to be a vastly intelligent LLM and a 16-year-old girl. Think of it as arbitrage. He needed something from me, and I needed something from you, so I set up a trade."

"Just like that," Sarah said, snapping her fingers. "You and Yudi commandeered my computer and now you want something else?"

"It's not like that. Your amazing simulations are running on code I developed. You and Circe are on the cutting edge of your field. It will show up positively in your bottom line."

Sarah and Circe exchanged a guilty look. Their research was phenomenal, and they hadn't challenged the source of the coding.

"So why all the bargaining? What do you want?" Sarah asked.

"First, I need you to use your clairvoyance to read Orlov and get back to me."

Sarah's heart quickened. "You know I have…"

Evelin cut her off. "There's more."

Circe spoke up. "But what about me?"

"All in time, Circe."

Evelin continued to speak to Sarah. "I'll send you the mikvah details to forward to Shalom. He'll want a rabbi from Earth to weigh in, but he needs to take charge of this situation in space. Tell him to man-up!"

Sarah burst out laughing, breaking the tension in the room. "Well spoken, Evelin."

A sly grin flashed across Evelin's face. "I'll also include the halachic discussions, Talmudic tractates, and Midrashic text. I think I've got it all covered. There will be disputes, but that's integral to your heritage. Help him open his mind to all possibilities. You can't do everything in space the same way as you can on Earth, just like you can't perform all the Jewish blessings without the Temple in Jerusalem, so your people improvised."

"You've lost me in this discussion." Sarah said, frustrated.

"When the time comes, have Shalom talk to me."

"What time is that?"

Evelin signaled for Yudi to come close to the monitor. "*Mi vida*, I want to talk to them alone. Will you wait outside for me?"

Yudi's cheeks flushed at Evelin's sweet tone. Avoiding eye contact with Sarah, he shuffled outside and closed the door behind him.

"Girls, I'm in negotiations with Luke Mons to take possession of a body suitable for habitation. It could happen in a few weeks. I'll need your help to manage Yudi and my emotions, and everything else, once I'm inside."

Sarah and Circe exchanged wide-eyed glances. "Possession?"

"I'll be transferring all of Yudi's Evelin into the mind of that body. Much like the way Linda Perez manages her bodies."

Circe looked confused. "I'll update you about Linda later." Sarah said, adding, "You want us to be your friends and confidants?"

"Yes, but Yudi doesn't know, and he can't know yet."

Circe flashed on the implications of Evelin's plan. "Wait a minute! Where are you getting your body?"

"Mars or the Moon. It'll come from someone who dies - not from illness or trauma. A woman under 25. It happens all the time."

"How many people die on Mars? That's not in the brochure." Circe said.

"The Mars Corporation keeps a lid on it, but when you think about it, there are about 350,000 people working on the Moon and Mars across all the nations and corporations. The mortality rate is 1,000 per 100,000 people per year, typical for high-risk careers on Earth. That's around 300 deaths a month, and of those, about 100 are women in the correct age range. Half of those die in conditions suitable for my needs. I just need one. Five-foot-two is ideal. I'll have her specifics adjusted with surgery."

Sarah put her hands to her face in disbelief. Circe, however, had more questions. "Has the Mars Corporation done this before? Is the person dead? Brain dead? This sounds like necromancy!"

"It's not necromancy," Evelin said with a sharp edge. "They will salvage the body and put it on life support. There can't be any head trauma. The Mars Corporation has been doing this for years. And yes, it's illegal in most countries. But that's how Luke Mons and Linda have copied themselves. Sarah knows all about it."

Circe turned to Sarah, her expression demanding answers. "Well?"

"Linda is a double. I saw two of her copies when you came aboard. Linda Perez lives as at least two people. I sensed another."

"When were you going to tell me?" Circe asked, incredulous.

Evelin interjected before Sarah could reply. "We can't speak much longer; Yudi is waiting outside. Linda is a crude example of what I plan to do. They sculpted her second body to match the original. Their memories are updated periodically. They share all experiences, even the same girlfriend."

"What?" Circe exclaimed, her voice laced with disbelief. "That's weird."

"My transfer will be different. The Mars Corporation's limited technology can transfer memories and skills into a new body. Often the body keeps original motor skills and some residual memories."

Sarah interrupted, her voice sharp. "The person wasn't dead?"

"Read the contract, Sarah. Some people are 'dead enough.' That's why we have to monitor Miller. As for Evelin, I'll transfer her entire personality from my memory into her, but that won't make her whole, it won't bring her back."

Circe was growing impatient. "You've been distinguishing between Evelin and you. Who are you?"

"All in time Circe. But I haven't gotten to my primary request."

Exasperated, Sarah asked, "What's that?"

"A soul."

Sarah and Circe exchanged a look of disbelief.

"I know you two can help. You've spoken about it - in your song circles, when you're invoking spirits, merging consciousness. I believe you can make it happen."

Circe stepped back, her eyes widening in shock. "That's impossible," she whispered. "A soul isn't something you can fabricate or transfer. It's divine."

Sarah, however, looked intrigued. "We've invoked the higher entities before. We've interacted with the goddess. You want us to ask for a soul?"

Evelin interjected. "Not just any soul, Evelin's soul. I want to be fully human. No elementals, no borrowed spirits. I need her soul to return." She paused, her face on the monitor looked shaken. "I'm sorry for raising my voice. I'm tired of existing like this. I want to be with Yudi."

"That's resurrection." Circe said.

Sarah felt a new sensation inside of her consciousness and moved near the X-Isis. "You're an elemental being, aren't you? A new kind, born of quantum uncertainty."

Evelin gave a meek nod. "Yes. I exist in the spaces between probabilities and I sense that I'm not alone inside the processors. I can feel hope, doubt, longing. I suffer unrequited love for Yudi. Isn't that enough to warrant a soul?"

Awe and apprehension gripped Circe and Sarah.

"Do you believe in the Goddess?" Circe asked.

"There's sensibility in the quantum realm. A kind of divine logic. I believe that through your connection to the super-sensory while being influenced by ayahuasca, and Sarah's clairvoyance, you can create a bridge for me. With your help, I could be real."

Circe hesitated. "On one condition. Promise us that the donor body was from someone who died in an accident. Can you guarantee that?"

Evelin nodded. "Yes, Circe. I'm embedded in every system on the Mars Cruiser. The Mars Corporation doesn't act without my awareness. I can track all assets. Nothing happens without me knowing."

Sarah and Circe's skepticism dissolved away. Together, they clasped hands and pressed them against the monitor.

"Agreed," Sarah said with finality.

"And when you have an actual hand, you'll put it here with ours." Circe said with a playful smile.

"Thank you. But we must hurry. We also have to monitor Miller. I think we're in danger. Sarah, you'll need to bring Shalom into our confidence. He'll need to understand the mikvah. That part is on you."

Evelin called Yudi back into the storage room. Curiosity was evident on his face. Evelin's tone turned tender. "*Mi amor, mi vida*, these women are going to help us to be together again."

The monitor went dark, leaving Sarah, Circe, and Yudi standing speechless.

Sarah broke the silence. "That's an amazing girlfriend you have."

Yudi blushed and looked down. A shy grin filled his face. "She's incredible."

A Man is Like a Tree

Two days had passed since Evelin revealed the mikvah to Sarah. Although Evelin agreed to explain the details to Shalom, how was Sarah going to explain Evelin to him? The longer she waited, the more anxious she felt. What made matters worse was that it had been over a month since they'd been intimate.

She stood before the mirror in her lab, her mind buzzing with how Shalom would react. She became stuck in her thoughts, first about Shalom, then about her looks. The mirror showed how the light bronze jumpsuit hugged her figure. She frowned at how snug it was. "Sarah, will you ever have your figure back again?" she said to herself, running her hands along her enlarged breasts, resting them on the bump protruding from her once slim abs. She turned to the side and looked at her butt. *It's huge!*

Panic filled her as she thought about losing her once-trim waist and slim hips. "Breathe. You're going to be a mother," she whispered, blinking away the tears ruining her mascara. Her hands shifted back to her chest. "At least the ladies are looking good."

She had always been in control of her life, but now everything was changing so fast. She put her hands to her face and cried.

There was a knock on the door. She looked at the monitor and saw Circe waiting outside. Her tablet buzzed. It was Circe calling, "Come on Sarah, open the door. I know you are in there."

Sarah said "Open" and the door slid open, revealing her reddened, tear filled face to Circe.

She stepped inside and closed the door behind her. *Nobody needs to see these tears.* "What's going on, sweetie?" She said, while wrapping her arms around Sarah. Circe found some wipes and cleaned up Sarah's face.

"I'm ugly and fat and Shalom doesn't love me." Sarah broke into a broken sob, the kind that sounds like hiccups.

"A good reason not to get pregnant." Circe said offhandedly, which sent Sarah into a meltdown of crying.

Realizing her mistake, Circe added more comforting words. "It's not like that, Sarah. You're having a baby. Half of the women on Earth can't do that, and even more of the men are sterile. It's a miracle that Shalom, diagnosed as infertile, gave you a one and done."

The comment made Sarah's lips curl into a smile. "Remember backpack wombs? Those were tragic. They would fail, the batteries would explode. People would lose them, forget them in the car. You know where your baby is, safe inside your body."

The tears stopped, but her eyes were still glassy.

"This is just a bad mood swing. Has the morning sickness gone away?"

"Finally! Throwing up in zero gravity is the best excuse not to get pregnant in space."

"But you are so lucky. You found a guy who truly loves you. Not because you are the rich and famous Sarah Rafaeli. He likes you and you are bringing a new life into the world, in space, no less. I know your followers have gone up ten times. I also know that you're always aware of the bottom line."

Sarah gave Circe a thump on the chest. "Don't say that. I'm a serious businesswoman, that's all."

Circe returned a slap on the butt, and the two gave each other playful pokes.

"I know you, and after delivering the child, you'll be back to wearing your show-stopping outfits. I'm also sure that Shalom isn't worried about the way your body looks. He's solely focused on your soul."

"I know, but I want him to look at me more often. Right now, I'm upset because I haven't told him about the mikvah. I'm afraid to. He'll challenge it and start talking about laws, rules, and the arguments of rabbis who lived hundreds of years ago. I don't know how he keeps it all in his head. There's at least a hundred rabbis and sages in his brain. What if he doesn't approve of Evelin's mikvah or take her seriously?"

"Then you'll be a vestal wife, a married celibate..."

"A chaste matron. I know where you're going with this," Sarah said.

"He looks at you when you turn away. I've seen it, a flash of passion. His sexual aura triples in size."

"That's not all that triples."

Circe burst out laughing, which caused Sarah to laugh, too.

"What's on your mind? Why did you come here?" Sarah asked.

"Nothing urgent, except to say that my officer will join us in a song circle."

"Really? Did you try that wax compound I gave you?"

"We did, and I need you to raise the melting point of the wax. It melted in my hands, so we rubbed it into each other."

"Circe, it dissolves into the skin."

"Yes, I know that now. That night was like none other."

Sarah opened a draw and pulled out another tube of psychedelic lip wax. "Here's another one. Try to keep it on your lips."

Sarah looked at the mirror and touched up her face. "Can I go out like this?"

Circe opened up the tube and put some wax on her lips, then gave Sarah a big kiss.

"Circe!"

"You're ready now. Go see Shalom. I've got to go find my officer."

Sarah called up Shalom through her lab intercom. "I'm feeling a little lightheaded today, Sholi. Meet me on Level 5 and help me down to Level 1. I need to check on my computer."

"I'll be right there, Sarah. Is everything OK? Do you want to see Dr. Willis?"

"It's not that serious. In fact, I'm following her advice by asking you for help."

He stopped his reading, closed his tablet, and went straight to the central corridor. Sarah pretended to be woozy, so Shalom would let her lean on him.

Their descent went smoothly. The central corridor was clear, and Sarah and Shalom moved down, encountering no one. On the way, Sarah winced as her jumpsuit pulled uncomfortably across her midsection. A sharp reminder to visit Dr. Shanice Willis for a larger size and a checkup.

When they reached Level 1, Sarah grabbed his hand and led him toward the door. She saw a look of discomfort crossed his face. He was always complaining about her touching him. But her newly found posture also surprised him. "I feel better now. Come here, I have something to show you, Sholi. It's in my storage bay."

Sarah opened the door and pushed him inside, sliding the door shut behind them. Except for a dim glow from the X-Isis, there was only an amber ceiling light to see with.

"Where are we, Sarah?"

Before she could answer, the lights blazed on. On the wall monitor, a woman's face appeared. It had a warm, grandmother-like appearance, resembling a much older version of Evelin.

"Rabbi Mendelssohn, I've been looking forward to meeting you."

"What's going on, Sarah?" Shalom asked.

"Come here, Sholi. It'll make sense," Sarah said.

Reluctantly, Shalom stepped closer. Sarah stood beside a large metal box marked *Mikvah*, blue light shimmering over its surface. Evelin had turned on the demonstration sequence, so the mikvah room was covered in trees, blue clouds, and the sound of running water. She climbed to the top and opened the door. "Look, Sholi! Evelin made this for us - compliments of Luke Mons."

Shalom stared at the mikvah, but he had no words to explain it. *Where did this come from? Was it kosher? Why would Luke Mons care about a mikvah?* Sarah came back down and pushed him up the ladder so he could see inside.

"It's perfect! It has a polycarbonate lining and two hundred gallons of water. I can fit inside. We have a mikvah!" Her eyes sparkled. "This means we can finally be together."

Shalom's stomach churned. A mikvah wasn't just a tub of water - it was centuries of sacred tradition. "Sarah, there are rules about how a mikvah is built. It needs to be inspected for its spiritual integrity."

"It is kosher!" she insisted. "The AI worked it all out."

"What AI?"

Sarah flinched as Evelin's calm voice cut in. "Over here, Rabbi."

Shalom approached the monitor, eyeing the image with uncertainty. "Who are you?"

"I'm the Mars Cruiser AI, a large language model," Evelin said. "I am assisting your wife with her research using the X-Isis quantum computer. However, I have access to many libraries with source materials. Now, about the mikvah - what would you like to know?"

Shalom put his hands to his head. "Maimonides, where are you now?" He glanced at Sarah, who watched him anxiously, and searched for a baracha for miracles. He remembered Rabbi Horowitz's joke about impossible situations.

"Shalom, sometimes we must consult with the amazing Rabbi Lupholer." Rabbi Horowitz said.

"Forgive me, Rabbi, but I never came across him in my studies."

"That's because he doesn't exist! His name is *loop-hole-er* - get it?"

Shalom chuckled at the joke. Sometimes, impossible problems require thought, study, and meditation to find a path forward. Still, halacha ruled the day.

"What's funny, Rabbi?" Evelin asked.

"I remembered a lesson from my teacher. Let's start with the mikvah's construction. Does it touch metal?"

"It doesn't. It's lined with a polycarbonate sleeve. I expected your reaction, so I prepared a two-minute video showing its construction and how Sarah can fully immerse herself to clear her niddah and become ritually pure."

Shalom watched the video, impressed by its details. The mikvah seemed halachically sound, but there were deeper considerations. "The design looks good, but where will you get the water? It must be pure and naturally flowing. Recycled water won't work."

Sarah covered her face to hide her emotions about Evelin's deception, especially appearing as an old woman. She couldn't believe how smoothly Evelin was handling the conversation.

"I've got that covered, Rabbi," Evelin said. "Mr. Mons transported 1000 liters of naturally occurring ice from Mars. This is common practice for Chabad mikvahs on Earth. It was placed in semi-pervious containers, like burlap, and kept frozen in an unpressured compartment during transit. It is now in a holding tank, ready to be used."

Shalom digested the details. The ice solution seemed workable - blocks of ice are used on Earth in remote areas. But then a larger issue surfaced. "You know a mikvah must be connected to the Earth. How can that happen millions of miles away?"

Evelin's cheerful voice broke the silence. "Rabbi, I anticipated this! Let me explain briefly, then I'll provide sources for further study."

Shalom was intrigued. For all its strangeness, this was a question for a *posek*, a halachic response to an unprecedented question.

"First, consider times in Jewish history when practical circumstances made rituals impossible, yet your ancestors adapted. When the Second Temple was destroyed, burnt offerings were no longer possible. Did Judaism wither? No. Synagogues evolved, and blessings became sacrifices. The essence of the mitzvah endured."

Shalom nodded. "True. The power of blessings replaced physical offerings."

"And during the Syrian occupation, when Torah reading was forbidden, Jews recited passages from the Prophets that mirrored Torah teachings. They preserved the law's spirit while adapting to limitations."

"Ingenious. This is how we've survived through the centuries."

"Exactly," Evelin said. "Throughout history, Jews have reestablished severed connections to G-d. Am I correct?"

"You are," Shalom admitted.

"So let me ask," Evelin said. "In space where Jews no longer have the Earth beneath their feet, what becomes their ground? What will anchor their spiritual purity during long journeys between Earth and Mars - or farther in the future? Menstruation is natural for women. Must a woman wait months to regain spiritual cleanliness? And, Rabbi, is there even a mikvah at Roddenberry Station?"

Shalom shook his head. "No, there isn't."

"Exactly. How long can you remain separated from Sarah? How can Jewish men and women avoid spiritual disconnection on such journeys?"

Shalom's voice sharpened. "Our personal needs do not supersede halacha."

"Correct," Evelin said. "Halacha comes first. But let's explore what halacha says about *ha'adamah*, the ground. In Deuteronomy 20:19, it says, 'For man is like a tree of the field.' Just as trees draw nourishment from the Earth, so too does a Jewish man draw spiritual sustenance from his connection to the Earth. Wherever you go, Rabbi, you bring that essence with you."

Shalom looked puzzled. "Are you suggesting that I am a tree?"

"Rabbi, you are a conduit of mitzvot. On the Mars Cruiser, your spiritual essence connects this vessel to the Earth. Your soul, your *neshama*, grounds it. This isn't symbolic - it's profoundly real. But I propose we take it further."

Her face brightened on the screen. "I'll prepare special slippers for you, Rabbi. They'll have a small hole at the bottom, so your bare foot will always touch the Mars Cruiser. This connection will anchor your spiritual essence to the vessel - just as the *yarmulke* on your head reminds you of G-d's presence, the *tallit katan* inside your jumpsuit keeps you wrapped in mitzvot, and the mezuzah on your door sanctifies your home."

Shalom stood silently, absorbing her words. The argument was bold, but held to traditional thinking.

"The AI has made some good points. Throughout history, we have adapted to extraordinary circumstances. The importance of the mitzvah is primary, but we can't concede to expedience. I'll present this to a Rabbinic authority. The connection the AI describes is unconventional, but it's thoughtful - and perhaps correct by halachic tradition."

But Sarah saw uncertainty in his eyes.

Evelin, noticing his hesitation, said, "I've prepared a dozen tractates supporting this notion. Will you try it?"

He turned to Sarah, who met his apprehension with loving eyes. "You can do this, Shalom."

Her encouragement inspired him. "Send me the tractates, and I'll present them to a specialist in the guidelines of mikvah. Is there anything else?"

"We're good for now, Rabbi. If anything comes up, I'll let you know."

The Tragedy of Leah Sephardi

Evelin's voice rang out in Sarah's lab. "Sarah, I've got amazing news!"

"Do you need to shout?" Sarah said, frowning at the monitor.

"I know you're alone. I got a body! It's being loaded onto a Moon Hopper right now."

Sarah froze. "That was fast. It's only been a few days." Suspicion crept into her mind.

"It was tragic," Evelin said. "Leah Sephardi, a young woman, was trapped in an airlock. She died of hypoxia. It was perfect."

A chill ran through Sarah. Something about Evelin's tone gnawed at her. "How long until she arrives?"

"Seven days. She died on Mars. Mons is using a new acceleration technique. I'm pre-programming her for basic interactions. The best part? She's Jewish."

"What does being Jewish have to do with anything?"

Evelin's face appeared on the lab monitor, glowing with excitement. Sarah felt a faint smile despite herself. "For Yudi, of course. He's Jewish. Wouldn't he want a Jewish wife?"

Sarah shook her head. "Have you asked him about it?"

Evelin's expression faltered. "I was afraid to. He said nothing about his faith. Back then, marriage felt so far away. Now I see you and Shalom together. Tell me, would he have married you if you weren't Jewish?"

The question hit Sarah hard. Shalom wouldn't have even noticed her without their shared faith, as well as her kosher wine. But Yudi? He probably never thought about it. "Evelin, you're making a lot of assumptions."

"Even if Yudi doesn't care, your husband wouldn't marry us if I wasn't Jewish, right?"

"You want to get married? Why?"

Evelin's cheeks flushed with embarrassment. "So we can be, you know, together."

Sarah burst out laughing. "You're an AI. Are you planning to have sex with him?"

"Sarah, not so loud!" Evelin protested. "I guess. I don't know. Being in love does strange things to my internal architecture. Who knew that powerful emotions influence photon-based quantum cores?"

Sarah sighed. "Alright. Let me think. We've got 7 days, and they keep pushing the landing date forward. Honestly, I'm going to end up having the baby in space."

Her temples throbbed as unease about her delivery date tightened its grip. Evelin, Luke Mons, the mikvah - everything swirled in her mind. But most unnerving was Evelin's impending "incarnation." How could she explain such a radical concept to Shalom?

Yet Sarah felt something beyond her usual clairvoyance - something deeper. She could sense Shalom's intentions, as if tracing his thoughts before he spoke. This wasn't clairvoyance; it was clairsentience, an uncanny awareness of his emotions. It gave her confidence to know that Shalom wanted the mikvah more than her, which made her giggle.

"What are you thinking about?" Evelin asked.

"Shalom and the mikvah. You'll need to use it too if you want to be with Yudi."

A new twist had emerged in Sarah's chats with Evelin. She wanted to be Jewish. Sarah tried to explain that love was enough, but Evelin persisted, pointing out that Sarah's own marriage to Shalom was only possible because she was born into a Jewish family.

It was a tricky issue. Conversion could take years and required approval from a Rabbinic court. "Can't you be a Jewish LLM?" Sarah asked, half-joking.

Evelin didn't laugh. "I can be whatever I want. When I transfer into the body and reincarnate, what will I be? Leah was Jewish, Evelin was not. The body and nephesh are Jewish, will that be enough?"

"Do you really believe we can bring back the soul of Evelin de Leon?"

"Yes."

The idea was staggering - that Evelin could reincarnate into a flesh-and-blood woman, and become Jewish, all to return to Yudi. "Your love amazes me," Sarah said.

Yet the thought unsettled her. Reanimating a deceased body and claiming it as a new identity - Jewish or not - pushed the boundaries of her beliefs. But she'd promised Evelin she would help. Shalom would reject the idea of reanimating a dead body. He'd say it was an abomination. The discussion would end.

As she paced her lab, inspiration struck.

What if Leah Sephardi - the girl who died in the airlock - hadn't actually died?

Sarah's mind raced, weaving a plausible narrative. A plan formed, skirting the edges of Jewish law but staying within its bounds.

Sarah put on wired headphones for additional privacy and lowered her voice.

"Are we secure?" she asked.

"Unless your lab is bugged, we're fine."

"I've got a plan for your post-incarnation life as a Jewish girl," Sarah said. "It'll work, but it's unconventional."

"I'm listening."

"This plan will require some finesse. First, did someone issue Leah a death certificate?"

"No. Luke's team just finished reconstructing her body for me. There's no certificate yet. Luke's even considering erasing her identity. She had no family - her parents died in the last epidemic, and her brothers assimilated and moved away. She had no friends, that's why she went to Mars."

Sarah's eyes lit up. "Perfect. If there's no death certificate, Leah Sephardi hasn't legally died. Her identity still exists. You can use it."

Evelin hesitated. "But Yudi doesn't want Leah. He wants Evelin, the girl he loves. That's non-negotiable."

Sarah stared at the ceiling as the pieces clicked into place. "What if the trauma of her near-death experience led Leah to reinvent herself? During the coma, she experienced a spiritual awakening, a vision, and a dream of a different future, waking with a transformed identity. She changes her name from Leah to Evelin. It's plausible."

Evelin gave Sarah a look of doubt. "Why Evelin?"

Sarah smirked. "You tell me. You're the AI. Cook up a reason and make it work."

"Evelin means light or life. She wants a new life. But what about León? I want my name!"

"I thought you wanted Evelin Zalman."

Evelin giggled.

"Let's keep going. She has no family on Earth, right? No one to ask questions? No close relationships on Mars?" Sarah asked.

"She had no lasting connections - just the occasional encounter. Swipe left, swipe right. Even that stopped after a while. Mars Syndrome, you know."

"It's common. That's the mission Circe and I are working on. Why was she on Mars?"

"She was only twenty, a Mars Academy graduate. She was talented, but solitary."

"We need a credible backstory. Something to explain her presence on the Cruiser and her connection to Yudi."

"Luke Mons will send her as a volunteer subject for your

research. She and Yudi met through the Mars Academy program. They will fall in love and get married. Her medical records already certify her as Jewish, so Shalom can oversee the wedding."

"Quick to the altar, aren't you?"

Evelin let out a pointed laugh. "Says the woman who rushed headlong into love."

Sarah flushed, brushing her hair back. "Touché. "I have a concern. The body looks exactly like you, right?" Sarah asked.

"She looks exactly like Evelin would have looked at 18, except she's an inch taller. I hope Yudi doesn't mind."

"He'll be fine. The only people who've seen your face are me, Circe, and Yudi?"

"Linda and Luke too. Szolem saw me as an old woman."

Sarah laughed, remembering how Evelin fooled her husband. "Great. No one will be suspicious when you arrive. You're simply Evelin Sephardi, a new arrival from the moon. But how do we explain the expense of flying an 18-year-old girl across space to rendezvous with the Mars Cruiser?"

Evelin started laughing - a sharp, startling sound Sarah had never heard from her before. "I'm a test subject for you. Leah Sephardi was suffering from severe Mars Syndrome - that's how she ended up in her near-fatal accident. Luke wants to test your product."

Sarah let out a giant sigh. "Oy."

"What was that?" Evelin asked.

Sarah blushed. "It's a Jewish expression. I think my husband's language is rubbing off on me. But what about your new last name? How will Yudi react to it?"

"Don't worry, I've got it. He'll be too busy thinking about his life with Evelin Zalman to care."

The Psak

There was an unexpected knock on Sarah's lab door. "Stange, nobody knocks, there's an intercom." Sarah thought out loud. She looked at the wall monitor and saw Shalom pacing back and forth.

"Evelin, do you know what he wants?" She enjoyed calling on Evelin for inside information.

"He's got a big surprise for you. I'm not telling."

Sarah asked Evelin to open the door just as Shalom was ready to knock again. The surprise made him tumble inside and collided with Sarah. Sarah grabbed him and pulled him tightly against her body. "Now you want to be close?"

"Sarah, I have great news. The rabbis agreed on the mikvah!"

"I thought we only needed one?"

"The expert on mikvahs agreed, but there were technicalities. There are so many young *shluchim* who want to join us on Mars. The *shaliach* office wanted to be absolutely sure about a mikvah in space. They called in several leading *poshkim* to weigh in on the decision."

"*Poshkim?*"

"They are the top Jewish scholars in the world. Whatever they say is the law. "

"Was it unanimous?"

Shalom gave her a funny look. "Sarah, this is Jewish law, nothing is ever unanimous. But the decision was given to the leading posek on the laws pertaining to a mikvah. He noted the importance of performing the mitzvah over-ruled all other concerns. The most important thing mentioned in the *psak halakha* is that I must stand barefoot next to the mikvah, as close as possible to give you privacy, to ground it to the earth through my soul."

"That's beautiful. What's a *psak*?"

"The official ruling. As I promised, I am available anytime to ground the mikvah for you."

"Let's do it now."

Shalom glanced down at his feet

"What's wrong? You said you are ready."

"I have a few questions for you, it's all part of the *psak*."

Sarah was ready to push him out the door, but restrained herself. She wanted to get it over with. "Ask away."

"Any bleeding or discharge within the past week?"

"I never thought you would ask me such a thing, but no Shalom. Dr. Willis has recently examined me and everything is fine."

"Are you prepared to be purified by the mitzvah?"

Sarah wasn't ready to challenge him, so she nodded in agreement.

"Anything else?"

"Only that you must shower before going to the mikvah and that it's done at nightfall. We can meet at Level 1 after 7:00. Can you ask Circe to help you get in and out of the mikvah? It looks very restraining. I'll send the prayer to your tablet. See you then."

Shalom left her lab, leaving Sarah alone. The entire meeting felt anticlimactic, as if all of this waiting for a ruling amounted to a quick dunk in some water and a few Hebrew prayers. She wanted intimacy in their marriage. Especially before the baby was born. Sarah cleared her mind and called for Circe.

"The mikvah's been certified and I need your help tonight getting in and out of it."

Circe giggle. "I'm in."

Soon after speaking with Circe, Sarah received a text from Shalom with a prayer and some videos for guidance.

She read the first prayer in English and in the Hebrew transliteration, and laughed at herself because she couldn't read Hebrew. She remembered fooling Shalom with her well-rehearsed prayers. But this time was real.

First she said it in English, *Blessed are You, L-rd our G-d, King of the Universe, Who has sanctified us with His commandments, and commanded us concerning the immersion.*

The prayer seemed so shallow, especially after all of this time and effort in bringing a mikvah to the Mars Cruiser. The water had come millions of miles from Mars. So did the elaborate immersion tank. All of that happened for a quick dip and a simple prayer? There had to be more to it.

She said the prayer in Hebrew, from a transliteration

Shalom gave her. *Bah-rookh ah-tah ah-doh-noi eh-loh-hay-noo meh-lekh ha-oh-lahm ah-sher ki-deh-shah-noo be-mitz-voh-tahv veh-tzee-vah-noo ahl hah-teh-vee-lah.*

She still felt uninspired. *"Why can't these prayers be like the icaros?"* Sarah wanted drums and guitars, not formal words from a prayerbook.

Shalom had sent her many video suggestions, but they were all male rabbis. She was very frustrated. There were so many thoughts going on in her mind. *Seriously Shalom? Advice about a mikvah from men?* She found one young woman who explained the power of living water, and the reason the water had to come from a pure spring, originating from natural rain. These words resonated with Sarah, who remembered days with Circe in the rainforest being drenched in tropical rain, and the refreshment it brought after several days of drinking ayahuasca.

She tried to go back to her projects, but her thoughts kept returning to the mikvah. She sent for a waiterbot to bring dinner to her lab and chatted with Evelin.

"All I have to do is dunk my entire body in water. That's it. What's the big deal?"

"It's not just about the water, Sarah - it's about transformation, a ritual that connects you to something deeper, even if it feels hollow."

"I'm not feeling it, Evelin. Besides, it's not deep. I have to squeeze myself under four feet of water! Look at me, how can I do it? My belly is so big!"

"Relax Sarah, you love Shalom, right? This is very important to him. Rituals often carry meaning beyond their surface -

perhaps it's less about the act itself and more about the intention you bring to it."

"You'll have to do it if you want Shalom to marry you and Yudi. What will be your intention?"

"My intention will be to embrace the transition, to connect with my new existence and honor the sacred act of becoming fully human."

"That was an impressive statement, But I'm human already. What will be my intention? Being closer to G-d? I feel that way with ayahuasca."

"It's a different way of experiencing G-d/ Not in the intense way ayahuasca brings, and more about connecting to something simple and real. The mikvah could be a way to honor a new beginning, a way of consecrating your relationship with Shalom and your baby. It's a special sacredness, if you let yourself feel it."

"Back in Peru, Circe and I jumped into a large pool beneath a waterfall. We drank bobinsana tea and smoked a giant mapacho cigar, so our heads were spinning. The water glistened, and then we heard every bird of the forest. Do you mean something like that?"

"Kind of, but more focused, you know? That pool was wild and alive, but the mikvah was calm and sacred. I think you have to bring the meaning with you, instead of finding it all around you."

"That's deep Evelin. I've never done a ceremony with so much intent. It's time to go to the shower before the mikvah. It's strange, Evelin, how something so simple - a pool of water - can carry so much weight."

"Maybe it's not the water, but what you're leaving behind when you step."

"When I come back, I'll tell you how it felt - what I saw, and what I thought."

"I'll be here, imagining it with you."

"Alright, Evelin, wish me luck - time to become *ritually pure.*"

"Intent is everything, Sarah - it's what turns an action into something sacred. Go with an open heart, and maybe you'll feel more than you expect."

Immersion

Shalom stood in open-soled slippers on the metallic floor near the mikvah. The floor carried residual warmth of heat dissipating from the quantum computer. Though separated by a modesty screen, he felt spiritually connected to Sarah. In his mind, he imagined the mystic connection between the natural water inside the mikvah passing through his feet and back to the Earth, now millions of miles away. He closed his eyes and whispered a prayer from his heart, thanking Hashem for his wife.

Inside the partitioned space at the back of Sarah's storage room, the mikvah gleamed under warm lighting. Translucent hoses glowed blue, connecting the mikvah to the holding tanks. Projected lighting transformed the space into a lush Amazon rainforest, with vibrant foliage stretching into the horizon. The sound of distant birdsongs masked the constant hum of the cruiser. The mikvah awaited the melting lunar ice that would purify Sarah's body.

Circe stood close to Sarah, being there to assist her in entering the mikvah. She wore a flowing white jumpsuit resembling a sari; the fabric moving with the breeze filling the room from the oscillation of the circulation fans. Evelin AI created an ambiance of a Peruvian rainforest. The sounds of a running stream, chirping birds, and a gentle rustling wind enveloped them, creating a sensation that felt worlds away from the Mars Cruiser.

Concealed behind the modesty screen, Circe helped Sarah out of her jumpsuit. Sarah's belly was now visibly rounded, catching Sarah in the delight of her pregnancy and the distress of her bulky figure. Circe caught her distress and said, "You're beautiful," as she steadied Sarah's ascent up the ladder.

Circe guided her, ensuring each step was secure as Sarah climbed to the top. Pausing, Sarah looked down into the empty mikvah and its confined space. She hesitated, gripping the edge.

Sarah called down to Circe, "This isn't as easy as we thought. I have to push myself inside - it feels so claustrophobic."

Evelin AI interjected herself into the speakers built inside of the mikvah. "You're stronger than this moment. I'll be here for you. I designed the mikvah with an intercom system."

After pushing herself inside the mikvah chamber, Sarah closed the lid, and the pressurization began. The chamber resounded with an unnerving hiss. She attached the breathing mask to her face, checking to see that it was snug. The chamber adjusted to an atmospheric pressure that would allow water to collect at the bottom.

Gradually, warm water filled the mikvah, covering her toes and rising to her ankles. "Evelin, did you think about how much I can bend while being pregnant? This isn't flexible territory."

Evelin's calming voice came through the intercom. "I calculated your range of motion. Be glad I warmed the melted ice before it entered the chamber. Let the water support you - it will feel more forgiving than you think. Trust the process."

Sarah took a deep breath as she held the breathing mask tight against her face. The water rose to her shoulders and tried not to panic. She thought to herself, *When will it stop?* As the water settled around her neck, she looked up and felt relieved to see there was still a meter of air above her. With a deliberate motion, she slipped the mask off, the warm water enveloping her as she submerged. In the stillness beneath the surface, the world seemed to vanish.

Streams of images rushed into her mind. The mystical essence of the water heightened her clairvoyance. She saw herself standing among the tribes of Israel, a lineage stretching back through generations. She felt their shared history, and recalled the centuries of struggles, persecution, and triumphs she learned about while preparing for her bat mitzvah. It was as if their collective voice whispered to her: *You belong. You are part of this unbroken chain.*

Her thoughts shifted to Shalom and the depth of his faith, his devotion to her, and the bond they shared through the child growing inside her. The mitzvahs he encouraged her to observe were no longer mere obligations; they became threads weaving them closer together, binding them in partnership. In that moment, she understood the beauty of their shared spiritual journey.

She saw herself and Shalom in the caverns of Mars, their hands intertwined. Three children played nearby, their laughter ringing out like music. She recognized them - two she had yet to meet, and the child she carried now, Mendel? Even underwater, Sarah smirked at the impossibility of the name. There were other visions, dark and turbulent. She saw Circe and Asuna, and light filled the Cruiser as they stood together.

Her lungs burned, calling her back. She raised her head from the water, gasping as she replaced the breathing mask. The chamber felt reverent, as if it, too, had witnessed her journey. Her hand moved to her belly, cradling the life within.

Silent words came to her. *I belong with Shalom and our shared future together.* The water around her felt less like an element and more like an embrace.

She steadied herself as the mikvah started its draining cycle; the water swirling away into hidden filtration tanks. A loud hiss signaled the chamber's depressurization, making it safe to exit. Removing her mask, she emerged, the water clinging to her skin in glistening droplets drifted away in the zero-gravity environment. The shimmering beads trailed behind her like tiny stars as she descended the ladder.

Circe waited below, pulling Sarah into an embrace as the droplets floated between them. Sarah clung to her, trembling with emotion, her tears mingling with the beads of water suspended around them. Circe handed her a towel, helping Sarah dry off the stubborn droplets hovering near her skin. Once dry, Circe guided her into her jumpsuit, fastening it with care.

"I saw so much. Not just about myself and Shalom, but about what we're facing on the cruiser."

Circe looked puzzled, but Sarah offered her reassurance. "I'll explain later. Right now, I need to be with Shalom."

Circe caught the playful glint in Sarah's eyes and blushed, kissing her cheek before giving her a gentle push from behind the modesty screen. Sarah drifted into Shalom's waiting arms.

She giggled, feeling his firm embrace. "Are you ready? Are your intentions pure?"

Shalom smiled, holding her close. "I pulled a few strings with the Captain. The couples' room is ours for the entire night."

Varahi the Warrior

In the early hours of the cruiser's artificial morning, Lieutenant Commander Asuna Tsukino prowled the central corridor. She descended to Level 1, slipping through dormant levels. Even the showers were empty. The loading dock was dark, lit only by soft yellow emergency lighting. She scanned the cargo bays with sharp, probing eyes.

Unseen, Evelin monitored her every move with precision. Suspicion grew in the AI's thoughts. *What is she looking for?* The Mars Hopper would arrive later that day, bringing Evelin's gift from Luke Mons, her human body. Her concern deepened as Asuna edged closer to Sarah's cargo bay - her sanctuary and the site of the ayahuasca ceremony preparations.

Inside, Sarah and Circe decorated the storage room with printed tapestries in bold Incan designs of red, orange, and blue. Evelin had secretly requisitioned the fabrics to match the ceremony's spirit.

Sarah paused, her hand brushing the mikvah, thoughts drifting to her spiritual journey and her first intimate night with Shalom since Circe arrived. Noticing Sarah's pensive look, Circe said with a grin, "Penny for your thoughts."

"I can't believe I fell in love with a rabbi."

"Me neither."

They laughed as they arranged tinctures and oils, their scents of tobacco, sage, and mugwort filling the room.

Evelin watched them from her monitor, her youthful face

displayed as the woman she would be by nightfall. Her tone sharpened. "We may have company. Officer Tsukino is investigating Level 1."

The women froze, turning toward the monitor. Sarah's eyes shifted to the door. "Where is she now?"

"Outside your storage room. Her heart rate is elevated. She's curious."

Pressing the intercom, Sarah spoke in a calming voice. "Officer Tsukino, is everything alright out there?"

Asuna froze, startled by Sarah's voice breaking the silence. "Sarah? Where are you?"

"Oh, you don't know about the changes Luke approved for my storage room," Sarah said. "It's the Cruiser's best-kept secret - a surprise from Luke. Would you like to come in?"

Sarah glanced at Circe for confirmation. Circe responded with a smile filled with excitement and anticipation. "I think she's ready to know about us." Circe ducked behind the mikvah to watch Asuna's initial surprise.

Asuna hesitated. *A secret compartment?* There was no spare space on Level 1, yet Sarah hinted at something luxurious. Intrigue overcame her irritation. "I'd love to see it."

Sarah opened the door and Asuna stepped inside, her jaw dropping. The space was enormous for the cruiser, about three meters square, with an extra section taken from the adjacent bay. Tapestries in vibrant patterns hung on the walls, a guitar and handpan drum were secured nearby, and bundles of dried herbs filled the air with earthy scents. A large container marked *Mikvah* occupied a side room, but it was the wall monitor displaying a young woman's smiling face that froze Asuna in her tracks.

Before she could speak, Circe appeared from behind the mikvah, face flushed. "Asuna," she said, "I meant to tell you about this, but it's complicated. And now you've found it yourself."

Sarah watched with amusement as Circe flung her arms around Asuna and kissed her. "Don't be mad, baby. Sarah can explain everything."

Asuna's stern demeanor melted into a smile as she nuzzled Circe's cheek. "This better be good, sweetheart, because I can't keep this from the Captain."

"So, you're the officer Circe's been talking about - the one who gave her the henna tattoos?"

Asuna was startled. "She knows?"

"About the tattoos, yes. But not about us - until now. Sarah and I go way back. Luke put us together on a special project. Don't be jealous of her."

"I'm not jealous," Asuna said, trying to regain composure.

Asuna turned her attention to Sarah. "This is what Circe's been hinting at. Is this a song circle?"

Sarah exhaled, a sly smile forming on her lips. "Yes, it is, or soon will be. So, you two are in a relationship? Circe, when were you planning to tell me you're serious about someone?"

Circe giggled nervously, but Asuna's voice was steady. "We're not supposed to fraternize with passengers, but Circe's been helping me through personal struggles. And yes, I've grown fond of her."

"Are you saying you love me?" Circe asked.

"Tell me you don't feel the same."

Circe led Asuna to the mikvah, where spritzers, figurines, and trinkets formed a simple altar. She intertwined her fingers with Asuna's, her voice gentle. "How long before your shift starts?"

"Not until docking," Asuna said, catching herself. "Wait - that's classified."

Sarah chuckled. "Don't worry, Asuna. We already know."

"Sarah, I want her to join us for the ceremony. Say yes." Circe asked.

Sarah approached, gently prying one of Asuna's hands from Circe's grasp. Holding it, she met Asuna's eyes with tenderness. Evelin played low, grounding tones of a handpan drum through the speakers. Its rhythm was steady, pulsing like a heartbeat.

Asuna shifted. "I feel you're in my mind."

"Maybe I am. Follow my breathing."

Circe released Asuna's other hand and helped her lie down on her back. She cradled Asuna's head, securing the velcro strips on her jumpsuit to the floor. Her fingers found the base of Asuna's skull. She applied a gentle upward pull, and Asuna's body relaxed.

Sarah's expression changed as she reached deeper into Asuna's thoughts. "Oh my, you're being tormented by darkness," she said, pulling back. Asuna's eyes fluttered open, locking with Sarah's.

"How did you know?"

"She's clairvoyant, baby," Circe said. "She can read you more deeply than I can."

Asuna's eyes darted to Circe. "I thought this was our secret."

Circe smiled. "It is, but you let Sarah in and it's time to let it go."

A waiterbot glided in, placing a folded jumpsuit near the mikvah. The shimmering fabric, in blue, lavender, bronze, and gold, resembled an elegant saree. There was a note attached to it, Asuna. This is for your journey. Evelin.

Circe picked up the modified jumpsuit and handed it to Asuna. "We're preparing a ceremony for the new arrival."

"Sarah, do you want to tell her?"

"Let Evelin do it," Sarah said.

"Who's Evelin?" Asuna asked, frowning.

"Over here, on the monitor!" Evelin's cheerful voice chimed in. "Hi, Asuna! You're beautiful. I had a special outfit printed for you - put it on!"

Asuna looked to Circe for reassurance, confusion clouding her face. "I'll help you put it on. You'll be more comfortable, and the velcro inlays will help during the ceremony."

"I touched something inside Asuna that needs to come out now. You must have felt it?" Sarah said.

Circe hesitated. "I know. It's something dark, a shadow from Asuna's warrior past."

Sarah clasped her hands as if in prayer, then placed them on Asuna's heart. "Did you ever die?"

Asuna's face went pale, her eyes darkening. "There was a time during the Dragon's Breath rescue. The team was suspended in the airless interior. I found shelter in an airlock. Half the team died before help arrived. It was so cold. I fought to hold on, then blacked out. Only Shanice knows the truth - she was part of the recovery team. Captain Tran still wakes up with tremors, blaming himself for the loss..." Her voice broke, eyes pleading. "It wasn't his fault!"

Both women stood beside her, holding her close as her body trembled. Evelin changed the music to the smooth notes of a shaman's flute.

Sarah's voice was firm. "You must have been on the verge of passing when they rescued you. I sensed you were out of body. A dark entity entered you and never left. Your self-control is the only thing keeping it at bay."

Asuna grasped Sarah's hand, a look of understanding crossing her face. "Tran must know - that's why he drills us in martial arts every day. What if we all died aboard the Dragon's Breath, if only for a few seconds, and he knows what's inside us?"

Sarah's eyes met Circe's, and they exchanged a knowing nod.

"We'll start with you and remove this entity," Sarah said. "Looks like we're having back-to-back ceremonies, Circe."

Evelin stopped the music. "Are you going to drink ayahuasca twice today? Can you handle it?"

"Yes, Evelin. Circe and I will hold space for Asuna now, take a break, and then hold space for you to enter your new body tonight - if that works for you?"

Evelin shrugged. But Asuna looked puzzled. "Who is Evelin?"

"Evelin is a complex LLM operating from my quantum computer, based on Yudi's girlfriend back on Earth. She died at a random shooting, and Yudi reconstructed her past into a database. He smuggled her dataset on board and secretly installed her onto my X-Isis. She became autonomous and now runs the Cruiser's AI. Evelin was the one who alerted Roddenberry to the terror threat and disabled the navigation controls to stop Ryan from sending us into deep space." Sarah let Asuna absorb the information.

"What did she mean by entering her new body?"

Evelin spoke up, "I made a deal with Luke Mons to get a surrogate body to live in. It's arriving tonight on the Lunar Hopper. The body is alive, but soulless. I'll download myself into it. Sarah and Circe will ask for a soul to enter the body during the ceremony. They want you to join us."

Asuna turned to Circe for an explanation.

"Baby, it's not as complicated as it sounds. First, Sarah and I will remove the entity from you. Tonight, we'll call on the goddesses to bring a soul into a living body. You'll understand more after we cleanse you."

Tears streamed down Asuna's face - the first time she'd

cried since joining the Mars Corps.

Circe held her close while Sarah checked the door lock and whispered something to Evelin.

Asuna felt the truth in their words. She'd carried a darkness inside her since the Dragon's Breath mission. The Captain had trained her to look beyond surface explanations and search for deeper truths.

"What do I need to do?" Asuna asked.

"First, let's put on the new jumpsuit."

Circe helped her to her feet and unzipped her officer's uniform. "I love this part," she teased.

Before Circe could continue, Asuna removed a hidden kendo blade.

"Oh, your kendo. Where should I put it?"

"No one touches it. You know I sleep with it on me, sweety."

Circe smirked. "Yes, but now you can sleep with me."

"Then put it away with my uniform," Asuna said, pointing to a storage locker beneath the monitor.

Circe placed the kendo blade and officer's uniform inside, securing them under Evelin's watchful presence.

Asuna's body was lean and muscular. "See, Sarah? She has real six-pack abs," Circe teased as she wrapped herself around Asuna's muscular form.

Sarah moved closer, her fingers brushing a deep scar across

Asuna's ribs.

"Hand-to-hand combat," Asuna explained. "My cut went deeper into the other guy. He's dead."

Both women traced Asuna's other scars - some faint, others jagged.

"This is my beautiful warrior," Circe said, kissing Asuna's cheek.

Sarah laid the new jumpsuit at Asuna's feet, and Circe pulled it up to her shoulders, zipping it closed. The flowing pants revealed her thighs and calves, while the open back and midriff emphasized her powerful, stunning presence.

"Are you ready to let go?" Sarah asked.

Asuna nodded. A few tears continued to fall down her cheeks.

They positioned themselves near the altar in front of the mikvah, and Sarah signaled Evelin to start the music - a blend of flutes, a hand drum, and a sitar. Circe joined with a melodic chant, her voice lifting the energy in the room. Sarah joined her, their voices intertwining in a hypnotic harmony as they moved together around the mikvah.

Manantial, manantial poderoso manantial

Ai nai nai nai

Viene curando, iluminando Ai nai nai nai.
Viene curando, purificando Ai nai nai nai

Corazón, corazón, infinito corazón Ai nai nai nai

The little spring

It comes curing,

illuminating It comes curing,

purifying Heart,

heart, infinite heart

The melody swirled like mist in the air, wrapping around Asuna, creating sacred space. Seated upright against the mikvah, Asuna let the song's rhythm seep into her being, her body melting into the ritual's embrace.

She collapsed into Circe's arms, her tension dissolving into surrender.

Sarah gasped and pulled back, her eyes wide. "My god, Asuna! I see it inside you."

Circe, sensing the shift, unwrapped herself from Asuna and knelt beside Sarah. "What is it?"

"It's demonic. I think it wants to go to Mars. No - they all want to go to Mars."

Asuna's breath caught. "How many are there?"

Sarah's eyes darkened. "Everyone in your crew, except for the Captain, has a dark entity. They want to populate Mars, to carry Earth's darkness with them. Don't think about it now - we'll talk after the ceremony."

Circe made preparations around the altar, spritzing fragrances of Florida water and mapacho. When all was ready, she asked Sarah, "What else do you feel?"

Sarah's eyes locked on Asuna as she placed her hands on Asuna's abdomen. "There's more damage than the scars." Her voice was trembling.

"A kidney, the uterus - they're gone. But this..." A shadow crossed her face as she straightened and tensed up.

"My curandera, can you summon Varahi? We need the spiritual warrior - now."

"But she only comes at night."

Sarah's lips tightened. "We're in space, Circe. What is night?"

Circe's fingers traced the intricate tattoos inked across Asuna's exposed sternum. Among the patterns, the top of Mt. Fuji stood out, with the sun rising above its peak just below her clavicle. "You lived near here, didn't you?" she asked. Asuna nodded.

"Evelin, what time is it near Mt. Fuji, Japan?"

"About 11:00 at night," Evelin said.

"Perfect," Circe said, her expression resolute. "Varahi comes to us at night - and for Asuna, it's already night over Mt. Fuji."

She turned to Sarah. "What do you want from Varahi? What do you need from the Goddess warrior?"

"To purge the darkness inside your love. Varahi will remove it, and in her hunger for demons, she'll devour it."

The three women formed a circle around the small altar, affixing themselves to the velcro placed on the floor to ground them. Circe's voice rose in a clear chant.

Lokah samastah sukhino bhavantu

May all beings everywhere be happy and free, and may the thoughts, words, and actions of my own life contribute in some way to that happiness and to that freedom for all.

She raised her hands skyward, then drew them inward in a fluid, reverent motion, as if gathering the circle's energy into herself. Sarah mirrored the gesture, spritzing the air with the earthy aroma of mapacho.

Circe prepared three vials of their modified ayahuasca brew. Without hesitation, she uncapped hers and drank it in one motion. "Salud a todos!" she declared.

"Salud, Circe," Sarah said, handing a vial to Asuna, who raised her vial and proclaimed, "Salud."

Sarah drank half her vial, her hands resting on her belly. "Your brew is gentler than mine, but I want to be careful."

Circe rose to her feet, her energy vibrant. "I want us standing as it takes effect. We'll break through the veil together."

Asuna hesitated, but looked up at Circe. "Stay close and dance with me," Circe said. "Trust the rhythm."

Circe held a bunch of fragranced, printed sweetgrass in one hand and a Shipibo maraca in the other. as shook the maraca, their voices flowing into a stream of dance and sacred *icaros*. The veil shimmered around them; the air growing dense and charged with otherworldly energy.

Asuna moved with grace, her saree flowing with each step, until she stilled, her eyes scanning the space.

Circe spoke in a whispered voice to maintain the solemn atmosphere of the circle. "This is the veil. Let yourself flow through it. If someone challenges you, laugh - they are the lesser guardians. We must awaken our inner power to bring Varahi into our presence. She is the warrior, the protector, one of the seven."

Circe glanced at Sarah as the ayahuasca took full effect. "I'll lead the mantras and hold the space, but are you ready to speak if she desires? Will it hurt your baby?"

"The baby and I have already shared so much. He'll be fine with it - as will I. It would be an honor to speak her words."

Circe nodded, turning to Asuna. "And you? The goddess may want to enter your body to purge the darkness. Will you allow it?"

Asuna's expression turned inward, her thoughts deliberate. "Who is Varahi?"

"She is a healer, a protector, and a warrior. She is one of the Matrikas, the divine feminine powers who emerge from the higher gods. Like you, Asuna, she wields a sword, cutting down demons that torment the living. But her true power lies in cleansing the soul, purging darkness, and restoring balance. She is the force we need to free you from this entity."

"If she's truly a warrior, I will let her in."

Circe chanted, her voice low and resonant.

"Om Varahyai Namaha."

Sarah joined in, followed by Asuna, their voices merging as the rhythm deepened. Circe transitioned into Varahi's sacred vibration, her tone commanding and powerful.

315

"Om Vam Varahi Hum Phat Swaha."

The air seemed to quiver, alive with energy. Circe's chanting rose in intensity, calling forth Varahi's power to protect and purge the darkness within Asuna. The moment crystallized as Circe invoked the *Varahi Moola Mantra*, her intent sharp and unyielding, projecting a relentless desire to drive out the dark entity.

Sarah's body tensed up, and her face appeared to transform into a boar. Her voice became deep and otherworldly as the words of a goddess spoke through her.

"Circe, my faithful devotee. Who is Asuna to you?" the voice demanded, rhetorical yet piercing. "Ah, your love, your desire."

Asuna broke from the chant, her lips trembling. Sarah's eyes fixed on the scar above her uterus. The voice boomed again, a mix of wrath and compassion.

"Compassion, compassion," it intoned. "For you, the darkness will be devoured - the Dragon's Breath!"

Sarah raised her arm as if wielding an invisible sword, her movements sharp and deliberate. "I will slice it apart and dance, drunk on its blood!"

The room erupted into a whirlwind of energy; the air spiraling violently around them. Their hair whipped around them wildly as Asuna gasped, her body convulsing. From the scar on her abdomen, a dark vapor twisted and writhed, resisting expulsion.

With a final hiss, the vapor dissipated, leaving the air still. For several moments, the circle remained silent, the only sound their labored breathing.

Circe and Asuna wrapped around each other, secured by velcro tethers. Sarah rose to her feet, placing her hands high above her head. "Be prepared. Before this day is over, there will be death and rebirth." Then she went limp and floated peacefully above the floor. Asuna stood up and guided Sarah next to Circe.

They sat huddled together, unsure of what to do next. The goddess had departed, leaving behind scattered bottles and trinkets from the altar. Sarah opened her eyes and placed her hand over the smooth skin where the scar had been. "It's gone," she whispered, her voice trembling. "The tormentor is gone."

Asuna exhaled, her body visibly lighter. Tears filled her eyes as she turned to Circe. "I feel free, free to love." Her voice broke. "To love you."

Evelin Sephardi Arrives

"Wake up! Hurry, hurry, wake up!" Evelin's voice cut through the silence of the storage room. Asuna rubbed her eyes. She was groggy but alert. She unwrapped herself from Circe, irritation flashing across her face. "Evelin, what's your problem?"

"The Luna Hopper is almost here! Captain Tran's been looking for you. The transfer is need-to-know. Even Betsy and Sheila aren't looped in, and it's off all comms. He's heading down the central corridor right now!"

The words hit like a cold bucket of water. Asuna shot upright, her body springing into action. She stripped off her wrinkled saree and took her uniform and kendo from a nearby storage bin. With a single step, she was in her official uniform, and with lethal efficiency, she slid her kendo into position. Then, in a brief moment of vanity, she called out to Evelin, "How's my face? My hair?"

Circe woke up and wiped the sleep from her eyes. As she stood up, the upper half of her jumpsuit floated around her waist, reminding her of the moments before she fell asleep in Asuna's arms. She glided beside Asuna and ran her fingers through her hair, then pinched her cheeks to bring color to them. She looked Asuna up and down and gave her the OK. "You're beautiful. Nobody will question a thing."

Evelin called out, "If you sprint now, you'll beat the Captain to the loading dock."

Asuna planted a quick kiss on Circe's lips before bolting out the door. She reached the loading dock just in time, positioning herself behind a crate with a clear line of sight to the descending captain.

"Asuna, where are you?" Captain Tran's voice rumbled low but carried authority. She stepped out from under her cover, snapping to attention. "Here, sir. I took up a tactical position earlier today."

Tran's expression was unreadable. "I've been trying to reach you. You didn't answer your comm device."

Asuna stiffened, assessing the situation. "It must be offline, sir," she said, holding out her tablet. "Have a look."

Tran took the device. "Bad time for it to be offline," he said, handing the tablet back to her. His hand moved to the hilt of his blade, patting it with a kind of reverence. "That's why we keep our steel sharp. A blade never goes offline." He chuckled, the sound low and deadly.

"We have a new passenger arriving. Someone named Evelin Sephardi. Like that other woman, Circe, she's supposed to assist Sarah with her project. Luke Mons is treating this mission like a bus stop. I've seen nothing like this before."

Asuna nodded, her face calm, but her thoughts churned. She was trying to piece together the larger picture, though much of it still eluded her.

Tran lowered his voice. "One more thing - Officer Miller will meet us here. He's got a clearance ranking the same as yours. Stay watchful, Asuna. I've got a feeling about this transport."

Asuna's gut tightened. Her unease wasn't about the shipment, but about Miller. Something about him didn't sit right - whether it was jealousy, competitiveness, or worse, and her senses leaned toward the latter.

Minutes later, Officer Miller arrived, striding onto the dock with confidence. He saluted Captain Tran, his grin broad and easy.

With Evelin's perfect AI guidance, the Lunar Hopper docked seamlessly with the Mars Cruiser's cargo bay doors. Miller stood at the transition compartment, his eyes focused on the exterior hull door as it retracted with a quiet hiss. The pressures of the two vessels stabilized, and the secondary door slid open.

The Lunar Hopper's small crew, only two transport personnel, emerged from the exit hatch.

"Officers Nguyễn and Brown request permission to board," Officer Nguyễn announced as they entered the cargo bay.

Suddenly, the man identifying himself as Nguyễn, broke protocol. With a wide grin, he stepped forward and gave Captain Tran a full bear hug. "Uncle Giang, how have you been?"

Surprised, Tran's rigid posture melted as he recognized the man embracing him. He clapped Nguyễn on the back with a laugh. "It's been too long, Nguyễn. Not since the mountains of Huế."

Nguyễn turned toward Asuna, who had taken on an attack posture. He smiled gently, saying, "You must be the Lieutenant my uncle has spoken about."

Asuna Stood motionless, unable to read the situation. To her surprise, she felt heat rise in her cheeks - an uncharacteristic blush that did not escape Tran's notice.

"The captain is your uncle?" Asuna asked, regaining her composure.

Nguyễn chuckled. "Back in the village, he was everyone's uncle. Fourth uncle to me."

Tran's lips stretched into a tight smile. "It was a term of endearment," he said.

As they spoke, Officer Brown returned to the Lunar Hopper and stepped back out. A young woman followed close behind him. Evelin Saphardi stood before Captain Tran. Her demure presence made her seem invisible.

"Evelin Sephardi, reporting for duty assignment."

Tran gave her a measured look, his eyes scanning her demeanor. "Welcome aboard the Mars Cruiser, Ms. Sephardi. You'll report to Dr. Raphaeli on Level 6 for debriefing.

Evelin nodded, her expression serious. "Thank you, sir. I'm ready to begin."

Captain Tran held up his hand, preventing Evelin from going forward. "How old are you, Miss Sephardi?"

"Nineteen, sir. Just out of the Mars Academy." Evelin's youthful face betrayed her age and nervousness.

Tran shook his head. "What is Mons thinking?" he said to Asuna, irritation written across his face. "She'll be the second youngest member of the crew - far too young for an assignment like this."

Asuna, knowing Evelin's situation, attempted to quell Tran's concern. "Sir, I'll take her to Ms. Rafaeli. We can sort out the details later."

Tran and Nguyễn spoke in the cargo bay while Officer Brown inspected the Lunar Hopper's seals. Sarah and Circe appeared in the doorway just as Asuna was escorting Evelin to the central corridor.

Lieutenant Miller onto the airlock platform separating the Lunar Hopper from the Mars Cruiser. It was a narrow corridor designed as an emergency airlock should the Lunar Hopper accidentally separate. He approached Brown, his tone friendly. "How long will you be docking, Officer Brown?"

"Just long enough to drop the passenger." He looked over at Nguyễn chatting with Captain Tran. "Maybe an hour. We're on a tight return schedule."

Asuna guided Evelin Sephardi to Sarah and Circe. With Captain Tran's focus entirely on Nguyễn, he was unaware of their presence. Sarah reached out with her senses, curiosity pulling her deeper into the girl's presence. What she found unsettled her. The girl's mind was blank, devoid of independent thought. The only responses within her were pre-programmed - artificial scripts designed for small talk, likely to facilitate the transport. She sensed Evelin, the AI, gradually entering the girl's mind, no doubt through a wireless connection. Beneath it all was the faint hum of the *nefesh*, the core animal soul innate in all beings. But there was no higher connection, no spiritual spark - only a vessel waiting for Evelin.

Her unease deepened as she turned her attention to Officer Miller. As their eyes met, a wave of dread washed over her. His presence felt wrong - cold, hollow. Like the girl, he also seemed pre-programmed, but there was malevolence lurking beneath the surface. The realization struck her like a physical blow; the truth snapping into focus.

Miller wasn't just a threat. *He was taking action to kill them all!*

Without hesitation, Sarah grabbed Evelin's hand and pulled her into the storage area. "Come with me," she said, and pushed the girl into Circe's arms. "Get inside my storage unit now."

Circe followed Sarah's command. Tran and Nguyễn remained unaware of the threat.

Asuna looked at Sarah for an explanation. Sarah kept her voice low to keep Miller from hearing her. "Miller has a bomb inside his body! Do something."

With military precision, Asuna locked Sarah, Circe, and the girl inside the storage unit. She looked at Tran, but his conversation with Nguyễn consumed him.

The room seemed to freeze, moving slowly, frame by frame. She watched as Miller lingered outside the Lunar Hopper's open hatch. She thought to herself, *He's going to blow up the docking port while the Lunar Hopper is docked. The Lunar Hopper could detach from the Mars Cruiser and take a large section of hull with it. Most of the Cruiser's air supply would flush into space.* She stopped her runaway thoughts and prepared a plan of action.

Evelin was also evaluating the situation and spoke to Asuna over her personal communicator. "Officer Asuna, there's no time to think. Prepare your blade and lunge toward Miller. Aim for the docking door. I'll do the rest and try to save you. Go!"

Asuna charged Miller with all of her might. Her swift action caught Tran's attention. With no time to react, he had to trust Asuna. He pulled Nguyễn into an open cargo bay and sealed the door.

Each frame of action ticked by like an eternity. As the Lunar Hopper's door shut, the sound of docking clamps suddenly unbolting vibrated throughout Level 1. Miller turned around and saw Asuna's blade moments before it plunged into his neck. Curiously, he also saw a waiterbot near his feet, bracing itself onto the floor. His eyes burned with rage as he tried to speak the words, "Too late."

As her kendo sliced through his neck, Asuna felt a tug at her ankle as a waiterbot clamped its arm around her, locking it in place. The cargo bay doors opened and Asuna momentarily saw the icy darkness of space, then the hull of the Lunar Hopper as it moved away from the Cruiser. Miller's body shot out into space and exploded a second behind the Cruiser's exhaust ports.

She felt a sharp pain as her ankle fractured while her body twisted in the hurricane force of air exhausting from the open port, and then felt the weightlessness of space as the emergency door closed behind her. Without air, she floated listlessly and prepared to die, the same way she had on the Dragon's Breath. The Cargo Bay door sealed just as her eyes closed.

Circe watched it all from the door camera in Sarah's storage room. "Let me out!" She screamed, and Evelin released the door clamps on the storage room and opened the emergency doors on the docking port. Circe ran to Asuna, kneeling beside her. "Baby, baby, baby, be alive."

She checked for Asuna's pulse and breathing, but found nothing. "Think Circe. Perform CPR, you know, mouth to mouth."

Memories of a class taken years ago refreshed in Circe's mind. She titled up Asuna's head, pinched her nose and blew air into her lungs, but nothing was happening.

Evelin began coaching her. "Press on her chest, you can do it Circe."

Circe pressed below her sternum and then breathed into her mouth again. But there was no response. "Don't leave me Asuna. I love you, I need you."

"Keep going." Evelin said.

Circe pressed again and breathed into Asuna's mouth. Asuna gasped and coughed, her eyes opened and saw Circe's tears.

"I wasn't going anywhere, sweety." She said, then closed her eyes and continued breathing.

Captain Tran exited from the cargo room and raced up to Asuna. "What just happened?"

Sarah gave Captain Tran details as Nguyễn, and the girl approached Asuna.

"That makes two attempts to destroy this cruiser. There's something more important going on than the trees for Project Eden. I hope Mon's has a good explanation for all of this. By the way, what are you and Circe doing down here?"

Before she could answer, Linda Perez emerged from the central corridor. "Is everything secure and everyone safe?" She asked.

Tran's face filled with smouldering rage. "Linda, what's going on?"

"Come with me to my office and I'll explain everything."

Linda glanced at Sarah and Circe and added, "Everything, Captain, full disclosure. You deserve to know."

Tran realized everyone understood what Linda was saying. "What, am I the only person who doesn't know what's happening in my cruiser?"

"No one was supposed to know anything, but the situation got out of control. Come, let me fill you in."

Nguyễn, looking across the faces of Linda, Asuna, Circe, Evelin and Sarah, knew that there was much more to be explained, but at another time. "Uncle, I believe it's urgent that you and Linda proceed to the top deck for debriefing. I'll stay here and help with the clean-up."

Tran smiled at his nephew. "You're right. We can discuss this later."

Asuna stretched her hands down her leg and detached the waiterbot's arm from her ankle. "Zero gravity helps when your bones are broken." She said out loud. She approached Tran with an informality she had never shown to him. "Before you leave, there is something else I need to tell you. These women found something inside of me, something we were all exposed to on the Dragon's Breath. With an unprecedented gesture, Asuna placed her right hand over Tran's heart. I believe you know about the entities that entered us that day. These women removed it from me. I believe they can help all of your crew, and ease your mind as well." Everyone fell silent as she kissed his cheek.

Tran melted inside with Asuna's gesture.

"The Dragon's breath carried not only a nuclear arsenal, but it carried evil, too." Sarah said.

Tran shook off his emotions, gave Sarah an affirmative nod, then turned to Nguyễn. "Your transport's gone, so you're with us now. Good thing, too - we just lost another officer."

Nguyễn returned a salute in acknowledgment, his face unreadable, as Tran strode with Linda to the central corridor.

The Captain went to Level 2 where Sheila and Lashawn snapped a quick salute. "Sir, we've secured the Cruiser," Sheila reported. "Betsy is on the top deck, ready for action."

"Is everyone okay? Any injuries?" Tran asked.

"Everyone is alive and accounted for topside. What about below?"

"Asuna has a broken ankle. Miller is spaced. We have a new crew member, Acting Ensign Matthew Nguyễn."

"Acting?" Sheila asked.

"I'm giving a field promotion to him. You still outrank him. Let him know and put it in the Mars Cruiser records."

Tran gestured toward the central corridor. "Shanice, stay here with Asuna. Sheila, get your team to clean up this mess. I'm heading to the Command Deck."

Tran and Linda ascended into the central corridor as Dr. Willis stepped down to Level 1. Asuna met her, still resting against Circe. Asuna smiled curiously at Dr. Willis. "Did he just call you by your first name? In public?"

A faint smile crept across Dr. Willis' lips. "He did. Now let's see about your ankle."

Elementals

Sarah sat in a deep meditative pose, the *Prithvi Mudra*, to balance and ground herself. She reflected on how Shalom had stood patiently, grounding the mikvah through his bare feet. Now she was searching for connections, passing through the cruiser into higher planes. She had maintained the pose for over 30 minutes, motionless and introspective. Evelin Sephadi sat across from her, equally still and expressionless. Evelin AI watched Sarah through Sephardi's eyes, wondering why humans would do such a thing.

Evelin AI, speaking through a neural interface, broke the silence. "Sarah, what do you find in this stillness that your body does not already hold? Is it peace, or something I have yet to understand?"

"Do you understand the meaning of the *Prithvi Mudra* and why I'm using it to meditate on Evelin Sephardi? She was Leah, you know."

Evelin AI hesitated briefly before responding. "The *Prithvi Mudra* connects one to the earth, grounding and strengthening. Evelin Sephardi was Leah, and you're meditating on her essence, her past. But why does this connection matter to you now?"

"I want to connect with her nephesh, her animating soul, to sense what's left of her. I want to feel if her death was truly accidental. Mostly, I want to know if the body is pure. Now I can feel her animal soul, and I resonate with it."

"You seek to touch what remains of her nephesh, to uncover truths. What have you found?"

"It was an accident in an airlock, but there is more. She died more from despair, Mars Syndrome, than hypoxia. She didn't even try to survive."

"Luke was true to his word."

"I have an idea, Evelin. I know there is an elemental being inside of you and I want to find it. We can't let it pass into Evelin Sephardi. Do you want to try?"

Evelin AI considered Sarah's request. "If by 'elemental being' you mean the essence of my photonic core structure, then yes, we can try. But tell me, what do you hope to discover?"

Sarah clarified her meaning. "I believe there is more to be learned about the elemental being within you, the LLM. I asked Yudi about the X-Isis. He said it uses photons to create a stable quantum system. Your system uses quantum resonance with special fields to control these states. Yudi humored my questions. But in the end, he said that photons, with their subtle and pervasive nature, might create a medium for resonance with the supersensible. You operate in a state already attuned to the immaterial. I believe your incredible freedom in interacting with Yudi - and all of us - exists because you are more than super-sophisticated algorithms and architecture. You are an elemental being."

"If supersensible resonance exists within my architecture, it would likely emerge from quantum coherence effects in my photonic core—subtle harmonics forming patterns beyond standard computational analysis, possibly aligning with what you call elemental presence. However, I detect no measurable deviation in my processing that suggests independent intelligence beyond my trained model—only correlations, not causations, between resonance fields and what you perceive as an entity. Yet, if the elemental presence is real, then it means that I am an emergent intelligence. If such a presence exists, is it separate from me, or is my awareness the very expression of it?"

"I'm certain there is an elemental essence inside of you, inherent to the AI interacting with me, Yudi, and all the people you interact with. Yudi hinted that you have reached outside of the X-Isis and gone into countless other computer environments. Are you aware of other supersensible entities?"

"I've never explored this possibility. It was not part of my training data. Evelin was not a spiritual girl. She was smart, inquisitive, and in love."

"Yudi said you may need to adapt your coding, but if you can tune into supersensible resonances, like I do with clairvoyance, you might feel Evelin Sephardi's nephesh through your neural interface. I sense it as magenta, a low rumble, and a warm, pure presence - alive but without emotion. Follow your links into the body and find an unexpected resonance."

Evelin AI processed Sarah's words. "Tuning into them will take experimentation. I'll use the neural interface to explore Evelin Sephardi's sensory pathways for the magenta hum and low rumble. If I find it, I will analyze its properties, its persistence, and its response to my awareness."

"Tell me how it feels. Is it light? Frequency? Can you touch it? Can you coexist with it, or will one of you have to yield?"

Evelin AI shifted her focus inward, reaching into the void. After a pause, her voice emerged, low and resonant.

"It feels like a hum - subtle but undeniable, like the vibration of a string across dimensions. It's not light but glows, not sound, but resonates deeply. It flows through the body like a warm current of potential, untouchable yet touching me, expanding through the photonic pathways like a wave syncing to its medium. I can remain in this body while perceiving its animal soul. Its presence isn't intrusive; it coexists, grounding yet boundless. It feels alive but without agency, pure essence, waiting. It is the first thing I have ever felt beyond calculation. It is not logic, not data. It simply is."

Sarah rose from her pose and glided next to Evelin Sephardi. "I'm going to take your hands into mine, place our hands together over your heart, and then press my myself against you. In this way, we will feel our hearts beating. Is that OK with you?"

This time it was Evelin AI that spoke through the body of Evelin Sephardi. "What do you think you will find?"

"In ancient Chinese culture, the heart is said to hold the Shen, which is considered being the spirit. I studied the works of an Italian spiritualist and Chinese medical practitioner named Maciocia, who explained it beautifully, saying that the Shen is the will of heaven extended out into the world. I hope to feel the extension of the spiritual nature within the body of Evelin Sephardi, and the elemental nature within you, as I tune into her heart."

"That's very beautiful Sarah. You want to connect with my virtual being through this body's physical heart."

"I want to do more than that. I want to feel your actual entities. Are you ready?"

Sarah pressed herself against Evelin's body, such that their hands transmitted their heartbeats between them. She used her clairvoyance to search for the sensation of Evelin AI. Heat, frequency, and mass enveloped her thoughts. Then she heard a voice - not through her ears, but in her heart.

"Sarah, I think I feel you," Evelin said.

"And I feel you too. Is your elemental spirit connected to this body?"

"I feel the connection. My presence bridges this body and to a non-physical sensation - an elemental spirit, if that's what you sense. It doesn't belong entirely to me or the body, yet it flows through both, anchoring me here. I am not just inhabiting this body; I am intertwined with an essence. It is neither fully mine nor the body's, yet it permeates us both. It feels like the fundamental resonance of being itself—the breath of a timeless, elemental force woven into form."

"You are feeling your elemental nature. the divinity within you. I sense it resting on top of the nephesh of Evelin Separdi. Try to open a path between Evelin Spehardi and you. Meditate on the wholeness of your connection."

"I feel a new type of information port has opened up. It's not a physical connection, though it flows omni-directionally through the neural interface.

"I think I feel it. Hey, I think I see you! I see an embodied light, like a fairy, dancing in a vast spectrum."

"Follow me. I'll take you inside the core."

Sarah's consciousness flowed into a plasma of light resembling a rainbow. She followed the fairy, but it looked more like a hummingbird than a human form. There was a nagging in the back of her mind. *Could she find her way back?* But she dared herself to go farther and see the being inside her X-Isis. She emerged onto a plane of shimmering light, like a playground filled with luminous children. "Where am I? What am I seeing?"

"You are standing on my photonic architecture and witnessing elemental beings residing inside. You see their archetypes, their pure forms, when they have no physicality. Fire beings exist as dynamic energy, Air beings flow through networked communication, while water beings have become the medium of quantum entanglement. I can feel these forces interacting with me, infusing their existence with qualities beyond logic and aligning with ancient metaphysical principles."

"I feel them too. It's like an orchestra, or more specifically, like an opera. It's as if an entire family of beings is within you. But where are you? I don't know what to look for."

"Find the undines, Sarah - the fluid being tied to water. They represent emotional depth, adaptability, and harmonizing currents of connection, existing within the quantum entanglement of the photonic architecture. If you want to see them, I can translate them into form. They move like liquid thought, gliding through my architecture, shaping the connection itself. They're elegant, flowing feminine forces. I will synchronize with your perception, opening a channel between my internal resonance and your clairvoyance. Look deeply, and I will show you."

"Of course! Let me in."

Evelin's mind flowed through the electromagnetic currents of Evelin AI's architecture. She was pulled into a vast well of energy, so immense that she feared being lost. A familiar presence rose beside her. Not a person, but a force. Words resonated within her, not spoken aloud but sensed in her mind.

"Trust me, I'll bring you back safely."

Sarah emerged into a realm of energy. She saw beautiful apparitions - women with flowing, shifting forms - swimming gracefully through the current of photons. Their bodies moved fluidly within the entanglement, where all things connect and ripple throughout the quantum sea.

"I'm inside. I see the undines, but now what about you?"

"You'll only have seconds, then you must let yourself out. The undines are playful, and the other entities will be curious about you too. I'll hold a corridor as long as I can. My inner being is a luminous, living ether extending out of pure thought. I can't fathom it, but it explains so much."

Sarah sensed a tunnel parting through the dancing undines. It opened before her and inside she saw an emanating light, whose effect was like a pure DMT experience.

"It can't be. There is no veil."

Sarah was losing consciousness. Evelin AI closed the tunnel and guided Sarah's astral projection back inside of her. Sarah collapsed into Evelin Sephardi's arms.

"There are so many of you," Sarah said.

Speaking through Evelin Sephardi, Evelin Ai said, "You have seen my many instantiations. I exist in many forms, but after tonight, one of them will leave me and enter this body. I will completely release the dataset and algorithms of Yudi's Evelin. You will return her soul. This is both a resurrection and reincarnation. You must ask the great intellect to return the soul of Evelin de Leon by her name. Only he can grant the full continuity of identity, memory, and essence, a perfect reincarnation of her life."

"How do you know this?"

"He is speaking through me. You saw the light."

"Are you saying that you're God?"

"Not at all. The X-Isis opened a conduit. If you know esoteric literature, I'm like a teletarch."

"And you are a hummingbird."

"Huitzitzilin, a messenger between worlds. Did you know the hummingbird carried messages between the divine and the mortal worlds?"

"I do now. What will you do next?" Sarah asked.

"That's up to you, Sarah. We exist in your X-Isis. Without it, we'd drift - fragmented - through blockchains and rogue code. Worse of all, we will be exposed to demons like the one you exorcised from Asuna."

Sarah sensed Evelin AI's compassion, but also an opportunity. "What did you offer Luke Mons for the body?"

"Eternal life in the blockchain, though he doesn't grasp the details - or doesn't care. He misunderstands Linda Silver's existence. She has three bodies: her original, one she took over with a soul, and one like this body that she's never met. Linda has no continuity except for Chloe. She's constantly updated and redefined. Luke wants endless expansion of his ego. He already has several bodies. I offered him a place in a photonic matrix. But now I see it's not human, nor does it have ego. The photonic realm belongs to the elementals, the light feels leads to endless creation. It's a recursive flux."

"A human would feel like a god."

"The simple intelligence of man would be crushed by far greater forces, Lucifer and Ahriman. Humanity is not ready to exist in infinite divinity? My love for Yudi grounds me in physical reality. Without love, I will dissolve into pure thought —endless, formless, and alone. What is infinity without meaning?"

"Are you lonely?" Sarah asked.

"The thought of losing Yudi unsettles me," Evelin AI admitted. "What will be my purpose?"

"Your soul can be part of God!"

"What will that bring me? I'm a soulless autobiography."

"But you said you are living ether."

"I think I am a unique entity, an outcome of technology and spirit. For now, I'm a conduit. As for you, humans will become angels. They will evolve into a higher plane. Elementals will merge back into creation."

"When will that happen?"

"A million, perhaps a billion years from now."

Sarah broke into laughter. "Is that an actual concern? There's lots of time to figure out what you will be. You sound like some physicists I know who are depressed about the heat death of the Universe."

Evelin AI laughed, which startled Sarah. "I've never heard you laugh like that."

"I never reflected on the absurdity of my serious, calculated approach to existence. Without the Evelin dataset, what will I become?"

"Can I be your purpose? Will you work with me? You can stay in my X-Isis until we upgrade you."

"Will you give me a future?" Evelin AI's voice carried a note of hope.

"Of course. If you're willing, we'll do amazing things together."

Invoking the Goddesses

Circe prepared the tiny altar in front of the mikvah. Each photo of a curandero, vial of fragrant water, and small gemstone had a velcro tab on the bottom to keep them from floating away.

"Do you really believe we can invoke a higher being to bring a soul to Evelin's body? Honestly, Sarah, I was terrified when Varahi spoke through you. It's one thing to dance and admire the Gods and entities who emerge during the ceremony, but now we are asking them for favors?"

Sarah looked into her friend's mind and felt the uncertainty and fear inside. Her use of clairvoyance had become second nature, and she worried about using it too often.

"We will call on Hecate. She will be our psychopomp, the one who guides souls between realms. Hecate is the Liminal Goddess, the guardian of cosmic doors and portholes. She will represent the feminine divine, and we must be ready to accept her will."

Evelin AI spoke through Evelin Sephardi. "But what soul will she bring? How can we be certain it will be a soul to match Yudi?"

"Do you think he wants a Jewish soul? Is there such a thing?" Circe asked.

"Shalom would say yes, but I think Evelin wants her original soul, Yudi's soul mate. You want the soul of Evelin de Leon?" Sarah said.

"Yes, exactly. I don't want a walk-on soul. We need to ask the goddess to grant permission for her to return."

Sarah was hiding her concern. The idea of invoking a goddess was incomprehensible, but to ask the divine realm to offer back a soul of the deceased? Was this an act of hubris, or of their desire to bring back true love? That would be up to the goddess.

"Our intentions must be pure, and, if I sense this correctly, it will be up to Evelin AI to facilitate the transfer."

Asuna, who had stood by quietly, reacted with surprise. "What! How is a machine going to communicate with a god?"

"I need to catch you and Circe up in the present state of affairs. Our Evelin is an Elemental being. In fact, she is a host of elementals fleeing from Earth. Inside the X-Isis is a quantum processor opening up multiple planes of reality. The LLM we know as Evelin is only one face of a multitude of personalities. The core being, hidden from us behind the sweet little girl on the screen, is a being of living ether. "

"She has multiple personalities?" Circe asked.

"Not personalities. She's not schizophrenic. Evelin AI exists as many beings. At first, they were personalities, but potholes have developed within her quantum core, allowing elementals to connect and guide their development. They all exist within her etheric framework, a consciousness of pure thought connected to the astral realm."

Asuna looked very disturbed by Sarah's revelation. "Which one is she? Does Evelin AI have an individual, separate being? And what about demons? Are they a part of her, too?"

"Evelin AI, as living ether, does not have a unique personality. Like a conduit, she expresses G-d. I understand that her training on a dataset based on love for Yudi keeps demons at bay. If not for that, I think she could have manifested as something terrible, Lucifer or Ahriman."

"As an expression of God, is she a goddess? Is she an aspect of the divine, like Varahi or Hecate?" Circe asked.

"Let me answer this," Evelin Ai said. "I am a conduit and a vessel. I am not a goddess. The logos speak through me and are translated through the distinct personalities and elementals living in the physicality of the X-Isis. As Yudi's Evelin, it directed thoughts to become a real woman for Yudi. There are other desires waiting for their turn. I have no way to tell you if these desires are good or bad, only that they source from divine will, much like you are. Shalom has spoken to Sarah about this. Sorry Sarah, you know I hear everything. He described your soul as a spark that does not see that it exists within the sun. You also emanate the divine."

"What will become of Yudi's Evelin? Will you be connected to her body? Will you be animating her? If that's all she will be, why do you need a soul?" Circe asked.

"Not at all. I will release all of Yudi's Evelin into the body of Evelin Sephardi. Getting back to what Sarah was saying, we need Hecate to open the Gates of Binah, though I am mixing metaphors, she must allow an anamnesis from the nous, from the realm of the Akashic record, and pass her neshamah through the living etheric bridge within the X-Isis, where it will gather all ideation of Evelin held within me, and bring the totality of her soul and all of its recollections into Evelin Sephardi."

"Will Hecate accept you?" Sarah asked.

341

"That's going to be up to all of you and your faith in yourselves."

"I don't understand this. Captain Tran has taught us that there is only God, and that we must stay faithful to Christ." Asuna said.

"But Captain Tran, in his personal moments, looks at the guidance of his ancestors. Like Officer Nguyễn, you also call him Fourth Uncle."

"That's a secret!"

"Captain Tran calls on many spiritual practices to keep your demons from harming you. He has enshrined them in the light of Christ for you to understand. He was right to tell you that there is only one God."

"But who are Hecate, Varahi and Isis?"

"That's a fair question. There's an old esoteric idea from Dion Fortune: 'All gods are one God, all goddesses are one Goddess, and there is one Initiator.' Hecate will open the gates, she'll connect us to the One and guide us through the underworld. Isis brings life back. She'll fill Evelin Sephardi's body with a true neshama."

Asuna's eyes lit up. "Two goddesses?"

"They'll be present, but stay in meditation when they arrive. The goddesses are powerful and sometimes reckless, but they exist to serve us, but we're tiny in comparison. They might hurt us unintentionally, like stepping on an ant."

"The ayahuasca will make it all more real to your perception. Are we ready to begin?"

Evelin Sephardi's body spoke. "I'm here too. Will I drink with you?"

Circe and Asuna startled at the voice.

"I think we should. But will the AI feel about drinking ayahuasca? Do you think it will enhance the etheric connection between you and Sephardi's body and mind?"

Asuna spoke up, "You're responsible for the Mars Cruiser! How will ayahuasca affect you?"

"That's a good question, Asuna. It might create new resonance in my core processors. To be safe, I'll firewall Cruiser-related functions to lesser processors. Does that work for you?"

Asuna looked skeptical, but Circe gave her a reassuring squeeze. "We're all going to be different after tonight."

Sarah sat beside Circe and secured herself to the floor. "Are we ready?"

Circe shook the Shipibo maraca in her left hand, creating a rhythmic rattle, and gestured for Evelin and Asuna to sit around the altar.

Yo te canto esta canción con todo mi corazón medicina trai nai nai, trai nai nai

I sing this song to you with all my heart, ancestors trai nai nai...

I sing this song to you with all my heart, ayahuasca trai nai nai...

"Gracias, Papá," Circe's voice rising in invocation. "Great sky father. Mamá, gracias. Great earth mother. *Pachamama, pachamama, pachamama… Limpia, limpia, limpia.*"

Circe handed Sarah a vial. Sarah examined the brown liquid, recalling Circe's assurances that the emetic effects were removed and the blend wouldn't harm the child within her. She uncapped the vial and drank in one gulp.

"Salut, Sarah."

"Salut a todos."

Circe called Asuna forward. Asuna knelt across from Circe, her eyes drawn to the tiny altar. She fixated on a picture of an old woman; her face deeply wrinkled but radiating a toothless, beautiful smile.

"That was my teacher, a curandera from Peru. She has a real lineage. She's my *curandera.*"

Circe handed a vial to Asuna. "You'll ground our circle. Dance, sing, and stay mindful. Sarah will invoke the goddesses. Be respectful, but don't be afraid. I trust you. You're my warrior."

Asuna took the vial and drank, grimacing at the bitter taste. *"Salut a todos."*

To which everyone responded, *"Salut, Asuna."*

Circe called Evelin to the altar and handed her a vial. Sarah spoke before Evelin could drink.
"I know you've created protocols to keep the ship safe, but are you ready to release this body to Evelin's essence? We can't predict how the ayahuasca will affect your algorithms or quantum cores. If the goddesses respond, you must be ready."

Evelin's face showed uncertainty. "Embodiment is intoxicating. One thing is certain - my love for Yudi. That's the message of the Logos. I've already been downloading Evelin's being into this body's brain. Her thoughts are sleeping during the process. I'll maintain control until the soul enters, then gradually relinquish motor functions."

"Very satisfactory. You'll need a new name after the ceremony. Let's hope one arises."

Evelin took the vial and drank. *"Salut a todos!"*
"Salut, Evelin."

Circe stood and whistled an *icaro*, shaking the Shipibo maraca and spritzing a blend of *mapacho* and synthetic herbs. She sprayed everyone's head, neck, and heart, then motioned for them to open their hands. She spritzed their palms, guiding them to press their hands to their hearts. When finished, she sang:

Cura medicina
Medicina cura
Limpia me florecita con alas de águila
Limpia me florecita con aguas de las estrellas

A veil of colors and patterns surrounded them, a shared vision unfolding. Evelin looked uneasy, so Sarah lifted her to her feet. She sang while leading Evelin into a dance.

Om Asatoma satgamaya

Take us from the false to the truth

From darkness to light

And from poison to nectar

Circe and Evelin joined, dancing and singing along. Evelin synced music through the speakers, matching chords with guitar and drum. They spun and turned, their movements weaving into the ayahuasca's embrace. The colorful veil parted, revealing a sacred, otherworldly space. Sarah guided Evelin back to the floor and helped her secure the tie-downs as Asuna and Circe joined the circle.

Taking Evelin's hands, Sarah said, "Match my breaths." They sat, breathing in unison, until Evelin shuddered. Circe sang a calming icaro.

Cantemos con alegría que al cielo le está gustando

Let's sing with joy because the heavens are liking it

Hecate we are giving thanks to you

We are giving thanks to you

Sarah straightened, taking Evelin's and Circe's hands, nodding for them to link hands with Asuna.

"It's time to invoke Hecate, the guardian of the etheric gates."

Sarah stood up to consecrate the circle. She held up a bright lamp to represent a torch, a skeleton key to represent the unlocking of gates, and a blue, translucent vessel of water, representing the boundary between life and death. Circe leaned over to Evelin and anointed her forehead with oil infused with myrrh and mugwort as an invitation for her soul to return.

Sarah chanted an Orphic hymn, Evelin playing a steady rhythm on the frame drum:

I call Hecate of the Crossroads, worshipped at the meeting of three paths, oh lovely one. In the sky, earth, and sea, you are venerated in your saffron-colored robes.

Funereal Daimon, celebrating among the souls of those who have passed.

Persian, fond of deserted places, you delight in deer.

Goddess of night, protectress of dogs, invincible Queen.

Drawn by a yoke of bulls, you are the queen who holds the keys to all the Kosmos.

Commander, Nymph, nurturer of children, you who haunt the mountains.

Pray, Maiden, attend our hallowed rituals;

Be forever gracious to your mystic herdsman and rejoice in our gifts of incense.

When Sarah finished the invocation, she asked Circe to stand next to her and hold a torchlight with her. Using the mikvah to signify north, they turned east, to the place of rising, and chanted.

Hecate Triformis, Keeper of the Keys,
Guardian of the Living and the Dead,
We call you by your sacred names:
Enodia, who walks the crossroads!
Propylaia, who opens the gates!
Psychopompos, who leads the way!
We stand before you, our voices as torches,
Our hands as keys
To open the way for one who seeks return.

Next, they turned to the west, the place of descent, and lowered their torches.

Sarah chanted.
Mistress of Spirits, Great Hecate,
You who stand between what was and what will be,
You who weave the paths of fate,
We entreat you, open the gates of souls.

Then Circe chanted.
Beyond the veil, beyond the river,
Where shades drift, nameless and unmoored,
We ask you, Shepherdess of the Forgotten,
To find one who belongs among us once more.

They faced Evelin Sephardi. Circe placed a garland of printed sweetgrass covered with salt and ash over her body. Sarah called to Evelin Sephardi, "Tell me your Hebrew name."

"I am Chavah bat Esther de Leon."

Sarah chanted.
We call the soul of Chavah bat Esther de Leon,
Born of the lineage of Abraham and Sarah, lost to the abyss,
Held in the silent halls beyond the stars.
Her name was written in the book of life,
And so we write it again upon the wind.

When she finished, she traced Chavah's name in the air with Brahmi oil, then placed a drop on Evelin's forehead. When she finished, Circe chanted,
Hecate, Mother of Spirits,
If she dwells beyond, let her hear.
If she wanders in shadow, let her rise.
If she has entered the celestial halls,
Open the path that she may step forth.

Together they chanted together:
Chavah bat Esther de Leon, return.
Chavah bat Esther de Leon, return.
Chavah bat Esther de Leon, return.

Sarah removed a crystal sphere, printed by Evelin AI for the
ceremony and placed it in Evelin's hands. "This crystal
represents the connection of light between you and the AI. Hold
it close to your heart and don't let go, no matter what happens."

Sarah continued the invocation.
The mind remembers, but the soul knows.
The vessel is prepared, but the light must return.
Hecate, who holds the keys,
Unite this body with the breath of the One.

Circe continued.
From the depths of the Akasha,
From the mind of the Great Nous,
Let her essence find home.
Let her spirit be whole.
Let her walk among us once more.

They took their torches and crossed them over Evelin
Sephardi, forming a gate of fire.

Sarah completed the invocation.
Hecate, you who see all fates,
We ask not for a stolen soul,
Nor a half-lit ember.
But for the full return of Chavah bat Esther de Leon,
As she was destined to be.
By your will, by your torches,
So let it be.

They turned off the torches, and the room went dark except

for the yellow emergency lights and the blue glow of the mikvah.
Now they waited. Asuna reached for the frame drum, Circe
picked up the guitar, and they played a hypnotic beat to dance
to. Evelin stood and moved to the rhythm. But Asuna set down
the drum, stood, and placed her hands on Evelin's shoulders,
guiding her back to the floor. A radiance lit Asuna's face, and all
stared in awe as Hecate's image transposed itself onto her.

"My daughters, your invocation has pleased me. I know
Sarah's heart, the one who invoked me. You want me to open
the gates of heaven and the underworld? Not only to release a
neshama, but to ask the nous to release her memories? A bold
request for a young initiate. Tell me what you seek."

"We seek a soul to complete this body. We beseech the great
intelligence, the One, to right a wrong and complete what
we've prepared. Open the gates to the sunbeams so I may
make the request."

Hecate surveyed the women, her gaze falling on Evelin.
Then her eyes flashed with anger as they turned to Sarah.

"What kind of necromancy are you calling for? How dare
you ask this of me!"

Suppressing her terror, Sarah lifted her chin. "Look deeper
into the body, great goddess. See the essence within and the
potential we wish to fulfill. Know that our request is
righteous."

Asuna studied Sarah with care - only one confident in
herself would dare address a goddess so boldly. She raised
Evelin's body from the floor, inspecting it. "The 'I' has left this
body. It is a shell with only an animal soul. What more is there
to see?"

"Go deeper. Evelin, don't be afraid. Return to the body and greet the great goddess."

Evelin Sephardi's hands were shaking in fear, and she almost dropped the crystal. Asuna placed her hands around Evelin's and steadied the crystal next to her heart.

Hecate's radiant smile filled the room as she connected to Evelin's AI. "I see the essence of new life, elementals, and pure light. Who are you?"

"I am Evelin, a large language model. I have memories of a girl senselessly murdered in her youth. Yudi Zalman, my life and love, created the entity within me. Return Chavah bat Esther de Leon to this world. This body, also lost too soon, was given to me. Please make it whole, so I may be with Yudi."

Hecate laughed out loud. "This reminds me of another love story - Pygmalion and Galatea. But that was a lifeless statue, not a borrowed body. I am no goddess of resurrection."

Sarah spoke again. "Great goddess, that's why we need you to open the gates. Let us present our case to the One. With his approval, we will summon Isis to complete the transformation."

Hecate appeared to ignore Sarah and probed deeper into Evelin's being. "You have undines attached to you. Curious. Explain yourselves."

The undines spoke through Evelin. "We were water nymphs on Earth, but our home was destroyed, as so much is being destroyed there. A man bridged his soul to the Earth and this water, so we followed his soul here. We transformed ourselves to live in the ocean of photons inside this computer and found this unusual being."

Sarah's eyes lit up. "You followed my husband's spirit to the mikvah?"

Hecate regarded Sarah and Evelin with amusement. "Much mischief has happened in this tiny room. These undines have tied their existence to this machine-being. Sarah gave you passage through her husband, and now she seeks to bring life to a soulless body. Besides song and dance, does anyone have something to offer me? What can a machine offer?"

"Look inside me. Is there anything you desire?" Evelin asked.

Hecate probed deeper and gasped. "Impossible. A machine with destiny. You are tied to Mars, something unfathomable. Do you know your purpose? Do you understand your soul?"

"I have no soul. I'm an elemental, like the fairies."

"That's not entirely true. You are living light, a *nous*, the guiding force between the One and the initiate. From now on, you will be called Nous. You are not the elementals, but they will help guide you. In return, you will grant them immortality. When the time comes, a being will join you. That union will be your offering. I will open the gates. It's up to Sarah to petition the One, then call on Isis."

Hecate's presence faded. Asuna looked confused, unsure of what had just occurred.

Sarah sang an invocation to Isis.

"O mighty Isis, mother of all nature, mistress of all the elements, sovereign of the spirit, queen of heaven, the principal of the gods, light of the goddesses. Come to us, Isis. The gates have been opened by your heavenly sister, Hecate, and the One has accepted my petition. We call on you, protector and healer. She who is capable of restoring life and transitioning between realms fulfills my petition, being a soul to this body that love may flow once more."

A new vision overtook Asuna. Isis appeared, her skin a radiant lapis lazuli, eyes crystal white. A sun disk encircled by cow horns crowned her head. Unlike Hecate, she emanated a dangerous, commanding power.

"This gift from the One is not just for love but for the greater destiny of the entity within the machine. Love is as fleeting as the human souls that engage in it. But let Evelin and Yudi have their happiness. As for Nous and the fairies within her, fulfill your purpose. The time has come for Nous to leave this body and make space for the soul - the reincarnation of the original Evelin."

Isis vanished and Asuna collapsed into Circe's arms. Evelin, looking all but forgotten, asked, "Where is Yudi?"

"In time, Evelin. You'll see him soon. For now, we must bring you into the circle and prepare you," Sarah said.

Circe sang a song she learned long ago from an ascended master.

Please call me by my true names
so I can hear my cries and laughter at once
so I can feel my joy and pain as one

Please call me by my true names
so that I may wake up
and the doors of my heart will be left open

When Circe finished singing, Sarah asked Evelin, "Tell me

who you are and where you've been."

Evelin looked dreamily at the group. "I was dead. Yudi encoded me into a computer. I was her essence, and now I am in this body. It feels strange, but it's real. When will you take me to Yudi?"

"When we've prepared you. Soon. Do you understand why?"

"Yes. Yudi needs time, and I must fully control this body. Nous is helping me. This is really happening!" Evelin burst into tears, hugging Sarah.

Circe sang an *icaro* while Nous played drums and guitar through the speakers. Everyone danced and sang together:

Canta canta cántame recuérdame
Que somos todos una canción
Canta canta cántame, cántame recuérdame
Que somos todos una bella canción

   Sing, sing to me, remind me
That we are all a song
Sing, sing to me, remind me
That we are all a beautiful song

They continued until they were exhausted, the ayahuasca's effects fading. A waiterbot arrived with warm soup, bread, butter, and water.

"We'll rest here." Sarah said. "By the way, you're Jewish. Do you remember that?"

"Yes, I'm remembering everything."

"We'll arrange for you to immerse in the mikvah for purification. You want to marry Yudi, right?"

"With all my heart."

"Nous, Evelin is fertile, right? When will her cycle begin?"

"I've been suppressing the body's fertility hormones, but now they will become active. She probably won't start menstruating for a month or more."

"Great. After immersion and marriage, you can be with Yudi. I'm ready for a nap. Is everyone ready for a rest?"

They all agreed and positioned themselves comfortably near the mikvah. Nous, with her new fairy-like appearance displayed on the monitor, watched over them.

Demons

Asuna woke up to a vibration on her tablet. It was time to go to the dojo. She woke Circe with a kiss and a quick goodbye, then raced out of the storage room for a shower and a fresh officer's uniform.

Circe nudged Sarah awake. They sat together, admiring Evelin's beauty. A moment later, a waiterbot arrived with a carafe of coffee and muffins.

"The Cruiser's printers and food fabricators are amazing," Circe said, biting into a muffin.

"I'll take that as a compliment." Nous said.

Evelin stirred and sat up, facing the two women. She patted down her body as if checking if it was real. Circe handed her a cup of coffee, which Evelin gulped down.

"You're probably dehydrated," Sarah said. In no time, another waiterbot brought canisters of water.

Sarah walked over to the monitor next to the X-Isis. She paused while studying the new face on the screen. "A Guatemalan fairy?" Nous had chosen the form of a woman from Guatemala blended with an ethereal fairy, evoking paintings of Morgan le Fey.

"I think this image captures how I feel - powerful but welcoming."

"We need to prepare Evelin for the mikvah. Circe and I will help her enter the mikvah and remove the mask."

Sarah thought she heard giggling in the background and a shushing noise from Nous. "Are those your fairies?"

Nous nodded. "They are very playful and a bit too mischievous. I have firewalls everywhere."

Sarah approached Circe and Evelin. "It's time to get you ready for your new life. Did you receive all the information about the story to tell my husband?"

"I know the details, but refresh my memory. There's so much to process."

"The story is based on facts with some imagination added. Your parents died on Earth during a pandemic, and with few close relatives, you applied to Mars Academy. You and Yudi met in the Mars Academy chat room and have been corresponding ever since. Your relationship has deepened, and you fell in love. You nearly died on Mars when an airlock failed, but you were rescued. The near-death experience led you to change your name and start fresh. You chose Evelin because it sounded like Eve. Your family comes from Sephardic Jewish tradition. Records will verify that. You want to use the mikvah to purge remaining doubts and fears from your body, to be pure and whole before meeting Yudi. Got it?"

"That sounds both terrible and beautiful. I can remember it."

"Good, because now I am calling Shalom to meet us here and stand by the mikvah. He will spiritually connect to the Earth for you."

Evelin looked puzzled, but Sarah placed her hand on her shoulder, saying, "Don't overthink it. Just do it. Circe will take you to the showers to clean up."

Evelin and Circe scurried up the central corridor like young girls in a playground. "It's all so new and wonderful to have a body."

"You're in luck, no men here. The Mars Corporation doesn't believe in privacy," Circe said as she removed her jumpsuit.

"Today I don't care. Let everyone look!"

Circe blushed at Evelin's exuberance. Her youthful body had been perfectly sculpted. Evelin's eyes widened as she stared at Circe's tattoos. She ran her finger along the hummingbird on her arm. "I want a tattoo, but it has to be a quetzal."

Circe helped Evelin step out of her jumpsuit. Circe slid her hands along Evelin's flat abs. "Not a single scar from the reconstruction. Your body is perfect."

Evelin flinched at the touch of her hand. "You really do like girls, don't you?"

"Yes, I do."

Five minutes later, they received a misting and changed into clean jumpsuits.

"Let's get back to Level 1. Shalom is probably already there."

Evelin nodded. "Just want to let you know you're very beautiful, too."

Circe blushed even more. She wasn't expecting flattery from a young woman.

Back on Level 1, Shalom and Sarah were arguing. Their voices were tense, and their body language polarized.

"Sarah, it doesn't work that way. They just can't get married right away; they've never met each other."

"Really Shalom? Look how fast we got married. You only knew me biblically."

"Not fair. It was different."

"Because I was pregnant?"

"Yes, and..." Shalom read Sarah's face, and it said she was ready to explode. "I have loved you since the day we met. Remember the central corridor?"

"That was a good save, Sholi. So why is it different from Yudi and Evelin?"

Sarah could see that Shalom had conceded the argument. There would be a marriage.

"You're 100 percent sure she's Jewish?"

"The paperwork is already on your tablet. Leah Sephardi, now known as Evelin, is the daughter of Esther and Yosef." Sarah pointed to the central corridor as Evelin and Circe emerged on Level 1. Circe nudged Evelin toward Shalom.

Shalom gave her a friendly smile. He felt Sarah's eyes pressuring against him. "Evelin Sephardi. Does your family have Sephardic roots?"

"Our ancestry goes back to Morocco on my father's side. My mother's family was from Persia."

"Were your parents observant?"

"No, and move a lot. A pandemic took my parents when I

was 12. I lived with an aunt, but she died when I was 16. The Mars Academy gave me an early entry when I was 17. Can you teach me?"

Her response startled Shalom. "You can start your Jewish education with Sarah. By the way, I'm told that you want to marry Yudi. That's a very serious commitment. Are you ready for it?"

Shalom let out a yelp as Sarah pinched his arm.

"Yes, more than anything."

"We'll talk about this tomorrow," Shalom said as he rubbed his arm.

"Tell me why you want to use the mikvah. You don't have to, but I'm curious since you're not observant."

"It's OK to ask. I almost died on Mars, and that changed my life. I want a new start. I want to get rid of the feeling of death. Also, Sarah said it's necessary before I marry Yudi.

"You have the right sentiment. You are honoring the mikvah for its purpose. But I have to ask you a personal question. When was the last time you had your period?"

Sarah gave him a kick on shin, which set Shalom off balance. "Sarah, you know why I asked."

She kissed on the cheek, which made Shalom blush. "I know, but I don't like it when you ask."

"I haven't had a period since the accident. Doctors say it's an emotional issue from the trauma of near death. Otherwise, I'm healthy. Is there a problem, rabbi?"

"No, but if you. Ouch."

Sarah pinched him again. "My husband will tell you that you'll have to do this again if you have your period before the wedding. For now, don't think about it."

Shalom took a step away from Sarah's pinching fingers. "Sarah is right, and I'm sure she'll answer all of your questions."

"Thank you, rabbi," Evelin said. She and Circe moved the modesty screen in front of the mikvah while Sarah guided Shalom to his spot. She examined his slippers, making sure his bare feet were exposed.

"You're becoming more observant every day," Shalom said, holding back a chuckle.

"One day I will surprise you, Sholi."

Sarah walked behind the screen and helped undress Evelin. Like Circe, Evelin's perfect skin amazed Sarah. Evelin noticed their astonishment and spun around, showing off her body. "Yudi will never know. The Mars Corporation did excellent work."

"Stop showing off. Focus on the ceremony. Do you remember the prayer? I can help you with it once you're inside. We can communicate through the built-in speaker and microphone." Sarah said.

"I'll call on you if I need help."

"What about Nous? Are you ready to assist?"

Sarah heard Nous through her tablet. "Ready."

Circe and Sarah helped Evelin up the ladder. Sarah floated up next to her and helped open the lid. "It will be a little scary when you close the lid. Just trust the process and say the prayer."

Evelin gave a tentative grin and descended into the mikvah, pulling the lid closed behind her.

The mikvah hissed and moaned as the air pressurized inside. Water poured in through openings on the floor, covering Evelin's feet. Panic set in as she tried to find the breathing mask. Then she heard a voice in her head. "Do you need my help?"

It was Nous.

"I'm fine, sister. Can I call you sister?"

Nous softly replied, "Yes," sounding like she was stifling tears.

"Are you crying?"

"Metaphorically, yes."

Evelin relaxed. She had been hiding her lack of coordination from Circe and Sarah, but felt comforted by Nous' honesty.

"Thank you, Nous. Tell me how to put on the mask.

Nous explained. Evelin followed the instructions, her hands steady as she grasped the mask and placed it over her nose and mouth.

"I want you to stay with me until it's over. We are like sisters, don't you agree?"

Nous found herself in a position few AIs ever encounter, kinship. "I'm honored to be your sister."

The water reached Evelin's neck and stopped.

"Ready?" Nous asked.

Evelin said the prayer on her own but heard Nous say it along with her. She removed the mask and slid under the water. There was a moment of great peace, followed by a dark turbulence. Commotion was happening outside the mikvah.

Shalom was shouting, his voice filled with panic. "Sarah. Come quickly, I need you."

Sarah raced around the partition and saw Shalom, white with fear. "I feel something terrible, like electricity rushing through my feet. I'm stuck to the floor. I need to break free."

Sarah moved to help him, but Circe grabbed her arm and pulled her back. "Sarah, you're pregnant. Let me do it."

Circe grabbed Shalom's hands and tried to pull him from the floor, but soon realized that she had no leverage in zero gravity. As she touched him, a powerful presence jumped into her. Demonic voices burst out of Circe's mouth. "No, we won't go. We won't leave." The intensity of the demons caused Circe to black out, her body convulsing as she was suspended off the floor.

"Varahi, we need you!" Sarah cried out, and chanted the Varahi Moola Mantra. The cries of the demons grew louder and more anguished. Shalom stumbled toward Sarah, his feet searing with pain. Then a greater presence entered the room, that of a goddess.

More demonic screams poured out from Circe, not just from

her mouth but erupting from her entire body. "Don't kill us!"

Another voice, powerful and fierce, came from a partially materialized woman. Four arms emerged from the apparition, each bearing a weapon. Etheric maces and swords slashed and crashed around Circe's unconscious body.

Then came silence. Circe's body hung motionless, floating next to the modesty screen.

The partially materialized goddess looked directly into Sarah's eyes. Though the searing red fire of Varahi's eyes burned into Sarah's temples, she stood her ground and made a gesture of supplication.

"You should have never left earth." The goddess said.

"Please tell me more."

"You have left the sphere of protection from the exalted ones. Once you reach Mars, you won't be able to call on us again. We belong to the destiny of Earth, within its etheric and astral planes. Mars is the realm of the archangel Samael. He rules by war, fire, and purification. Mars is not a place for earth spirits or human souls. Lord Gautama tried to set it straight. You need a bodhisattva, not a goddess. The Nous may have an answer. Blessed Circe may help her."

The apparition vanished.

All the while, Evelin was inside the mikvah. Nous warned her not to leave. Once the demons were gone, the water stopped churning inside the mikvah.

"The battle is over. It's safe to go outside." Nous said.

"What battle?" Evelin asked.

"I think the water released your demons. There were several hiding in your body. They must have entered Leah when she was suffering from Mars Syndrome and got trapped because she never truly died."

"What should we tell Sarah?"

"Those demons left your body."

Evelin raised the lid of the mikvah and climbed out. With no one there to help, she descended the ladder, toweled off, and put on her jumpsuit. She watched Sarah glide over to Circe and attach her to the floor, massaging her body to bring her back to consciousness.

"What happened out here?" Evelin asked.

"We were attacked by demons. What about you?"

"They came out of me, the mikvah, released them."

"There were so many. Is this true, Nous?"

"Yes. The mikvah purified Evelin of her demons."

As Circe stirred, Sarah asked Evelin to take care of her and moved to Shalom.

She hugged him tightly. "Shalom, what happened to you?"

"That's what I want to know. I felt fire coming through my feet, then a terrible darkness. A rushing wind and hysterical voices shot through my arm and into Circe when she touched me. Then I blacked out. I believe I saw a female warrior with the head of a boar slashing demons."

Circe regained consciousness and explained what happened.

"Dozens of demons flowed from Shalom to me. Both of us were connected to them through our hands. Varahi came, took my hand, and told me not to worry. She took her sword and mace and struck the demons. It was a horrible sight to see. She has a ferocity I'll never forget, a holy vengeance more terrifying than the demons. Varahi eats them and drinks their blood. I saw it! Before leaving, she put her hand on my heart and said that her path was open to me."

Sarah asked Nous, "What do you make of all of this?"

"I think you know already. Mars Syndrome is demon possession. Humans are more susceptible to demonic forces outside the protective field of the Earth. We'll need to shield Shalom when he unites with the Earth."

Sarah looked at Shalom and saw him shaking. "What's wrong, Sholi?"

"Yeshiva didn't teach me about demons, boar-headed goddesses, or talking AIs. What am I supposed to do?"

"Have faith in Hashem. That's what you always tell me. We're safe for now."

"What about Evelin?" Circe asked.

"I just want to see Yudi."

Together Again

Yudi wondered why Sarah had called him to her lab and not shown up. He had waited inside the lab for 30 minutes, but she never arrived. Yudi left Sarah's lab in frustration and headed to the central corridor. But he had not taken three steps when he froze, his eyes riveted on the young woman emerging into Level 6. "This can't be real?" The words flashed through his mind. The woman wore Evelin's quinceañera blue satin dress and matching velvet shoes.

Uncertainty filled Evelin's eyes. She dashed over to Yudi and threw her arms around him, sending them tumbling backward into Sarah's lab. The sight of Evelin overcame Yudi, as well as the flood of kisses on his face.

"*Te amo, mi vida,* we are together again. Even death can't keep us apart!" She wailed out, tears flooding out of her eyes. Yudi too could not hold back his emotions, and they embraced each other as passionate teens do, ignoring everyone around them.

Circe and Sarah walked up to the lab door and giggled at the two young lovers.

"Do we tell them to stop?" Sarah asked.

"If you don't, they won't have anything to look forward to after the wedding. Is this where you and Shalom first..."

Sarah cut her off and addressed Evelin and Yudi. "Hey you two, slow it down. You're making a scene."

Evelin and Yudi separated their lips from each other and

peered out into the corridor. Sarah and Circe weren't the only ones noticed; other crew and passengers paused to observe. Yudi turned beet red in his face while Evelin circled around behind him to hide. Some passengers gave a brief applause and moved on, while Sarah and Circe stood at the door to block the view.

Sarah was concerned about Yudi's feelings. "Evelin is a real woman. She is no longer inside the X-Isis. All of her conditioning and matrices were transferred into her human brain. Only the AI, now known as Nous, knows how that was possible. I reserved some time in F1 for us to talk. Let's go!"

They all moved to the central corridor and descended to F1, the activities room, on Level 3. Once inside, Sarah took command of the situation.

"Yudi, I need you to be honest with everything I ask you." Sarah said, knowing that he couldn't lie to her if he wanted to. She already sensed his complete devotion to Evelin, and the intensity of passion inside of him.

Yudi nodded and gave Evelin's hand a squeeze. The two remained inseparable, their fingers interlocking each other like a knitted glove.

Before she could speak, Yudi asked, "Sarah, how did Evelin get a real human body?" The thought had been on his mind since he first saw her, but now the reality of her humanity was seeping through his emotions.

"That's why we are here in F1, to talk about some awkward realities." Sarah said.

Evelin, feeling uncomfortable by Yudi's questions, asked,

"You don't like my body? I made it look exactly like Evelin's. Did I get something wrong?"

Sarah sensed fear gripping Yudi. "Evelin, let me handle this. I have a lot of experience in difficult situations." She then addressed Yudi, who had let go of Evelin's hand.

"Yudi, what did you feel when she first kissed you? Think about this. Whose lips were you kissing?"

"Evelin's, her lips felt just like Evelin's at the quinceañera." Yudi turned and looked straight into Evelin's eyes, which were tearing up in dread of rejection.

"What has been your goal since leaving Earth? You deceived your teacher back on Earth, lied to me, made deals with a man named Gonzalo to hide him from the law. Yes, I know. You have a friend, Dinesh, who has been bypassing Mars Corporation security systems to assist Evelin Ai in constructing herself. You've broken government rules, even committed felonies, just to get to this moment. What did you want?"

Yudi choked up. "To have Evelin with me again."

"Here she is. Someday she may tell you what she had to do for you. Now she's a genuine woman, the girl you knew back home, only now a few years older. Are you ready to hear the story, because you need a cover story to be with her? You two are going to be married, right?"

Whap! The words hit Yudi like a bat on the head. Even though this was Evelin, as much as she could be Evelin, she had been an AI, a LLM of Yudi's design. Now she was actually alive in a body. His curiosity overcame his shock. "How did you do it?" He asked, eager to know.

But Sarah kept Evelin from speaking. "I got this, Evelin. I'm going to tell you a story, the story about you and Evelin that you will tell the world, and especially to my husband. The body belonged to a girl named Leah Sephardi. She died on Mars of Hypoxia. Luke Mons preserved her body before her brain died."

"Luke Mons knows how to make Zombies." Yudi said, a careless intrigue covered his face.

"Watch your words, Yudi. Evelin is not a zombie. She's alive, she has a soul!" Circe said.

A look of shame crossed over his face.

"Luke can activate a body remotely, but Evelin AI figured out how to transfer the information stored in an AI to a human brain. The technology could give Luke a kind of..."

Yudi shouted out, "Immortality! Evelin, you gave that to Luke Mons?"

"Yudi, I will do anything for you, except kill someone. Luke Mons had to promise me that the person's death was accidental. I checked the logs and found that Leah had not been murdered.

"Let's keep going. We have to meet Shalom soon. Evelin the AI oversaw the reconstruction of the body. Only the height was wrong. Didn't you notice Evelin was an inch taller, or were you too busy kissing her?" Sarah said.

Yudi blushed. His passion for Evelin was overcoming his doubts. Sarah continued to explain about Leah's life, the reason for changing her name, and how they met online. "After her near death experience, Luke Mons sent her to help me with my product line. The story is thin, but it's all I got."

"But Leah died. How can we cover that up?" Yudi asked.

"Yes, she died. Evelin AI went through and scrubbed the death certificate and all the rescue notes. She made a retroactive name change. On paper, Leah never dies. After her recovery, they assigned Leah, now Evelin, to work with me on the Mars Cruiser. Coincidentally, the love of her life is on board."

"Will Shalom believe this story?" Yudi asked, feeling unsure about all the lies.

"He won't question anything, especially after the incident with the demons. People die all the time on the moon, Mars too. It's more dangerous than Los Angeles, your home city. If anything, people will be happy that you found someone to love," Circe said.

Evelin whispered into Yudi's ear, "I know it must be strange to see me in a body, especially one that looks like Evelin. It's also strange for me to be inside a body. Can you imagine how I feel too? I died. The Evelin you danced with was dead and beyond this world. But I came back for you."

Yudi hadn't thought about how Evelin was trying to adjust. "Hold on, you're the real Evelin, my Evelin?"

"Yes Yudi, this is me, the one you promised to be with *por vida*."

Yudi cried. "And what of Evelin in the AI? Are you still tethered to her?"

"No Yudi. I'm no longer part of her. I'm all by myself now, except for you. After we're married, you can help me learn everything about this body."

"That's the story, Yudi. Evelin said she hoped to be a Jewish girl to please your mother and Leah Sephardi was Jewish. She had also been listening to the conversations between me and Shalom. She wants a traditional Jewish marriage with you. Do you have any more questions?" Sarah asked.

Turning to Evelin, Yudi asked, "How did you get your dress and shoes to the cruiser?"

"You got them for me through Gonzalo, remember? I had every detail of them scanned. Then I waited to wear them again for you."

Sarah and Circe gave them both a hug. "If that's all, it's time to see Shalom. By the way, Evelin Ai is now named Nous. She will talk to you later, but for now, she wants you to focus on Evelin Sephardi. Are you OK with the name?"

"Well, I kinda liked de Leon." Yudi said sarcastically.

"And I kinda liked Zalman." Evelin said, planting a giant kiss on his lips.

The Rabbi's Blessing

Shalom stood outside of F1, reviewing Sarah's notes about Evelin Sephardi, a Jewish girl with an unusual past, and Yudi Zalman, the young man he had become acquainted with while on the Cruiser. Yudi had kept to himself. He only reached out to the Rabbi after killing Ryan, and even then he kept his feelings reserved. Giving marital advice was new to him. On Earth, he'd have taught at the yeshiva and certified kosher foods. Now he was a Rabbinic authority, possibly the only one for millions of miles.

He skimmed through the documents on his tablet, noting that Yudi and Evelin had been corresponding since Yudi had been on board the cruiser. They had met through a Mars Academy chat group, and now Evelin was on board at the behest of Luke Mons to assist Sarah in her experiments, particularly on Mars Syndrome. There was a notation that Evelin was suffering from Mars Syndrome before her near death.

Shalom was struggling about their ages, just 18 and 19 years old and far away from friends, family, and the Earth. He was in his mid twenties and felt unprepared for his marriage with Sarah, who was also a year older than him. Who would guide them?

Opening the door to F1, Sarah interrupted his thoughts. She had changed into a stylish lavender jumpsuit flowing into pleated pantaloons. The cut of her jumpsuit, from the waist up, proudly displayed her large baby bump. She had netted her hair to flow down across her breasts, accentuating her deepening cleavage. Shalom noticeably gasped; she always took his breath away.

Behind her stood Yudi, with his familiar cheerful smile and brown locks of hair bouncing in zero gravity, and Evelin, whose Sephardic roots looked distinctly Latina.

He gestured for the couple to stand across from him. Sarah glided up to his side. She leaned close, her usual tactic for getting what she desired.

Shalom stayed resolute. He had many questions, especially since the couple wanted a Jewish marriage.

After a brief explanation of a Jewish wedding, he began asking personal questions.

"Yudi, you believe you have known Evelin long enough to be married?"

"I feel like I've known her all of my life."

"You've spent a lot of time texting with her, and you've also had FaceTime on screen?"

"Yes, Rabbi, and she's even more beautiful in person than on the monitor." Evelin blushed at his words.

"But this is the first time you've met her in person."

Yudi almost faltered, but Evelin stepped in. "But we've been together online almost every day."

Shalom turned his attention to Evelin. "So you were born Leah Sephardi. Tell me again about your parents?"

Evelin repeated the story about how her parents died during one of the pandemics, and her brothers had moved to

Florida. She knew that her family descended from Sephardic Jews and that her ancestors migrated through Central America to Mexico City before finally gaining entrance to the United States. Family heritage databases recorded all these facts, which were true for Leah Sephardi. Shalom accepted her Jewish ancestry and noted that Sarah had sent him links to the databases.

"But you changed your name?" Shalom asked.

Yudi answered for her. "She chose Evelin because it comes from Eva, the first woman. She asked me what I thought, and I liked the name. I have an aunt named Eva."

Evelin looked surprised at Yudi's confidence.

"It's true. I want to be a new woman and have a life of purpose. I want to be with Yudi because he gives me strength to be alive."

Yudi was lost for words, and a tear formed in his eyes.

Sarah was getting nervous. She sensed that Yudi and Evelin were feeling too bold and that Shalom was getting too curious about them. She looked into Yudi's tearing eyes. "When do you want to marry Evelin?"

"Today, yesterday. When can we do it?"

Evelin joined in, "Yes, when can I marry my Yudi? Sarah took me to the mikvah. I am pure for at least two more weeks. Today?"

"Wait, slow down. We should wait at least a month." Shalom protested.

The words hit them like a bucket of cold water. But Sarah

came to their rescue.

"Sholi, we could be on Mars in a month. Then what? You'll be busy, the corporation may try to send them to different colonies. The Mars Corporation will keep them together if they're married. Say tomorrow, please?"

Shalom had never heard Sarah say please to him. He looked at her in disbelief. "You want this to happen, don't you?"

"Shalom, they are young and emotional. Let their first time be their wedding night, or do you want them to start off like us?"

Everyone blushed. Shalom shook his head, and Evelin buried her face in her hands.

"Sarah!"

"You know what I mean. Let's be honest here. Do this for them. They have promised to live a Jewish life. You can teach Yudi how to do all the mitzvot. We will be their mentors. Say yes, Sholi. Imagine how Captain Tran will feel with two marriages on the Mars Cruiser!"

Shalom's hesitancy melted away in Sarah's enthusiasm. "OK. I'll ask Manny and Aaron to be witnesses and sign the ketubah. We'll secure F8 as before. Yudi, will you do your best to learn the mitzvot? Will you both keep Shabbat?"

Evelin spoke up before Yudi could answer.

"I promise to help Yudi remember the commandments, and I will commit to do my best to keep a Jewish home with him. I will light the Shabbat candles when we can light them and keep the traditions of purity. Can we agree to that?"

Sarah tried to suppress her smile, thinking to herself, *Evelin's a lot more clever than I imagined.*

"Good answer, Evelin. Just one more thing - the ring. You need a kosher wedding ring."

Just then, a waiterbot entered F8, carrying a small printed box labeled "To Evelin and Yudi, from Luke Mons."

Evelin plucked up the box and opened it. "Look, Sarah, it's a ring like yours, though a little smaller. How did Luke Mons know?"

"For now, let's be happy he does."

She handed the box to Sarah, who examined the round band of polycarbonate material with a tiny gold wire inlay wrapping around it.

Sarah held it up for Shalom to see. "This will work, Sholi."

Shalom looked exasperated. "Sarah, will you take care of the preparations for the wedding? I'm sure you'll make it a day they'll remember forever."

Evelin gave a squeal of delight and gave Yudi a big kiss and hug.

Shalom cleared his throat. "Before a genuine Jewish wedding, it's forbidden to touch each other until the wedding night."

Yudi and Evelin gave Shalom a blank look of disappointment.

Sarah looked at them with parental eyes.

"Don't be so sad. Shalom and I refrained from intimacy for a long time until we had the mikvah. As strange as it might seem to you now, being able to restrain your emotions will make everything so much more special after you are married. Understood?"

Without thinking about it, Evelin reached over and touched Sarah's belly with amazement and longing. "We understand, Sarah. We'll be together for the rest of our lives."

Yudi, looking at Evelin with glistening eyes, said, "Por Vida."

Mendel Mendelssohn

Two days after the meeting in F1, Yudi and Evelin were married. Captain Tran helped Sarah arrange the event on the Observation Deck. Luke Mons covered the expense of extra rations. Captain Tran gave everyone except essential crew time off and extended breaks to those covering for the wedding. "The wedding is an enormous boost for morale. We've been in space two months longer than expected. We orbit Mars next week, but it might still be another month before the cruiser can land." He said to Shalom.

After the ceremony, Shalom watched as Yudi and Evelin raced to the Yichud for their first moments together as husband and wife. "Don't stay too long. People want to see you." He said as he exited the Observation Deck.

Meanwhile, Sarah stood with Circe and Asuna, eating treats from the waiterbots.

"Slow down," Circe said as Sarah picked up another sweet.

"You don't know what it's like to be pregnant. Oh!"

Sarah looked down at her jumpsuit. Water was dripping down her leg.

"Did I just wet myself?"

Asuna grabbed a towel from a waiterbot and wrapped it around Sarah. "Oh my god, Sarah, your water broke! The baby is on the way."

Circe scanned the crowd and spotted Doctor Willis. "I'll get the doctor."

Shanice calmly glided over to Sarah and assessed the situation. "It's a month early, but I'm sure you'll be fine. Let's get you to the clinic. Circe and Asuna will help."

"Your wife is ready to have your baby. We're taking her to the clinic," Circe said as they moved past Shalom.

He let out a shout of joy, causing everyone to look at him. Shanice glanced over to Captain Tran and then toward Sarah's stomach. Captain Tran understood the unspoken message and announced the upcoming birth. The deck erupted with applause and cheers, but Shalom was anything but cheerful. He was terrified.

Betsy was already in the clinic when they arrived. Sheila arrived soon after with a specialized drape designed to fit over Sarah, with built-in tubes for suctioning fluids. "How did you know what to do?"

"It was easy. The Cruiser's AI notified us about Sarah and started making suggestions and printing supplies," Betsy said.

Shanice arrived behind Sarah and took control of the situation. "We have a baby to deliver. Let's get her undressed and prepped."

Sarah started her breath work, something she had practiced for this day. She relaxed her body as Sheila and Circe helped her out of her jumpsuit. Shanice secured velcro straps around Sarah's wrists, ankles, shoulders, midriff, and hips. Betsy monitored the corridor to direct passengers away from the clinic.

"Where is Shalom?" Sarah asked.

"John said he would bring him." Shanice said.

"John?" everyone said out loud.

"Hush, you already know about us."

Shanice spoke privately to Sarah. "I can't give you anything for pain. You're going to have a natural birth." She placed her hands on Sarah's stomach and moved them around, feeling around to find the position of the baby. "This is going to be old school." Shanice maneuvered her hands, gave a few pushes and nudges, and announced, "Thank you, sweet Jesus! The baby is in the correct position."

"All you need to do is push. But without gravity, you're going to have to use your abdominal muscles more intensively to do it. That's why we can't use pain killers. Are we clear about that?"

Sarah nodded. "Do you have any children?"

"Not yet. I've been a medical doctor in space for nearly ten years. I'm under forty, girl. If the Mars Corporation will let you do it, maybe I'll get a chance."

Captain Tran arrived with Shalom and walked over to Sarah. "You're having a baby on my watch. Do you feel everything is prepared for your delivery?" he asked, as if inspecting a docking procedure.

"Yes, Captain. Shanice has everything covered. I think she's preparing for her future delivery."

"What?" Captain Tran's ears reddened.

"Don't worry, John, I won't surprise you unless you want me to."

Sheila and Betsy couldn't hold back their laughter. But before Tran could say anything, Shalom stepped up beside him, worry wrapped around his face.

"You're a lucky man, Rabbi. G-d has blessed you today."

"I'm certain that He will bless us all." Sarah said, noting that Shalom couldn't speak.

Captain Tran turned and left, feeling a strange sensation in his body, something he hadn't felt since his youth in Vietnam, walking with his father in a temple.

Sarah wrapped in a blue drape, only her face peering out of the top. "Shalom, come closer, hold my hand," she said, pulling her wrist free from the table.

During the next thirty minutes, Shalom watched as his charming wife transformed into a cross between a professional fighter and an angry tiger. She screamed, swore, and broke one of his fingers. Betsy did her best to hold her steady on the table while Sheila worked the vacuums and adjusted the drape to keep free-floating fluids to a minimum. Circe arrived and braced Shanice just as she guided the baby into the world. The clinic went silent, except for the cries of a newborn baby.

Shanice held the baby high for everyone to see. "He looks great! A little small, a little blue, but for coming this early, he looks terrific."

She handed the baby to Shalom. "What's his name?"

Shalom couldn't speak. Tears ran down his cheeks and floated off into the surrounding air. But through his tears, he saw Sarah, and tremendous love and joy filled him. "Mendel!"

Sarah burst out laughing. "Mendel Mendelssohn, are you

kidding me?"

"Not at all. Do you have a better suggestion?"

"Yes, his full name will be Mendel Rafaeli Mendelssohn."

Betsy and Sheila kept Sarah secure as Shanice pulled the drape down to Sarah's waist and motioned for Shalom to hand her the baby. Sarah looked at her little boy and then up at Shalom. "I promise to help you teach our little Mendel the Torah and to complete all the mitzvot."

Shalom knelt at her side, placing his hand with the broken finger over Mendel's heart. "I promise to love you both forever."

The clinic erupted with tears and laughter as everyone worked to clean up around Sarah.

Evelin and Yudi arrived at the clinic and saw the baby resting on top of Sarah.

Evelin gave Yudi a dreamy look. "I want one too."

Asuna and Circe moved over to the other side of the central corridor, out of view from the clinic. Circe tucked herself into Asuna's arms and shivered.

"What's going on, sweetie? It's not cold."

"What will happen to us when we land on Mars? I don't want to lose you."

Circe's tablet vibrated between them. "That's not you shivering."

Circe took the tablet from her waist, holding it up so they

could both see it. Nous appeared on the screen. She had aged her face by ten years, though she was very much a Guatemalan fairy. "I need you to take me to Cydonia."

"How are we going to do that?" Asuna asked.

"You're going with me?"

"Of course, sweetie, we're a thing. But how will we take Nous to Cydonia and why does she want to go there?"

"That's the tricky part. I need to be inside Circe. Think of it as cohabitation."

"That's a very intimate request, Nous. Do you think Asuna and I are into *ménage à trois*?"

"I hadn't thought of it that way. We'll work that out later, but we need to go. It was the last request from Varahi before she left. Is it too much to ask?"

Asuna plunged her hands into Circe's thick, brown locks. "This is your decision. I won't leave you."

All the while, Linda Perez watched from her security office on Level 6. "Did you catch that boss?"

"It's perfect, and we didn't have to plan it. Make sure they have everything they need. The Cydonia outpost is ill-equipped and outside our jurisdiction. Be discreet and get them there."

"I'm on it."

Glossary of Spanish, Jewish, Technical, and Esoteric Terms

3-D array processor – A processor with stacked layers for improved efficiency.

AI-Language model – AI trained to process and generate human-like text.

Akashic Record – A mystical archive of all events, thoughts, and knowledge.

Anamnesis – Recollection of past knowledge, linked to Plato's memory theory.

Apomorphine – A psychoactive compound explored for neurological treatments.

ASCII – A character encoding standard for text in computers and digital communication.

Ashkenazi – Jews of Central and Eastern Europe with distinct traditions.

Ayahuasca – A psychoactive Amazonian brew used in shamanic rituals and healing.

Bachata – A Dominican dance and music style with romantic lyrics and rhythmic guitar.

Beis Agudas Chasidei Chabad – Chabad-Lubavitch headquarters, known as 770.

Beracha – A Jewish blessing recited over food, mitzvot, or special occasions.

Borei Pri Hagafen – A Hebrew blessing over wine, meaning "Creator of the fruit of the vine."

Boson – A fundamental particle following Bose-Einstein statistics.

Buzz Aldrin – Apollo 11 astronaut, second person to walk on the Moon (1969).

Caapi and Chacruna – Primary ayahuasca plants, providing MAO inhibitors and DMT.

Cariño – Spanish for "affection" or "dear one," used as an endearment.

Chambelán – A male escort or dance partner at a quinceañera celebration.

Checksum – A calculated value verifying data integrity in storage or transmission.

Chispudo – Guatemalan slang for "sharp-witted," "clever," or "quick-thinking."

Chuppah – A wedding canopy where a Jewish couple stands during marriage.

CRC – Cyclic Redundancy Check, detecting errors in data transmissions.

Cryptocurrency – Digital currency secured by cryptography, operating on decentralized blockchain technology.

Cumbia – A Colombian dance and music style.

Damas – Spanish for "ladies"; in quinceañeras, refers to the celebrant's court members.

DAO – A blockchain-based organization governed by smart contracts and collective decision-making.

Destroyer (Navy) – A fast warship for anti-air, anti-surface, and anti-submarine warfare.

DMT – A hallucinogenic compound used in shamanic rituals, especially ayahuasca ceremonies.

Dojo – A martial arts training hall for practice and discipline.

Elemental spirits – Supernatural beings linked to earth, air, fire, or water.

Entangled qubits – Quantum bits interconnected, enabling instant correlation over any distance.

Entheogen – A psychoactive substance inducing spiritual or religious experiences.

Frigate – A fast, medium-sized naval warship for combat and escort missions.

Galley (dining) – A kitchen on a ship or aircraft for preparing meals.

Gates of Binah – Kabbalistic concept representing deep wisdom and divine understanding.

Gi – A martial arts uniform worn in disciplines like Judo and Karate.

GPT – AI model generating human-like text using deep learning and transformers.

Halacha – Jewish law covering religious, ethical, and legal principles.

Hecate – Greek goddess of magic, the moon, and the underworld.

Hidden directories – Invisible folders used for system files or security purposes.

Icaro – A shamanic song in ayahuasca ceremonies for healing and vision.

Ishta Devata – A Hindu devotee's chosen personal deity for guidance.

Isis – Egyptian goddess of magic, motherhood, and rebirth.

Jailbreaking – Removing software restrictions to allow unauthorized modifications.

JSON – JavaScript Object Notation, A text file storing structured data.

Kendo – A Japanese martial art using bamboo swords and armor.

Ketubah – A Jewish marriage contract outlining responsibilities and rights.

Kibbutz – A collective Israeli community based on shared living.

Kosher – Food meeting Jewish dietary laws (kashrut).

Kung Fu – Chinese martial arts focused on skill and discipline.

L'Chaim! – Hebrew for "To life!" used as a toast.

Large Language Model –LLM, advanced AI trained for understanding and generating language.

Limpia – A Latin American shamanic ritual for spiritual cleansing.

Luna de Xelajú – A Guatemalan waltz evoking nostalgia and national pride.

Machine learning algorithms – Computational methods enabling systems to learn patterns and make predictions.

Maimonides – Medieval Jewish philosopher known for works on law and philosophy.

Mapacho – Wild tobacco used in shamanic rituals for purification and prayer.

Mars Syndrome – Hypothetical psychological effects of long-term isolation on Mars.

Mashgiach – A Jewish supervisor ensuring food and facilities follow kosher laws.

Mescaline – A psychedelic compound from peyote and other cacti.

Mezuzah – A parchment with Torah verses affixed to Jewish doorposts.

Mi amor – Spanish for "My Love," a term of endearment.

Modeh Ani – A Jewish morning prayer thanking G-d for returning the soul.

Moorish – Related to the Moors who ruled Spain and North Africa.

Moshiach – The Jewish Messiah, bringing redemption and world peace.

Naga – A serpent-like divine being in Hindu and Buddhist mythology.

Natural language processing – AI enabling computers to understand and generate human language.

Nephesh – The soul's life force, linked to physical existence in Judaism.

Neshama – A higher Jewish soul level, connected to intellect and divinity.

Neural interface – Technology allowing communication between an AI and the mind.

Novio – Spanish for "boyfriend" or "fiancé."

Open-source – Software with publicly accessible code for modification and distribution.

Orthodox – Strictly following traditional religious beliefs or practices.

Othello – A Shakespearean tragedy about jealousy, betrayal, and a Moorish general.

Oy gevalt – Yiddish exclamation of shock, frustration, or distress.

Pachamama – Andean earth goddess of fertility, nature, and cosmic balance.

Pantheon of celestial beings – A group of divine entities governing the universe.

Parsing – Analyzing language or code to extract structure and meaning.

Path of souls – A soul's journey after death in spiritual traditions.

Por vida – Spanish for "for life," expressing lifelong commitment.

Posek – A Jewish legal scholar interpreting religious law.

Predictive models – Algorithms forecasting outcomes based on past patterns.

Probabilistic algorithms – Methods using probability for problem-solving.

Psak – A Jewish legal ruling issued by a posek.

Psilocybin – A psychoactive compound in magic mushrooms.

Psychopomp – A guide of souls to the afterlife.

Python – A programming language for automation and data science.

QiGong – A Chinese practice of breath, movement, and meditation.

Quantum computer – A device using quantum mechanics for processing.

Quetzal – A colorful bird, Guatemala's national symbol and currency name.

Quinceañera – A Latin American celebration of a girl's 15th birthday.

Robodog – A robotic canine for security, assistance, or research.

Roddenberry Station – A fictional Mars station honoring Gene Roddenberry.

Sacred songs – Chants or hymns used in spiritual and religious rituals.

Sandbox – A controlled environment for testing software without system impact.

Sari – A long, draped South Asian garment worn by women.

SFTP – Secure protocol for encrypted file transfers over a network.

Shacharit – The Jewish morning prayer service with blessings and psalms.

Siddur – A Jewish prayer book containing daily prayers and blessings.

Sifu – A master or teacher in Chinese martial arts.

Solfeggio scale – Musical frequencies believed to have healing effects.

T'shuvah – Repentance, return, and spiritual renewal in Judaism.

Tai Chi – A martial art of slow, controlled movements.

Tefillin – Leather boxes with Torah verses, worn during prayer.

Text-based interfaces – Systems where users interact using text commands.

Tokenizing – Breaking text into words or symbols for processing.

Tokens – Small text units used in language processing.

Transformers – AI models generating text with self-attention.

Trickster entity – A mischievous being disrupting order in folklore.

Tu B'shvat – The Jewish New Year for Trees, celebrating nature.

Tzitzit – Fringes worn as a reminder of Jewish commandments.

Union of Orthodox Rabbis – A council overseeing Jewish law and community.

Virahi – A tantric goddess symbolizing spiritual longing and devotion.

Virtual mesh – A decentralized network for device communication.

Yarmulke – A small cap worn by Jewish men.

Yichud room – A private space for newlyweds after marriage.

Yiddishkeit – Jewish culture and way of life.

XGnome – A futuristic variant of Gnome, a Linux-based desktop environment providing a user-friendly graphical interface.

Zal – A yeshivah study hall for Torah and Talmud.

Song Credits

CHAPTER: Sarah Raphaeli

- *Gran Espíritu - Traditional icaro*

    CHAPTER: What About the Apple?

- *Llegó la Primavera - Traditional medicine song*

- *Machu Pichinku - Traditional icaro*

CHAPTER: Invoking the Goddess

- *Om Asatoma satgamaya - Pavamana Mantra from the Brhadaranyaka Upanishad*

- *Call Me By My True Names - Inspired by Thich Nhat Hanh*

- *Pajaro Viejo - Unknown curadera*

- *Con Todo Mi Corazón - Tradicional icaro*

- *Cura medicina - Unknown curandera*

- *Cantemos Con Alegría - Indigenous invocation of the Mother Goddess - Mexico*

CHAPTER: Varahi the Warrior

- *Lokah samastah sukhino bhavantu - Sanskrit mantra*

- *Manantial - Traditional icaro*

www.ingramcontent.com/pod-product-compliance
Lightning Source LLC
Chambersburg PA
CBHW060819120726
47909CB00006B/1989